"Earth brought life

to the Luanae, and the Luanae enlisted themselves in Earth's search for life . . .

"I had faith in my solution; I liked its math. I had little or no hope that it would be tried—really tried full-scale, and done right. People don't know enough. They don't think really straight. They turn the wrong valves and push the wrong buttons . . .

"I shall be bungled out of history, I told myself as we ground along in the nothingness of subspace—the Luanae subspace, given us by the Luanae cold-fusion generators. I'm coming, I'm coming, I told the Luanae silently, but I bring the enemy; I bring bungling; and, my marvels, you'll succumb to stupidity as will I, for it's the last and strongest enemy of them all, against which you and I might not prevail."

From *The Pod in the Barrier*, just one of the memorable science-fantasy stories of Theodore Sturgeon. There are eight more in this treasure box.

THEODORE STURGEON

A Touch of Strange

DAW BOOKS, INC.
DONALD A. WOLLHEIM, PUBLISHER

1301 Avenue of the Americas
New York, N. Y. 10019

Copyright ©, 1958, by Theodore Sturgeon

A DAW Book, by arrangement with
Doubleday & Co., Inc.

All Rights Reserved.

Cover art by Hans Arnold.

All of the characters in this book are fictitious, and any resemblance to actual persons, living or dead, is purely coincidental. The author and publisher are grateful to *The Magazine of Fantasy and Science Fiction* for the right to publish "A Touch of Strange," and to *Venture Science Fiction* for the right to publish "Affair with a Green Monkey," "The Girl Had Guts," and "It Opens the Sky."

Acknowledgments: "Mr. Costello, Hero," Copyright 1953 by Galaxy Publishing Corp.; "The Touch of Your Hand," Copyright 1953 by Galaxy Publishing Corp.; "The Other Celia," Copyright © 1957 by Galaxy Publishing Corp.; "The Pod in the Barrier," Copyright © 1957 by Galaxy Publishing Corp.

FIRST DAW PRINTING, APRIL 1978

3 4 5 6 7 8 9

PRINTED IN U.S.A.

CONTENTS

Mr. Costello, Hero	7
The Touch of Your Hand	33
Affair with a Green Monkey	77
A Crime for Llewellyn	88
It Opens the Sky	118
A Touch of Strange	160
The Other Celia	174
The Pod in the Barrier	192
The Girl Had Guts	232

For Grandma Sal

Mr. Costello,
Hero

"Come in, Purser. And shut the door."

"I beg your pardon, sir?" The Skipper never invited anyone in—not to his quarters. His office, yes, but not here.

He made an abrupt gesture, and I came in and closed the door. It was about as luxurious as a compartment on a spaceship can get. I tried not to goggle at it as if it was the first time I had ever seen it, just because it was the first time I had ever seen it.

I sat down.

He opened his mouth, closed it, forced the tip of his tongue through his thin lips. He licked them and glared at me. I'd never seen the Iron Man like this. I decided that the best thing to say would be nothing, which is what I said.

He pulled a deck of cards out of the top-middle drawer and slid them across the desk. "Deal."

I said, "I b—"

"And don't say you beg my pardon!" he exploded.

Well, all right. If the skipper wanted a cozy game of gin rummy to while away the parsecs, far be it from me to... I shuffled. Six years under this cold-blooded, fish-eyed automatic computer with eyebrows, and this was the first time that he—

"Deal," he said. I looked up at him. "Draw, five-card draw. You do play draw poker, don't you, Purser?"

"Yes, sir." I dealt and put down the pack. I had three threes and a couple of court cards. The skipper scowled at his hand and threw down two. He glared at me again.

I said, "I got three of a kind, sir."

He let his cards go as if they no longer existed, slammed

out of his chair and turned his back to me. He tilted his head back and stared up at the see-it-all, with its complex of speed, time, position and distance-run coordinates. Borinquen, our destination planet, was at spitting distance—only a day or so off—and Earth was a long, long way behind. I heard a sound and dropped my eyes. The Skipper's hands were locked behind him, squeezed together so hard that they crackled.

"Why didn't you draw?" he grated.

"I beg your—"

"When *I* played poker—and I used to play a hell of a lot of poker—as I recall it, the dealer would find out how many cards each player wanted after the deal and give him as many as he discarded. Did you ever hear of that, Purser?"

"Yes, sir, I did."

"You *did*." He turned around. I imagine he had been scowling this same way at the see-it-all, and I wondered why it was he hadn't shattered the cover glass.

"Why, then, Purser," he demanded, "did you show your three of a kind without discarding, without drawing—without, mister, asking me how many cards I might want?"

I thought about it. "I—we—I mean, sir, we haven't been playing poker that way lately."

"You've been playing draw poker without drawing!" He sat down again and beamed that glare at me again. "And who changed the rules?"

"I don't know, sir. We just—that's the way we've been playing."

He nodded thoughtfully. "Now tell me something, Purser. How much time did you spend in the galley during the last watch?"

"About an hour, sir."

"About an hour."

"Well, sir," I explained hurriedly, "it was my turn."

He said nothing, and it suddenly occurred to me that these galley-watches weren't in the ship's orders.

I said quickly, "It isn't *against* your orders to stand such a watch, is it, sir?"

"No," he said, "it isn't." His voice was so gentle, it was ugly. "Tell me, Purser, doesn't Cooky mind these galley-watches?"

"Oh, no, sir! He's real pleased about it." I knew he was thinking about the size of the galley. It was true that two men made quite a crowd in a place like that. I said, "That way, he knows everybody can trust him."

"You mean that way you know he won't poison you."

"Well—yes, sir."

"And tell me," he said, his voice even gentler, "who suggested he might poison you?"

"I really couldn't say, Captain. It's just sort of something that came up. Cooky doesn't mind," I added. "If he's watched all the time, he knows nobody's going to suspect him. It's all right."

Again he repeated my words.

"It's all right." I wished he wouldn't. I wished he'd stop looking at me like that. "How long," he asked, "has it been customary for the deck officer to bring a witness with him when he takes over the watch?"

"I really couldn't say, sir. That's out of my department."

"You couldn't say. Now think hard, Purser. Did you ever stand galley-watches, or see deck-officers bring witnesses with them when they relieve the bridge, or see draw poker played without drawing—before this trip?"

"Well, no, sir. I don't think I have. I suppose we just never thought of it before."

"We never had Mr. Costello as a passenger before, did we?"

"No, sir."

I thought for a moment he was going to say something else, but he didn't, just: "Very well, Purser. That will be all."

I went out and started back aft, feeling puzzled and sort of upset. The Skipper didn't have to hint things like that about Mr. Costello. Mr. Costello was a very nice man. Once, the Skipper had picked a fight with Mr. Costello. They'd shouted at each other in the day-room. That is, the Skipper had shouted—Mr. Costello never did. Mr. Costello was as good-natured as they come. A good-natured soft-spoken man, with the kind of a face they call open. Open and honest. He'd once been a Triumver back on Earth—the youngest ever appointed, they said.

You wouldn't think such an easygoing man was as smart as that. Triumvers are usually life-time appointees, but Mr. Costello wasn't satisfied. Had to keep moving, you know. Learning all the time, shaking hands all around, staying close to the people. He loved people.

I don't know why the Skipper couldn't get along with him. Everybody else did. And besides—Mr. Costello didn't play poker; why should he care one way or the other how *we* played it? He didn't eat the galley food—he had his own stock in his cabin—so what difference would it make to him if the cook poisoned anyone? Except, of course, that he cared about *us*. People—he *liked* people.

Anyway, it's better to play poker without the draw. Poker's a good game with a bad reputation. And where do you suppose it gets the bad reputation? From cheaters. And how do people cheat at poker? Almost never when they deal. It's when they pass out cards after the discard. That's when a shady dealer knows what he holds, and he knows what to give the others so he can win. All right, remove the discard and you remove nine-tenths of the cheaters. Remove the cheaters and the honest men can trust each other.

That's what Mr. Costello used to say, anyhow. Not that he cared one way or the other for himself. He wasn't a gambling man.

I went into the dayroom and there was Mr. Costello with the Third Officer. He gave me a big smile and a wave, so I went over.

"Come on, sit down, Purser," he said. "I'm landing tomorrow. Won't have much more chance to talk to you."

I sat down. The Third snapped shut a book he'd been holding open on the table and sort of got it out of sight.

Mr. Costello laughed at him. "Go ahead, Third, show the Purser. You can trust him—he's a good man. I'd be proud to be shipmates with the Purser."

The Third hesitated and then raised the book from his lap. It was the *Space Code* and expanded *Rules of the Road*. Every licensed officer has to bone up on it a lot, to get his license. But it's not the kind of book you ordinarily kill time with.

"The Third here was showing me all about what a captain can and can't do," said Mr. Costello.

"Well, you asked me to," the Third said.

"Now just a minute," said Mr. Costello rapidly, "now just a minute." He had a way of doing that sometimes. It was part of him, like the thinning hair on top of his head and the big smile and the way he had of cocking his head to one side and asking you what it was you just said, as if he didn't hear so well. "Now just a minute, you *wanted* to show me this material, didn't you?"

"Well, yes, Mr. Costello," the Third said.

"You're going over the limitations of a spacemaster's power of your own free will, aren't you?"

"Well," said the Third, "I guess so. Sure."

"Sure," Mr. Costello repeated happily. "Tell the Purser the part you just read to me."

"The one you found in the book?"

"You know the one. You read it out your own self, didn't you?"

"Oh," said the Third. He looked at me—sort of uneasily, I thought—and reached for the book.

Mr. Costello put his hand on it. "Oh, don't bother looking it up." he said. "You can remember it."

"Yeah, I guess I do," the Third admitted. "It's a sort of safeguard against letting the skipper's power go to his head, in case it ever does. Suppose a time comes when a captain begins to act up, and the crew gets the idea that a lunatic has taken over the bridge. Well, something has to be done about it. The crew has the power to appoint one officer and send him up to the Captain for an accounting. If the Skipper refuses, or if the crew doesn't like his accounting, then they have the right to confine him to his quarters and take over the ship."

"I think I heard about that," I said. "But the Skipper has rights, too. I mean the crew has to report everything by space-radio the second it happens, and then the Captain has a full hearing along with the crew at the next port."

Mr. Costello looked at us and shook his big head, full of admiration. When Mr. Costello thought you were good, it made you feel good all over.

The Third looked at his watch and got up. "I got to relieve the bridge. Want to come along, Purser?"

"I'd like to talk to him for a while," Mr. Costello said. "Do you suppose you could get somebody else for a witness?"

"Oh, sure, if you say so," said the Third.

"But you're going to get someone."

"Absolutely," said the Third.

"Safest ship I was ever on," said Mr. Costello. "Gives a fellow a nice feeling to know that the watch is never going to get the orders wrong."

I thought so myself and wondered why we never used to do it before. I watched the Third leave and stayed where I was, feeling good, feeling safe, feeling glad that Mr. Costello wanted to talk to me. And me just a Purser, him an ex-Triumver.

Mr. Costello gave me the big smile. He nodded toward the door. "That young fellow's going far. A good man. You're all good men here." He stuck a sucker-cup in the heater and passed it over to me with his own hands. "Coffee," he said. "My own brand. All I ever use."

I tasted it and it was fine. He was a very generous man. He sat back and beamed at me while I drank it.

"What do you know about Borinquen?" he wanted to know.

I told him all I could. Borinquen's a pretty nice place, what they call "four-nines Earth Normal"—which means that the climate, gravity, atmosphere and ecology come within .9999 of being the same as Earth's. There are only about six known planets like that. I told him about the one city it had and the trapping that used to be the main industry. Coats made out of *glunker* fur last forever. They shine green in white light and real warm ember-red in blue light, and you can take a full-sized coat and scrunch it up and hide it in your two hands, it's that light and fine. Being so light, the fur made ideal space-cargo.

Of course, there was a lot more on Borinquen now—rare isotope ingots and foodstuffs and seeds for the drug business and all, and I suppose the *glunker* trade could dry right up and Borinquen could still carry its weight. But furs settled the planet, furs supported the city in the early days, and half the population still lived out in the bush and trapped.

Mr. Costello listened to everything I said in a way I can only call respectful.

I remember I finished up by saying, "I'm sorry you have to get off there, Mr. Costello. I'd like to see you some more. I'd like to come see you at Borinquen, whenever we put in, though I don't suppose a man like you would have much spare time."

He put his big hand on my arm. "Purser, if I don't have time when you're in port, I'll make time. Hear?" Oh, he had a wonderful way of making a fellow feel good.

Next thing you know, he invited me right into his cabin.

He sat me down and handed me a sucker full of a mild red wine with a late flavor of cinnamon, which was a new one on me, and he showed me some of his things.

He was a great collector. He had one or two little bits of colored paper that he said were stamps they used before the Space Age, to prepay carrying charges on paper letters. He said no matter where he was, just one of those things could get him a fortune. Then he had some jewels, not rings or anything, just stones, and a fine story for every single one of them.

"What you're holding in your hand," he said, "cost the life of a king and the loss of an empire half again as big as United Earth." And: "This one was once so well guarded that most people didn't know whether it existed or not. There was a whole religion based on it—and now it's gone, and so is the religion."

It gave you a queer feeling, being next to this man who had so much, and him just as warm and friendly as your favorite uncle.

"If you can assure me these bulkheads are soundproof, I'll show you something else I collect," he said.

I assured him they were, and they were, too. "If ships' architects ever learned anything," I told him, "They learned that a man has just got to be by himself once in a while."

He cocked his head to one side in a way that he had. "How's that again?"

"A man's just got to be by himself once in a while." I said. "So, mass or no, cost or no, a ship's bulkheads are built to give a man his privacy."

"Good," he said. "Now let me show you." He unlocked a handcase and opened it, and from a little compartment inside he took out a thing about the size of the box a watch comes in. He handled it very gently as he put it down on his desk. It was square, and it had a fine grille on the top and two little silver studs on the side. He pressed one of them and turned to me, smiling. And let me tell you, I almost fell right off the bunk where I was sitting, because here was the Captain's voice as loud and clear and natural as if he was right there in the room with us. And do you know what he said?

He said, "My crew questions my sanity—yet you can be sure that if a single man aboard questions my authority, he will learn that I am master here, even if he must learn it at the point of a gun."

What surprised me so much wasn't only the voice but the words—and what surprised me especially about the words was that I had heard the Skipper say them myself. It was the time he had had the argument with Mr. Costello. I remembered it well because I had walked into the dayroom just as the Captain started to yell.

"Mr. Costello," he said in that big heavy voice of his, "In spite of your conviction that my crew questions my sanity . . ." and all the rest of it, just like on this recording Mr. Costello had. And I remember he said, too, "Even if he must learn it at the point of a gun. *That, sir, applies to passengers —the crew has legal means of their own.*"

I was going to mention this to Mr. Costello, but before I could open my mouth, he asked me, "Now tell me, Purser, is that the voice of the Captain of your ship?"

And I said, "Well, if it isn't, I'm not the Purser here. Why, I heard him speak those words my very own self."

Mr. Costello swatted me on the shoulder. "You have a good ear, Purser. And how do you like my little toy?"

Then he showed it to me, a little mechanism on the jeweled pin he wore on his tunic, a fine thread of wire to a pushbutton in his side pocket.

"One of my favorite collections," he told me. "Voices. Anybody, anytime, anywhere." He took off the pin and slipped a tiny bead out of the setting. He slipped this into a groove in the box and pressed the stud.

And I heard my own voice say, "I'm sorry you have to get off there, Mr. Costello. I'd like to see you some more." I laughed and laughed. That was one of the cleverest things I ever saw. And just think of my voice in his collection, along with the Captain and space only knows how many great and famous people!

He even had the voice of the Third Officer, from just a few minutes before, saying, "A lunatic has taken over the bridge. Well, something has to be done about it."

All in all, I had a wonderful visit with him, and then he asked me to do whatever I had to do about his clearance papers. So I went back to my office and got them out. They are kept in the Purser's safe during a voyage. And I went through them with the okays. There were a lot of them—he had more than most people.

I found one from Earth Central that sort of made me mad. I guess it was a mistake. It was a *Know All Ye* that warned consular officials to report every six months, Earth time, on the activities of Mr. Costello.

I took it to him, and it was a mistake, all right—he said so himself. I tore it out of his passport book and adhesed an official note, reporting the accidental destruction of a used page of fully stamped visas. He gave me a beautiful blue gemstone for doing it.

When I said, "I better not; I don't want you thinking I take bribes from passengers," he laughed and put one of those beads in his recorder, and it came out, in my voice, "I take bribes from passengers." He was a great joker.

We lay at Borinquen for four days. Nothing much happened except I was busy. That's what's tough about pursering. You got nothing to do for weeks in space, and then, when you're in spaceport, you have too much work to do even to go ashore much, unless it's a long layover.

I never really minded much. I'm one of those mathematical geniuses, you know, even if I don't have too much sense otherwise, and I take pride in my work. Everybody has something he's good at, I guess. I couldn't tell you how the gimmick works that makes the ship travel faster than light, but I'd hate to trust the Chief Engineer with one of my interplanetary cargo manifests, or a rate-of-exchange table, *glunker* pelts to U.E. dollars.

Some hard-jawed character with Space Navy Investigator credentials came inboard with a portable voice recorder and made me and the Third Officer recite a lot of nonsense for some sort of test, I don't know what. The SNI is always doing a lot of useless and mysterious things. I had an argument with the Port Agent, and I went ashore with Cooky for a fast drink. The usual thing. Then I had to work overtime signing on a new Third—they transferred the old one to a corvette that was due in, they told me.

Oh, yes, that was the trip the Skipper resigned. I guess it was high time. He'd been acting very nervous. He gave me the damnedest look when he went ashore that last time, like he didn't know whether to kill me or burst into tears. There was a rumor around that he'd gone beserk and threatened the crew with a gun, but I don't listen to rumors. And anyway, the Port Captain signs on new skippers. It didn't mean any extra work for me, so it didn't matter much.

We upshipped again and made the rounds. Boötes Sigma and Nightingale and Caranho and Earth—chemical glassware, blackprints, *sho* seed and glitter crystals; perfume, music tape, *glizzard* skins and Aldebar—all the usual junk for all the usual months. And round we came again to Borinquen.

Well, you wouldn't believe a place could change so much in so short a time. Borinquen used to be a pretty free-and-easy planet. There was just the one good-sized city, see, and then trapper camps all through the unsettled area. If you liked people, you settled in the city, and you could go to work in the processing plants or maintenance or some such. If you didn't, you could trap *glunkers*. There was always something for everybody on Borinquen.

But things were way different this trip. First of all, a man with a Planetary Government badge came aboard, by God, to censor the music tapes consigned for the city, and he had the credentials for it, too. Next thing I find out, the municipal authorities have confiscated the warehouse—*my* warehouses—and they were being converted into barracks.

And where were the goods—the pelts and ingots for export? Where was the space for our cargo? Why, in houses —in hundreds of houses, all spread around every which way, all indexed up with a whole big new office full of conscripts and volunteers to mix up and keep mixed up! For the first time since I went to space, I had to request layover so I could get things unwound.

Anyway it gave me a chance to wander around the town, which I don't often get.

You should have seen the place! Everybody seemed to be moving out of the houses. All the big buildings were being made over into hollow shells, filled with rows and rows of mattresses. There were banners strung across the streets: ARE YOU A MAN OR ARE YOU ALONE? A SINGLE SHINGLE IS A SORRY SHELTER! THE DEVIL HATES A CROWD!

All of which meant nothing to me. But it wasn't until I noticed a sign painted in whitewash on the glass front of a barroom, saying—TRAPPERS STAY OUT!—that I was aware of one of the biggest changes of all.

There were no trappers on the streets—none at all. They used to be one of the tourist attractions of Borinquen, dressed in *glunker* fur, with the long tailwings afloat in the wind of their walking, and a kind of distance in their eyes that not even spacemen had. As soon as I missed them, I began to see the TRAPPERS STAY OUT! signs just about everywhere—on the stores, the restaurants, the hotels and theaters.

I stood on a street corner, looking around me and wondering what in hell was going on here, when a Borinquen cop yelled something at me from a monowheel prowl car. I didn't understand him, so I just shrugged. He made a U-turn and coasted up to me.

"What's the matter, country boy? Lose your traps?"

I said, "What?"

He said, "If you want to go it alone, *glunker*, we got solitary cells over at the Hall that'll suit you fine."

I just gawked at him. And, to my surprise, another cop poked his head up out of the prowler. A one-man prowler, mind. They were really jammed in there.

This second one said, "Where's your trapline, jerker?"

I said, "I don't have a trapline." I pointed to the mighty tower of my ship, looming over the spaceport. "I'm the Purser off that ship."

"Oh, for God's sakes!" said the first cop. "I might have known. Look, Spacer, you'd better double up or you're liable to get yourself mobbed. This is no spot for a soloist."

"I don't get you, Officer. I was just—"

"I'll take him," said someone. I looked around and saw a tall Borinqueña standing just inside the open doorway of one of the hundreds of empty houses. She said, "I came back here to pick up some of my things. When I got done in here, there was nobody on the sidewalks. I've been here an hour, waiting for somebody to go with." She sounded a little hysterical.

"You know better than to go in there by yourself," said one of the cops.

"I know—I know. It was just to get my things. I wasn't going to stay." She hauled up a duffelbag and dangled it in front of her. "Just to get my things," she said again, frightened.

The cops looked at each other. "Well, all right. But watch yourself. You go along with the Purser here. Better straighten him out—he don't seem to know what's right."

"I will," she said thankfully.

But by then the prowler had moaned off, weaving a little under its double load.

I looked at her. She wasn't pretty. She was sort of heavy and stupid.

She said, "You'll be all right now. Let's go."

"Where?"

"Well, Central Barracks, I guess. That's where most everybody is."

"I have to get back to the ship."

"Oh, dear," she said, all distressed again. "Right away?"

"No, not right away. I'll go in town with you, if you want." She picked up her duffelbag, but I took it from her and heaved it up on my shoulder. "Is everybody here crazy?" I asked her, scowling.

"Crazy?" She began walking, and I went along. "I don't *think* so."

"All this," I persisted. I pointed to a banner that said, NO LADDER HAS A SINGLE RUNG. "What's that mean?"

"Just what it says."

"You have to put up a big thing like that just to tell me . . ."

"Oh," she said. "You mean what does it *mean!*" She looked at me strangely. "We've found out a new truth about humanity. Look, I'll try to tell it to you the way the Lucilles said it last night."

"Who's Lucille?"

"*The* Lucilles," she said, in a mildly shocked tone. "Actually, I suppose there's really only one—though, of course, there'll be someone else in the studio at the time," she added quickly. "But on trideo it looks like four Lucilles, all speaking at once, sort of in chorus."

"You just go on talking," I said when she paused. "I catch on slowly."

"Well, here's what they say. They say no one human being ever did *anything*. They say it takes a hundred pairs of hands to build a house, ten thousand pairs to build a ship. They say a single pair is not only useless—it's *evil*. All humanity is a thing made up of many parts. No part is good by itself. Any part that wants to go off by itself hurts the whole main thing—the thing that has become so great. So we're seeing to it that no part ever gets separated. What good would your hand be if a finger suddenly decided to go off by itself?"

I said, "And you believe this—what's your name?"

"Nola. *Believe* it? Well, it's true, isn't it? Can't you see it's true? Everybody *knows* it's true."

"Well, it *could* be true," I said reluctantly. "What do you do with people who want to be by themselves?"

"We help them."

"Suppose they don't want help?"

"Then they're trappers," she said immediately. "We push them back into the bush, where the evil soloists come from."

"Well, what about the fur?"

"*No*body uses furs any more!"

So that's what happened to our fur consignments! And I was thinking those amateur red-tapers had just lost 'em somewhere.

She said, as if to herself, "All sin starts in the lonesome dark," and when I looked up, I saw she'd read it approvingly off another banner.

We rounded a corner and I blinked at a blaze of light. It was one of the warehouses.

"There's the Central," she said. "Would you like to see it?"

"I guess so."

I followed her down the street to the entrance. There was a man sitting at a table in the doorway. Nola gave him a card. He checked it against a list and handed it back.

"A visitor," she said. "From the ship."

I showed him my Purser's card and he said, "Okay. But if you want to stay, you'll have to register."

"I won't want to stay," I told him. "I have to get back."

I followed Nola inside.

The place had been scraped out to the absolute maximum. Take away one splinter of vertical structure more and it wouldn't have held a roof. There wasn't a concealed corner, a shelf, a drape, an overhang. There must have been two thousand beds, cots and mattresses spread out, cheek by jowl, over the entire floor, in blocks of four, with only a hand's-breadth between them.

The light was blinding—huge floods and spots bathed every square inch in yellow-white fire.

Nola said, "You'll get used to the light. After a few nights, you don't even notice it."

"The lights never get turned off?"

"Oh, dear, no!"

Then I saw the plumbing—showers, tubs, sinks and everything else. It was all lined up against one wall.

Nola followed my eyes. "You get used to that, too. Better to have everything out in the open than to let the devil in for one secret second. That's what the Lucilles say."

I dropped her duffelbag and sat down on it. The only thing I could think of was, "Whose idea was all this? Where did it start?"

"The Lucilles," she said vaguely. Then, "Before them, I don't know. People just started to realize. Somebody bought a warehouse—no, it was a hangar—I don't know," she said again, apparently trying hard to remember. She sat down next to me and said in a subdued voice, "Actually, some people didn't take to it so well at first." She looked around. "*I* didn't. I mean it, I really didn't. But you believed, or you had to act as if you believed, and one way or another everybody just came to this." She waved a hand.

"What happened to the ones who wouldn't come to Centrals?"

"People made fun of them. They lost their jobs, the schools wouldn't take their children, the stores wouldn't honor their ration cards. Then the police started to pick up soloists—like they did you." She looked around again, a sort of contented familiarity in her gaze. "It didn't take long."

I turned away from her, but found myself staring at all that plumbing again. I jumped up. "I have to go, Nola. Thanks for your help. Hey—how do I get back to the ship, if the cops are out to pick up any soloist they see?"

"Oh, just tell the man at the gate. There'll be people waiting to go your way. There's always somebody waiting to go everywhere."

She came along with me. I spoke to the man at the gate, and she shook hands with me. I stood by the little table and watched her hesitate, then step up to a woman who was entering. They went in together. The doorman nudged me over toward a group of what appeared to be loungers.

"*North!*" he bawled.

I drew a pudgy little man with bad teeth, who said not one single word. We escorted each other two-thirds of the way to the spaceport, and he disappeared into a factory. I scuttled the rest of the way alone, feeling like a criminal, which I suppose I was. I swore I would never go into that crazy city again.

And the next morning, who should come out for me, in an armored car with six two-man prowlers as escort, but Mr. Costello himself!

It was pretty grand seeing him again. He was just like always, big and handsome and good-natured. He was not alone. All spread out in the back corner of the car was the most beautiful blonde woman that ever struck me speechless. She didn't say very much. She would just look at me every once in a while and sort of smile, and then she would look out of the car window and bite on her lower lip a little, and then look at Mr. Costello and not smile at all.

Mr. Costello hadn't forgotten me. He had a bottle of that same red cinnamon wine, and he talked over old times the same as ever, like he was a special uncle. We got a sort of guided tour. I told him about last night, about the visit to the Central, and he was pleased as could be. He said he knew I'd like it. I didn't stop to think whether I liked it or not.

"Think of it!" he said, "All humankind, a single unit. You know the principle of cooperation, Purser?"

When I took too long to think it out, he said, "You know. Two men working together can produce more than two men working separately. Well, what happens when a thousand—a million—work, sleep, eat, think, breathe together?" The way he said it, it sounded fine.

He looked out past my shoulder and his eyes widened just a little. He pressed a button and the chauffeur brought us to a sliding stop.

"Get that one," Mr. Costello said into a microphone beside him.

Two of the prowlers hurtled down the street and flanked a man. He dodged right, dodged left, and then a prowler hit him and knocked him down.

"Poor chap," said Mr. Costello, pushing the *Go* button. "Some of 'em just won't learn."

I think he regretted it very much. I don't know if the blonde woman did. She didn't even look.

"Are you the mayor?" I asked him.

"Oh, no," he said. "I'm a sort of broker. A little of this, a little of that. I'm able to help out a bit."

"Help out?"

"Purser," he said confidentially, "I'm a citizen of Borinquen now. This is my adopted land and I love it. I mean to do everything in my power to help it. I don't care about the cost. This is a people that has found the *truth,* Purser. It awes me. It makes me humble."

"I . . ."

"Speak up, man. I'm your *friend.*"

"I appreciate that, Mr. Costello. Well, what I was going to say, I saw that Central and all. I just haven't made up my mind. I mean whether it's good or not."

"Take your time, take your time," he said in the big soft voice. "Nobody has to *make* a man see a truth, am I right? A real truth? A man just sees it all by himself."

"Yeah," I agreed. "Yeah, I guess so." Sometimes it was hard to find an answer to give Mr. Costello.

The car pulled up beside a building. The blonde woman pulled herself together. Mr. Costello opened the door for her with his own hands. She got out. Mr. Costello rapped the trideo screen in front of him.

He said, "Make it a real good one, Lucille, real good. I'll be watching."

She looked at him. She gave me a small smile. A man came down the steps and she went with him up into the building.

We moved off.

I said, "She's the prettiest woman I ever saw."

He said, "She likes you fine, Purser."

I thought about that. It was too much.

He asked, "How would you like to have her for your very own?"

"Oh," I said, "she wouldn't."

"Purser, I owe you a big favor. I'd like to pay it back."

"You don't owe me a thing, Mr. Costello!"

We drank some of the wine. The big car slid silently along. It went slowly now, headed back out to the spaceport.

"I need some help," he said after a time. "I know you, Purser. You're just the kind of man I can use. They say you're a mathematical genius."

"Not mathematics exactly, Mr. Costello. Just numbers—statistics—conversion tables and like that. I couldn't do astrogation or theoretical physics and such. I got the best job I could have right now."

"No, you haven't. I'll be frank with you. I don't want any more responsibility on Borinquen than I've got, you understand, but the people are forcing it on me. They want order, peace and order—tidiness. They want to be as nice and tidy as one of your multiple manifests. Now I could organize them, all right, but I need a tidy brain like yours to keep them organized. I want full birth-and death-rate statistics, and then I want them projected so we can get policy. I want calorie-counts and rationing, so we can use the food supply the best way. I want—well, you see what I mean. Once the devil is routed—"

"What devil?"

"The trappers," he said grayly.

"Are the trappers really harming the city people?"

He looked at me, shocked. "They go out and spend weeks alone by themselves, with their own evil thoughts. They are wandering cells, wild cells in the body of humanity. They must be destroyed."

I couldn't help but think of my consignments. "What about the fur trade, though?"

He looked at me as if I had made a pretty grubby little mistake. "My dear Purser," he said patiently, "would you set the price of a few pelts above the immortal soul of a race?"

I hadn't thought of it that way.

He said urgently, "This is just the beginning, Purser. Borinquen is only a start. The unity of that great being, Humanity, will become known throughout the Universe." He closed his eyes. When he opened them, the organ tone was gone. He said in his old, friendly voice, "And you and I, we'll show 'em how to do it, hey, boy?"

I leaned forward to look up to the top of the shining spire of the spaceship. "I sort of like the job I've got. But—my contract *is* up four months from now . . ."

The car turned into the spaceport and hummed across the slag area.

"I think I can count on you," he said vibrantly. He laughed. "Remember this little joke, Purser?"

He clicked a switch, and suddenly my own voice filled the tonneau. *"I take bribes from passengers."*

"Oh, that," I said, and let loose one *ha* of a *ha-ha* before I understood what he was driving at. "Mr. Costello, you wouldn't use that against me."

"What do you take me for?" he demanded, in wonderment.

Then we were at the ramp. He got out with me. He gave me his hand. It was warm and hearty.

"If you change your mind about the Purser's job when your contract's up, son, just buzz me through the field phone. They'll connect me. Think it over until you get back here. Take your time." His hand clamped down on my biceps so hard I winced. "But you're not going to take any longer than that, are you, my boy?"

"I guess not," I said.

He got into the front, by the chauffeur, and zoomed away.

I stood looking after him and, when the car was just a dark spot on the slag area, I sort of came to myself. I was standing alone on the foot of the ramp. I felt very exposed.

I turned and ran up to the airlock, hurrying, hurrying to get near people.

That was the trip we shipped the crazy man. His name was Hynes. He was United Earth Consul at Borinquen and he was going back to report. He was no trouble at first, because diplomatic passports are easy to process. He knocked on my door the fifth watch out from Borinquen. I was glad to see him. My room was making me uneasy and I appreciated his company.

Not that he was really company. He was crazy. That first time, he came busting in and said, "I hope you don't mind, Purser, but if I don't talk to somebody about this, I'll go out of my mind." Then he sat down on the end of my bunk and put his head in his hands and rocked back and forth for a long time, without saying anything. Next thing he said was, "Sorry," and out he went. Crazy, I tell you.

But he was back in again before long. And then you never heard such ravings.

"Do you know what's happened to Borinquen?" he'd demand. But he didn't want any answers. He had the answers. "I'll tell you what's wrong with Borinquen—Borinquen's gone mad!" he'd say.

I went on with my work, though there wasn't much of it in space, but that Hynes just couldn't get Borinquen out of his mind.

He said, "You wouldn't believe it if you hadn't seen it done. First the little wedge, driven in the one place it might exist—between the urbans and the trappers. There was never any conflict between them—never! All of a sudden, the trapper was a menace. How it happened, why, God only knows. First, these laughable attempts to show that they were an unhealthy influence. Yes, laughable—how could you take it seriously?

"And then the changes. You didn't have to prove that a trapper had done anything. You only had to prove he was a trapper. That was enough. And the next thing—how could you *anticipate* anything as mad as this?"—he almost screamed—"the next thing was to take anyone who wanted to be alone and lump him with the trappers. It all happened so fast—it happened in our sleep. And all of a sudden you were afraid to be alone in a room for a *second*. They left their homes. They built barracks. Everyone afraid of everyone else, afraid, afraid ...

"Do you know what they *did?*" he roared. "They burned the paintings, every painting on Borinquen they could find that had been done by one artist. And the few artists who survived as artists—I've seen them. By twos and threes, they work together on the one canvas."

He cried. He actually sat there and cried.

He said, "There's food in the stores. The crops come in. Trucks ran, planes fly, the schools are in session. Bellies get full, cars get washed, people get rich. I know a man called Costello, just in from Earth a few months, maybe a year or so, and already owns half the city."

"Oh, I know Mr. Costello," I said.

"Do you now! How's that?"

I told him about the trip out with Mr. Costello. He sort of backed off from me. *"You're* the one!"

"The one what?" I asked in puzzlement.

"You're the man who testified against your Captain, broke him, made him resign."

"I did no such a thing."

"I'm the Consul. It was my hearing, man! I was *there!* A recording of the Captain's voice, admitting to insanity, declaring he'd take a gun to his crew if they overrode him. Then your recorded testimony that it was his voice, that you were present when he made the statement. And the Third Officer's recorded statement that all was not well on the bridge. The man denied it, but it was his voice."

"Wait, wait," I said. "I don't believe it. That would need a trial. There was no trial. I wasn't called to any trial."

"There would have been a trial, you idiot! But the Captain started raving about draw poker without a draw, about the crew fearing poisoning from the cook, about the men wanting witnesses even to change the bridge-watch. Maddest thing I ever heard. He realized it suddenly, the Captain did. He was old, sick, tired, beaten. He blamed the whole thing on Costello, and Costello said he got the recordings from you."

"Mr. Costello wouldn't do such a thing!" I guess I got mad at Mr. Hynes then. I told him a whole lot about Mr. Costello, what a big man he was. He started to tell me how Mr. Costello was forced off the Triumverate for making trouble in the high court, but they were lies and I wouldn't listen. I told him about the poker, how Mr. Costello saved us from the cheaters, how he saved us from poisoning, how he made the ship safe for us all.

I remember how he looked at me then. He sort of whispered, "What has happened to human beings? What have we done to ourselves with these centuries of peace, with confidence and cooperation and no conflict? Here's distrust by man for man, waiting under a thin skin to be punctured by just the right vampire, waiting to hate itself and kill itself all over again . . .

"My *God!*" he suddenly screamed at me. "Do you know what I've been hanging onto? The idea that, for all its error, for all its stupidity, this One Humanity idea on Borinquen was a *principle?* I hated it, but because it was a principle, I could respect it. It's Costello—Costello, who doesn't gamble, but who uses fear to change the poker rules—Costello, who doesn't eat your food, but makes you fear poison—Costello, who can see three hundred years of safe interstellar flight, but who through fear makes the watch officers doubt themselves without a witness—Costello, who runs things without being seen!

"My God, Costello doesn't *care!* It isn't a principle at all. It's just Costello spreading fear anywhere, everywhere, to make himself strong!"

He rushed out, crying with rage and hate. I have to admit I was sort of jolted. I guess I might even have thought about the things he said, only he killed himself before we reached Earth. He was crazy.

We made the rounds, same as ever, scheduled like an interurban line: Load, discharge, blastoff, fly and planetfall.

Refuel, clearance, manifest. Eat, sleep, work. There was a hearing about Hynes. Mr. Costello sent a spacegram with his regrets when he heard the news. I didn't say anything at the hearing, just that Mr. Hynes was upset, that's all, and it was about as true as anything could be. We shipped a second engineer who played real good accordion. One of the inboard men got left on Caránho. All the usual things, except I wrote up my termination with no options, ready to file.

So in its turn we made Borinquen again, and what do you know, there was the space fleet of United Earth. I never guessed they had that many ships. They sheered us off, real Navy: all orders and no information. Borinquen was buttoned up tight; there was some kind of fighting going on down there. We couldn't get or give a word of news through the quarantine. It made the skipper mad and he had to use part of the cargo for fuel, which messed up my records six ways from the middle. I stashed my termination papers away for the time being.

And in its turn, Sigma, where he lay over a couple of days to get back in the rut, and, same as always, Nightingale, right on schedule again.

And who should be waiting for me at Nightingale but Barney Roteel, who was medic on my first ship, years back when I was fresh from the Academy. He had a pot belly now and looked real successful. We got the jollity out of the way and he settled down and looked me over, real sober. I said it's a small Universe—I'd known he had a big job on Nightingale, but imagine him showing up at the spaceport just when I blew in!

"I showed up *because* you blew in, Purser," he answered.

Then before I could take that apart, he started asking me questions. Like how was I doing, what did I plan to do.

I said, "I've been a purser for years and years. What makes you think I want to do anything different?"

"Just wondered."

I wondered, too. "Well," I said, "I haven't exactly made up my mind, you might say—and a couple of things have got in the way—but I did have a kind of offer." I told him just in a general way about how big a man Mr. Costello was on Borinquen now, and how he wanted me to come in with him. "It'll have to wait, though. The whole damn Space Navy has a cordon around Borinquen. They wouldn't say why.

But whatever it is, Mr. Costello'll come out on top. You'll see."

Barney gave me a sort of puckered-up look. I never saw a man look so weird. Yes, I did, too. It was the old Iron Man, the day he got off the ship and resigned.

"Barney, what's the matter?" I asked.

He got up and pointed through the glass door-lights to a white monowheel that stood poised in front of the receiving station. "Come on," he said.

"Aw, I can't. I got to—"

"Come *on!*"

I shrugged. Job or no, this was Barney's bailiwick, not mine. He'd cover me.

He held the door open and said, like a mind reader, "I'll cover you."

We went down the ramp and climbed in and skimmed off.

"Where are we going?"

But he wouldn't say. He just drove.

Nightingale's a beautiful place. The most beautiful of them all, I think, even Sigma. It's run by the UE, one hundred per cent; this is one planet with no local options, but *none.* It's a regular garden of a world and they keep it that way.

We topped a rise and went down a curving road lined with honest-to-God Lombardy poplars from Earth. There was a little lake down there and a sandy beach. No people.

The road curved and there was a yellow line across it and then a red one, and after it a shimmering curtain, almost transparent. It extended from side to side as far as I could see.

"Force-fence," Barney said and pressed a button on the dash.

The shimmer disappeared from the road ahead, though it stayed where it was at each side. We drove through it and it formed behind us, and we went down the hill to the lake.

Just this side of the beach was the coziest little Sigma cabana I've seen yet, built to hug the slope and open its arms to the sky. Maybe when I get old they'll turn me out to pasture in one half as good.

While I was goggling at it, Barney said, "Go on."

I looked at him and he was pointing. There was a man down near the water, big, very tanned, built like a space-tug. Barney waved me on and I walked down there.

The man got up and turned to me. He had the same wide-spaced, warm deep eyes, the same full, gentle voice.

A TOUCH OF STRANGE

"Why, it's the Purser! Hi, old friend. So you came, after all!"

It was sort of rough for a moment. Then I got it out. "Hi, Mr. Costello."

He banged me on the shoulder. Then he wrapped one big hand around my left biceps and pulled me a little closer. He looked uphill to where Barney leaned against the monowheel, minding his own business. Then he looked across the lake, and up in the sky.

He dropped his voice. "Purser, you're just the man I need. But I told you that before, didn't I?" He looked around again. "We'll do it yet, Purser. You and me, we'll hit the top. Come with me. I want to show you something."

He walked ahead of me toward the beach margin. He was wearing only a breech-ribbon, but he moved and spoke as if he still had the armored car and the six prowlers. I stumbled after him.

He put a hand behind him and checked me, and then knelt. He said, "To look at them, you'd think they were all the same, wouldn't you? Well, son, you just let me show you something."

I looked down. He had an anthill. They weren't like Earth ants. These were bigger, slower, blue, and they had eight legs. They built nests of sand tied together with mucus, and tunneled under them so that the nests stood up an inch or two like on little pillars.

"They look the same, they act the same, but you'll see," said Mr. Costello.

He opened a synthine pouch that lay in the sand. He took out a dead bird and the thorax of what looked like a Caránho roach, the one that grows as long as your forearm. He put the bird down here and the roach down yonder.

"Now," he said, "watch."

The ants swarmed to the bird, pulling and crawling. Busy. But one or two went to the roach and tumbled it and burrowed around. Mr. Costello picked an ant off the roach and dropped it on the bird. It weaved around and shouldered through the others and scrabbled across the sand and went back to the roach.

"You see, you *see?*" he said, enthusiastic. "Look."

He picked an ant off the dead bird and dropped it by the roach. The ant wasted no time or even curiosity on the piece of roach. It turned around once to get its bearings, and then went straight back to the dead bird.

I looked at the bird with its clothing of crawling blue, and I looked at the roach with its two or three voracious scavengers. I looked at Mr. Costello.

He said raptly, "See what I mean? About one in thirty eats something different. And that's all we need. I tell you, Purser, wherever you look, if you look long enough, you can find a way to make most of a group turn on the rest."

I watched the ants. "They're not fighting."

"Now wait a minute," he said swiftly. "Wait a minute. All we have to do is let these bird-eaters know that the roach-eaters are dangerous."

'They're not dangerous," I said. "They're just different."

"What's the difference, when you come right down to it? So we'll get the bird-eaters scared and they'll kill all the roach-eaters."

"Yes, but why, Mr. Costello?"

He laughed. "I like you, boy. I do the thinking, you do the work. I'll explain it to you. They all look alike. So once we've made 'em drive out these—" he pointed to the minority around the roach—"they'll never know which among 'em might be a roach-eater. They'll get so worried, they'll do anything to keep from being suspected of roach-eating. When they get scared enough, we can make 'em do anything we want."

He hunkered down to watch the ants. He picked up a roach-eater and put it on the bird. I got up.

"Well, I only just dropped in, Mr. Costello," I said.

"I'm not an ant," said Mr. Costello. "As long as it makes no difference to me what they eat, I can make 'em do anything in the world I want."

"I'll see you around," I said.

He kept on talking quietly to himself as I walked away. He was watching the ants, figuring, and paid no attention to me.

I went back to Barney. I asked, sort of choked, "What is he doing, Barney?"

"He's doing what he has to do," Barney said.

We went back to the monowheel and up the hill and through the force-gate. After a while, I asked, "How long will he be here?"

"As long as he wants to be." Barney was kind of short about it.

"Nobody wants to be locked up."

He had that odd look on his face again. "Nightingale's not a jail."

"He can't get out."

"Look, chum, we could start him over. We could even make a purser out of him. But we stopped doing that kind of thing a long time ago. We let a man do what he wants to do."

"He never wanted to be boss over an anthill."

"He didn't?"

I guess I looked as if I didn't understand that, so he said, "All his life he's pretended he's a man and the rest of us are ants. Now it's come true for him. He won't run human anthills any more because he will never again get near one."

I looked through the windshield at the shining finger that was my distant ship. "What happened on Borinquen, Barney?"

"Some of his converts got loose around the System. That Humanity One idea had to be stopped." He drove a while, seeing badly out of a thinking face. "You won't take this hard, Purser, but you're a thick-witted ape. I can say that if no one else can."

"All right," I said. "Why?"

"We had to *smash* into Borinquen, which used to be so free and easy. We got into Costello's place. It was a regular fort. We got him and his files. We didn't get his girl. He killed her, but the files were enough."

After a time I said, "He was always a good friend to me."

"Was he?"

I didn't say anything. He wheeled up to the receiving station and stopped the machine.

He said, "He was all ready for you if you came to work for him. He had a voice recording of you large as life, saying 'Sometimes a man's just *got* to be by himself.' Once you went to work for him, all he needed to do to keep you in line was to threaten to put that on the air."

I opened the door. "What did you have to show him to me for?"

"Because we believe in letting a man do what he wants to do, as long as he doesn't hurt the rest of us. If you want to go back to the lake and work for Costello, for instance, I'll take you there."

I closed the door carefully and went up the ramp to the ship.

I did my work and when the time came, we blasted off. I was mad. I don't think it was about anything Barney told me. I wasn't especially mad about Mr. Costello or what happened to him, because Barney's the best Navy psych doc there is and Nightingale's the most beautiful hospital planet in the Universe.

What made me mad was the thought that never again would a man as big as Mr. Costello give that big, warm, soft, strong friendship to a lunkhead like me.

The Touch of Your Hand

"Dig there," said Osser, pointing.

The black-browed man pulled back. "Why?"

"We must dig deep to build high, and we are going to build high."

"Why?" the man asked again.

"To keep the enemy out."

"There are no enemies."

Osser laughed bitterly. "I'll have enemies."

"Why?"

Osser came to him. "Because I'm going to pick up this village and shake it until it wakes up. And if it won't wake up, I'll keep shaking until I break its back and it dies. Dig."

"I don't see why," said the man doggedly.

Osser looked at the golden backs of his hands, turned them over, watched them closing. He raised his eyes to the other.

"This is why," he said.

His right fist tore the man's cheek. His left turned the man's breath to a bullet which exploded as it left him. He huddled on the ground, unable to exhale, inhaling in small, heavy, tearing sobs. His eyes opened and he looked up at Osser. He could not speak, but his eyes did; and through shock and pain all they said was "Why?"

"You want reasons," Osser said, when he felt the man could hear him. "You want reasons—all of you. You see both sides of every question and you weigh and balance and cancel yourselves out. I want an end to reason. I want things done."

He bent to lift the bearded man to his feet. Osser stood

half a head taller and his shoulders were as full and smooth as the bottoms of bowls. Golden hairs shifted and glinted on his forearms as he moved his fingers and the great cords tensed and valleyed. He lifted the man clear of the ground and set him easily on his feet and held him until he was sure of his balance.

"You don't understand me, do you?"

The man shook his head weakly.

"Don't try. You'll dig more if you don't try." He clapped the handle of the shovel into the man's hand and picked up a mattock. "Dig," he said, and the man began to dig.

Osser smiled when the man turned to work, arched his nostrils and drew the warm clean air into his lungs. He liked the sunlight now, the morning smell of the turned soil, the work he had to do and the idea itself of working.

Standing so, with his head raised, he saw a flash of bright yellow, the turn of a tanned face. Just a glimpse, and she was gone.

For a moment he tensed, frowning. If she had seen him she would be off to clatter the story of it to the whole village. Then he smiled. Let her. Let them all know. They must, sooner or later. Let them try to stop him.

He laughed, gripped his mattock, and the sod flew. So Jubilith saw fit to watch him, did she?

He laughed again. Work now, Juby later. In time he would have everything.

Everything.

The village street wound and wandered and from time to time divided and rejoined itself, for each house was built on a man's whim—near, far, high, small, separate, turned to or away. What did not harmonize contrasted well, and over all it was a pleasing place to walk.

Before a shop a wood-cobbler sat, gouging out sabots; and he was next door to the old leatherworker who cunningly wove immortal belts of square-knotted rawhide. Then a house, and another, and a cabin; a space of green where children played; and the skeleton of a new building where a man, his apron pockets full of hardwood pegs, worked knowledgeably with a heavy mallet.

The cobbler, the leatherworker, the children and the builder all stopped to watch Jubilith because she was beautiful and because she ran. When she was by, they each saw the others watching, and each smiled and waved and laughed a little, though nothing was said.

A puppy lolloped along after her, three legs deft, the fourth in the way. Had it been frightened, it would not have run, and had Jubilith spoken to it, it would have followed wherever she went. But she ignored it, even when it barked its small soprano bark, so it curved away from her, pretending it had been going somewhere else anyway, and then it sat and puffed and looked after her sadly.

Past the smithy with its shadowed, glowing heart she ran; past the gristmill with its wonderful wheel, taking and yielding with its heavy cupped hands. A boy struck his hoop and it rolled across her path. Without breaking stride, she leaped high over it and ran on, the glass-blower's lips burst away from his pipe, for a man can smile or blow glass, but not both at the same time.

When at last she reached Wrenn's house, she was breathing deeply, but with no difficulty, in the way possible only to those who run beautifully. She stopped by the open door and waited politely, not looking in until Oyva came out and touched her shoulder.

Jubilith faced her, keeping her eyes closed for a long moment, for Oyva was not only very old, she was Wrenn's wife.

"Is it Jubilith?" asked Oyva, smiling.

"It is," said the girl. She opened her eyes.

Oyva, seeing their taut corners, said shrewdly, "A troubled Jubilith as well. I'll not keep you. He's just inside."

Juby found a swift flash of smile to give her and went into the house, leaving the old woman to wonder where, where in her long life she had seen such a brief flash of such great loveliness. A firebird's wing? A green meteor? She put it away in her mind next to the memory of a burst of laughter—Wrenn's, just after he had kissed her first—and sat down on a three-legged stool by the side of the house.

A heavy fiber screen had been set up inside the doorway, to form a sort of meander, and at the third turn it was very dark. Juby paused to let the sunlight drain away from her vision. Somewhere in the dark before her there was music, the hay-clean smell of flower petals dried and freshly rubbed, and a voice humming. The voice and the music were open and free, but choked a listener's throat like the sudden appearance of a field of daffodils.

The voice and the music stopped short, and someone breathed quietly in the darkness.

"Is . . . is it Wrenn?" she faltered.

"It is," said the voice.

"Jubilith here."

"Move the screen," said the voice. "I'd like the light, talking to you, Jubilith."

She felt behind her, touched the screen. It had many hinges and swung easily away to the doorside. Wrenn sat crosslegged in the corner behind a frame which held a glittering complex of stones.

He brushed petal-dust from his hands. "Sit there, child, and tell me what it is you do not understand."

She sat down before him and lowered her eyes, and his widened, as if someone had taken away a great light.

When she had nothing to say, he prompted her gently: "See if you can put it all into a single world, Jubilith."

She said immediately, "Osser."

"Ah," said Wrenn.

"I followed him this morning, out to the foothills beyond the Sky-tree Grove. He—"

Wrenn waited.

Jubilith put up her small hands, clenched, and talked in a rush. "Sussten, with the black brows, he was with Osser. They stopped and Osser shouted at him, and, when I came to where I could look down and see them, Osser took his fists and hammered Sussten, knocked him down. He laughed and picked him up. Sussten was sick; he was shaken and there was blood on his face. Osser told him to dig, and Sussten dug, Osser laughed again, he laughed . . . I think he saw me. I came here."

Slowly she put her fists down. Wrenn said nothing.

Jubilith said, in a voice like a puzzled sigh, "I understand this: when a man hammers something, iron or clay or wood, it is to change what he hammers from what it is to what he wishes it to be." She raised one hand, made a fist, and put it down again. She shook her head slightly and her heavy soft hair moved on her back. "To hammer a man is to change nothing. Sussten remains Sussten."

"It was good to tell me of this," said Wrenn when he was sure she had finished.

"Not good," Jubilith disclaimed. "I want to understand."

Wrenn shook his head. Juby cocked her head on one side

like a wondering bright bird. When she realized that his gesture was a refusal, a small paired crease came and went between her brows.

"May I not understand this?"

"You *must* not understand it," Wrenn corrected. "Not yet, anyway. Perhaps after a time. Perhaps never."

"Ah," she said. "I—I didn't know."

"How could you know?" he asked kindly. "Don't follow Osser again, Jubilith."

She parted her lips, then again gave the small headshake. She rose and went out.

Oyva came to her. "Better now, Jubilith?"

Juby turned her head away; then, realizing that this was ill-mannered, met Oyva's gaze. The girl's eyes were full of tears. She closed them respectfully. Oyva touched her shoulder and let her go.

Watching the slim, bright figure trudge away, bowed with thought, drag-footed, unseeing, Oyva grunted and stomped into the house.

"Did she have to be hurt?" she demanded.

"She did," said Wrenn gently. "Osser," he added.

"Oh," she said, in just the tone he had used when Jubilith first mentioned the name. "What has he done now?"

Wrenn told her. Oyva sucked her lips in thoughtfully. "Why was the girl following him?"

"I didn't ask her. But don't you know?"

"I suppose I do," said Oyva, and sighed. "That mustn't happen, Wrenn."

"It won't. I told her not to follow him again."

She looked at him fondly. "I suppose even you can act like a fool once in a while."

He was startled. "Fool?"

"She loves him. You won't keep her from him by a word of advice."

"You judge her by yourself," he said, just as fondly. "She's only a child. In a day, a week, she'll wrap someone else up in her dreams."

"Suppose she doesn't?"

"Don't even think about it." A shudder touched his voice.

"I shall, though," said Oyva with determination. "And you'd do well to think about it, too." When his eyes grew troubled, she touched his cheek gently, "Now play some more for me."

He sat down before the instrument, his hands poised. Then into the tiny bins his fingers went, rubbing this dried-petal powder and that, and the stones glowed, changing the flower-scents into music and shifting colors.

He began to sing softly to the music.

They dug deep, day by day, and they built. Osser did the work of three men, and sometimes six or eight others worked with him, and sometimes one or two. Once he had twelve. But never did he work alone.

When the stone was three tiers above ground level, Osser climbed the nearest rise and stood looking down at it proudly, at the thickness and strength of the growing walls, at the toiling workers who lifted and strained to make them grow.

"Is it Osser?"

The voice was as faint and shy as a fern uncurling, as promising as spring itself.

He turned.

"Jubilith," she told him.

"What are you doing here?"

"I come here every day," she said. She indicated the copse which crowned the hill. "I hide here and watch you."

"What do you want?"

She laced her fingers. "I would like to dig there and lift stones."

"No," he said, and turned to study the work again.

"Why not?"

"Never ask me why. 'Because I say so'—that's all the answer you'll get from me—you or anyone."

She came to stand beside him. "You build fast."

He nodded. "Faster than any village house was ever built." He could sense the 'why' rising within her, and could feel it being checked.

"I want to build it, too," she pleaded.

"No," he said. His eyes widened as he watched the work. Suddenly he was gone, leaping down the slope in great springy strides. He turned the corner of the new wall and stood, saying nothing. The man who had been idling turned quickly and lifted a stone. Osser smiled a quick, taut smile and went to work beside him. Jubilith stood on the slope, watching, wondering.

She came almost every day as the tower grew. Osser

never spoke to her. She watched the sunlight on him, the lithe strength, the rippling gold. He stood like a great tree, squatted like a rock, moved like a thundercloud. His voice was a whip, a bugle, the roar of a bull.

She saw him less and less in the village. Once it was a fearsome thing to see. Early in the morning he appeared suddenly, overtook a man, lifted him and threw him flat on the ground.

"I told you to be out there yesterday," he growled, and strode away.

Friends came and picked the man up, held him softly while he coughed, took him away to be healed.

No one went to Wrenn about it; the word had gone around that Osser and his affairs were not to be understood by anyone. Wrenn's function was to explain those few things which could not be understood. But certain of these few were not to be understood at all. So Osser was left alone to do as he wished—which was a liberty, after all, that was enjoyed by everyone else.

Twilight came when Jubilith waited past her usual time. She waited until by ones and twos the workers left the tower, until Osser himself had climbed the hill, until he had paused to look back and be proud and think of tomorrow's work, until he, too, had turned his face to the town. Then she slipped down to the tower and around it, and carefully climbed the scaffolding on the far side. She looked about her.

The tower was now four stories high and seemed to be shaping toward a roof. Circular in cross-section, the tower had two rooms on each floor, an east-west wall between them on the ground floor, a north-south wall on the next, and so on up.

There was a central well into which was built a spiral staircase—a double spiral, as if one helix had been screwed into the other. This made possible two exits to stairs on each floor at the same level, though they were walled off one from the other. Each of the two rooms on every floor had one connecting doorway. Each room had three windows in it, wide on the inside, tapering through the thick stone wall to form the barest slit outside.

A portion of the castellated roof was already built. It overhung the entrance, and had slots in the overhang through which the whole entrance face of the tower could be covered by one man lying unseen on the roof, looking straight down.

Stones lay in a trough ready for placing, and there was some leftover mortar in the box. Jubilith picked up a trowel and worked it experimentally in the stuff, then lifted some out and tipped it down on the unfinished top of the wall, just as she had seen Osser do so many times. She put down the trowel and chose a stone. It was heavy—much heavier than she had expected—but she made it move, made it lift, made it seat itself to suit her on the fresh mortar. She ticked off the excess from the joint and stepped back to admire it in the fading light.

Two great clamps, hard as teeth, strong as a hurricane, caught her right thigh and left armpit. She was swung into the air and held helpless over the unfinished parapet.

She was utterly silent, shocked past the ability even to gasp.

"I told you you were not to work here," said Osser between his teeth. So tall he was, so long were his arms as he held her high over his head, that it seemed almost as far to the parapet as it was to the ground below.

He leaned close to the edge and shook her. "I'll throw you off. This tower is mine to build, you hear?"

If she had been able to breathe, she might have screamed or pleaded with him. If she had screamed or pleaded, he might have dropped her. But her silence apparently surprised him. He grunted and set her roughly on her feet. She caught at his shoulder to keep her balance, then quickly transferred her hold to the edge of the parapet. She dropped her head between her upper arms. Her long soft hair fell forward over her face, and she moaned.

"I told you," he said, really seeing her at last. His voice shook. He stepped toward her and put out his hand. She screamed. "Be *quiet!*" he roared. A moan shut off in mid-breath. "Ah, I told you, Juby. You shouldn't have tried to build here."

He ran his great hands over the edge of the stonework, found the one she had laid, the one that had cost her such effort to lift. With one hand, he plucked it up and threw it far out into the shadows below.

"I wanted to help you with it," she whispered.

"Don't you understand?" he cried. "No one builds here who *wants* to help!"

She simply shook her head.

She tried to breathe deeply and a long shudder possessed her. When it passed, she turned weakly and stood, her back partly arched over the edge of the parapet, her hands behind her to cushion the stone. She shook the hair out of her face; it fell away on either side like a dawnlit bow-wave. She looked up at him with an expression of such piteous confusion that his dwindling rage vanished altogether.

He dropped his eyes and shuffled one foot like a guilty child. "Juby, leave me alone."

Something almost like a smile touched her lips. She brushed her bruised arm, then walked past him to the place where the scaffolding projected above the parapet.

"Not that way," he called. "Come here."

He took her hand and led her to the spiral staircase at the center of the tower. It was almost totally dark inside. It seemed like an age to her as they descended; she was alone in a black universe consisting of a rhythmic drop and turn, and a warm hard hand in hers, holding and leading her.

When they emerged, he stopped in the strange twilight, a darkness for all the world but a dazzle to them, so soaked with blackness were their eyes. She tugged gently, but he would not release her hand. She moved close to see his face. His eyes were wide and turned unseeing to the far slopes; he was frowning, yet his mouth was not fierce, but irresolute. Whatever his inward struggle was, it left his face gradually and transferred itself to his hand. Its pressure on hers became firm, hard, intense, painful.

"Osser!"

He dropped the hand and stepped back, shamed. "Juby, I will take you to . . . Juby, do you want to understand?" He waved at the tower.

She said, "Oh, yes!"

He looked at her closely, and the angry, troubled diffidence came and went. "Half a day there, half a day back again," he said.

She recognized that this was as near as this feral, unhappy man could come to asking a permission. "I'd like to understand," she said.

"If you don't, I'm going to kill you," he blurted. He turned to the west and strode off, not looking back.

Jubilith watched him go, and suddenly there was a sparkle in her wide eyes. She slipped out of her sandals, caught them up in her hand, and ran lightly and silently after him. He planted his feet strongly, like the sure, powerful teeth of the millwheel gears, and he would not look back. She sensed how immensely important it was to him not to look back. She knew that right-handed men look back over their left shoulders, so she drifted along close to him, a little behind him, a little to his right. How long, how long, until he looked to see if she was coming?

Up and up the slope, to its crest, over . . . down . . . ah! Just here, just at the last second where he could turn and look without stopping and still catch a glimpse of the tower's base, where they had stood. So he turned, and she passed around him like a windblown feather, unseen.

And he stopped, looking back, craning. His shoulders slumped, and slowly he turned to his path again—and there was Jubilith before him.

She laughed.

His jaw dropped, and then his lips came together in a thin, angry seal. For a moment he stared at her; and suddenly, quite against his will, there burst from him a single harsh bark of laughter. She put out her hand and he came to her, took it, and they went their way together.

They came to a village when it was very late and very dark, and Osser circled it. They came to another, and Jubilith thought he would do the same, for he turned south; but when they came abreast of it, he struck north again.

"We'll be seen," he explained gruffly, "but we'll be seen coming from the south and leaving northward."

She would not ask where he was taking her, or why he was making these elaborate arrangements, but already she had an idea. What lay to the west was—not forbidden, exactly, but, say discouraged. It was felt that there was nothing in that country that could be of value. Anyone traveling that way would surely be remembered.

So through the village they went, and they dined quickly at an inn, and went northward, and once in the darkness, veered west again. In a wood so dark that she had taken his hand again, he stopped and built a fire. He threw down springy boughs and a thick heap of ferns, and this was her bed. He slept sitting up, his back to a tree trunk, with Jubilith between him and the fire.

Jubilith awoke twice during the long night, once to see him with his eyes closed, but feeling that he was not asleep; and once to see him with his eyes open and the dying flames flickering in the pupils, and she thought then that he was asleep, or at least not with her, but lost in the pictures the flames painted.

In the morning they moved on, gathering berries for breakfast, washing in a humorous brook. And during this whole journey, nothing passed between them but the small necessary phrases: "You go first here." "Look out—it drops." "Tired yet?"

For there was that about Jubilith which made explanations unnecessary. Though she did not know where they were going, or why, she understood what must be done to get them there within the framework of his desire: to go immediately, as quickly as possible, undetected by anyone else.

She did only what she could to help and did not plague him with questions which would certainly be answered in good time. So: "Here are berries." "Look, a red bird!" "Can we get through there, or shall we go around?" And nothing more.

They did well, the weather was fine, and by mid-morning they had reached the tumbled country of the Crooked Hills. Jubilith had seen them from afar—great broken mounds and masses against the western sky—but no one ever went there, and she knew nothing about them.

They were in open land now, and Jubilith regretted leaving the color and aliveness of the forest. The grasses here were strange, like yet unlike those near her village. They were taller, sickly, and some had odd ugly flowers. There were bald places scored with ancient rain-gullies, as if some mighty hand had dashed acid against the soil. There were few insects and no animals that she could see, and no birds sang. It was a place of great sadness rather than terror; there was little to fear, but much to grieve for.

By noon, they faced a huge curved ridge, covered with broken stones. It looked as if the land itself had reared up and pressed back from a hidden something on the other side —something which it would not touch. Osser quickened their pace as they began to climb, although the going was hard Jubilith realized that they were near the end of their journey, and uncomplainingly struggled along at the cruel pace he set.

At the top, they paused, giving their first attention to their wind, and gradually to the scene before them.

The ridge on which they stood was nearly circular, and perhaps a mile and a half in diameter. In its center was a small round lake with unnaturally bare shores. Mounds of rubble sloped down toward it on all sides, and farther back was broken stone.

But it was the next zone which caught and held the eye. The weed-grown wreckage there was beyond description. Great twisted webs and ribs of gleaming metal wove in and out of the slumped heaps of soil and masonry. Nearby, a half-acre of laminated stone stood on the edge like a dinner plate in a clay bank. What could have been a building taller than any Jubilith had ever heard about lay on its side, smashed and bulging.

Gradually she began to realize the peculiarity of this place —All the larger wreckage lay in lines directly to and from the lake in a monstrous radiation of ruin.

"What is this place?" she asked at last.

"Don't know," he grunted, and went over the edge to slip down the steep slope. When she caught up with him near the bottom, he said, "There's miles of this, west and north of here, much bigger. But this is the one we came to see. Come."

He looked to right and left as if to get his bearings, then plunged into the tough and scrubby underbrush that vainly tried to cover those tortured metal bones. She followed as closely as she could, beating at the branches which he carelessly let whip back.

Just in front of her, he turned the corner of a sharp block of stone, and when she turned it no more than a second later, he was gone.

She stopped, turned, turned again. Dust, weeds, lonely and sorrowful ruins. No Osser. She shrank back against the stone, her eyes wide.

The bushes nearby trembled, then lashed. Osser's head emerged. "What's the matter? Come on!" he said gruffly.

She checked an impulse to cry out and run to him, and came silently forward. Osser held the bushes briefly, and beside him she saw a black hole with broken steps leading downward.

She hesitated, but he moved his head impatiently, and she passed him and led the way downward. When he followed, his wide flat body blocked out the light. The darkness was so heavy, her eyes ached.

He prodded her in the small of the back. "Go on, go on!"

The foot of the steps came sooner than she expected and her knees buckled as she took the downward step that was not there. She tripped, almost fell, then somehow got to the side wall and braced herself there, trembling.

"Wait," he said, and the irrepressible smile quirked the corners of her mouth. As if she would go anywhere!

She heard him fumbling about somewhere, and then there was a sudden aching blaze of light that made her cry out and clap her hands over her face.

"Look," he said. "I want you to look at this. Hold it."

Into her hands he pressed a cylinder about half the length of her forearm. At one end was a lens from which the blue-white light was streaming.

"See this little thing here," he said, and touched a stud at the side of the cylinder. The light disappeared, came on again.

She laughed delightedly, took the cylinder and played its light around, switching it on and off. "It's wonderful!" she cried. "Oh, wonderful!"

"You take this one," he said, pleased. He handed her another torch and took the first from her. "It isn't as good, but it will help. I'll go first."

She took the second torch and tried it. It worked the same way, but the light was orange and feeble. Osser strode ahead down a slanting passageway. At first there was a great deal of rubble underfoot, but soon the way was clear as they went farther and deeper. Osser walked with confidence, and she knew he had been here before, probably many times.

"Here," he said, stopping to wait for her. His voice echoed strangely, vibrant with controlled excitement.

He turned his torch ahead, swept it back and forth.

They were at the entrance to a room. It was three times the height of a man, and as big as their village green. She stared around, awed.

"Come," Osser said again, and went to the far corner.

A massive, boxlike object stood there. One panel, about eye-level, was of a milky smooth substance, the rest of black metal. Projecting from the floor in front of it was a lever. Osser grasped it confidently and pulled. It yielded sluggishly, and returned to its original position. Osser tugged again. There was a low growling sound from the box. Osser pulled, released, pulled, released, each time a little faster. The sound rose in pitch, higher and higher.

"Turn off your light," he said.

She did so and blackness snapped in around them. As the dazzle faded from her eyes, she detected a flicker of silver light before her, and realized that it came from the milky pane in the box. As Osser pulled at the lever and the whine rose and rose in pitch, the square got bright enough for her to see her hands when she looked down at them.

And then—the pictures.

Jubilith had never seen pictures like these. They moved, for one thing; for another, they had no color. Everything in them was black and white and shades of gray. Yet everything they showed seemed very real.

Not at first, for there was flickering and stopped motion, and then slow motion as Osser's lever moved faster and faster. But at last the picture steadied, and Osser kept the lever going at the same speed, flicking it with apparent ease about twice a second, while the whine inside the box settled to a steady, soft moan.

The picture showed a ball spinning against a black, light-flecked curtain. It rushed close until it filled the screen, and still closer, and Jubilith suddenly had the feeling that she was falling at tremendous velocity from an unthinkable height. Down and down the scene went, until at last the surface began to take on the qualities of a bird's-eye view. She saw a river and lakes, and a great range of hills—

And, at last, the city.

It was a city beyond fantasy, greater and more elaborate than imagination could cope with. Its towers stretched skyward to pierce the clouds themselves—some actually did. It had wide ramps on which traffic crawled, great bridges across the river, parks over which the buildings hung like mighty cliffs. Closer still the silver eye came to the scene, and she realized that the traffic was not crawling, but moving faster than a bird, faster than the wind. The vehicles were low and sleek and efficient.

And on the walks were people, and the scene wheeled and slowed and showed them. They were elaborately clothed and well-fed; they were hurried and orderly at the same time. There was a square in which perhaps a thousand of them, all dressed alike, were drawn up in lines as straight as stretched string. Even as she watched, they all began to move together, a thousand left legs coming forward, a thousand right arms swing back.

Higher, then, and more of the city—more and more of it, until the sense of wonder filled her lungs and she hardly breathed; and still more of it, miles of it. And at last a great open space with what looked like sections of road crossing on it—but such unthinkable roads! Each was as wide as her whole village and miles long. And on these roads, great birdlike machines tilted down and touched and rolled, and swung and ran and took the air, dozens of them every minute. The scene swept close again, and it was as if she were in such a machine herself; but it did not land. It raced past the huge busy crossroads and out to a coastline.

And there were ships, ships as long as the tallest buildings were high, and clusters, dozens, hundreds of other vessels working and smoking and milling about in the gray water. Huge machines crouched over ships and lifted out cargoes; small, agile machines scurried about the docks and warehouses.

Then at last the scene dwindled as the magic eye rose higher and higher, faster and faster. Details disappeared, and clouds raced past and downward, and at last the scene was a disc and then a ball floating in starlit space.

Osser let the lever go and it snapped back to its original position. The moan descended quickly in pitch, and the motion on the screen slowed, flickered, faded and went out.

Jubilith let the darkness come. Her mind spun and shook with the impact of what she had seen. Slowly she recovered herself. She became conscious of Osser's hard breathing. She turned on her dim orange torch and looked at him. He was watching her.

"What was it?" she breathed.

"What I came to show you."

She thought hard. She thought about his tower, about his refusal to let her work on it, about his cruelty to those who had. She looked at him, at the blank screen. And this was to supply the reason.

She shook her head.

He lowered himself slowly and squatted like an animal, hunched up tight, his knees in his armpits. This lifted and crooked his heavy arms. He rested their knuckles on the floor. He glowered at her and said nothing. He was waiting.

On the way here, he had said, "I'll kill you if you don't understand." But he wouldn't really, would he? Would he?

If he had towered over her, ranted and shouted, she would not have been afraid. But squatting there, waiting, silent, with his great arms bowed out like that, he was like some patient, preying beast.

She turned off the light to blot out the sight of him, and immediately became speechless with terror at the idea of his sitting there in the dark so close, waiting. She might run; she was so swift . . . but no; crouched like that, he could spring and catch her before she could tense a muscle.

Again she looked at the dead screen. "Will you . . . tell me something?" she quavered.

"I might."

"Tell me, then: When you first saw that picture, did you understand? The very first time?"

His expression did not change. But slowly he relaxed. He rocked sidewise, sat down, extended his legs. He was man again, not monster. She shuddered, then controlled it.

He said, "It took me a long time and many visits. I should not have asked you to understand at once."

She again accepted the timid half-step toward an apology, and was grateful.

He said, "Those were men and women just like us. Did you see that? Just like us."

"Their clothes—"

"Just like us," he insisted. "Of course they dressed differently, lived differently! In a world like that, why not? Ah, how they built, how they built!"

"Yes," she whispered. Those towers, the shining, swift vehicles, the thousand who moved like one . . . "Who were they?" she asked him.

"Don't you know? Think—think!"

"Osser, I want to understand. I truly want to!"

She hunted frantically for the right thing to say, the right way to catch at this elusive thing which was so frighteningly important to him. All her life she had had the answers to the questions she wanted to understand. All she had ever had to do was to close her eyes and think of the problem and the answers soon came.

But not this problem.

"Osser," she pleaded, "where is it, the city, the great complicated city?"

"Say, 'Where *was* it?' " he growled.

She caught his thought and gasped. "This? These ruins, Osser?"

"Ah," he said approvingly. "It comes slowly, doesn't it? No, Juby. Not here. What was here was an outpost, a village, compared with the big city. North and west, I told you, didn't I? Miles of it. So big that . . . so big—" He extended his arms, dropped them helplessly. Suddenly he leaned close to her, began to talk fast, feverishly. "Juby, that city—that world—was built by *people*. Why did they build and why do we not? What is the difference between those people and ours?"

"They must have had . . ."

"They had nothing we don't have. They're the same kind of people; they *used* something we haven't been using. Juby, I've got that something. I can build. I can make others build."

A mental picture of the tower glimmered before her. "You built it with hate," she said wonderingly. "Is that what they had—cruelty, brutality, hatred?"

"Yes!"

"I don't believe it! I don't believe anyone could live with that much hate!"

"Perhaps not. Perhaps they didn't. But they *built* with it. They built because some men could flog others into building for them, building higher and faster than all the good neighbors would ever do helping one another."

"They'd hate the man who made them build like that."

Osser's hands crackled as he pressed them together. He laughed, and the echoes took everything that was unpleasant about that laughter and filled the far reaches of the dark room with it.

"They'd hate him," he agreed. "But he's strong, you see. He was strong in the first place, to make them build, and he's stronger afterward with what they built for him. Do you know the only way they can express their hatred, once they find he's too strong for them?"

Jubilith shook her head.

"They'd build," he chuckled. "They'd build higher and faster than he did. They would find the strongest man among them and *ask* him to flog them into it. That's the way a great city goes up. A strong man builds, and strong men follow, and soon the man who's strongest of all makes all the other strong ones do his work. Do you see?"

"And the ... the others, the weak?"

"What of them?" he asked scornfully. "There are more of them than strong ones—so there are more hands to do the strong man's work. And why shouldn't they? Don't they get the city to live in when it's built? Don't they ride about in swift shining carriers and fly through the air in the bird machines?"

"Would they be—happy?" she asked.

He looked at her in genuine puzzlement. "Happy?" He smashed a heavy fist into his palm. "They'd have a *city!*" Again the words tumbled from him. "How do you live, you and the rest of the village? What do you do when you want a—well, a garden, food from the ground?"

"I dig up the soil," she said. "I plant and water and weed."

"Suppose you want a plow?"

"I make one. Or I do work for someone who has one."

"Uh," he grunted. "And there you are, hundreds of you in the village, each one planting a little, smithing a little, thatching and cutting and building a little. Everyone does everything except for how many—four, five?—the leather-worker, old Griak who makes wooden pegs for house beams, one or two others."

"They like to do just one work. But anyone can do any of the work. Those few, we take care of. Someone has to keep the skills alive."

He snorted. "Put a strong man in the village and give him strong men to do what he wants. Get ten villagers at once and make them all plant at once. You'll have food then for fifty, not ten!"

"But it would go to waste!"

"It would not, because it would all belong to the head man. He would give it away as he saw fit—a lot to those who obeyed him, nothing to those who didn't. What was left over he could keep for himself, and barter it out to keep building. Soon he would have the biggest house and the best animals and the finest women, and the more he got, the stronger he would be. And a city would grow—a *city!* And the strong man would give everyone better things if they worked hard, and protect them."

"Protect them? Against what?"

"Against the other strong ones. There would be others."

"And you—"

"I shall be the strongest of all," he said proudly. He waved at the box. "We were a great people once. We're ants now—less than ants, for at least the ants work together for a common purpose. I'll make us great again." His head sank onto his hand and he looked somberly into the shadows. "Something happened to this world. Something smashed the cities and the people and drove them down to what they are today. Something was broken within them, and they no longer dared to be great. Well, they will be. *I* have the extra something that was smashed out of them."

"What smashed them, Osser?"

"Who can know? I don't. I don't care, either." He tapped her with a long forefinger to emphasize. "All I care about is this: They were smashed because they were not strong enough. I shall be so strong I can't be smashed."

She said, "A stomach can hold only so much. A man asleep takes just so much space. So much and no more clothing makes one comfortable. Why do you want more than these things, Osser?"

She knew he was annoyed, and knew, too, that he was considering the question as honestly as he could.

"It's because I . . . I want to be strong," he said in a strained voice.

"You *are* strong."

"Who knows that?" he raged, and the echoes giggled and whispered.

"I do. Wrenn. Sussten. The whole village."

"The whole world will know. They will all do things for me."

She thought, But everyone does everything for himself, all over the world. Except, she added, those who aren't able . . .

With that in mind, she looked at him, his oaken shoulders, his powerful, bitter mouth. She touched the bruises his hands had left, and the beginnings of the understanding she had been groping for left her completely.

She said dully, "Your tower . . . you'd better get back there."

"Work goes on," he said, smiling tightly, "whether I'm there or not, as long as they don't know my plans. They are afraid. But—yes, we can go now."

Rising, he flicked the stud of his torch. It flared blue-white, faded to the weak orange of Jubilith's, then died.

"The light . . ."

"It's all right," said Jubilith. "I have mine."

"When they get like that, so dim, you can't tell when they'll go out. Come—hurry! This place is full of corridors; without light, we could be lost here for days."

She glanced around at the crowding shadows. "Make it work again," she suggested.

He looked at the dead torch in his hand. "You," he said flatly. He tossed it. She caught it in her free hand, put her torch on the floor, and held the broken one down so she could see it in the waning orange glow. She turned it over twice, her sensitive hands feeling with every part rather than with fingertips alone. She held it still and closed her eyes; and then it came to her, and she grasped one end with her right hand and the other with her left, and twisted.

There was a faint click and the outer shell of the torch separated. She drew off the butt end of it; it was just a hollow shell. The entire mechanism was attached to the lens end and was now exposed.

She turned it over carefully, keeping her fingers away from the workings. Again she closed her eyes and thought, and at last she bent close and peered. She nodded, fumbled in her hair, and detached a copper clasp. She bent and broke off a narrow strip of it and inserted it carefully into the light mechanism. Very carefully, she pried apart two small strands of wire, dipped a little deeper, hooked onto a tiny white sphere, and drew it out.

"Poor thing," she murmured under her breath.

"Poor what?"

"Spider's egg," she said ruefully. "They fight so to save them; and this one will never hatch out now. It's been burned."

She picked up the butt-end housing, slipped the two parts together, and twisted them until they clicked. She handed the torch to Osser.

"You've wasted time," he complained, surly.

"No, I haven't," she said. "We'll have light now."

He touched the stud on the torch. The brilliant, comforting white light poured from it.

"Yes," he admitted quietly.

Watching his face as he handled the torch, she knew that if she could read what was in his mind in that second, she would have the answer to everything about him. She could not, however, and he said nothing, but led across the room to the dark corridor.

He was silent all the way back to the broken steps.

They stood halfway up, letting their eyes adjust to the daylight which poured down on them, and he said, "You didn't even try the torch to see if it would work, after you took out that egg."

"I knew it would work." She looked at him, amazed. "You're angry."

"Yes," he said.

He took her torch and his and put them away in a niche in the ruined stair-well, and they climbed up into the noon light. It was all but intolerable, as the two suns were all but in syzygy, the blue-white midget shining through the great pale gaseous mass of the giant, so that together they cast only a single shadow.

"It will be hot this afternoon," she said, but he was silent, steeped in some bitterness of his own, so she followed him quietly without attempting conversation.

Old Oyva stirred sleepily in her basking chair, and suddenly sat upright.

Jubilith approached her, pale and straight. "Is it Oyva?"

"It is, Jubilith," said the old woman. "I knew you would be back, my dear. I'm sore in my heart with you."

"Is he here?"

"He is. He has been on a journey. You'll find him tired."

"He should have been here, with all that has happened," said Jubilith.

"He should have done exactly as he has done," Oyva stated bluntly.

Jubilith recognized the enormity of her rudeness, and the taste of it was bad in her mouth. One did not criticize Wrenn's comings and goings.

She faced Oyva and closed her eyes humbly.

Oyva touched her. "It's all right, child. You are distressed. Wrenn!" she called. "She is here!"

"Come, Jubilith," Wrenn's voice called from the house.

"He knows? *No* one knew I was coming here!"

"He knows," said Oyva. "Go to him, child."

Jubilith entered the house. Wrenn sat in his corner. The musical instrument was nowhere in sight. Aside from his cushions, there was nothing in the room.

Wrenn gave her his wise, sweet smile. "Jubilith," he said. "Come close." He looked drawn and pale, but quite untroubled. He put a cushion by him and she crossed slowly and sank down on it.

He was quiet, and when she was sure it was because he waited for her to speak, she said, "Some things may not be understood."

"True," he agreed.

She kneaded her hands. "Is there never a change?"

"Always," he said, "when it's time."

"Osser—"

"Everyone will understand Osser very soon now."

She screwed up her courage. "Soon is not soon enough. I must know him now."

"Before anyone else?" he inquired mildly.

"Let everyone know now," she suggested.

He shook his head and there was no appeal in it.

"Then let me. I shall be a part of you and speak of it only to you."

"Why must you understand?"

She shuddered. It was not cold, or fear, but simply the surgings of a great emotion.

"I love him," she said. "And to love is to guard and protect. He needs me."

"Go to him then." But she sat where she was, her long eyes cast down, weeping. Wrenn said, "There is more, then?"

"I love . . ." She threw out an arm in a gesture which enfolded Wrenn, the house, the village. "I love the people, too, the gardens, the little houses; the way we go and come, and sing, and make music, and make our own tools and clothes. To love is to guard and protect . . . and I love these things, and I love Osser. I can destroy Osser, because he would not expect it of me; and, if I did, I would protect all of you. But if I protect him, he will destroy you. There is no answer to such a problem, Wrenn; it is a road," she cried, "with a precipice at each end, and no standing still!"

"And understanding him would be an answer?"

"There's no other!" She turned her face up to him, imploring. "Osser is strong, Wrenn, with a—new thing about him, a thing none of the rest of us have. He has told me of it. It is a thing that can change us, make us part of him. He will build cities with our hands, on our broken bodies if we resist him. He wants us to be a great people again—he says we were, once, and have lost it all."

"And do you regard that as greatness, Jubilith—the towers, the bird-machines?"

"How did you know of them? . . . Greatness? I don't know, I don't know," she said, and wept. "I love him, and he wants to build a city with a wanting greater than anything I have ever known or heard of before. Could he do it, Wrenn? Could he?"

"He might," said Wrenn calmly.

"He is in the village now. He had about him the ones who built his tower for him. They cringe around him, hating to be near and afraid to leave. He sent them one by one to tell all the people to come out to the foothills tomorrow, to begin work on his city. He wants enough building done in one hundred days to shelter everyone, because then, he says, he is going to burn this village to the ground. Why, Wrenn—why?"

"Perhaps," said Wrenn, "so that we may all face his strength and yield to it. A man who could move a whole village in a hundred days just to show his strength would be a strong man indeed."

"What shall we do?"

"I think we shall go out to the foothills in the morning and begin to build."

She rose and went to the door.

"I know what to do now," she whispered. "I won't try to understand any more. I shall just go and help him."

"Yes, go," said Wrenn. "He will need you."

Jubilith stood with Osser on the parapet, and with him stared into the dappled dawn. The whole sky flamed with the loom of the red sun's light, but the white one preceded it up the sky, laying sharp shadows in the soft blunt ones. Birds called and chattered in the Sky-tree Grove, and deep in the thickets the seven-foot bats grunted as they settled in to sleep.

"Suppose they don't come?" she asked.

"They'll come," he said grimly. "Jubilith, why are you here?"

She said, "I don't know what you are doing, Osser. I don't know whether it's right or whether you will keep on succeeding. I do know there will be pain and difficulty and I—I came to keep you safe, if I could . . . I love you."

He looked down at her, as thick and dark over her as his tower was over the foothills. One side of his mouth twitched.

"Little butterfly," he said softly, "do you think *you* can guard *me?*"

Everything beautiful about her poured out to him through her beautiful face, and for a moment his world had three suns instead of two. He put his arms around her. Then his great voice exploded with two syllables of a mighty laugh. He lifted her and swung her behind him, and leaped to the parapet.

Deeply shaken, she came to follow his gaze.

The red sun's foggy limb was above the townward horizon, and silhouetted against it came the van of a procession. On they came and on, the young men of the village, the fathers. Women were with them, too, and everything on wheels that the village possessed—flat-bed wagons, two-wheeled rickshaw carts, children's and vendors' and pleasure vehicles. A snorting team of four tiger-oxen clawed along before a heavily laden stone-boat, and men shared packs that swung in the center of long poles.

Osser curled his lip. "You see them," he said, as if to himself, "doing the only thing they can think of. Push them, they yield. The clods!" he spat. "Well, one day, one will push back. And when he does, I'll break him, and after that I'll use him. Meantime—I have a thousand hands and a single mind. We'll see building now," he crooned. "When they've built, they'll know what they don't know now—that they're men."

"They've all come," breathed Jubilith. "All of them. Osser—"

"Be quiet," he said, leaning into the wind to watch, gloating. With the feel of his hard hands still on her back, she discovered with a crushing impact that there was no room in his heart for her when he thought of his building. And she knew that there never would be, except perhaps for a stolen moment, a touch in passing. With the pain of that realization came the certainty that she would stay with him always, even for so little.

The procession dipped out of sight, then slowly rose over and down the near hill and approached the tower. It spread and thickened at the foot of the slope, as men cast about, testing the ground with their picks, eying the land for its color and vegetation and drainage . . . or was that what they were doing?

Osser leaned his elbows on the parapet and shook his head pityingly at their inefficiency. Look at the way they went about laying out houses! And their own houses. Well, he'd let them mill about until they were completely confused, and then he'd go down and make them do it his way. Confused men are soft men; men working against their inner selves are easy to divert from outside.

Beside him, Jubilith gasped.

"What is it?"

She pointed. "There—sending the men to this side, that side. See, by the stone-boat? It's Wrenn!"

"Nonsense!" said Osser. "He'd never leave his house. Not to walk around among people who are sweating. He deals only with people who tell him he's right before he speaks."

"It's Wrenn, it is, it is!" cried Jubilith. She clutched his arm. "Osser, I'm afraid!"

"Afraid? Afraid of what? . . . By the dying Red One, it *is* Wrenn, telling men what to do as if this was *his* city." He laughed. "There are few enough here who are strong, Juby, but he's the strongest there is. And look at him scurry around for me!"

"I'm afraid," Jubilith whimpered.

"They jump when he tells them," said Osser reflectively, shading his eyes. "Perhaps I was wrong to let them tire themselves out before I help them do things right. With a man like him to push them . . . Hm. I think we'll get it done right the first time."

He pushed himself away from the parapet and swung to the stairway.

"Osser, don't, please don't!" she begged.

He stopped just long enough to give her a glance like a stone thrown. "You'll never change my mind, Juby, and you'll be hurt if you try too often." He dropped into the opening, went down three steps, five steps . . .

He grunted, stopped.

Jubilith came slowly over to the stairwell. Osser stood on the sixth step, on tiptoe. Impossibly on tiptoe, the points of his sandals barely touched the step at all.

He set his jaw and placed his massive hands one on each side of the curved wall. He pressed them out and up, forcing himself downward. His sandals touched more firmly; his toes bent, his heels made contact. His face became deep red, and the cords at the sides of his neck ridged like a weathered fallow-field.

A strained crackle came from his shoulders, and then the pent breath burst from him. His hands slipped, and he came up again just the height of the single stair-riser, to bob ludicrously like a boat at anchor, his pointed toe touching and lifting from the sixth step.

He gave an inarticulate roar, bent double, and plunged his hands downward as if to dive head-first down the stairs. His wrists turned under and he yelped with the pain. More cautiously he felt around and down, from wall to wall. It was as if the air in the stairway had solidified, become at once viscous and resilient. Whatever was there was invisible and completely impassable.

He backed slowly up the steps. On his face there was fury and frustration, hurt and a shaking reaction.

Jubilith wrung her hands. "Please, please, Osser, be care—"

The sound of her voice gave him something to strike out at, and he spun about, raising his great bludgeon of a fist. Jubilith stood frozen, too shocked to dodge the blow.

"Osser!"

Osser stopped, tensed high, fist up, like some terrifying monument to vengeance. The voice had been Wrenn's— beyond belief. The echoes of it rolled off and were lost, Wrenn speaking quietly, even conversationally, but magnified in the hills.

"Come watch men building, Osser!"

Dazed, Osser lowered his arm and went to the parapet.

Far below, near the base of the hill, Wrenn stood, looking up at the tower. When Osser appeared, Wrenn turned his back and signaled the men by the stone-boat. They twitched away the tarpaulin that covered its load.

Osser's hands gripped the stone as if they would powder it. His eyes slowly widened and his jaw slowly dropped.

At first it seemed like a mound of silver on the rude platform of the ox-drawn stone-boat. Gradually he perceived that it was a machine, a machine so finished, so clean-lined and so businesslike that the pictures he had shown Jubilith were clumsy toys in comparison.

It was Sussten, a man Osser had crushed to the ground with two heavy blows, who sprang lightly up on the machine and settled into it. It backed off the platform, and Osser could hear the faintest of whines from it. The machine rolled and yet it stepped; it kept itself horizon-level as it ran, its long endless treads dipping and rising with the terrain, its sleek body moving smooth as a swan. It stopped and then went forward, out to the first of a field of stakes that a crew had been driving.

The flat, gleaming sides of the machine opened away and forward and locked, and became a single blade twice the width of the machine. It dropped until its sharp lower edge just touched the ground, checked for a moment, and then sank into the soil.

Dirt mounded up before it until flakes fell back over the wide moldboard. The machine slid ahead, and dirt ran off the sides of the blade to make two straight windrows. And behind the machine as it labored, the ground was flat and smooth; and it was done as easily as a smoothing hand in a sandbox. Here it was cut and there it was filled, but everywhere the swath was like planed wood, all done just as fast as a man can run.

Osser made a sick noise far back in his tight throat.

Guided by the stakes, the machine wheeled and returned, one end of the blade now curved forward to catch up the windrow and carry it across the new parallel cut. And now the planed soil was twice as wide.

As it worked, men worked, and Osser saw that, shockingly, they moved with no less efficiency and certainty than the machine. For Osser, these men had plodded and sweated, drudged, each a single, obstinate unit to be flogged and pressed. But now they sprinted, sprang; they held, drove, measured and carried as if to swift and intricate music.

A cart clattered up and from it men took metal spikes, as thick as a leg, twice as tall as a man. Four men to a spike, they ran with them to staked positions on the new-cut ground, set them upright. A man flung a metal clamp around the spike. Two men, one on each side, drove down the clamp with heavy sledges until the spike would stand alone. And already those four were back with another spike.

Twenty-six such spikes were set, but long before they were all out of the wagon, Sussten spun the machine in its own length and stopped. The moldboard rose, hinged, folded back to become the silver sides of the machine again. Sussten drove forward, nosed the machine into the first of the spikes, which fitted into a slot at the front of the machine. There was the sound of a frantic giant ringing a metal triangle, and the spike sank as if the ground had turned to bread.

Leaving perhaps two hand's-breadths of the spike showing, the machine slid to the next and the next, sinking the spikes so quickly that it had almost a whole minute to wait while the spike crew set the very last one. At that a sound rolled out of the crowd, a sound utterly unlike any that had ever been heard during the building of the tower—a friendly, jeering roar of laughter at the crew who had made the machine wait.

Men unrolled heavy cable along the lines of spikes; others followed right behind them, one with a tool which stretched the cable taut, two with a tool that in two swift motions connected the cable to the tops of the sunken spikes. And by the time the cable was connected, two flatbeds, a buckboard and a hay wagon had unloaded a cluster of glistening machine parts. Men and women swarmed over them, wrenches, pliers and special tools in hand, bolting, fitting, clamping, connecting. Three heavy leads from the great ground cable were connected; a great parabolic wire basket was raised and guyed.

Wrenn ran to the structure and pulled a lever. A high-pitched scream of force dropped sickeningly in pitch to a jarring subsonic, and rose immediately high out of the audible range.

A rosy haze enveloped the end of the new machine, opposite the ground array and under the basket. It thickened, shimmered, and steadied, until it was a stable glowing sphere with an off-focus muzziness barely showing all around its profile.

The crowd—not a group now, but a line—cheered and the line moved forward. Every conceivable village conveyance moved in single file toward the shining sphere, and, as each stopped, heavy metal was unloaded. Cast-iron stove legs could be recognized, and long strips of tinning solder, a bell, a kettle, the framing of a bench. The blacksmith's anvil was there, and parts of his forge. Pots and skillets. A ratchet and pawl from the gristmill. The weights and pendulum from the big village clock.

As each scrap was unloaded, exactly the number of hands demanded by its weight were waiting to catch it, swing it from its conveyance into the strange sphere. They went in without resistance and without sound, and they did not come out. Wagon after wagon, pack after handsack were unloaded, and still the sphere took and took.

It took heavy metal of more mass than its own dimensions. Had the metal been melted down into a sphere, it would have been a third again, half again, twice as large as the sphere, and still it took.

But its color was changing. The orange went to burned sienna and then to a strident brown. Imperceptibly this darkened until at last it was black. For a moment, it was a black of impossible glossiness, but this softened. Blacker and blacker it became, and at length it was not a good thing to look into— the blackness seemed to be hungry for something more intimate than metal. And still the metals came and the sphere took.

A great roar came from the crowd; men fell back to look upward. High in the west was a glowing golden spark which showed a long blue tail. It raced across the sky and was gone, and moments later the human roar was answered by thunder from above.

If the work had been swift before, it now became a blur. Men no longer waited for the line of wagons to move, but ran back along it to snatch metal and stagger forward again to the sphere. Women ripped off bracelets and hammered earrings and threw them to the implacable melanosphere. Men threw in their knives, even their buttons. A rain of metal was sucked silently into the dazzling black.

Another cry from the crowd, and now there was hurried anguish in it; again the craning necks, the quick gasp. The golden spark was a speed-blurred ovoid now, the blue tail a banner half a horizon long. The roar, when it came, was a smashing thunder, and the blue band hung where it was long after the thing had gone.

A moan of urgency, caught and maintained by one exhausted throat after another, rose and fell and would not leave. Then it was a happy shout as Sussten drove in, shouldering the beautiful cutting machine through the scattering crowd. Its blade unfolded as it ran, latched high and stayed there like a shining forearm flung across the machine's silver face.

As the last scrambling people dove for safety, Sussten brought the huge blade slashing downward and at the same time threw the machine into its highest speed. It leaped forward as Sussten leaped back. Unmanned, it rushed at the sphere as if to sweep it away, crash the structure that contained it. But at the last microsecond, the blade struck the ground; the nose of the machine snapped upward, and the whole gleaming thing literally vaulted into the sphere.

No words exist for such a black. Some people fell to their knees, their faces covered. Some turned blindly away, unsteady on their feet. Some stood trembling, fixed on it, until friendly hands took and turned them and coaxed them back to reality.

And at last a man staggered close, squinting, and threw in the heavy wrought-iron support for an inn sign—

And the sphere refused it.

Such a cry of joy rose from the village that the sleeping bats in the thickets of Sky-tree Grove, two miles away, stirred and added their porcine grunting to the noise.

A woman ran to Wrenn, screaming, elbowing, unnoticed and unheard in the bedlam. She caught his shoulder roughly, spun him half around, pointed. Pointed up at the tower, at Osser.

Wrenn thumbed a small disc out of a socket in his belt and held it near his lips.

"Osser!" The great voice rang and echoed, crushing the ecstatic noises of the people by its sheer weight. *"Osser, come down or you're a dead man!"*

The people, suddenly silent, all stared at the tower. One or two cried, "Yes, come down, come down . . ." but the puniness of their voices was ludicrous after Wrenn's magnified tones, and few tried again.

Osser stood holding the parapet, legs wide apart, eyes wide—too wide—open. His hands curled over the edge, and blood dripped slowly from under the cuticles.

"Come down, come down . . ."

He did not move. His eyeballs were nearly dry, and unnoticed saliva lay in a drying streak from one corner of his mouth.

"Jubilith, bring him down!"

She was whimpering, begging, murmuring little urgencies to him. His biceps were as hard as the parapet, his face as changeless as the stone.

"Jubilith, leave him! Leave him and come!" Wrenn, wise Wrenn, sure, unshakable, imperturbable Wrenn had a sob in his voice; and under such amplification the sob was almost big enough to be voice for the sobs that twisted through Jubilith's tight throat.

She dropped to one knee and put one slim firm shoulder under Osser's wrist. She drove upward against it with all the lithe strength of her panicked body. It came free, leaving a clot of fingertip on the stone. Down she went again, and up again at the other wrist; but this was suddenly flaccid, and her tremendous effort turned to a leap. She clutched at Osser, who tottered forward.

For one endless second they hung there, while their mutual center of gravity made a slow deliberation, and then Jubilith kicked frantically at the parapet, abrading her legs, mingling her blood with his on the masonry. They went together back to the roof. Jubilith twisted like a falling cat and got her feet down, holding Osser's great weight up.

They spun across the roof in an insane staggering dance; then there was the stairway (with its invisible barrier gone) and darkness (with his hand in hers now, holding and leading) and a sprint into daylight and the shattering roar of Wrenn's giant voice: *Everybody down, down flat!"*

And there was a time of running, pulling Osser after her, and Osser pounding along behind her, docile and wide-eyed as a cat-ox. And then the rebellion and failure of her legs, and the will that refused to let them fail, and the failure of that will; the stunning agony of a cracked patella as she went down on the rocks, and the swift sense of infinite loss as Osser's hand pulled free of hers and he went lumbering blindly along, the only man on his feet in the wide meadow of the fallen.

Jubilith screamed and someone stood up—she thought it was old Oyva—and cried out.

Then the mighty voice again, *"Osser! Down, man!"* Blearily, then, she saw Osser stagger to a halt and peer around him.

"Osser, lie down!"

And then Osser, mad, drooling, turning toward her. His eyes protruded and he slashed about with his heavy fists. He came closer, unseeing, battling some horror he believed in with great cuts and slashes that threatened elbow and shoulder joints by the wrenching of their unimpeded force.

His voice—but not his, rather the voice of an old, wretched crone—squeaking out in a shrill falsetto, "Not down, never down, but up. I'll build, build, build, break to build, kill to build, and all the ones who can do everything, anything, everything, they will build everything for me. I'm strong!" he shrieked, soprano. "All the people who can do anything are less than one strong man . . ."

He jabbered and fought, and suddenly Wrenn rose, quite close by, his left hand enclosed in a round flat box. He moved something on its surface and then waved it at Osser, in a gesture precisely like the command to a guest to be seated.

Down went Osser, close to Jubilith, with his face in the dirt and his eyes open, uncaring. On him and on Jubilith lay the invisible weight of the force that had awaited him in the stairway.

The breath hissed out of Jubilith. Had she not been lying on her side with her face turned skyward in a single convulsive effort toward air, she would never have seen what happened. The golden shape appeared in the west, seen a fraction of a second, but blazoned forever in tangled memories of this day. And simultaneously the earth-shaking cough of the machine as its sphere disappeared.

She could not see it move, but such a blackness is indelible, and she sensed it when it appeared in the high distances as its trajectory and that of the golden flyer intersected.

Then there was—*Nothing*.

The broad blue trail swept from the western horizon to the zenith, and sharply ended. There was no sound, no concussion, no blaze of light. The sphere met the ship and both ceased to exist.

Then there was the wind, from nowhere, from everywhere, all the wind that ever was, tearing in agony from everywhere in the world to the place where the sphere had been, trying to fill the strange space that had contained exactly as much matter as the dead golden ship. Wagons, oxen, trees and stones scraped and flew and crashed together in the center of that monstrous implosion.

The weight Wrenn had laid on Jubilith disappeared, but her sucking lungs could find nothing to draw in. There was air aplenty, but none of it would serve her.

Finally she realized that there was unconsciousness waiting for her if she wanted it. She embraced it, sank into it, and left the world to its wailing winds.

Ages later, there was weeping.

She stirred and raised her head.

The sphere machine was gone. There was a heap of something down there, but it supported such a tall and heavy pillar of roiling dust that she could not see what it was. There, and there, and over yonder, in twos and threes, silent, shaken people sat up, some staring about them, some just sitting, waiting for the shock-stopped currents of life to flow back in.

But the weeping . . .

She put her palm on the ground and inched it, heel first, in a weak series of little hops, until she was half sitting.

Osser was weeping.

He sat upright, his feet together and his knees wide apart, like a little child. He rocked. He lifted his hands and let them fall, lifted them and punctuated his crying with weak poundings on the ground. His mouth was an O, his eyes were single squeezed lines, his face was wet, and his crying was the most heartrending sound she had ever heard.

She thought to speak to him, but knew he would not hear. She thought to go to him, but the first shift of weight sent such agony through her broken kneecap that she almost fainted.

Osser wept.

She turned away from him—suppose, later, he should remember that she had seen this?—and then she knew why he was crying. He was crying because his tower was gone. Tower of strength, tower of defiance, tower of hope, tower of rebellion and hatred and an ambition big enough for a whole race of city-builders, gone without a fight, gone without the triumph of taking him with it, gone in an instant, literally in a puff of wind.

"Where does it hurt?"

It was Wrenn, who had approached unseen through the blinding, sick compassion that filled her.

"It hurts there." She pointed briefly at Osser.

"I know," said Wrenn gently. He checked what she was about to say with a gesture. "No, we won't stop him. When he was a little boy, he never cried. He has been hurt more than most people, and nothing ever made him cry, ever. We all have a cup for tears and a reservoir. No childhood is finished until all the tears flow from the reservoir into the cup. Let him cry; perhaps he is going to be a man. It's your knee, isn't it?"

"Yes. Oh, but I can't stand to hear it, my heart will burst!" she cried.

"Hear him out," said Wrenn softly, taking medication from a flat box at his waist. He ran feather-fingers over her knee and nodded. "You have taken Osser as your own. Keep this weeping with you, all of it. It will fit you to him better through the healing time."

"May I understand now?"

"Yes, oh yes . . . and since he has taught you about hate, you will hate me for it."

"I couldn't hate you, Wrenn."

Something stirred within his placid eyes—a smile, a pointed shard of knowledge—she was not sure. "Perhaps you could."

He kept his eyes on his careful bandaging, and as he worked, he spoke.

"Stop a man in his work to tell him that each of his fingers bears a pattern of loops and whorls, and you waste his time. It is a thing he knows, a thing he has seen for himself, a thing which can be checked on the instant—in short, an obvious, unremarkable thing. Yet, if his attention is not called to it, it is impossible to teach him that these patterns are exclusive, original with him, unduplicated anywhere. Sparing him the truism may cost him the fact.

"It is that kind of truism through which I shall pass to reach the things you must understand. So be patient with me through the familiar paths; I promise you a most remarkable turning.

"We are an ancient and resourceful species, and among the many things we have—our happiness, our simplicity, our harmony with each other and with ourselves—some are the products of intelligence, per se, but most of the good things spring from a quality which we possess in greater degree than any other species yet known. That is—logic.

"Now, there is the obvious logic: you may never have broken your knee before, but you knew, in advance, that if you did it would cause you pain. If I hold this pebble so, you may correctly predict that it will drop when I release it, though you have never seen this stone before. This obvious logic strikes deeper levels as well; for example, if I release the stone and it does not fall, logic tells you not only that some unpredicted force is now acting on it, but a great many things about that force: that it equals gravity in the case of this particular pebble; that it is in stasis; that it is phenomenal, since it is out of the statistical order of things.

"The quality of logic, which we (so far as is known) uniquely possess, is this: any of us can do literally anything that anyone else can do. You need ask no one to solve the problems that you face every day, providing they are problems common to all. To cut material so that a sleeve will fit a shoulder, you pause, you close your eyes; the way to cut the material then comes to you, and you proceed. You never need do anything twice, because the first way is the most logical. You may finish the garment and put it away without trying it on for fit, because you know you have done it right and it is perfect.

"If I put you before a machine which you had never seen before, which had a function unknown to you, and which operated on principles you had never heard of, and if I told you it was broken and needed repairing, you would look at it carefully, inside, outside, top and bottom, and you would close your eyes, and suddenly you would understand the principles. With these and the machine, function would explain itself. The step from that point to the location of a faulty part is self-evident.

"Now I lay before you parts which are identical in appearance, and ask you to install the correct one. Since you thoroughly understand the requirements now, the specifications for the correct part are self-evident. Logic dictates the correct tests for the parts. You will rapidly reject the tight one, the heavy one, the too soft one, and the too resilient one, and you will repair my machine. And you will walk away without testing it, since you now know it will operate."

Wrenn continued, "You—all of us—live in this way. We build no cities because we don't need cities. We stay in groups because some things need more than two hands, more than one head, or voice, or mood. We eat exactly what we require, we use only what we need.

"And that is the end of the truism, wherein I so meticulously describe to you what you know about how you live. The turning: Whence this familiar phenomenon, this closing of the eyes and mysterious appearance of the answer? There have been many engrossing theories about it, but the truth is the most fascinating of all.

"We have all spoken of telepathy, and many of us have experienced it. We cannot explain it, as yet. But most of us insist on a limited consideration of it; that is, we judge its success or failure by the amount of detail sent and received. We expect *facts* to be transmitted, *words,* idea sequences—or perhaps pictures; the clearer the picture, the better the telepathy.

"Perhaps one day we will learn to do this; it would be diverting. But what we actually *do* is infinitely more useful.

"You see, we *are* telepathic, not in the way of conveying details, but in the much more useful way of conveying *a manner of thinking.*

"Let us try to envisage a man who lacks this quality. Faced with your broken machine, he would be utterly at a loss, unless he had been specially trained in this particular field. Do not overlook the fact that he lacks the conditioning of a whole life of the kind of sequence thinking which is possible to us. He would probably bumble through the whole chore in an interminable time, trying one thing and then another and going forward from whatever seems to work. You can see the tragic series of pitfalls possible for him in a situation in which an alternate three or four or five consecutive steps are possible, forcing step six, which is wrong in terms of the problem.

"Now, take the same man and train him in this one job. Add a talent, so that he learns quickly and well. Add years of experience—terrible, drudging thought! —to his skill. Face him with the repair problem and it is obvious that he will repair it with a minimum of motion.

"Finally, take this skilled man and equip him with a device which constantly sends out the habit-patterns of his thinking. Long practice has made him efficient in the matter; in terms of machine function he knows better than to question whether a part turns this way or that, whether a rod or tube larger than *x* diameter is to be considered. Furthermore, imagine a receiving device which absorbs these sendings whenever the receiver is faced with an identical problem. The skilled sender controls the unskilled receiver as long as the receiver is engaged in the problem. Anything the receiver does which is counter to the basic patterns of the sender is automatically rejected as illogical.

"And now I have described our species. We have an unmatchable unitary existence. Each of us with a natural bent—the poets, the musicians, the mechanics, the philosophers—each gives of his basic thinking method every time anyone has an application for it. The expert is unaware of being tapped—which is why it has taken hundreds of centuries to recognize the method. Yet, in spite of what amounts to a veritable race intellect, we are all very much individuals. Because each field has many experts, and each of those experts has his individual approach, only that which is closest both to the receiver *and* his problem comes in. The ones without special talents live fully and richly with all the skills of the gifted. The creative ones share with others in their field as soon as it occurs to any expert to review what he knows; the one step forward then instantly presents itself.

"So much for the bulk of our kind. There remain a few specializing *non*-specialists. When you are faced with a problem to which no logical solution presents itself, you come to one of these few for help. The reason no solution presents itself is that this is a new line of thinking, or (which is very likely) the last expert in it has died. The non-specialist hears your problem and applies simple logic to it. Immediately, others of his kind do the same. But, since they come from widely divergent backgrounds and use a vast variety of methods, one of them is almost certain to find the logical solution. This is your answer—and through you, it is available to anyone who ever faces this particular problem.

"In exceptional cases, the non-specializing specialist encounters a problem which, for good reason, is better left out of the racial 'pool'—as, for example, a physical or psychological experiment within the culture, of long duration, which general knowledge might alter. In such cases, a highly specialized hypnotic technique is used on the investigators, which has the effect of cloaking thought on this particular matter.

"And if you began to fear that I was never coming to Osser's unhappy history, you must understand, my dear, I have just given it to you. Osser was just such an experiment.

"It became desirable to study the probable habit patterns of a species like us in every respect except for our unique attribute. The problem was attacked from many angles, but I must confess that using a live specimen was my idea.

"By deep hypnosis, the telepathic receptors in Osser were severed from the rest of his mind. He was then allowed to grow up among us in real and complete freedom.

"You saw the result. Since few people recognize the nature of this unique talent, and even fewer regard it as worth discussion, this strong, proud, highly intelligent boy grew up feeling a hopeless inferior, and never knowing exactly why. Others did things, made things, solved problems, as easily as thinking about them, while Osser had to study and sweat and piece and try out. He had to assert his superiority in some way. He did, but in as slipshod a fashion as he did everything else.

"So he was led to the pictures you saw. He was permitted to make what conclusions he wished—they were that we are a backward people, incapable of building a city. He suddenly saw in the dreams of a mechanized, star-reaching species a justification of himself. He could not understand our lack of desire for possessions, not knowing that our whole cultural existence is based on sharing—that it is not only undesirable, but impossible for us to hoard an advanced idea, a new comfort. He would master us through strength.

"He was just starting when you came to me about him. You could get no key to his problem because we know nothing about sick minds, and there was no expert you could tap. I couldn't help you—you, of all people—because you loved him, and because we dared not risk having him know what he was, especially when he was just about to take action.

"Why he chose this particular site for his tower I do not know. And why he chose the method of the tower I don't know either, though I can deduce an excellent reason. First, he had to use his strength once he became convinced that in it lay his superiority. Second, he had to *try out* this build-with-hate idea—the bugaboo of all other man-species, the trial-and-error, the inability to *know* what will work and what will not.

"And so we learned through Osser precisely what we had learned in other approaches—that a man without our particular ability must not live among us, for, if he does, he will destroy us.

"It is a small step from that to a conclusion about a whole race of them coexisting with us. And now you know what happened here this afternoon."

Jubilith raised her head slowly. "A whole ship full of . . . of what Osser was?"

"Yes. We did the only thing we could. Quick, quite painless. We have been watching them for a long time—years. We saw them start. We computed their orbit—even to the deceleration spiral. We chose a spot to launch our interceptor." He glanced at Osser, who was almost quiet, quite exhausted. "What sheer hell he must have gone through, to see us build like that. How could he know that not one of us needed training, explanation, or any but the simplest orders? How could he rationalize to himself our possession of machines and devices surpassing the wildest dreams of the godlike men he admired so? How could he understand that, having such things, we use them only when we must, and that otherwise we live in ways which will not violate the walking, working animal we are?"

She turned to him a mask so cold, so beautiful, he forgot for a moment to breathe. "Why did you do it? You had other logics, other approaches. Did you have to do *that* to him?"

He studiously avoided a glance at Osser. "I said you might hate me," he murmured. "Jubilith, the men in that ship were so like Osser that the experiment could not be passed by. We had astronomical data, historical, cultural—as far as our observations could go—and ethnological. But only by analogy could we get such a psychological study. And it checked too well. As for having him see this thing, today . . . building, Jubilith, is sometimes begun by tearing down."

He looked at her with deep compassion. "This was not the site chosen for the launching of the interceptor. We uprooted the whole installation, brought it here, rebuilt it, just for Osser; just so that he could stand on his tower and see it happen. He had to be broken, leveled to the earth. Ah-h-h . . ." he breathed painfully, "Osser has earned what he will have from now on."

"He can be—well again?"

"With your help."

"So very right, you are," she snarled suddenly. "So sure that this or that species is fit to associate with superiors like us." She leaned toward him and shook a finger in his startled face. The courtly awe habitual to all when speaking to such as Wrenn had completely left her.

"So fine we are, so mighty. And didn't we build cities? Didn't we have giant bird-machines and shiny carts on our streets? Didn't we let our cities be smashed—haven't you seen the ruins in the west? Tell me," she sparked, "did we ruin them ourselves, because one superior city insisted on proving its superiority over another superior city?"

She stopped abruptly to keep herself from growling like an animal, for he was smiling blandly, and his smile got wider as she spoke. She turned furiously, half away from him, cursing the broken knee that held her so helpless.

"Jubilith."

His voice was so warm, so kind and so startling in these surroundings, held such a bubbling overtone of laughter that she couldn't resist it. She turned grudgingly.

In his hand he held a pebble. When her eye fell to it he rolled it, held it between thumb and forefinger, and let it go.

It stayed motionless in mid-air. "Another factor, Jubilith."

She almost smiled. She looked down at his other hand, and saw it aiming the disc-shaped force-field projector at low power.

He lifted it and, with the field, tossed the pebble into the air and batted it away. "We have no written history, Jubilith. We don't need one, but once in a while it would be useful."

"Jubilith, our culture is one of the oldest in the Galaxy. If we ever had such cities, there are not even legends about it."

"But I saw—"

"A ship came here once. We had never seen a humanoid race. We welcomed them and helped them. We gave them land and seeds. Then they called a flotilla, and the ships came by the hundreds.

"They built cities and, at that, we moved away and left them alone, because we don't *need* cities. Then they began to hate us. They couldn't hate us until they had tall buildings to do it in. They hated our quiet; they hated our understanding. They sent missionaries to change our ways. We welcomed the missionaries, fed them and laughed with them, but when they left us glittering tools and humble machines to amuse us, we let them lie where they were until they rotted.

"In time they sent no more missionaries. They joked about us and forgot us. And then they built a city on land we had not given them, and another, and another. They bred well, and their cities became infernally big. And finally they began to build that one city too many, and we turned a river and drowned it. They were pleased. They could now rid themselves of the backward natives."

Jubilith closed her eyes, and saw the tumbled agony of the mounds, radiating outward from a lake with its shores too bare. "All of them?" she asked.

Wrenn nodded. "Even one might be enough to destroy us." He nodded toward Osser, who had begun to cry again.

"They seemed . . . good," she said, reflectively. "Too fast, too big . . . and it must have been noisy, but—"

"Wait," he said. "You mean the people in the picture Osser showed you?"

"Of course. They were the city-builders you—we—destroyed, weren't they?"

"They were not! The ones who built here were thin, hairy, with backward-slanting faces and webs between their fingers. Beautiful, but they hated us . . . The pictures, Jubilith, were made on the third planet of a pale star out near the Rim; a world with one Moon; a world of humans like Osser . . . the world where that golden ship came from."

"How?" she gasped.

"If logic is good enough," Wrenn said, "it need not be checked. Once we were so treated by humanoids, we built the investigators. They are not manned. They draw their power from anything that radiates, and they home on any planet which could conceivably rear humans. They are, as far as we know, indetectible. We've never lost one. They launch tiny flyers to make close searches—one of them made the pictures you saw. The pictures and other data are coded and sent out into space and, where distances warrant it, other investigators catch the signal and add power and send them on.

"Whenever a human or humanoid species builds a ship, we watch it. When they send their ships to this sector, we watch their planet *and* their ship. Unless we are sure that those people have the ability we have, to share all expertness and all creative thinking with all who want it—they don't land here. And no such species will ever land here."

"You're so sure."

"We explore no planets, Jubilith. We like it here. If others like us exist—why should they visit us?"

She thought about it, and slowly she nodded. "I like it here," she breathed.

Wrenn knelt and looked out across the rolling ground. It was late, and most of the villagers had gone home. A few picked at the mound of splinters at the implosion center. Their limbs were straight and their faces clear. They owned little and they shared their souls.

He rose and went to Osser, and sat down beside him, facing him, his back to Jubilith. "M-m-mum, mum, mum, mum, mum-mum-mum," he intoned.

Osser blinked at him. Wrenn lifted his hand and his ring, green and gold and a shimmering oval of purple, caught the late light. Osser looked at the ring. He reached for it. Wrenn moved it slightly. Osser's hand passed it and hit the ground and lay there neglected. Osser gaped at the ring, his jaws working, his teeth not meeting.

"Mum, mum, *mummy*, where's your mummy, Osser?"

"In the house," said Osser, looking at the ring.

Wrenn said, "You're a good little boy. When we say the word, you won't be able to do anything but what *you* can do. When we say the key, you'll be able to do anything *anybody* can do."

"All right," Osser said.

"Before I give the word, tell me the key. You must remember the key."

"That ring. And 'last 'n' lost.' "

"Good, Osser. Now listen to me. Can you hear me?"

"Sure." He grabbed at the ring.

"I'm going to change the key. It isn't 'last'n' lost' any more. 'Last 'n' lost' is no good now. Forget it."

"No good?"

"Forget it. What's the key?"

"I—forgot."

"The key," said Wrenn patiently, "is this." He leaned close and whispered rapidly.

Jubilith was peering out past the implosion center to the townward path. Someone was coming, a tiny figure.

"Jubilith," Wrenn said. She looked up at him. "You must understand something." His voice was grave. His hair reached for an awed little twist of wind, come miles to see this place. The wind escaped and ran away down the hill.

Wrenn said, "He's very happy now. He was a happy child when first I heard of him, and how like a spacebound human he could be. Well, he's that child again. He always will be, until the day he dies. I'll see he's cared for. He'll chase the sunbeams, a velvet red one and a needle of blue-white; he'll eat and he'll love and be loved just as is right for him."

They looked at Osser. There was a blue insect on his wrist. He raised it slowly, slowly, close to his eyes, and through its gauze wings he saw the flame-and-silver sunset. He laughed.

"All his life?"

"All his life," said Wrenn. "With the bitterness and the trouble wiped away, and no chance to mature again into the unfinished thing that fought the world with the conviction it had something extra."

Then he dropped the ring into Jubilith's hand. "But if you care to," he said, watching her face, the responsive motion of her sensitive nostrils, the most delicate index of her lower lip, "if you care to, you can give him back everything I took away. In a moment, you can give him more than he has now; but how long would it take you to make him as happy?"

She made no attempt to answer him. He was Wrenn, he was old and wise; he was a member of a unique species whose resources were incalculable; and yet he was asking her to do something he could not do himself. Perhaps he was asking her to correct a wrong. She would never know that.

"Just the ring," he said, "and the touch of your hand."

He went away, straight and tall, quickening his pace as, far away, the patient figure she had been watching earlier rose and came to meet him. It was Oyva.

Jubilith thought, "He needs her."

Jubilith had never been needed by anyone.

She looked at her hand and in it she saw all she was, all she could ever be in her own right; and with it, the music of ages; never the words, but all of the pressures of poetry. And she saw the extraordinary privacy of love in a world which looked out through her eyes, placed all of its skills in her hands, to do with as she alone wished.

With a touch of her hand . . . what a flood of sensation, what a bursting in of voices and knowledge, for a child!

How long a child?

She closed her eyes, and quietly the answer came, full of pictures; the lute picked up and played; the instant familiarity with the most intricate machine; the stars seen otherwise, and yet again otherwise, and every seeing an honest beauty. A thousand discoveries, and manhood with a rush.

She slipped the ring on her finger, and dragged herself over to him. She put her arms around him and his cheek came down to the hollow of her throat and burrowed there.

He said, sleepily, "Is it nighttime, Mummy?"

"For just a little while," said Jubilith.

Affair with a Green Monkey

There was this trained nurse who retired at 24 to marry a big guy, six foot seven, top brass in a Government agency. He was home only weekends. His name was Fritz Rhys. About sick people, wrong people, different people, he was a very understanding guy. It was his business to understand them.

So one night he went for a walk with his wife Alma down to this little park on the river front where they could get some air. There was a fountain and a bench where they could sit and see the lights across the water and flower-beds and all that, and this particular Sunday night there was a bunch of punks, eight of them, kicking someone to death over by the railing. Fritz Rhys understood right away what was happening and what to do, and in three big jumps he was right in the middle of it. He snatched a hunk of broom-handle away from one of the kids just before it got buried in the victim, and then they all saw him and that was the end of that. They cut out of there, ducking around Alma where she stood as if she was dangerous too.

Alma ran over to where Fritz knelt and helped him turn the man over. She got Fritz's display handkerchief and sponged the blood and broken teeth out of the slack mouth and turned the head to one side, and did the other things trained nurses are trained to do.

"Anything broken?"

She said yes. "His arm. Maybe internal injuries too. We'd better get an ambulance."

"Home's quicker. Hey boy! You're all right now. *Up* you

go!" So by the time the man got his eyes open Fritz had him on his feet.

They half carried him up the steps and over the footbridge that crosses the Drive, and Fritz was right, they had him back to their apartment forty minutes sooner than it would have taken to call a wagon.

She was going to phone but he stopped her. "We can handle it. Get some pajamas." He looked at the injured man draped over one big arm. "Get some of yours. He won't mind."

They cleaned him up and splinted the arm. It wasn't so bad. Bruises on the ribs and buttocks, and then the face, but he was lucky. "Give him one week and one dentist and you'll never know it happened."

"He will."

"Oh, that," Fritz said.

She said, "What do you suppose they did it for?"

"Green monkey."

"Oh," she said, and they left the man sleeping and went to bed. At five in the morning Fritz rose quietly and got dressed and she didn't wake up until he thumped his suitcase down by the bed and bent over to kiss her goodbye.

She gave him his kiss and then came all the way awake and said, "Fritz! You're not just—leaving, like always?"

He wanted to know why not, and she pointed at the guest room. "Leave me with—"

He laughed at her. "Believe me, honey, you haven't got a thing to worry about."

"But he . . . I . . . oh, Fritz!"

"If anything happens you can call me."

"In *Washington?*" She sat up and sort of hugged the sheet around her. "Oh, why can't I just send him to a hospital where—"

He had a way sometimes of being so patient it was insulting. He said, "Because I want to talk to him, help him, when he's better, and you know what hospitals are. You just keep him happy and tell him not to leave until I can have a talk with him." Then he said something so gentle and careful that she knew when to shut up: "And let's say no more about it, shall we?" so she said no more about it and he went back to Washington.

The pajamas were small for him but not much and he was about her age, too. (Fritz Rhys was quite a bit older.) He had a name that she got fond of saying, and small strong hands. All day Monday he was kind of dazed and didn't say much, only smiled thanks for the eggnog and bouillon and bedpan and so on. Tuesday he was up and about. His clothes were back from the cleaners and mended and he put them on and they sat around the whole day talking. Alma read books a good deal and she read aloud to him. She played a lot of music on the phonograph too. Whatever she liked, he liked even better. Wednesday she took him to the dentist, once in the morning to get the stubs ground down and impressions, and again in the afternoon to have the temporary acrylic caps cemented in. By this time the lip swelling was all but gone, and with the teeth fixed up she found herself spending a lot of time just looking at his mouth. His hair shone in the sun and she half believed it would shine in the dark too. He somehow never answered her when she wanted to know where he came from. Maybe there was too much laughing going on at the time. They laughed a whole lot together. Anyway it was some place where you couldn't get spaghetti. She took him to an Italian restaurant for dinner and had to teach him how to spin it on his fork. They had a lot of fun with that and he ate plenty of it.

On Wednesday night—late—she phoned her husband.

"Alma! What is it? Are you all right?"

She did not answer until he called her name twice again, and then she said, all whispery, "Yes, Fritz. I'm all right. Fritz, I'm *frightened*."

"Of what?"

She didn't say anything, though he could hear her trying.

"Is it the . . . what's his name, anyway?"

"Loolyo."

"Julio?"

She sang: "Lool-yo."

"Well, then. What's he done?"

"N-nothing."

"Well then—are you afraid of anything he might do?"

"Oh, *no!*"

"You're so right. I understood that when I left, or he wouldn't be there. Now then: he hasn't done anything, and you're sure he won't, and I'm sure he won't, so—why call me up at this time of night?"

She didn't say anything.

"Alma?"

"Fritz," she said. She was swift, hoarse: "Come home. Come right home."

"Act your age!"

"Your three minutes are up. Signal when through please."

"Yes operator."

"Alma! Are you calling from an outside phone? Why aren't you home?"

"I couldn't bear to have him hear me," she whispered. "Goodbye, Fritz." He might have said something more to her, but she hung up and went home.

On Thursday she phoned for the car and packed a picnic and they went to the beach. It was too cold to swim but they sat on the sand most of the day and talked, and sang some. "I'm frightened," she said again, but she said it to herself. Once they talked about Fritz. She asked him why those boys had clobbered him and he said he didn't know. She said Fritz knew. "He says you're a green monkey," and she explained it: "He says if you catch a monkey in the jungle and paint it green, all the other monkeys will tear it to pieces because it's different. Not dangerous, just different."

"Different how?" Loolyo asked, in a quiet voice, about himself.

She had a lot of answers to that, but they were all things of her own and she didn't mention them. She just said again that Fritz knew. "He's going to help you."

He looked at her and said, "He must be a good man."

She thought that over and said, "He's a very understanding man."

"What does he do in Washington?"

"He's an expert on rehabilitation programs."

"Rehabilitation of what?"

"People."

"Oh... I'm looking forward to Saturday."

She told him, "I love you." He turned to her as she sat round-eyed, all her left knuckles in her mouth so that the ring hurt her.

"You don't mean that."

"I didn't mean to say it."

After that, and on Friday, they stayed together, but like the wires on your lamp cord, never touching. They went to the zoo, where Loolyo looked at the animals excited as a child, except the monkeys, which made them be quiet and go quickly to something else. The longer the day got the quieter they were together, and at dinner they said almost nothing, and after that they even stopped looking at each other. That night when it was darkest she went to his room and opened the door and closed it again behind her. She did not turn on the light. She said, "I don't care . . ." and again, "I don't care," and wept in a whisper.

Loolyo was alone in the apartment when Fritz came home. "Shopping," he answered the big man's question. "Good afternoon, Mr. Rhys. I'm glad to see you."

"Fritz," instructed Fritz. "You're looking chipper. Alma been good to you?"

Loolyo smiled enough to light up the place.

"What'd you say your name was? Julio? Oh yeh, Loolyo, I remember. Well, Lou m'lad, let's have our little talk. Sit down over there and let me have a good look at you." He took a good long look and then grunted and nodded, satisfied. "You ashamed of yourself, boy?"

"Wh . . . ? Ashamed? Uh—no, I don't think so."

"Good! That means this doesn't have to be a long talk at all. Just to make it even shorter, I want you to know from the start that I know what you are and you don't have to hide it and it doesn't matter a damn to me and I'm not going to pry. Okay?"

"You *know?*"

Fritz boomed a big laugh. "Don't *worry* so, Louie! Everybody you meet doesn't see what I see. It's my business to see these things and understand them."

Loolyo shifted nervously. "What things are you talking about?"

"Shape of the hands. Way you walk, way you sit, way you show your feelings, sound of your voice. Lots more. All small things, any one or two or six might mean nothing. But all together—I'm on to you, I understand you. I'm not asking, I'm telling. And I don't *care*. It's just that I can tell you how to behave so you don't get mobbed again. You want to hear it or don't you?"

Loolyo didn't look a thing in the world but puzzled. Fritz stood up and pulled off his jacket and shirt and threw them on the corner of the couch and fell back in the big chair, altogether relaxed. He began to talk like a man who loves talking and who knows what to say because he's said it all before, knows he's right, knows he says it well. "A lot of people live among people all their lives and never find out this one simple thing about people: human beings cease to be human when they congregate, and a mob is a monster. If you think of a mob as a living thing and you want to get its I.Q., take the average intelligence of the people there and divide it by the number of people there. Which means that a mob of fifty has somewhat less intelligence than an earthworm. No one person could sink to its level of cruelty and lack of principle. It thinks that anything that is different is dangerous, and it thinks it's protecting itself by tearing anything that's different to small bloody bits. The difference-which-is-dangerous changes with the times. Men have been mob-murdered for wearing beards, and for not wearing beards. For saying the right series of words in what the mob thinks is the wrong order. For wearing or not wearing this or that article of clothing, or tattoo, or piece of skin."

"That's . . . ugly," Loolyo said.

" 'That's . . . ugly,' " Fritz repeated, with completely accurate and completely insulting mimicry, then made his big roar of laughter and told Loolyo not to get mad. "You've just made a point for me, but wait a bit till I get to it." He leaned back and went on with his speech. "Now, of all 'dangerous' differences which incite the mob, the one that hits 'em hardest, quickest and nastiest is any variation in sex. It devolves upon every human being to determine which sex he belongs to and then to *be* that as loud as possible for as long as he lives. To the smallest detail men dress like men and women dress like women, and God help them if they cross the line. A man has got to look and act like a man. That isn't a right. It's a duty. And no matter how weird mankind gets in its rules and regulations—whether manhood demands shoulder-length hair for a Cavalier or waist-length for a Sikh or a crew-cut for a Bavarian, the rules must be followed or bloody well else.

"Now, as for you people," Fritz said, sitting up and flipping his long index finger down and forward, like a sharpshooter practicing a snap shot, "you are what you are just like everybody else. But I'm not talking about what you are —that's self-evident—only about how you're treated.

"The only big difference between you and normal people, in those terms, is that they must display their sex and insist on it, and you may not. But I mean, you one hundred percent by God *may* not, not in public. Among your own kind you can camp and scream and giggle to your heart's content, but don't let yourself get caught at it. It would be better not to do it at all."

"Now wait, wait, wait," Loolyo barked. "Hold on here. What has this got to do with me?"

Fritz opened his eyes big and round and then closed them and slumped into the cushions. He said in a very very tired voice, "Aw, now lookit. You're not going to bust into the middle of this and make me go all the way back to the beginning."

"I just want to know what makes you think—"

"Sit down and shut up!" Fritz bellowed, and he was the man who could do it. "Do you or do you not want to know how to go about among human beings without getting your girlish face kicked down your throat?"

Loolyo stood for a while, pale, his bright eyes drawn down to angry slits. It was as if Fritz's question didn't reach him all at once, but had to percolate in. Slowly he sat down again. "Go ahead then."

Fritz nodded approvingly. "I hate a bad liar, Louie, and you were about to try the one lie you could never get away with. Not with anyone who understands you. . . . All right then. My advice to you: Be a man. Not any old man, not mankind, but manhood. To do this you don't need to play pro football and grow hair on your chest and seduce every third woman you meet long as she's female. All you have to do is hunt, fish (or talk sense about 'em as if you had) and go bug-eyed when the girls go by. If a sunset moves you so much you *have* to express yourself, do it with a grunt and a dirty word. Or you say, 'That Beethoven, he blows a cool symphony.' Never champion a real underdog unless it's a popular type, like a baseball team. Always treat other men as if you were sore at something and will wipe it off on them if they give you the slightest excuse. I mean sore, Louie, not vexed or in a snit. And stay away from women. They have an intuition that'll find you out nine times out of ten. The tenth time she falls for you, and there's nothing funnier."

"I think," Loolyo said after a time, "that you hate human beings."

"I understand 'em, that's all. Do you think I hate you?"

"Maybe you should. I'm not what you think I am."

Fritz Rhys shook his head and quietly cursed. "All right. Wear your cellophane mask if it makes you feel better.

I don't give a damn about you or what you do. Do what I tell you and you can live in a man's world. Go on the way you are and in that last split second before they kick your brains in, you'll admit I was right."

"I'm glad you told me. It's what I came here to find out," Loolyo said finally.

At the sound of a key in the lock Fritz sprang up and ran to the door. It was Alma. Fritz took her packages and kissed her. While he was kissing her she looked past him to the living room and Loolyo, and as soon as he was finished she went and stood in the doorway. Fritz stood behind her, watching. Loolyo raised his head slowly and saw her and started and smiled shyly.

Fritz stepped up and took her shoulder and turned her around because just then he had to see her face. When he saw it he gently bit his lower lip and said, "Oh," and went back to his chair. He was a man who understood things real quick.

Alma ignored him, all eyes for Loolyo. "What has he been saying to you?"

He didn't answer. He looked at the carpet. Fritz jumped up and rapped, "Well, are you willing to tell the lady?"

"Why?"

"Promise me you will, every word, and I'll let her take the car and give you a lift out of town. You are from out of town? Yes. Well, I think you owe it to each other. What do you say, Louie?"

"Fritz! Have you gone cr—"

"You better persuade him to play it that way, honey. It's the last chance you'll have to see him alone."

"Loolyo . . ." she whispered, "come on, then."

Loolyo stared at the big man. Fritz grinned and said, "Every God damned word, mind. I'll quiz her when she gets back and take it out on her if you don't. Alma, try not to make it more'n two, three hours. Okay?"

"Come on then," she said stiffly, and they went out. Fritz went and got a beer and came back and flopped in the chair, drinking and laughing and scratching his chest.

In the car he said only "Uptown, over the bridge," and then fell into a silence that lasted clear to the toll-booths. They turned north and at last he began to talk. He told her all about it. She said nothing until he had quite finished; then: "How could you let him suggest such a filthy thing?"

He laughed bitterly. "Let him? . . . When he understands something, that—is—it."

There was nothing she could say to this; she knew it better than anything in life. He said, "But I guess I'm a green monkey anyhow. Well . . . I should be grateful. He told me where my kind can hide, and how to act when we're out in the open. I'd about given up."

"What do you mean?" He would not answer her, but rode with his face turned away. He seemed to be scanning the roadside to the right.

Suddenly: "Here," he said. "Stop here."

Startled, she pulled off the pavement and stopped. There's a new parkway north of the bridge, and for miles it parallels the old road. Between them is a useless strip of land, mauled by construction machines, weedy and deserted. She looked at it and at him, and if she was going to speak again the expression on his face stopped her. It was filled with sadness and longing and something else, a sort of blue-mood laughter. He said, "I'm going home now."

She looked at her hands on the wheel and suddenly could not see them. He touched her arm and said gently, "You'll have to get over it, Alma. It can't work. Nothing could make it work. It would kill you. Try to get back with your husband. He's better equipped for you. I'm not, not at all."

"Stop it," she whispered. "Stop it, stop it."

Loolyo sighed deeply, put his arms around her and kissed her, rough, gentle, thorough, face, mouth, tongue, ears, neck, touching her body hungrily while he did it. She clung to him and cried. He put her arms from him and pressed something into her hand and vaulted out of the car, ran across the shoulder, jumped over the retaining wall and disappeared. It was only a low wall. He didn't disappear behind anything or into anything or in the distance. He just disappeared. She called him twice and then got out and ran to the wall. Nothing—weeds, broken ground, a bush or two. She wrung her hands and became conscious of the object he had given her. It was a transparent disk, about like a plain flat flashlight lens. She turned it over twice, then impulsively looked through it.

She saw Loolyo crouched in a . . . machine.

She saw the machine leave, and when it was gone, her

glass disc ceased to exist also, so that she had nothing of his any more. For a while she thought she could not survive that. And in its time came the thing known to everyone who has had grief enough: that no matter what you've lost, the lungs and the heart go on, and all around, birds fly, cars pass, people make a buck and lose their souls and get hernia and happy and their hair cut just like before.

When she came through the other side of this, it was quite a bit later. She was weak and numb but she could drive again, so she did, very carefully, and soon she was able to think again, so she did, just as carefully, and by the time she got home her rehearsed 'Hel-*lo!*" was perfect and easy.

Maybe she forgot to rehearse her face. Fritz Rhys, shirtless, huge and understanding, came up out of the big chair like a cresting wave of muscles and kindliness. He took her hand and laughed quietly and brought her to the couch. She cowered back into the corner cushions and just sat, waiting for him to wash over her any way he wanted. He sat on the edge of the couch close to her, leaning forward to wall her away from the world, his heavy forearm and fist on the end table next to the couch; singlehandedly he surrounded her: "Alma . . ." he whispered, and waited, waited, until at last she met his eyes.

"I'm not angry," he told her. "Believe me, honey, I'm glad you can . . . love someone that much. It only means you're alive and . . . compassionate and—Alma." He laughed the quiet laugh again. "Of course I'll admit I'm glad he turned out to be a—one of the girls. I don't know what I'd do if you ever felt that way about a real man."

Her eyes had been fixed on his all the while, and now she moved them, let them drop to the heavy naked forearm which lay across the polished wood of the end table. She watched it with increasing fascination as he talked. "So let's chalk up one for the statistical mind, namely me, versus feminine intuition which sort of let you down. What are you staring at?"

She was staring at the forearm. Almost in spite of herself she reached for it. She didn't answer. He said, "It could have been worse. Imagine living with him. Imagine getting right to the point, drunk on poetry and shiny hair, and just when you were . . . ah, why go on. It would be impossible."

"It was impossible," she said in a low voice. She put her hand on his forearm, looked up and saw him watching her, and snatched the hand away self-consciously. She couldn't seem to keep her eyes off his arm. She began to smile, looking at it. He was a big man, and his forearm was about seventeen inches long and perhaps five and a half inches thick. "Quite impossible," she murmured, "and that's about the size of it." *Damn near exactly the size of it,* she thought wildly.

"Good girl!" he said heartily. "And now I'll give you forty-eight hours mooning time and then we'll be—"

His voice trailed off weakly as he watched the wildness transfer itself from somewhere inside her to her face and turn to laughter, floods, arrows, flights, peals, bullets of laughter.

"Alma!"

Her laughter ceased instantly but left her lips curled and her eyes glittering. "You better go back to killing the green monkeys," she said in a flat hard voice. "You've given them a beachhead."

"*What?*"

"There's something awfully small about you, Fritz Rhys," she said, and again the laughter, more and more of it, and he couldn't croon it down, he couldn't shout it down, and he couldn't stand it. He got dressed and packed his bag and said from the door, into the blare and blaze of her laughter, "I don't understand you. I don't understand you at all," and he went back to Washington.

A Crime for Llewellyn

I

He had a grey little job clerking in the free clinic at the hospital, doing what he'd done the day he started, and that was nineteen years back. His name was Llewellyn, and Ivy Shoots called him Lulu.

Ivy took care of him. He'd lived with Ivy ever since she was an owlish intellectual with an uncertain, almost little girl look about her and he was a scared, mixed up adolescent wilting in the interim between high-school and his first job. Ivy was in several senses his maiden experience—first date, first drink, first drunk, and first hangover in a strange hotel in a strange city accompanied by a strange girl. Strange or not— and she was—she was his Secret.

A man like Lulu needs a Secret. A sheltered background consisting of positive morality, tea-cosies, spinster aunts and the violent contrast of eighteen months as a public charge— after the aunts had burned to death, uninsured—had convinced him that he was totally incapable of coping with a world in which everybody else knew all the angles. So he fell joyfully into the arrangement with Ivy Shoots and the Secret that went with it.

He was small and he was pudgy, and he wasn't bright, and his eyes weren't too good, and the very idea of his stealing a nickel or crossing in the middle of the block was ridiculous. It seemed to him that all the men around him emanated the virtue of sin—the winks and whistles at the girls, the Monday tales (*boy did I tie one on Saturday night*), the legends of easy conquests and looseness and casual infidelity, the dirty jokes, and the oaths and expletives—and because they seemed to have no scruples they kept their stature as men in a world of men.

In this, Lulu could easily have drowned. Only his Secret kept him afloat. He told it to no one, partly because he sensed instinctively that he would treasure it more if he kept it to himself, and partly because he knew he would not be believed even if he proved it. He could listen contentedly to the boasting of the men he envied, thinking *if you only knew!* and *you think that's something!* hugging to himself all the while the realization that not one among them had committed the enormity of living in sin as he was doing.

When he first went to work at the hospital, he was the youngest clerk in the crowd. He had felt enormously superior to the other sinners who with all their triumphs had not been able to dye themselves as black as he had succeeded in doing. As the years went by, and he became one of the older ones, he patronized the young ones instead and pitied his contemporaries.

All this, of course, took place in his most inward self. On the surface he was an inconspicuous individual who was laughed at when noticed—which was seldom—and he took both the laughter and the anonymity as envious compliments. *You don't know it and you'd never guess, but you're talking to a pretty gay dog.*

Life with Ivy was, in some respects, as methodically guarded, as hedged about with limitations as his infancy with the aunts had been. In all their years together it never occurred to him that there was anything very unusual about the fact that they never entertained at home nor, for that matter, went anywhere together. She had her friends, and he had his acquaintances, and they seldom discussed them.

As a matter of fact they talked about very little. Ivy Shoots was a statistical typist, a strange breed to begin with. She was capable of meticulous accuracy without concentration and she spent her days rapidly typing long lists of bond issues and proofing drafts of catalogue numbers and patent listings.

She would arrive home within a few seconds of 5:45 each evening. Lulu, who went to work at six in the morning, would be waiting, with no variation in the pattern. Unvaryingly the potatoes would be on to boil. He had done the marketing; she cooked. They ate; he washed up. It was all very painless and almost completely automatic. He had eight shopping lists and she had eight menus, so that by using one each day they never ate the same food on successive Wednesdays.

He took out the laundry on Mondays, the dry-cleaning on Tuesdays and picked both bundles up on Fridays. She made the bed and handled all of the money. He dusted and swept and put the garbage out. On Saturday mornings she left the house at eight. Sunday evenings precisely at nine she returned.

He spent Saturday mornings cleaning the house, Saturday afternoons at the movies (a children's matinee, with 5 Cartoons) and all day Sunday listening to the radio tuned in loud. Ivy couldn't abide the radio, so out of consideration for her he used earphones on weekday evenings. And on weekday evenings she read novels—each a book club selection —from the lending library in the drugstore downstairs.

There were two things in all his life with her which he never opened. They were his pay envelope and the black steel box on the night table. Opening the first was unthinkable, and the second impossible, since she kept the key on a ribbon around her neck. Each of these closed matters was indicative of the total way her mind worked.

She pooled her wages with his pay envelope and kept track of every penny. Lulu neither smoked nor drank. He walked to and from work and brought his lunch in a paper bag. He had no use for cash and—except for his movie money on Saturdays—never touched it. Laundry and groceries were handled by monthly billing and paid for by mail. It is the literal truth that on nine hundred and ninety-one successive weeks he never once broke the seal on his pay envelope.

There was nothing in such self-control not compatible with the effortless routine of his life, and he put all temptation behind and away from him—along with U.S. foreign policy, baseball games, and the mating of the sapsucker, Ivy's whereabouts on week-ends, and all the other world's works in which he did not participate. Perhaps it would be more correct to say he simply filed it away, not so much forgotten as simply unremembered.

So life proceeded for nineteen years while wars and seasons crept by unnoticed, touching him no more than ambition or variety did. His life was a quiet succession of children's matinees with 5 Cartoons 5, of work in the morning and potatoes to peel at five in the afternoon, and, it may even be noted, the perfunctory performance, in the speechless dark, on three Tuesdays and three Fridays in each month, of an activity most essential to his secret status.

Evening after quiet evening was spent simply with the radio droning through the earphones into Lulu's lethargic and semi-conscious mind, while Ivy Shoots sat across the room from him in a straight-backed chair with her novel in one hand and her balsam inhalator—she was perpetually entering or leaving a head-cold—in the other. Whether or not they were happy is an argument for people who like definitions, but it can hardly be denied that a good many of the less restricted are unhappier than Lulu Llewellyn and Ivy Shoots.

In the nineteenth year of their arrangement, Ivy Shoots had a sort of colic of the conscience. Maybe it had something to do with the poor-man's Yoga she was hobbying at the time—a pseudo-mystic cult which dictated that the higher self, being chained to earth by lies and sin, must confess All to be cleaned and truly free itself. Anyway, she started to brood, and she brooded for three days and nights, and then one evening she began breathing hard—which made her cough—and at last came out with it: "Lulu, you're a good man. A *really* good man. You've never done anything wrong in your whole life. You couldn't. So you needn't be ashamed."

Lulu was, of course, no end startled. He pushed back his left earphone and blinked. "I'm not ashamed," he said. Then, in utter amazement, he watched her leap up, and go scrabbling for the key of her black box. In a moment she had opened the box and was fanning through the papers it contained. In another moment she had found the paper that was to explode a bomb-shell in Lulu's quiet life. She simply crossed the room and handed it to him.

"Well, read it," she said.

He blinked and did as he was told. And he honestly couldn't understand it. It was a legal form, apparently—all filled out with names and dates and witnesses and the like. He got as far as realizing that and then his mind refused to go on. He waved the paper and said inanely, "What's this?"

She expelled her breath slowly, looked up at the ceiling as if to remind herself that she could not expect him to understand all at once, and then gently took the certificate from him. She held it so that he could see it clearly, while she pointed out its significance. She explained each part to him— his signature, hers, the witnesses, the place, the official stamp, and finally the date, some nineteen years before. He nodded as each brick of structure fell into place, right up until she said, ". . . so you see, we were married that night." At that point he looked up.

"No we weren't," he said. "It's some kind of mistake."

"But I tell you we were, Lulu." She tapped the paper. "We were."

"No we weren't," he said again, but now with all of the assurance gone from his voice.

"Do you remember that night? Try to remember. Think back."

"Well, it was a long time ago."

"The very next day when you woke up there in the hotel. Start then."

"Well—" He tapped the paper, his eyes wide, and she nodded. He said, "Oh." And after a bit, his only defense, his only reference: "Fellow on the radio said . . ." He stopped, trying to remember exactly what the fellow had said. "He said you *can't* do that—get married all at once, drinking and all."

"It happened nineteen years ago, Lulu."

Lulu sat looking at the marriage certificate. It began to blur before his eyes. He whispered, "Why did you do it, Ivy?"

"I wanted to get married, that's all. I couldn't . . . do it any other way."

It wasn't really an answer to the question he had asked her, which concerned only him and an old piece of paper— not her at all. But he found he could not repeat the question and after a moment he didn't even try. She was nineteen years in the past, saying, "I was going to tell you, but I was afraid. I didn't know you, Lulu—the way I do now. I didn't know if you'd be angry or hate me, or leave, or what. I was going to tell you," she added after a pause, "but I waited so I could be sure you wouldn't be angry. And in a week . . ." She closed her eyes. ". . . you were *glad*. You said that. It was the only thing bad you ever did, or thought you did. It was the only thing. And now you see you didn't do anything bad after all. I—I know it must be a shock, but . . ." She shrugged then, opened her eyes, and smiled at him.

"Well!" she said briskly, "I'm glad you know now. At least you won't have that on your conscience. You!" she added, with the completely sincere but naïve fondness that often seems only a hair's breadth from scorn. "You doing *anything* bad. The very idea!"

He sat in his usual chair in his usual plump slump, with his feet in his shoes—he wiggled them to be sure—and his heart going not much faster than usual. He was all the parts of a man, alive and feeling, with the same name as before and the same weight cradled the same way on the bent springs of the same chair. Yet he could not have been more different had he become six feet tall or shrunk to midget size, or even if he had changed species and become a squirrel or a philodendron.

He just sat there wondering numbly where he had changed, and why so drastic a change seemed not to show somewhere. Something inside him had crumpled, but its precise nature eluded him. He put his hand on his round little stomach as if to find it, but everything felt the same to his touch.

Why did you do it, Ivy?

But he couldn't ask the question aloud. Instead he stood up suddenly, and because of some freak lack of control, his voice came out harsh, whiplike. "Ivy, you let me think—"

She whirled to face him, paling.

He was sorry his voice had done that, he was sorry he had frightened her. He was bewildered by the fact that he felt frightened too. He opened his lips to speak, and saw the absolute attention her sudden fright had gained him. He knew then that his next words would be words she would never forget. They came, and they were, "I guess I might's well turn in now." He shambled past her, saw the fright leave, and the color return to her face.

"Yes, you must be tired," she said cheerfully. "I felt funny there for a second. I guess what I need is a bite to eat!" She began to trim the crusts off some bread slices and to hum a no-tune she was fond of. Lulu had heard it for so long he was unaware of whether or not he liked it. It was a random sequence of notes within a range of about four tones. But unlike any other music, it was phrased not by bars nor melodic units, but by ladylike sniffs from her perpetually dripping nose.

Lulu found himself watching that nose as he slowly undressed. It was slightly bulbous at the tip, reddened and highly flexible, the results of years of blotting and mopping and repeated testing during the rare times when the drip was absent. He looked at the nose and he said to himself, *nineteen years,* and somehow that made sense to him. He got into bed and lay down to stare up at the ceiling until she retired.

She stopped by the bedroom door. She had the black box nestling in the crook of one elbow and a small sandwich in the other hand. She chewed and swallowed and then patted the black steel affectionately with the sandwich.

"Don't you ever forget, Lulu! Anybody tries to make out you did a wrong thing in your whole life, this box has all the proof in the world it's not so."

She came in and put the box down on the night table, and patted it again. She hummed for a moment longer, then took another bite out of the sandwich and said, "My, I feel so *good* now that it's in the open. Lulu, I'm filing that paper under M in the writing-desk. Don't forget—in case you ever need it for anything. It doesn't need to be in the box any more."

She washed up her things and put them on the rack to dry and after a while she came to bed. It wasn't Tuesday night or Friday night. It was Sunday night. They went to sleep without talking.

II

Lulu went to work on Monday. It was pretty bad. The talk was the same as every Monday and that was what made it so bad.

. . . about the ninth beer I was—
. . . only a high-school kid, Joe, but she—
. . . summagun rolled just one too many nines, so I—
. . . so I—
. . . pair of—
. . . Roseland—

Pretty bad. It washed and splashed and flooded around him, trickled away, and then came back, foaming and roaring to engulf him for the second time. He found that the Secret, in taking its departure, had left all its reflexes behind. He couldn't unlearn his defenses. Any anecdote which dealt in coarse, boastful fashion with sex, sin or scandal, he had been accustomed to counterbalance with a hidden loftiness, and from that take his pleasure.

But how could he experience pleasure when he had to remember that black steel box with its damnable certificate? Each time it happened he was emptied, and emptied again, and each time, it all had to happen again. *But we got married, we got married,* he told and told himself, and was then without sin to call his own.

Tuesday was much worse. The hairy-chested histories were fewer, of course, having nothing as eventful as a Saturday night to draw upon. But they were, by contrast, more unusual and unexpected. Lulu never knew when a charity-patient's face would appear in the grated arch above his desk, and give evidence of some riotous sin solely by its scars and contours, or drop before him some virile obscenity which he might repeat but could never hope to conceive. And when these things happened he was caught up in his hellish little chain, the reflex, the lofty pleasure, the recollection and the emptying.

What made it so much worse was that, unlike Monday, Tuesday's misery continued after quitting time. To be strictly accurate, the misery *re-emerged* after quitting time, after everything else, the homecoming, the potatoes, the dinner, the dishes, the radio and the reading. His last activity with Ivy on Tuesdays—and Fridays, except for every fourth—had regularized itself into a commonplace, and destroyed all piquancies but one. And that one had been Lulu's alone, his own special creation. It was the core crystal of his Secret.

He was able to conceal the change from himself until the very moment arrived, in its usual form of two firm taps on his shoulder as he lay in bed with his back to Ivy. He immediately, and with conscious decision, shook his head. The gesture in darkness was invisible, but conveyed itself quite clearly through the bed. Ivy's response was to stop breathing for a time. When she resumed, the sniffs which punctuated it were no more frequent, but they were much fuller in body, the oboe (as it were) replacing the clarinet.

This departure from routine was demoralizing in the extreme, and brought to Lulu his first dim awareness that the future was going to be quite different from the past. A miserable hour or two later he made the further distressing discovery that he missed tormentingly that which he had just refused, such being the tyranny of the habitual.

You, too? he demanded wistfully of his body as he had for two days of his mind. *Can't you understand that it's all changed now?* Somehow his body couldn't. He lay rigid and miserable until the window-sashes showed darker than the panes, and then got up and dressed and went to work. Ivy, who frequently showed signs of life when he got up in the morning, now lay with her eyes closed, too still to be asleep.

As might have been expected, Wednesday was a quiet day containing a stretch of hell. As quitting time approached, a couple of orderlies started horsing around in the employees' locker room which adjoined Lulu's office. Custom demanded that they have but one thing on their minds and three ways of getting rid of it—through comedy, insult, and loud-mouthed boasting. The location of their lockers—diagonally across from each other in the big room—made them fire their expletives at the tops of their voices. The position of the main exit set their course inevitably past the back of Lulu's chair.

They boiled out of the locker room into the office. Lulu didn't turn to look at them, even when one said, "Do you know what we ought to do some payday? We ought to take old Llewellyn out an' get his ashes hauled."

"He wouldn't know what to look for unless you dressed it up to look like a ledger book."

"Maybe he fool you. Maybe he set so quiet around here 'cause he keepin' all he can handle around home."

Lulu did not move, and his stillness seemed to force the orderlies' attention on him. One wisecrack, one grin over his shoulder, and they would have moved away. But he had no wisecrack and he didn't know how to make a grin. He could only sit still with his back to them.

"Nah. I'll tell you somethin'. He just ain't alive. Man don't chase a little ain't really livin'."

The uproarious laugh. Apparently the heartiness of their mirth was a good substitute for the missing reaction from Lulu, for they turned abruptly and moved to the exit.

Suddenly Lulu got to his feet excitedly. "I know what I'll do. I'll go out and pick up some actress," he told himself. And suddenly felt fine. He felt better than he had at any time since the night when he had first seen the marriage certificate. He couldn't explain why the idea had come so abruptly into his head—only that it had.

I'll pick up this actress, he told his image in the washroom mirror five minutes later. The image nodded encouragingly back at him. *No matter what happens then, I'll have it to* tell. Maybe I'll tell them and maybe I won't. Maybe it'll be all about how she steals my wallet and my watch, and that's funny. Or maybe it'll be about how she can't get enough of me, how she gives me her money and sells her ring.

I won't tell them a thing, he decided firmly as he left the hospital. I'll make it happen, that's all. They don't have to know. *I'll* know.

Halfway home he said to himself, *I don't even have a wallet. I'll have to buy one first.*

On the steps at home he added, *a watch too.*

Considerably sobered, he let himself into the apartment, hung up his jacket, and got the potatoes and the knife and a pan of water and a paper bag for the peels, and stood in front of the counter in the kitchenette.

How much money is a wallet and a watch—

He didn't know. It would have to be a whole lot, because he'd have to have money for the actress too.

He put down the potato he was peeling and pulled on his lower lip. There was one thing he could do—he could quit going to the movies on Saturdays.

"That's a lot of Saturdays," he murmured.

The idea of holding on to his own pay envelope simply did not occur to him. It had never been a reality to him, anyway. When he thought about money he thought about Ivy. In fact, it took him quite a while to dispose of the very direct idea of getting the money from her simply by asking for it. He decided against that very direct solution only because he didn't think she'd have any. He just couldn't erase from his mind the picture he had of her paying out money every month for electricity and gas and other household expenses.

The amount of money that could be accumulated by two people with steady jobs and a medium-low standard of living over nineteen uninterrupted years of employment, was completely beyond his comprehension. When he began to search her writing desk it was only with some vague recollection of one of his painful overheard anecdotes at the hospital— something about a boy who was eighty cents short rummaging in his mother's purse and finding forty dollars. "Lift it from the old lady's shopping money," he murmured.

Well, there wasn't any shopping money. There wasn't a thing in Ivy's desk but painfully neat stacks of writing paper and envelopes and the file of cancelled checks cross-indexed by number, date and alphabet—he recalled the incomprehensible ritual each New Year's Day when she burned every check seven years old—little boxes of paper clips, three sizes; rubber bands, two sizes; first and fourth class package labels; bottles of ink, red and blue-black; forty-two thousand dollars in bonds, three unopened boxes of pencils, and a file of correspondence. Lulu turned away in disappointment and went back to peeling the potatoes.

He sighed and turned on the radio and went on peeling the potatoes. He heard a commercial advertising wristwatches and paused midway in his task to listen to it. The man said they started at only $49.95. That didn't sound so "only" to Lulu. That much money would amount to—uh—He closed his eyes and moved his lips while he worked it out—about two years and nine months worth of Saturday movies. After that he'd have to get a wallet, and then more money—to give to the actress. He wondered how much money you had to give actresses. Oh well. He could certainly manage to find out in the next three years, or four—or however long it took him.

Bulletin. Five-state alarm for two men who had only an hour before held up a suite of offices on High Street. The robbers had made off with four thousand in cash and negotiable bonds and twelve thousand in securities.

All that money would be enough, thought Lulu. Good heavens! Imagine it—wanting money real bad, and going out and getting it, *just like that.* Imagine having a story like that to tell about yourself (whether you kept it to yourself or not.) *So I took out the gun and said all right, let's have them there securities.* He didn't quite know what securities were, but they sounded like fine things to have twelve thousand dollars invested in. Anyone with enough spunk to do a thing like that could make up for a good many years of sinlessness.

He wouldn't have to wait around for years counting every penny until he had enough money set aside to pick up an actress. (Much of Lulu's radio listening was in mid-afternoon, and the disruptive elements in the lives of decent people in the serials was very frequently an actress.) Matter of fact, if you could steal like that, you wouldn't even need the actress. The stealing would be sin enough. *All right, you, let's have those negotiable bonds. He* didn't know what bonds were either. And he didn't have a gun.

Suddenly his hands stopped moving and he looked down

at them and the long curl of potato skin depending from the paring-knife, and he said aloud, "I do so know what bonds are and I don't even need a gun."

III

At half-past two on Thursday afternoon he was standing timidly at the edge of a wide expanse of polished marble inside the First National Bank. He no longer carried the folder next to his skin, with his undershirt and outer shirt tucked over it. (Ivy had said, as he left, "Lulu, I do believe you're putting on more weight.") He had secured one of the hospital's big manila envelopes and crammed the bonds into it. The envelope was wet now where his hand grasped it. He peered all around and just didn't know what to do.

A man in a policeman's uniform—but grey instead of blue—crossed over to where Lulu was standing. He had a gun. "Can I help you, sir?" he asked.

Lulu swallowed heavily and tried to say, "I got some bonds." But no sound came out. He coughed and tried again.

"You want to talk to somebody about some securities," the guard almost miraculously divined.

Lulu managed to nod. The guard smiled and said, "All right, sir. Just step this way."

Lulu followed the guard to a low shiny wall with a mahogany gate that swung open both ways. Beyond the gate was an area containing a half-dozen desks and a half-dozen chairs, all very far apart like small islands in a big river. The guard pointed at one of the chairs beside one of the desks.

"Just sit down there, sir. Mr. Skerry will take care of you in a moment."

The guard turned away.

Lulu sidled through the gate, wondering with mounting alarm what 'take care of' might lead to, and sat down on the edge of the chair with the envelope on his lap. The man behind the desk was huge. He had snow-white hair and ice-blue eyes and nobody in the world could have had a collar that clean. He finished doing something with a ruled card on the desk and then hit the card hard with a rubber stamp. Then he looked at Lulu, who shrank under the impact of a truly frightening smile. The man asked, "What can I do for you?"

"Uh," said Lulu. He dropped his eyes, saw the envelope,

and remembered the bonds. He gave the envelope to the oversized Mr. Skerry.

Mr. Skerry looked at him almost accusingly before he took out the bonds, and after he took out the bonds, and a third time after he had riffled through the stack, and that final scrutiny was the worst. He said, "What are these?"

"Well," said Lulu. "Bonds."

"Hmm, I see."

Mr. Skerry took a glass-case out of his waistcoat and opened it with a snap and took out a pair of glasses and put them on. They hung to his face by biting the bridge of his nose with little gold lips. Lulu was fascinated. Mr. Skerry bent his iceberg of a head and looked at Lulu between the tops of the lenses and a frown. "Are these bonds yours?"

"Oh yes," said Lulu.

"Hmph," said Mr. Skerry to the bonds. He lifted them a little and let them fall to the desk and looked at the stack again.

"What I wanted," said Lulu timidly, "is the money."

"Oh?" said Mr. Skerry.

The phrase from the radio bulletin came to Lulu, and he pointed his finger. "They're *negotiable* bonds," he said, his voice quavering a little.

"Oh yes, they certainly are, Mr. Er-ump."

"Llewellyn," Lulu supplied.

"Llewellyn. Of course, naturally. Excuse me." Mr. Skerry picked up a yellow sheet with some very black typing on it, made three quick motions with his finger on the telephone dial, and said into the instrument, "I've got BW listing No. three seventy-eight. Is that the latest? You're sure, now? Very well." He hung up and studied the yellow sheet, and then put it down beside the bonds and began methodically to go through them, comparing numbers on the bonds with numbers on the list. "Well," he said after a while, "that part's all right, anyway."

He picked up the yellow sheet again and waved it at Lulu and smiled. Over the smile his eyes were precision-aimed— as ready as a pair of steel drills. "This is the latest list of stolen bonds," he said. "We always know."

He then did nothing for a moment but watch Lulu's face. Lulu's face remained utterly expressionless, because Lulu had gone utterly numb.

"Now then, you want to liquidate all of these bonds, Mr.

Llewellyn? I see. Well, I'm afraid it will take a while. If you'd be kind enough to wait over there..."

Lulu looked up at the big clock on the wall in panic. It was a minute or so of the bank's closing time. A brassy clang had started echoes all up and down the vast marble interior, and when he glanced toward the big door where he had come in he saw that the brass gates had been closed. The guard was herding people out a smaller door at the side of the building.

"Oh dear, I can't," he gasped. "I've got to get the potatoes on."

"Miss Fisher," said Mr. Skerry flatly.

Startled, Lulu said, "What?"

But before he could make a more disastrous blunder a homely ageless fat girl with thick glasses appeared at the other end of the desk and said, "Yes, sir?"

"Take these bonds and list the numbers on a receipt for Mr. Llewellyn here," said Mr. Skerry. "Mr. Llewellyn, can you come back tomorrow at about this time? We'll have everything taken care of by then." He added quickly, as if to override a protest (which Lulu would not have dared to interpose) "Not today, not today. There just isn't time. These things take a while, you understand? Miss Fisher, get his address. You can wait over there," he said to Lulu and pointed with his frown.

Lulu went "over there," which was a long leather bench against the opposite wall. Near it was a much smaller desk than Mr. Skerry's, where Miss Fisher sat enthroned. In front of her was an electric typewriter. She had the bonds at her elbow and was turning them over one by one with her left hand while her right danced frantically and apparently unnoticed on the top rows of keys.

Lulu watched her with awe. She had a flexible bulbous nose almost exactly like Ivy's, and he felt comforted. The tip of Miss Fisher's nose was the only remotely familiar thing in this cold busy place.

Much sooner than he would have thought possible, she was finished. She took down his name and home address and work address and asked him if he had a car registration —which gratified him—or any identification at all. He showed her his pay signature card, and she seemed satisfied. Then the guard with the grey uniform let him out the small door, and he hurried home to peel the potatoes.

It took Mr. Skerry just three phone calls and forty minutes of his costly time to discover the identity of the bonds' rightful owner. Shortly after that Ivy Shoots sat in the chair at the end of his desk. He had to tell her three times in a row and then show her the bonds before she could believe her ears.

IV

Lulu got up and dressed as quietly as he could. Maybe the difference was all in him, but Ivy had seemed painfully quiet all evening and he didn't like it and he wanted to get out of the apartment before he had to talk to her. But he got only as far as the bedroom door when her voice brought him up short.

"Lulu."

Slowly he turned back. He said, "I'm late already. It's half past—"

"That's all right. I want to talk to you." She turned on the lamp on the night table. "Lulu, anything to do with money, you ought to ask me first."

He didn't say anything. He found that he felt no fear, but only a fierce secret happiness. The money wasn't important, getting caught wasn't important. The important thing was stealing the bonds, and she couldn't change that. He hoped she would hurry up and get through accusing him, because he wanted to be at his cage at the hospital. He wanted to hear the people all around him talking, and be able to say silently, how long has it been since *you* stole three and a half pounds of negotiable bonds?

"It was really too silly of you. You just don't understand these things, Lulu. Do you know you came *that* close"—she showed him how close with a thumb and forefinger—"to getting arrested for *stealing* those bonds?"

Lulu made no reply, offered no defense. He simply poked out his lower lip and looked at his shoes. He didn't know what to say.

"You told yourself I was keeping all that money for myself, didn't you?" she said. "Isn't that what you thought?"

He remained silent.

"Oh dear, I suppose I can't blame you. I just never dreamed you'd misunderstand and you never said anything. It seemed the best way. You've got to believe me, Lulu! You *do* believe me?" She looked at him and sniffed unhappily, and blew her nose. "No—I guess you don't. Wait—I'll prove it."

He looked at her, and what she read in his face he had no way of knowing. But she scrabbled at her throat so roughly and suddenly that she tore off one of her shoulder-straps. She pulled out the key to the steel box by its ribbon, and put it in the keyhole and opened the box, and took out the top paper without looking at what she was doing and gave it to him.

"You take this with you when you go back there this afternoon, and give it to Mr. Skerry. He's a nice man, and he'll take care of everything."

Lulu looked down at the paper, and then quickly back at her. "It's called an assignment form. It signs over most of the bonds to you, Lulu. They're *yours*. Don't you understand? I worked it out to the penny—how much I've made, how much you've made, and all the expenses we shared. That's your money, Lulu. Only you've *got* to believe I wanted you to have it all along."

He looked at the assignment form, and slowly put it away in his breast pocket with the receipt that Miss Fisher had given him at the bank.

"You could have gone to jail, Lulu, you silly. For stealing your own money. Imagine you—*stealing!*"

He looked at her and at the black box. Suddenly he began to tremble. Something about him made Ivy pick up the bedclothes and clutch them to her breast. "Lulu!"

He whirled and ran out. He was panting even before he began to run. He pursed up his lips painfully and his cheeks went round and flat, round and flat, like a little plump bellows. His eyes began to water and his throat hurt him.

He hadn't stolen anything. He felt cheated, betrayed, lost.

And Mr. Skerry was nicer to him on Friday afternoon than anyone had ever been since his aunts died. He told Lulu that he now possessed a very respectable sum of money which he'd do well to—direct quote—"let that fine woman take care of for you." When he got no reaction from Lulu —who had gone numb again—he sighed and helped him deposit most of the money in a savings account and some of it in a checking account.

He even showed him how to make out a check and keep up the stubs. He really took a lot of trouble over Lulu, who absorbed perhaps a fifth of what he was saying and ultimately escaped into the sunlight again.

He found Friday's shopping list and blindly went through the routine of marketing and getting home, the stairs, the key, the putting away of the groceries. Then he went into the living room and sat, or collapsed, into his chair in the corner by the radio.

He was confused and despairing, lost especially in the once securely-blueprinted stretches of the future. More than anything else, he wanted back what he had lost—this apartment, this routine, Ivy's protective handling of everything. His hand strayed to the radio dial but he could not switch it on because of the envelope which was propped against it. The envelope had his name on it in Ivy's quick accurate handwriting. Wondering, he tore it open and unfolded the sheet of letter paper within and squared himself away to read the communication through. He read every word in quick succession without grasping the letter's meaning at all. He was just getting the feel of the words the first time around. Then he started over, reading each sentence slowly for the meaning alone.

Dear Lulu:

I am going away right from work today instead of tomorrow morning. So don't do so many potatoes and be sure to put my half of the liver in the freezer part.

I am going away early this week because I want to think about things. What happened about the bonds opened my eyes a whole lot, and I have to look around with my eyes open. You must believe me when I say I never meant to keep the savings away from you. You have got to believe me. Please. It's just that in arranging everything to suit myself I never thought you might feel hurt and not understand. It was all done to make everything simple for you but now I want to arrange everything to make it fair. I am very sorry Lulu. Don't worry if what I'm saying doesn't make sense right now. It will later. You'll see.

Lulu please, please don't do anything silly. Don't go away and leave me whatever you do. You don't know how to take care of yourself. If you want to go later, well, all right. But give me a chance to teach you how to do for yourself. I am so afraid you will get yourself into some awful trouble.

Lulu you are a good person, a very good person who could

not do a bad thing if you tried. I don't like myself very much just now, and I am not surprised if you don't either. I want to help you and do some things over I have done wrong. So please don't go away. I'll be worried sick. Believe me about the bonds, it's the truth. Now you have your share you can believe me, can't you? Only just don't go away anywhere.

Ivy

The last paragraph contained several crooked lines and words crossed out here and there and squinched up so that reading them took time. Lulu read the last part four times, and then he drew down the paper and glared at the radio. "I am not!" he barked in the same furious voice with which he had frightened Ivy by accident once.

... *a very good person who could not do a bad thing if you tried.* "I am *not!*" he shouted for the second time. He stamped across the room and back again, and what he felt uncurling somewhere in the region of his solar plexus was a new thing, a frightening thing. It was anger—and nothing that he had ever experienced in his entire life up to that instant had made him feel enraged before.

He scooped up the letter and glared at it. Next to that one infuriating statement—which he again denied out loud—the only other thing the letter had to say to him was the desperate, pleading request that urged him not to go away.

Leaving Ivy—leaving the only home he had—was something that would never have crossed his mind in thirty years' trying. But when Ivy said it, and said it over and over, it exploded inside him. "I will so," he told the piece of paper solemnly. "I will so leave."

And he did. He really did. He filled two paper shopping bags with his clothes and left on Saturday afternoon instead of going to the movies as he had planned. He got a furnished room right across the street from the hospital and down the street from the bank and up the street from the movies.

On Monday they called him in to the main office and sat him down in front of a telephone with the receiver off. He picked the receiver up and listened to it, and sure enough it was Ivy, calling him up at work for the very first time. She sounded terrible, with her squeaky pleading, her frequent sobbing, and another one of her head colds. He just listened in complete silence until there was a pause, unable to think of anything to tell her that would make even a little sense to himself.

He finally said, "No, no, I can't. I can't. You hear, I can't no more." He put the receiver on its cradle and sat there looking at it. He found he was trembling. He thought he ought to tell her at least that he wasn't sick or in any awful trouble. He picked up the phone again but it only buzzed at him. Ivy was gone out of it. He re-cradled the receiver.

The hospital cashier glanced at him, and then came over. "Anything wrong?" he asked.

Lulu stood up and wiped his upper lip with the back of his hand. "I can take care of myself," he said almost belligerently.

"Why, sure you can," said the cashier, backing off a pace. "You just didn't look so good, that's all."

"Well, I'm not going back there," said Lulu.

"Okay, *okay*," said the cashier, holding up placating hands. "I just wanted to help."

"No sense ever asking me no more," said Lulu. He shambled back to the receiving desk, leaving a very puzzled young man staring after him.

For a few weeks, getting adjusted to living alone took up so much of Lulu's life and thoughts that he had no time for his sins. Living in furnished rooms and eating in restaurants are not always completely simple matters even to the intelligent, and Lulu was a babe in the woods almost from the first. Keeping cash on his person was a habit he found complicated and very difficult to acquire.

He used his checkbook constantly, for a ten-cent cup of coffee, a sandwich, and once even for a newspaper so he could check the radio programs. Finally the manager of the restaurant where he ate came over to him with a sheaf of his checks and asked him plaintively to cut it out.

"Write a big one any time, and keep the cash in your pocket and use what you want. Okay? You got my girl spendin' a hour and a half every week listin' your checks in the deposit slip."

Lulu blushed painfully and promised to do better. To his amazement he found that he could. He tried the same thing at the grocery, where he had been writing a check every night for two soft rolls and six slices of liverwurst for his lunch. He wrote a check for ten dollars, and used the cash for a week. The proprietor was pleased and even increased the thickness of the liverwurst slices as a token of his esteem.

He passed Ivy twice in the street. She did not speak to him, and he was speechless even at the thought of her.

His new life wove in one unexpected thread. The second day of his liberation he was in a booth in the restaurant, and had just finished his soup when he became aware of someone standing next to the table. He looked up and there was Miss Fisher from the bank.

She said timidly, "I do beg your pardon. But I thought perhaps you wouldn't mind if I shared this table with you. There are no other seats in the restaurant . . ."

He got up hastily and made room at the little table and saw that she had the salt and he even stacked her cafeteria tray on top of his out of the way. When she was organized she looked at him with a wan thank-you smile that became recognition. "Why, it's Mr. Llewellyn!"

He didn't say anything more to her that evening—he couldn't. But the next night she was there ahead of him and when he came along with his tray, she called out to him and patted the table across from her. After that they always had dinner together. She was quiet and nice, and she let him be silent for as long as he wanted to be.

Six or seven weeks later something happened at the hospital that made a deep impression on Lulu. A furious young female face appeared at his wicket and demanded: "Where is George Hickenwaller? Where is he? I got to see him right away."

Lulu stared dumbly until she banged the palm of her hand on the shelf by the wicket, and repeated the question. Her face started darkening ominously and the blood-vessels on the sides of her neck began to stand out in the most alarming fashion.

He remembered then. George Hickenwaller was the married orderly who had annoyed him more than most of the others—although he wasn't quite sure why. "I'll find him. Just wait a minute," he promised. He got up, and went over to the doorway of the locker room, and saw at once that George Hickenwaller was in there with his back to the wall. He was making wild signals of distress and prayer, and moving his mouth strangely, giving vent to some exaggerated, silent, pleading syllables which Lulu could not understand.

He went back to his wicket. "He's in there," he said, thumbing at the door.

"In there, is he?" said the young woman. She turned angrily to the man behind her. Lulu saw that the man was a policeman. "He's in there," she relayed.

"In there, is he?" the policeman countered. He ran around to the front, to the general office door, and went sprinting across behind Lulu and into the locker room.

There came sounds of the chase and a cry for mercy, and then poor Hickenwaller was walked abjectly out by the policeman. The big, red-faced cop had a meaty hand on his collar and another in the back of his belt.

Quite a crowd had gathered by this time and Lulu found himself standing next to Hickenwaller's friend, the other orderly. This man shook his head sadly. "I tol' him he wasn't goin' to get away with it. 'I know what I'm doin',' he says. 'I got it made.'" The orderly shook his head again. "He got it made *now* all right, but good."

"What did he do?" Lulu asked.

"Got married."

"To that one?" Lulu pointed at the angry woman, who was ducking under the policeman's guard to punch Hickenwaller solidly on the ear.

"Yeah, an' another one too. I *tol'* him she'd find out."

"Two wives?"

"Bigamy," said the orderly knowledgeably.

"Is that very bad?" Lulu asked, really wanting to know.

The orderly cocked his head and squinted at him. "Lew old man, let me tell you. *One* is very bad."

"Yes, but this—uh—bigamy. It's *really* bad, huh."

"No way to get to heaven."

"Well," said Lulu, and got back to work.

V

Dinner time, comfortable with Miss Fisher in the booth. He wondered why she seemed so glad to have dinner with him all the time. What did she get out of it. He didn't ask her. But he continued to wonder.

"Oh, *there* you are!" someone said at his elbow. It was the manager. He half-filled the booth and loomed over them. "I thought I had all the trouble with you I was goin' to," he growled at Lulu.

Lulu went speechless. He made himself smaller in his seat, while Miss Fisher looked frightened at the manager and anxious at Lulu.

The manager banged a check with a bank slip stapled to it, banged it down directly in front of Lulu. "After all that trouble, now they're bouncing."

Lulu didn't know what to say. Miss Fisher stared at him, while the manager continued to glare. People began to crane and peer at them. Lulu slipped down another notch in his seat.

Suddenly Miss Shelly Fisher snatched up the check. "Just a minute, Mr. Grossman," she said firmly, "I'm sure this can be straightened out. Mr. Llewellyn, didn't you make a large deposit at the First National just a few weeks ago?"

Lulu nodded.

"Have you put any more money in the checking account since then?"

He shook his head sheepishly. "I didn't know I had to," he mumbled.

"Well, have you taken anything out of the savings account?"

He shook his head. Miss Fisher said, "I'll vouch for him, Mr. Grossman. He just isn't used to a checking account yet. He has a good balance in savings. You can take my word for it."

"You work at the bank?"

"You've seen me there."

He nodded slowly. "Well, all right then," he growled. He picked up the check and waved it in front of Lulu's nose. "You take care of it by this time tomorrow, you hear?"

"Of course he will. Of course," said Miss Fisher soothingly. She put her hand over Lulu's as he slipped yet another inch down in his chair, which put the table about breast-high to him. Grossman went away.

"It's all right now," she said. "It's all right. Sit up, Mr. Llewellyn."

He did, shamefaced. "I didn't know," he said feebly.

"You'd better let someone look over your checkbook. Do you want me to?"

"It's home," he said, regretfully, feeling that the simple statement had disposed of the matter.

"I don't mind," she said, surprisingly. "I have nothing else to do."

"You mean, you'd come to—"

She nodded while he fought his unwilling tongue. After a moment she got up. "Come on," she said.

Unbelievingly he followed her out of the restaurant, and then led the way to his rooming house.

The room was so small he had to sit on the bed if she was going to sit at the table. He kept it neat enough, but places that crummy are unconquerable. He found the checkbook and gave it to her. She riffled through the stubs, finding not a single entry.

"Well," she said, "no *wonder!*" Very carefully she explained to him how he must keep his record in the stubs and make an effort not to let checks bounce. He nodded humbly every three seconds while she talked. She did it kindly and did not laugh at him, or sneer.

"Yes, Mr. Skerry told me. I guess it didn't stick."

"*Lots* of people don't understand it at first."

This is a very fine lady, he told himself, and wished he could say it out loud.

"What are those?" She pointed to the top of the chest, where eleven cash envelopes lay in a neat row.

"Oh, that's my paydays," he said.

She picked one of the envelopes up, pressed it, shook it, and finally read the data typed on it. "Cash, my goodness. They pay you in cash. You shouldn't leave cash around."

He could only manage to get out a faltering, "I'm sorry."

"My, you do need someone to look after you." She counted the envelopes. "Don't you see, if you put these in your checking account every week you'd always have money to write checks against?"

He didn't see. He just waved at the envelopes and said unhappily, "I just never knew *what* to do with 'em."

He intercepted her look of astonishment and said abjectly, "I never could understand all this. You want to help me with it?"

So Miss Fisher began taking care of Lulu Llewellyn.

He began to be happier. Yet his relationship with Miss Fisher was so innocent, and she herself so different from any woman he'd ever met that some of his old torment began to return, and he found himself cringing again under the assault of other people's sins. Now, however, as his philosophy of sin began a slow evolution, there was a slightly different reaction. Instead of considering himself totally unfit and excluded, he began to match what he knew of himself against each of the sins he heard recounted. *Could I do that?* Could he ever gamble? Seduce? Steal, swear, assault, outwit? Always no and no and no, and the words in Ivy's letter trailing across his clear conscience: *a very good man who couldn't do a bad thing if he tried.*

And then one day he saw the face of Hickenwaller's friend go past his wicket—just that, a reminder. And belatedly, as all things did, the solution came to Lulu Llewellyn.

He went to Miss Fisher and asked her, and she cried. Then she said yes, she would marry him. Then she cried again and said pathetically that she had made up her mind when she was eight years old that nobody would ever want her and she might as well face it.

So they went down to City Hall and got a license, and three days later they were married. He chittered and jittered like the most eager of grooms. He was eager about something else than that which plagues most grooms, however, and it was more important—to him, at least.

That very evening he marched to Ivy's apartment and up the one flight of stairs. It made him feel a little strange to be knocking on the door instead of using his key, but somehow he felt that he should knock, that he owed her that courtesy. He waited happily, feeling the crackling comfort of the marriage license in his breast pocket.

The door opened.

"Lulu! Oh—*Lulu,* I'm so glad." She looked worn, sallow-cheeked, but her eyes were shining. She pulled him inside and shut the door. "I just knew you'd come back. I just knew you would, you had to."

He cleared his throat. "I—"

"Don't talk. Don't say anything. I've had a chance to think things out clearly. And oh, Lulu, it's all so senseless and I'm so sorry."

"But I didn't—"

"Don't say another word. You're going to listen to me now. I've waited too long. You just stay right there where you belong."

Half playfully but very firmly she nudged him over to his old chair and crowded him until he had to sit down.

"I won't be a second," she said, and ran out of the room.

He sat there, his backsides liking the old chair, and

thought excitedly: You're the first. Miss Fisher—she's the second. He wondered how that would sound if he ever told it at the hospital. He put the speculation aside to think about later.

After a moment she came out of the bedroom carrying the black metal box. "I'm not a stupid woman, Lulu," she said. "Really I'm not. I read and I think and I can keep my end up when I talk with well-educated people. But sometimes the brightest of us can be more stupid than the slowest witted. Well, anyway, I'll admit it. I finally had to talk it out with someone. I did, Lulu—and I got the answer." She inserted the key in the box, turned it, raised the black metal lid. "He's a dear man, a brilliant man. He's a psychiatrist. I told him everything, but you mustn't worry about that, Lulu, They're like *priests*. Anyway, I didn't even tell him your name."

She rummaged in the box and found a paper and began to gesture with it while she talked.

"There it was, right in front of my silly old eyes, and I never even saw it. He explained to me that it was *terribly* important to you to think we were living together *without* being married. He said it made a man of you. He said you had been very strictly brought up and that you had—well, he called it a 'black-and-white' morality. He said you took it so seriously when you were a child that you had nothing at all on the black side—not so much as cheating on a school examination, or hitting a puppy in your whole life. That's why, he said, when I finally told you that our living together was a 'white' thing, and had been from the beginning, it was a terrible blow to your self-confidence. You just couldn't stand it.

"Now I'm going to tell you something I never thought I'd ever tell to a living soul. I was on my own when I was fourteen, and I always had to think things out for myself. Sometimes I did well at that, and sometimes I failed. But I always thought things out for myself first—not for laws or anyone else or customs or anything like that, but just for myself alone. Well, never mind all that now. One of the main things was—I thought I had to have freedom. I made up my mind I'd do what I wanted with whom I wanted, just as long as I was discreet. As long as I put a partition that was like a high wall between the one thing and the other. You don't understand this, do you? Well, that's all right. You'll understand all you need to in just one more minute.

"Didn't you ever wonder what I did with my weekends for nineteen years, Lulu? Didn't you *care?*"

He started to answer, but she gave him no chance. "No, I don't suppose it ever occurred to you to wonder. It was just the way things were—like water running downhill and the sun coming up. You knew I was going to be away Saturday and Sunday, and you just accepted it. Poor Lulu! Well, I see I've got to tell you then. I was taking a course in economics for a while. Let me see—that would be about six years ago. Oh, I've done all *sorts* of things on weekends—and anyway, there was this man. You see, and I don't know what happened to me at all, but I'd never felt like that in my life before. And I guess I never will again," she added in a whisper, tragically.

Then she blew her nose. "I have the most awful cold, Lulu. I think I'm a bit feverish. So there I was, feeling like that about this man, you see, and for a while I thought he might feel the same way about me. So I saw a lawyer and showed him my papers, and I got this. Here, Lulu, this is yours. This is for you." She handed him the paper.

The whole episode was so reminiscent of the one which had blasted his quiet life once before that he took the paper without even glancing at it. He simply closed his eyes, and got up and stood trembling, waiting for he knew not what.

She understood and laughed happily. Then she coughed, and laughed again and took the paper away from him. "You're afraid of it, and I don't blame you. Here, I'll read it to you." Her hand touched his, and he felt the paper slip out of his fingers.

" 'There came before me in the County Court in the township of—' Oh, let's skip all that lawyers' talk. Here it is. 'Therefore by weight of evidence in camera—' that means secret and confidential—'the marriage of said L. Llewellyn and said Ivy Shoots is hereby annulled and held to be void and without existence.' "

She pushed the paper triumphantly back into his lap. "You understand that, Lulu? It isn't a divorce. A divorce says a marriage *was* and is no more. This says that in the eyes of the law and in my eyes, Lulu, and in *your* eyes, Lulu, the wedding never took place. You see? You see? So if that was what was bothering you, it needn't any longer. It's gone.

We're without benefit of clergy if that's how you'd like it to be. We can call it common-law if you want that instead. Lulu I just don't know—?"

He lay in a pressing welter of thoughts and scraps of thoughts. The one which came swirling to the top first had to do with the nature of the certificate in a modern culture. The thought wasn't quite that lucid in him, of course. He saw the blasting of his painless existence by a piece of paper. He saw people breaking the law and being broken by it—a piece of paper for each. A piece of paper for everything you did or didn't do, even the things which were truly and really done, just by changing the paper.

"Lulu," she whispered, "If you should want to—you can even m-marry someone else. You're free to do that, to hurt me that much if—" And then she began to cough. The wracking, all-too-familiar quality of the cough made him shift uneasily in his chair, and over his heart his new marriage license crackled gently.

Somewhere deep within him stirred the bitter, despairing thought that he was going to have to pick up an actress after all. Pick one up and marry her—or he would never be a bigamist. He put his knuckles slowly up to his forehead and closed his eyes. He stood like that for a long time while his lips tried futilely to shape words. Finally a half-sentence came. "Think about," he said. He went to the door. "Think about it, I'll . . . think about it."

"Come back . . . soon," she said. "It's not—good here now, Lulu. I didn't know what I—well, come back soon." She did not accompany him to the door. He knew she was going to cough, or cry, or let go again in some even more distressing way. He got out quickly.

VI

Lulu went upstairs to the pharmacy and said, "Joe, I don't sleep so good."

Joe said, "How long you want to sleep?"

"Just once, twelve hours. Like a cold shower couldn't wake me up."

"Can do, Lew. Take two of—"

"That's the trouble, Joe. Pills choke me up. You got powder that don't taste so bad?"

"I got better'n that. I got a liquid don't taste at all. Only, Lew, don' talk it around, right?"

"Me? Joe, I wouldn't do that."

"That's good. That's fine, Lew."

An hour later Lulu said, "Drink your milk."

Obediently, Shelly Fisher Llewellyn drank her milk. She was quite unhappy for a four-week bride. For the time being she was trying to escape from her unhappiness by doing everything she could think of that might please her husband. Lulu got up and stretched. "I don't know what you're going to do, but I'm going to turn in," he said. "Don't come now if you don't want to. Good night."

"Oh," she said, "I'll come."

He embraced her while she fell asleep. He said, "I'm going to hold you just like this all night long."

Just after two in the morning he silently mounted the steps at Ivy's place and let himself in with his key. She never had asked him for the key and never would. The chain lock wasn't on, either.

He was wearing gloves and sneakers. It was dark inside and he was as quiet as all the rest of it. He knew where it creaked and where it bumped. He drifted through the place and into the bedroom like a searching of wind.

She was peacefully in bed on her back, her lips slightly parted. He couldn't really see her, but he could sense her there, lying very, very still.

He got the second pillow, *his* pillow, from the bed, just the way he had thought about it. She wasn't touching it with her cheek or her hand, and she didn't stir when he lifted it away. Very carefully he tucked the end of the pillow under his chin, so that it hung down over the front of his chest like a bib. Then he fell across the bed with the pillow over her face and leaned his whole weight on it, with both hands pulling upward on the bed rail. For a couple of seconds it was as if the woman and the bed and even the floor were fighting back, but it passed quickly. He clung there, heavy on her, for a long time, till he was sure.

Panting, he rose and stood and held his breath and listened. The whole world was asleep.

It's done, he said silently. She always had an answer in her black box, she always made me lose. But I fooled her. Now I've done the biggest one of all.

The box. There it was. He crossed to it and tried the lid, feeling sure it would be locked. To his surprise, it wasn't.

He opened it. There was only one paper in it.

He began to tremble. If she'd had one paper she'd kept away from him, he told himself, it was a paper he didn't want to see. He took it in the dark and carried it to the bathroom and tore it into fragments and flushed it away.

Then he left—not by the front door, but by the fire escape. He left the bedroom window open and the lower section of the fire escape lowered—swung down and held by a tilted ashcan.

When he got back to his room he undressed quickly, silently, and climbed into bed. He was exalted, beside himself, a giant. Shelly said in the morning, very shyly, "Quite a man, aren't you?"

The detective sergeant had an old face and brand new eyes. He came to Lulu's window at the hospital and peered through the bars and said, "You're Llewellyn?"

Lulu said: "That's my name."

"Where were you at last night?" the detective asked.

"Home asleep."

"Well, that's all right. We checked already. You got an ex-wife who called herself Ivy Shoots?"

Whatever showed on Lulu's face must have looked all right to the detective, for he paused for only an instant before he said: "Well, she's dead."

I killed her, said Lulu. But to his own amazement he didn't say it aloud. He wanted to, but somehow he couldn't. He couldn't say anything.

"Don't take it so hard," said the detective. "We all got to go some time. What I want to know is—you goin' to plant her? The doctor, he didn't know who to notify, so he called us. We had to go through her stuff, and that's how we found your address. She didn't have much, but she left it all to you."

"Oh."

"You better get right down there, and check up. Somebody broke in there last night. Only thing we can find is missing is her death certificate. The doc says he wrote one and stuck it in a lockbox beside the bed. But we found only the box."

"Death certificate?" Lulu whispered.

"Yeah, there she lays stiff as a plank, dead of pneumonia. And somebody comes in and puts a pillow over her face and swipes the exit ticket. Must've took it in the dark, thinking it was worth something. Joke on him. But you better get down there and check."

"I killed her," said Llewellyn. "I did, I killed her."

"Cut it out," said the detective.

"Well I did," said Lulu.

"There's a nice legal duplicate piece of paper says you didn't," said the detective, and drove Lulu down to the apartment, where there were lots of people to tell him all the things he had to do. He did them and he died.

He's still working at the hospital behind his little iron grating, and he takes the laundry out on Mondays and the cleaning on Tuesdays and picks them all up on Fridays, and he has the potatoes on by the time his missus gets home from work every day. But he's dead all right.

It Opens the Sky

Opportunity knocked again, this time right on the eyeball, making him blink.

Deeming had stopped at a crosswalk—he lived in one of the few parts of town where streets still crossed on the same level—and was waiting for the light to change, when on the post by his head, right at eye level, a hand appeared. It wore a thin gold band and a watch. It was the watch that made him blink. He'd seen only one like it in his life before, a beautifully made little thing with slender carved-ruby numerals and, instead of hands, the ability to make its rubies glow one at a time for the hours, and a ruddy-amber pip of light float mysteriously at the right minute. It was geomagnetically powered and wouldn't wear out or run down for a thousand years. It came from someplace in the Crab Nebulae, where the smallest intelligent life form yet known to man did a brisk trade in precision engineering.

Deeming tore his gaze away from the watch and followed its wrist and arm down to its owner. Deeming was not especially fond of animals, but he categorized his women with a zoological code. They were chicks, fillies, bunnies, and dogs, in descending order of appeal.

This one was a goat.

She looked as if she had packed sixty years of living into thirty-five plus. She had half a bag on already, though it was still early in the evening, which accounted for her holding the pole up while she waited with him for the light to change. She had not noticed him, which was fine, and he acted just as abstracted as she was.

I'll give it two hours, he thought, and then, as she sagged

slightly and caught her balance too quickly and too much, as befits any drunk passing through dignity on the way to sloppiness, he made it ninety minutes. That watch is mine in ninety minutes. Bet?

The light changed and he strode out ahead of her. Just past the corner he stopped to look in a display window and see her reflection as she approached, stiff but listing a bit to port. He let her pass him and then to his delight saw her step into a cocktail bar. He went the other way, rounded the corner, entered a restaurant, and went straight back to the men's room. He had it to himself for the moment, and a moment was all he needed. Off came the stiff, clipped mustache; out came the golden-brown contact lenses, so that now his eyes were blue. He combed the part out of his flat black hair and set up waves. Half-inch inserts came out of his side pockets and were slipped into his heels, to change his gait and increase his already considerable height. He took off his jacket and turned it inside out, so that he was no longer drab and monochrome, as befitted Mr. Deeming, second assistant to the assistant desk man at the Rotoril Hotel, but sport-jacketed and cocky the way Jimmy the Flick ought to be. Jimmy the Flick always emerged and disappeared in men's rooms, not only because of their privacy, but because that was the one place you could count on not to see one of those damned Angels, who didn't eat, either.

Deeming was pleasantly certain, as he left the place, that no one had noticed him going in or Jimmy coming out. He went around the corner and into the cocktail joint.

Deeming sat on the edge of his bed, feeling glum. He tossed the watch up in the air and caught it.

It hadn't been ninety minutes after all—it had taken him nearly two and a half hours. He hadn't planned on her caring quite that much for the watch. She wouldn't take it off for him to admire and wouldn't agree that it was out of kilter and he could adjust it in just a second, so he had to use the old midnight-swim gimmick. He'd gotten her into the car all right, without her seeing the number plate, and he'd done a good clean job of parking by the river where it wouldn't be noticed. It was hard to judge how drunk she was. When she talked about her husband—the watch was all that she had of her husband's any more—she sobered up altogether too much, and it took a lot of oil and easy chatter to get her off the subject. But anyway he'd gotten the clothes off her and at last the watch, down there by the river, and then had managed to scoop up the lot and sprint back to the car before she could bleat, "Oh, Jimmy—Jimmy, you can't!" more than twice. He didn't know how she'd get back to town and it didn't worry him. He found six and a half in her pouch, and an I.D. card. He pocketed the money—it about covered the price of her drinks—and incinerated the rest of her stuff with the clothes. A good clean job, carrying the special virtue of being totally unlike anything he had ever done before; if there was anything in the cosmos that would bring a swarm of Angels down on a citizen, it was the habitual crime habitually performed. He should be proud.

He was, too, but he was also glum, and this irritated him. Both the glumness and the irritation were familiar feelings with him, and he could not for the life of him figure out why he always felt this way after a job. He had so much to be glad about. He was big and handsome and smart as an Angel —he might even say smarter; he'd been doing this for years now and they'd never come close to picking him up. Damn zombies. Some said they were robots. Some said supermen. People touched their cloaks for luck, or to help a sick child get better. They didn't eat. They didn't sleep. They carried no weapons. Just went around smiling and being helpful and reminding people to be kind to one another. There used to be police and soldiery, according to the books. Not any more. Not with the Angels popping up whenever they weren't wanted by the people concerned, with their sanctimony and their bullet-proof hides.

Sure, Deeming thought, I'm smarter than an Angel. What's an Angel anyway? Somebody with rules to abide by. (I've got a little more elbow room than that.) Somebody who is remarkable to begin with and makes himself more so with magic tricks and golden cloaks and all that jazz. (I'm an invisible clerk at a low-level flea bag, or a disappearing cockerel with a line like lightning and sticky fingers—whichever I want.)

He tossed the watch and caught it and looked at it and felt glum. He always felt glum when he succeeded, and he always succeeded. He never tried anything where he wouldn't succeed.

Maybe that's the trouble, he thought, falling back on the

bed and looking up at the ceiling. I got all this stuff and never use but a fraction of it.

Never thought of it like that before.

I break all the rules but I do it by playing safe. I play it safer than a civil servant buying trip insurance for a ride on a bus. I walk under a closed sky, he thought, like a bug under a rock. Course, I put the tight lid on myself, which is better than having a lid put on, even a large lid, by society or religion. But even so . . . my sky is closed. What I need, I need *reach*, that's what.

Or maybe, he thought, sitting up to glower at the watch in his hand, maybe I need a pay-off that's worth what brains and speed I put into it. How long have I been working respectably for peanuts and robbing carefully for—well, no more'n an occasional walnut?

Which reminds me, I better get this thing fenced out before that spaceman's relict finds herself a fig leaf and somebody with a whistle to blow.

He got up, slowly shaking his head in disgust and wishing that one time—just one lousy time—he could make a touch and feel as good as he had a right to feel.

He put out a hand to the door and it knocked at him.

Now, you see? he told himself out of the same sort of disgust, you see? Anybody else would freeze now, turn pale, start to sweat, throw the watch into the reclaimer, run up the wall like a rat in a box. But look at you, standing absolutely still thinking three times as fast as a Class Eight computer, checking everything, including all the things you have already done to handle just this situation—the mustache back on, the brown eyes again, the shorter stature again, the heel pads hidden in the reversible jacket and the jacket hidden in the secret panel behind the closet.

"Who is it?"

. . . And your voice steady and your pulse firm—yes, Deeming's voice and the pulse of innocence, not the jaunty Jimmy's tone or his rutty heartbeat. So what's to feel glum about, boy? What's the matter with you, to dislike yourself and every situation you get into, purely because you know before you start that you'll handle it so well?

"May I see you for a moment, Mr. Deeming?"

He didn't recognize the voice. That was good, or it was bad, depending. If good, why worry? And why worry if it was bad?

He dropped the watch into his side pocket and opened the door.

"I hope I'm not bothering you," said the pudgy man who stood there.

"Come in." Deeming left the door open and turned his back. "Sit down." He laughed the minor assistant's timid little laugh. "I hope you're selling something. I wouldn't be able to buy it but it's nice to have somebody to talk to for a change."

He heard the door close carefully. The pudgy man did not sit down and he did not laugh. Deeming did not care for the silence so he turned to look at the man, which was apparently what the man was waiting for. "You can have somebody to talk to," he said quietly. "You can talk to Richard E. Rockhard."

"Great," said Deeming. "Who might Richard E. Rockhard be?"

"You haven't . . . well, that isn't really surprising. When they're big, everybody knows them. When they're hiring and firing the big ones, they tend to be almost as quiet as assistant clerks, Mr. Deeming. . . . You know Antares Trading? And the Lunar and Outer Orbit Lines? And Galactic Mines?"

"You mean this Rockhard is——"

"In part, Mr. Deeming. In part."

Jimmy the Flick would have bugged his eyes and made a low whistle. Deeming put his finger tips together and whispered, "Oh, my goodness."

"Well?" said the man, after waiting for something more and not getting it. "Will you come and see him?"

"You mean, Mr. Rockhard? You mean—me? You mean—now?"

"I mean all those things."

"Why does he . . . what—well, why *me?*" asked Deeming, with becoming modesty.

"He needs your help."

"Oh, my goodness. I don't know what I could possibly do to help a man like . . . well, can you tell me what it's about?"

"No," said the man.

"No?"

"No, except that it's urgent, it's big, and it will be more worth your while than anything you have ever done in your life."

"Oh, my goodness," said Deeming again. "What you'd better do is go find an Angel. They help people. I can't——"

"You can do things an Angel couldn't do, Mr. Deeming?"

Deeming affected a laugh. It said a thousand words about the place and function of the Little Men of the world.

"Mr. Rockhard thinks you can, Mr. Deeming. Mr. Rockhard *knows* you can."

"He knows . . . about *me?*"

"Everything," said the pudgy man, absolutely without inflection.

Deeming had a vague swift wish that he had atomized the watch after all. It seemed to be as big and as spillable and as hot as a bowl of soup wedged into his side pocket. "Better get an Angel," he suggested again.

The man glanced at the door and then took a step closer. He dropped his voice and said earnestly, "I assure you, Mr. Deeming, Mr. Rockhard will not and cannot do that in this matter."

"It sounds like something I'd better not do," said Deeming primly.

The man shrugged. "Very well. If you don't want it, you don't want it." He turned to the door.

Deeming couldn't, for once, help himself. He blurted out, "What happens if I refuse?"

The pudgy man did not quite turn back to face him. "You promise me you will forget this interchange," he said casually, "especially if asked by one of the gentlemen in the pretty cloaks."

"And that's all?"

For the first time a glint of amusement crossed the bland features. "Except for wondering, for all the days of your life, what you might have missed."

Deeming wet his lips. "Just tell me one thing. If I go see your Mr. Rockhard, and have a talk, and still want to refuse . . . ?"

"Then of course you may. If you want to."

"Let's go," said Deeming. They were high over the city in a luxurious helicopter before it occurred to him that "If you want to," said the way the man had said it, might have many meanings. He turned to speak, but the man's face, by its very placidity, said that this was a man whose job was done and who would not add one syllable to cap it.

Richard E. Rockhard had blue-white hair and ice-blue eyes and a way of speaking that licked out and struck deep like a series of sharp skilled ax blows, cutting deep, careless of the chips. This tool's edge was honed so fine it was a gentleness. Deeming could well believe that this man was Galactic Mines and all those other things. He could also believe that Rockhard needed help. He was etched with anxiety and the scarlet webs of capillaries in his eyeballs were bloated with sleeplessness. He was a man who was telling the truth because he had not time to lie. "I need you, Deeming. I am supposing that you will help me and will speak my piece accordingly," he said, as soon as they were alone in a fabulous study in an unbelievable penthouse. "I give you my word that you will be in no danger from me unless and until you do help me. If you do proceed with it, you may be sure the danger is sizable." He nodded to himself and said again, "Sizable."

Deeming, the hotel clerk, got just this far with his clerkly posture: "Mr. Rockhard, I am absolutely mystified as to why you should turn to a man like me for any——" because Rockhard brought both hands down with a crash and leaned half across his desk. "Mr. Deeming," he said, in his gentle, edged voice, with all the power in the world throttled way back and idling at the ready, "I know about you. I know it because I needed to find such a man as you and I have the resources to do it. You may wear that comman-man pose if it makes you comfortable, but do not deceive yourself that it deceives me. You are not a common man or—to put it on the very simplest terms—you would not be in this room at this moment, because the common man will not be tempted by anything which he knows offends the Angels."

So Deeming dropped the invisibility, the diffidence, the courtesy and deference of an assistant to an associate, and said, "It is hardly safe for even an uncommon man to offend them."

"You mean me? I'm perfectly safe from you, Deeming. You wouldn't report me, even if you knew I couldn't strike back. You don't *like* Angels. You never met another man before who didn't like them. Therefore you like me."

Deeming had to smile. He nodded. He thought, But when is he going to point out that if I don't help him he will blackmail me?

"I will not blackmail you," said the old man surprisingly.

"I will pull you into this with rewards, not push you into it with penalties. You are a man whose greed peaks higher than his fear." But he smiled when he said it. Then without waiting for any response at all, he made his proposition.

He began to speak of his son. "When you have unlimited credit and an only son, you begin by being quite certain that you can extend yourself through him to the future; for he is your blood and bone, and he will of course want to follow in your footsteps. And if it occurs to you that he might veer from that course—it never does occur to you until late in the game, too late—then you let the situation get past curing by the smug assumption that the pressures you can put on him will accomplish what your genes could not.

"Ultimately you realize that you have a choice—not the choice of keeping or losing him; you've lost that already; but the choice of throwing him out or letting him go. If you care more for yourself and what you've built than you do for your son, you throw him out, and good riddance. I"—he stopped to wet his lips and glanced quickly at Deeming's face and back to his folded hands—"I let him go."

He was still a moment and then suddenly wrenched his hands apart and then laid them carefully and silently side by side before him. "I don't regret it, because we are friends. We are good friends, and I helped him in every way I could, including not helping him when he wanted to make his own way, and giving him whatever he asked me for whether or not I thought it was valuable." He smiled suddenly, and whispered more to his sleeping hands than to Deeming, "For a son like that, if he wants to paint his belly blue, you buy the paint."

He looked at Deeming. "The blue paint is archaeology, and I bought it for him. Dead diggings, pure knowledge, nothing that will make a dime to buy a bun with. That isn't my kind of work or my kind of thinking, but it's all Donald wants."

"There's glory," said Deeming.

"Not this trip. Now hear me out. That boy is willing to disappear, cease to exist, become nothing at all, just to follow a thread which almost certainly leads nowhere, but which, if it leads somewhere, can become only an erudite curiosity like the Rosetta stone or the Dead Sea scrolls or the frozen language in the piezo-crystals of Phygmo IV."

He spread his hands and immediately put them back to bed. "Blue paint. And I bought it."

"What do you mean 'cease to exist—become nothing'? You don't mean 'die,' you mean something else."

"Good, *good*, Deeming. Very perceptive. What it means is that in order to pursue this Grail of his, he must expose himself to the Angels. They can't stop him, but they can wait for him to come back. And I bought him another bucket of paint for that. He has a paid-up ticket to Grebd."

Deeming unhesitatingly released the low whistle. Grebd was the name of a sun, a planet and a city in the Coalsack matrix, where certain of the inhabitants had developed a method of pseudosurgery unthinkably far in advance of anything in the known cosmos. They could take virtually any living thing and change it as drastically as it wanted to be changed, even from carbon-base to boron-chain, or as subtly as it might want, like an alteration of all detectible brainwave characteristics or retinal patterns, or even a new nose. They could graft (or grow?) most of a whole man from a tattered lump, providing it lived. Most important, they could make these alterations, however drastic, and (if requested) leave the conscious mind intact.

But the cost of a major overhaul of this nature was beyond reason—unless a man had a reason compelling enough. Deeming looked at the old man with unconcealed awe. Not only had he been able to pay such a price, he had been willing—willing in a cause in which he could have no sympathy. To care that much for a son—to care so very much that the most he could ever hope for now would be to meet a total stranger in an unexpected place who might take him aside and whisper, *"Hello—Dad!"* but for whom he could do nothing further. For if he had transgressed some ruling of the Angels so drastically as to need a trip to Grebd, the Angels would have an eye on the old man for all time to come, and he would not dare even to smile at the new stranger. Such a transgression meant death. Could a father so much as clasp his son's hand under such circumstances?

"In the name of all that's holy," Deeming breathed, "what did he want so badly?"

Rockhard snorted. "Some sort of a glyph. There's a theory that the Aldebaranian stock sprang from the same ethnic roots as those in the Masson planets. It sounds like nonsense to me, and even if it's true, it's still nonsense. But certain vague evidence points to a planet called Revelo. There may be artifacts there to prove the point."

"Never heard of it," said Deeming. "Revelo . . . n-no. And so—he makes his discovery. And goes to Grebd. And gets his total disguise. And forever after, he can't claim the discovery he made."

"Now you know about Donald," said the old man wryly. "He just wants the discovery made. He doesn't care who makes it."

They looked at each other in shared bafflement. At last Deeming nodded slightly to convey the thought that it didn't matter if he understood. If Donald Rockhard was crazy, that was beside the point. He said, "Now where do the Angels come into this?"

"Revelo," said the old man, "is—Proscribed."

Well then, Deeming thought instantly, that seems to be that, and where's the problem? A Proscribed planet was surrounded by a field of such a nature that if it was penetrated by a flickership, anything organic aboard would instantly and totally cease to live. If Donald had gone to Revelo, Donald was dead. If he had been snapped out of hyperspace on the way there by the outer-limit warning field, and had heeded the warning, then he hadn't landed on Revelo, hadn't broken an Angel dictate, and wasn't in trouble. Deeming said so.

Slowly Rockhard shook his head. "He's on Revelo right now, and alive. Far as I know," he added.

"Not possible," said Deeming flatly. You just don't penetrate the field around a Proscribed planet and live.

"Very well," said the old man, "nevertheless he's there. Look, I'll tell you something that only four other men know. There *is* a way to get through to a Proscribed planet.

"About thirty years ago one of my ships happened on a derelict. God alone knows where it came from. It was a mess, but it contained two lifeboats intact. Lifeboats with flicker drive."

"Boats? They must be big as ships, then."

"Not these. They do the same thing as our flicks, but they don't do it the same way. It isn't understood yet just how, though I have a man working on it. The captain of my freighter brought 'em back for me, for my spacecraft collection, never knowing just what he had. We found that out by accident. We fitted them out with Earth-type controls, but although we know what button to push, we don't know what happens when we push it. It worked no better than our own flicks, so there was no point in filing the information with the Improvement Section. And when we found out the ships would penetrate the Proscribed planets, we just kept our mouths shut. I have my opinion of the Angels, but I will say that when they proscribe a planet, they do it for a good reason. It may have rock-plague aboard, or, worse still, yin-yang weed. Or it may be just that the planet is deadly to humans, because of its sun's radiation or the presence of some hormone poison."

"Yeah," agreed Deeming, "Nantha, Sirione, and that devil's world Keth." He shuddered. "Glad they keep us off *that* one. Guess you're right—the Angels know what they're doing just this once.... What's so special about Revelo, that it's Proscribed?"

"As usual, the Angels won't say. It might be anything. As I say, I trust them for that, and I'm not going to be the one who spreads around a device to make it possible for anyone to penetrate any of 'em."

"Except Donald."

"Except Donald," Rockhard conceded. "For that I have no excuse. If something there kills him, it's a chance he was willing to take. If he brings something out inadvertently, it will be taken care of on Grebd. And I know he won't bring out anything on purpose, like Yinyang seeds. Explain it all away, don't I?" His voice changed, as if some internal organist had shut down all the stops and grouped out new ones. "Don't tell me I shouldn't have done it. I know that. I knew it then. But I'd do it again, hear? I'd do it again if it was what he wanted."

There was silence for a time and Deeming turned his head away as a decent person might, offering privacy to another. Rockhard said, "We found out how the little alien flickers penetrate the Proscribed planets. They turn it inside out. An analogue might be the way a surge of current will reverse the polarity on a DC generator. We found out," he said bleakly, "that if that happens, the flicker goes in harmlessly. And then when it comes out, the field will kill anyone aboard." He raised his head and looked at Deeming blindly. "Don doesn't know that," he whispered.

Deeming said, "Oh."

After a while he spoke again, incredulously. "I think

you're saying that I . . . that somebody has to go there and tell him."

"Tell him? What would he do if you told him?"

"Wouldn't the flicker reverse the polarity a second time?"

"Not from the inside. Besides, that polarity reverse is only an analogy, Deeming. No, what has to be done is to take him this," and from the desk drawer he scooped two tiny cylindrical objects. Both together were less than the length of his little finger, smaller in diameter than a pen. Deeming rose and went to the desk and took one of them up. There were four separate coils rigidly mounted on the cylinder, toroids, each wound with what seemed to be thousands of precise turns of microscopically fine wire. At one end was an octagonal recess, meant apparently to receive a rotating shaft, as well as a spring collar designed to clamp the device down. The other end faded to insubstantiality, neither transparent nor opaque, but both and neither, and acutely unsettling to watch for more than a second or two.

"Replacement freak coils for the flickerfield," he diagnosed. "But I never saw them this tiny. Are they models?"

"The real thing," said Rockhard tiredly. "And actually an improvement on the one the aliens put on those boats. Apparently they never encountered the kind of deathtrap the Angels use, or they might well have designed one like this."

"What do they do?"

"Put a certain randomness in the frequency of the flickerfield, when it approaches a Proscribed area. Just as a flickerfield works by making a ship, in effect, exist and cease to exist in normal space, so that it doesn't exist at any measurable time as real mass, and can therefore exceed the velocity C, so this coil detects and analyzes the frequency of the Angel's death-field, and phases with it. The death-field doesn't kill anything because the approaching ship ceases to exist before it enters the field and does not exist again until it is through it. Unlike the one Donald used, it doesn't affect the field or reverse its direction."

"So if Donald gets one of these and replaces his frequency coil with it——"

"He can forget the existence of the Angel's field."

"On Revelo or any other Proscribed planet." Deeming tossed the coil and caught it. He held it up and sighted past it at Rockhard. "I've got a whole cosmos full of bad trouble here in my hand," he said steadily.

"You have every rotten plague and dangerous plant pest known to xenology, right here in your hand," agreed Rockhard.

"And yinyang weed. Lots of money in yinyang weed," said Deeming reflectively. Yinyang (derived from the old Chinese *yin* and *yang*), the two-colored disk divided by an S-shaped line, and representing all opposites—good and evil, light and dark, male and female, and so on—as well as the surprising fact that the flowers were an almost perfect representation of the symbol in red and blue, was by far the most vicious addictive drug ever known, because not only was it potent and virtually incurable, it increased the addict's intelligence fivefold and his physical strength two to three times, and he became an inhuman behemoth with the sole desire to destroy anything and everything between himself and his source of supply, able to outlast, outthink, outfight and outrun anyone of his species.

"If you're really thinking about making money out of yinyang, you're a swine," said Rockhard evenly, "and if that was meant as a joke, you're an oaf."

Deeming locked eyes with him for a moment, then dropped his eyes. "You're right," he muttered. He put the coil carefully down on the desk next to its mate.

Rockhard said, "You worry me, Deeming. If I thought you'd use these coils for any such thing I'd . . . well, Donald can die. He'd die gladly, if he knew."

Deeming said soberly, "Can you find a man willing to breach an Angel's command who is not also willing to take anything that comes his way?"

"*Touché*," said Rockhard, with a bitter and reluctant grin. "You have a head on your neck. Well, have you got the picture? You're to go to Revelo in the other alien lifeboat, equipped with this coil. Slip through the field, locate Donald, tell him what's happened, and see that his coil is replaced with this other one. Then off he goes to Grebd for his—his camouflage job."

"And what do I do?"

"Come back with a message from Don. He'll know which one. When I hear it I'll know if you've done the job."

"If I haven't I won't come back," said Deeming bluntly, and realized as he said it that, incredibly, he had at some point decided to do this crazy thing. "And what do you do if I come back and say 'Mission accomplished'?"

"I'm not going to name a figure. It's a little like the way top executives get paid, Deeming. After a certain point you stop talking salary, and a man begins drawing what he needs for expenses—any expenses—against the value of his holdings. When his holdings go up to a certain level the company stops keeping books on what he draws. It'll be like that with you. You just take what you want, as often as you like, for as long as you live. One man might break up this organization by throwing assets away, but he'd have to work all day every day for a good long while to do it."

"We . . . ah . . . have no contract, Mr. Rockhard."

"That's right, Mr. Deeming."

He's saying, thought Deeming, *you can trust me.* And I can. But I can't say that to him. He'd have to answer no. He said cruelly, "You ought to let him die."

"I know," said Rockhard.

"I'm a damn fool," said Deeming. "I'll do it."

Rockhard held out his hand and Deeming took it. It was a warm firm hand and when it let go it withdrew slowly as if it regretted the loss of contact, instead (like some) of falling away in relief. This was a man who meant what he said.

Which of course, he thought, is only another species of damn fool, when you get down to it.

Why me?

That was the base thought, the kingpin thought, the keystone thought of everything that happened between that first meeting and the day he coined off for Revelo. By that time he knew the answer.

Begin at Earth, go to Revelo, do a little job, and return. If it had been just that, and that's all, there wouldn't have been a reason for Deeming's presence in the matter. The nameless pudgy man could have done it; the old man could have done it himself. But there were—details.

There were the two interminable briefing sessions. He had the new coil; all he had to do was plug it into the alien ship.

But the alien ship was hidden far from Earth.

All right; given the ship, all he needed was to drop a Revelo course-coin into his autopilot and push the button.

But he didn't have a Revelo course-coin. Nobody had a Revelo course-coin. Few people even knew where it was.

There was a coin, certainly. In the files at Astro City on Ybo. He'd have to get that one. The files——

The files were in the Angel Headquarters building.

Well, if he got the ship, and if he got the coin, and if Rockhard was right and the new coil worked properly, not only to get him through the death-field but back out again, and if this could be done without alerting an Angel (Rockhard's reasoning was that by turning the field inside out, Don had almost certainly alerted them, but that the new design, which would not—he hoped—touch or affect the field, would permit Deeming to get in and both of them to get out again without activating any alarms. So that for an indeterminate time the Angels must operate on their original information —that one ship had gone in, none come out), and if Donald Rockhard were alive, and if he knew what message to give Deeming and if Deeming got back all right and if Rockhard understood the message properly and if, after all this, Rockhard paid off, why then, this looked like a pretty good deal. And also clearly something that only a man like Deeming could possibly accomplish.

So there were the two long briefings with Rockhard and his scientific assistant Pawling (of whose discourse Deeming caught not one word in nine), and a hurried trip back to his own quarters, where he wrote suitable letters to the hotel and to his housing and food depots and maintenance and communications services and so on and on, including the mailing of the goat's wrist-watch where it would do him the most good, and the paying of bills for liquor and clothing and garage, and, and . . . ("How doth the little busy bee/ Keep from flipping his lid like me?" he sang insanely to himself as he did all the things that would assure the hive that it could rest easy, nobody was doing anything unusual around here, honest.) When he was finished with it his affairs were ready for him to resume in a couple of weeks, or, if not, a small secondary wave of assurances to the trades, comforts, and services would go out announcing a minor accident, and making arrangements for another two weeks' absence, and then another ripple reporting a new job on Bluebutter, which was somewhere among the Crabs, and at last a line to a bartender, *How are you Joe?* to be mailed at the end of two years. If that one ever got mailed, he'd be eighteen months dead, and if he thought he had cold feet before, he was afraid to bend his toes when he wrote it.

The day came (was it really only four days since he started out to fence a watch and faced a knocking door?) for departure. Rockhard shook his hand, and Deeming for the second time felt that warm contact and, along with it, a thing in the old cold eyes that could only be covered by the word "pleading." If the pleading had words, what would they be? *Bring my boy out.* Or, *Let me trust you.* Or maybe, *Don't doubt me: don't ever doubt me.* Perhaps, *You're my kind, boy—a pretty sleazy edition, but anyway my kind, so . . . take care of yourself, whatever.* He handed Deeming more cash money than he had had in his hand since the night he gathered up the big pot at the poker game and handed it over to the guy who won it from him on the next hand. But this time it was only expense money, not even figured in. Rockhard probably never knew how close he came to losing his man by the size of that pittance. Or maybe he did. The pudgy man and the chauffeur were about as easy to shake from that moment until coin-off as a coat of shellac.

And did he lean back in cosy cushions and watch a band of loving friends waving from the blockhouse? He did not. He left the house in the back of a utility truck, which pulled up in utter darkness inside a building somewhere. He was hustled wordlessly into a side room, shoehorned into a power suit, and rammed into a space fully as tall as the underneath of a studio couch and round—torturously, about two handbreadths less than he was tall, so that he couldn't straighten out. They welded him in, at which point he discovered that his honey-pipe had not been giving the quarter turn necessary to open it to the converters. He spent almost the entire night trying to grip it with his southern cheeks, which he found indifferently prehensile and, as time went on, demanding of differential subtleties that he would have sworn were beyond his control. He was wrong; he succeeded by laborious fractions and got it open and at last lay sweat-drenched and limp with effort and relief. And then more time flowed through his prison than any small space ought to hold, when he had nothing to do but think.

And the only thing he could think about, and that over and over, was that he really wasn't too uncomfortable or distressed by this imprisonment, because he seemed to be conditioned to it. He had, after all, for some years lived huddled in mediocrity with his hotel job pulled no less tight around him than this welded steel pillbox. His excursions as the disappearing Jimmy the Flick were no less confined; confined by limited time, limited targets, and the ubiquitous golden Angels with their wise kind faces and understanding voices, God burn 'em all. They were supposed to be unkillable, but he'd sure like to get one for Christmas and make some simple tests lasting till, say, Midsummer Eve. They, more than anyone, kept the sky closed over him, so he had to walk everywhere with his head bent. He tried to imagine what it would be like to walk in a place where his personal sky had room for a whee of a jump and a holler that anyone could hear and the hell with them; but the wish was too far from his conditioning and bounced him right back to the uncomfortable thought that he was not uncomfortable here, and so around he went again on the synapse-closed box, closed sky. Damned strong gentle Angels—how would it be to run tall someplace? But I can't quite grasp that, here in this closed sky.

And then he slept, and then the surface under him rumbled and tipped, and, lo and behold, it was only the next morning after all.

He switched on his penetroscope and waited impatiently while the pseudo-hard radiation fumbled its way through the beryl hull metal and the image cleared. His prison was being lifted by a crane onto a lowboy trailer, which began to move as soon as it had its load. It rumbled out to the apron where the ship waited, belly down like some wingless insect, with its six jointed jacks, one of which was footless and supported by a tall gantry which had thrust out a boom to hold up the limb, like a groom holding up a horse's split hoof while the stableboy runs for the liniment.

The lowboy was positioned under the leg, and Deeming blinked at the pounding and screeching going on above him as his tomb was bolted to the landing jack and became a part of it. Then there was a quiet time as tools and ground hands got clear, ports and locks were battened, and the crew assumed coin-off stations. Somewhere a whistle was blowing; Deeming could hear it through his radio, picking it from the intercom, which in turn had it from an outside microphone in the hull. It stopped, and there was a rumbling purr as all six legs began to straighten, pushing the ship up off the ground so that most of the terrestrial matter included in its flicker-field would be air.

Then without warning the earth was gone, the vanished

ship lightyears away already before the gut-bumping boom of its air-implosion could sound. Deeming's stomach lurched, and then there was gravity again and a scene in his 'scope—a rolling gray-green landscape, with a few cylindrical buildings and a half dozen docking pads.

That's the trouble with space travel nowadays, he thought glumly. They've taken all the space out of it.

The ship hovered perhaps a thousand feet high, drawing anti-grav power from the beam generator down below. It drifted slowly downward, positioning itself over one of the empty pads.

Pad Four.

According to his briefing, the correct pad was number 6. With rising anxiety he saw that 6 was already occupied by a small sport flicker.

There was only one way he would ever get out of here, and that was in Pad 6. Nobody in the ship knew he was there. He was not even sure of the origin or destination of the ship, or on which planet they were now landing. If it set down in the wrong pad, he would stay right where he was, leave with the ship, and either starve or set up a howl with his radio and get dragged out at the wrong place at the wrong time by the wrong people.

He turned on his transmitter, fingered it to docking frequency, and said authoritatively, "Wear off, skipper. Pad 6 is ours." He waited tensely. He hoped the ground control would think it was hearing a crewman speaking to the captain, while the captain thought he was hearing ground control.

He heard murmurs in the intercom but could not pick them up clearly. The ship steadied, then began to sink again. He waited tensely, begging his brains to come up with something, anything, then literally sobbed with relief as a spacesuited figure tumbled out of the blockhouse and sprinted for the sportster in Pad 6. The little ship lifted and slid into 4, and Deeming's ship settled into its assigned berth.

For a moment Deeming lay trembling with reaction, and then grinned. He wondered if the captain and the control officer, sitting over a beer later, would think to ask each other who had called out to wear off. That, he said, is how fights start in bars.

He scanned once around him with the 'scope and thereafter ignored the scene. He grasped the metal ring in the center of the floor of his prison and turned it. Faintly, he felt the slight tapping of a relay sequence, and then the surface on which he lay began to descend. Down it went to ground level and still down. He snapped on his helmet light confidently; nothing would be seen from outside but the great round jack foot pressed solidly against the concrete pad. Who could know that its sole pressed a matched disk of concrete down into the ground?

The movement stopped and Deeming saw the niche in the concrete wall to his right. He swiftly rolled into it, the surface which had carried him down already starting back up. Silently it slid by him—he had not realized it was so thick— until it formed a roof for the underground room which now was revealed. He dropped down to the floor. The space was tiny, just enough for himself and the tiny alien lifeboat which lay welcoming him with glitters of gold from its polished, dust-bloomed surface.

It was a sphere, at first sight far too small to be good for anything. The single bucket seat had been designed for a being considerably shorter than he, and narrower too, he realized, grunting, as he wedged himself into it. The controls were few and simple. The hull material was, from inside, totally transparent. The entire power plant must be under the seat.

He thumbed the sensors at his waist, and settled back to wait. In a moment he heard the hiss of air as his power suit flooded the tiny cabin, and then the sensors, having analyzed the atmosphere and pressure-checked the seals, twinkled cheerfully. With a sigh of relief he wrung his helmet off and unclamped his gauntlets. From his pouch he found the course-coin for Ybo, an osmium disk with irregular edges like a particularly complicated cam. He dropped it in the slot of the course box, and confidently thumbed the red button.

There was no sound. The boat seemed to settle a little, and there was a measurable flash of that indescribable, discomfiting grayness to be seen outside. Deeming was not worried about the sudden vacuum he had created in the hole. It would hardly be noticed amid the rumblings and scrapings of dockside, and the chances were that air would seep in slowly enough to make the whole thing unnoticed.

He looked around him with pleasure. Rockhard's people had really set things up properly. Though a flickership could coin off from anywhere, on, over, or under the surface, planet falls were generally made high. Contact with anything on the ground from a child's toy to an innocent bystander could be unpleasant. It wouldn't hurt the ship, which would flick out of existence and remove itself automatically at the slightest sign of coexistent matter, but the less resilient planet-bound object would not be so fortunate. One solution was a landing plate, and that was what had been supplied here. It beamed the ship in and brought it to contact unless there was enough heavy matter in the way to be dangerous, in which case the beam operated but the landing guide did not, and the craft would appear with good safe altitude. The device was no larger than a dinner plate, and buried under a sprinkling of topsoil it was indetectable.

The lifeboat nestled near the bottom of a deep narrow cut in hilly land. It was night. A brook burbled pleasantly somewhere close by. Weeds nodded and swayed all about; a searcher would have to fall over the ship before he could see it. Deeming unhesitatingly unbuttoned the canopy and swung it back. He had been on Ybo before and knew it as one of the few "perfect" Terran planets. He breathed the soft rich air with real pleasure, then rose and shucked out of his power suit and stowed it on the seat. He pulled the creases out of his trustworthy reversible jacket, checked his pockets to see that he had everything he needed, closed and locked the canopy, and climbed the steep side of the gully.

He found himself at the edge of a meadow. A beautiful planet, he told himself cheerfully. He stretched, for a moment capturing that open-sky fantasy of his. Then he saw moving lights and shrank down into the long grass, and his personal sky was tight down over him again.

It was only a ground car, and he certainly could not be seen. He watched it veer closer to him and then pass not thirty paces away. Good; a road was just what he was looking for.

He took careful bearings of the bank on which he stood, and then followed the crest of it down to the road. He was gratified to see a milepost by the coping of a stone bridge which carried the road over the brook he had heard. Finding this place again would not be difficult.

He strode cheerfully along the road toward the loom of city lights that limned the wooded hills close ahead. He was still in his *why me?* phase, and he had a moment of real regret that Rockhard could not have shared this adventure with him, or even done it alone. Well . . . if he wanted to give away unlimited chunks of credit for work as pleasant as this, it was his hard luck.

He mounted the hill and suddenly the city was all around him. His landing spot wasn't at the edge of town—it was in Astro City's huge Median Park. Why, there was the Astro Center, not five minutes away!

It was an impressive building, one of those low, winged structures which seem to be so much larger on the inside than they are outside. Wide shallow steps led up to the multiple doors. It must have been early in their evening; the place was still busy, and ablaze with lights. Deeming knew it was open all night, but later the crowds of spacemen, shipping clerks, students of navigation, flicker techs and school children would thin out. Wonderful, he thought. If he need crowds, here they were. If not, not.

At the top of the steps a slender girl in her mid-teens emerged from the door and stopped to answer his automatic smile radiantly. And to his intense astonishment she sank to one knee and bowed her head.

"Ah, don't, my child—please don't," said a resonant voice behind him, and a tall Angel swept by him and lifted the girl to her feet. He touched her cheek playfully, smiled, and went into the building. The girl stood looking after him, her hand pressed to her cheek and her eyes bright "Oh," she murmured, "Oh, I wish . . ." Then she seemed to become aware of Deeming standing beside and behind her, and stepped to the side in confusion. "I'm so sorry. I'm in your way."

In spite of the fact that he wore the brown uniform of mediocrity—his nondescript suit and pathetic crisp mustache—he said with the voice of Jimmy the Flick, "Finish your wish, pretty. You'll never get a wish that you break in the middle." And he smiled the glittering happy smile that never belonged with the small silly mustache and desk clerk Deeming's invisible unnoticeable crowd's face. Inwardly he seethed He had been frightened by the sudden appearance of the Angel; captivated by the girl and the utter adoration which for a crazy moment he had thought was his; intoxicated by the nearness of this last barrier to his quest, hyperalert because of it. And so for the very first time Jimmy the Flick smiled from the desk drudge's face, creating a new person whose actions he could not quite predict. Like the swift glance he threw upward. Why that? Why, the sky, of course: he had felt the shuttering sky move upward a bit to give him room to move. *Well, sure,* he thought in a burst of astonishment, *there's much more room to move when you don't know what move you might make next.* A crazy moment, all this is a click of time, and the girl was taking from him his astonished smile in its mismatched face and giving it back to him hued with all the tints of herself, saying, "Breaking my wish . . . ? Oh, I did, didn't I?"

She put her hand to her hot throat and looked swiftly into the building where the Angel had disappeared. "I wish I were a boy."

He laughed so abruptly and so loudly that everyone on the steps stopped to catch a piece of it and go on, smiling. "That's a wish that deserves breaking," he said, making no slightest attempt to hide his admiration of her. She was slender and tall and had one of those rare gentle faces which can move untouched through any violence. "But who ever heard of a girl Angel?" she said.

"Oh, so that's your trouble. Now why would you want to be an Angel?"

"To do what they do. I never yet saw an Angel do a thing I wouldn't want to be doing. To help, to be kind and wise and strong for people who need something strong."

"You don't have to be one of them to learn all those things."

"Oh yes, you do!" she said, in a tone that would accept no argument or discussion. He understood, and grudgingly agreed. Thinking like an Angel did not give one the sheer strength nor the resources to act like one. "Well, even if you could become a man, that wouldn't make you an Angel."

"But then I could get to be one," she said, craning her neck to look far out over the plaza where there was a glimpse of gold from the cloak of another of the creatures. She glowed when she saw it, even so distantly, and brought the glow full on Deeming when she faced him again. It was unsettling as hyperspace.

"Are you sure of that? Were they just plain men before they were Angels?"

"Of course they were," she said with that devoted positiveness. "They couldn't be so much to humans without being human first of all."

"And how do they get to be Angels?" he bantered.

"No one knows that," she conceded. "But, you see, if a man can become one, and if I was a man, I'd find out and do it."

He stood in the full radiation of her intense feeling and irrationally admitted that if she were a man and wanted to be an Angel, or wanted anything else that much, she'd probably make it.

"I'd like to think they were just men, at that," he said.

"You can be sure of it. What's your name?"

"What? Uh———." The strange first fusion of Deeming the Invisible with Jimmy the Flick had him disoriented, and he could not answer. He covered it with a cough, and said, "I've just come in from Bravado to see this place I've heard so much about."

If she noticed that he had avoided her question, or wondered about such a place as Bravado, she gave no sign. The worlds were full of slightly odd people these days and the sky full of names. She said, "Oh, may I show it to you? I work here. I'm just off duty, and I really have nothing else to do."

He wished he knew what her name was. He soaked up this eagerness of hers, this total defenselessness, trust, earnest generosity, and felt a great choking wash of feeling of a kind quite alien to him. He cared suddenly, cared desperately about what might happen to her in the years to come, and wished he could spare her whatever would be wrong for her; wished he could run before her and remove anything over which she might stumble, kill anything which might sting her; guard her, warn her . . . He wanted to grip her shoulders and shake her and shout, look out for me, beware the stranger; trust no one, help no one, just look out for yourself! The feeling passed, and he did not touch her or speak of it. He glanced into the building and remembered that there was something he needed in there and must have, no matter what he had to use to get it. He would use this girl if he had to; he knew that too. He didn't like knowing it, but know it he most painfully did. He said, "Well, thanks! It's very kind of you."

"No it isn't," she said, with that faith-full ardor of hers. "I love this place. Thank *you*," and she turned and went in. He followed numbly.

Hours later he had what he wanted. Or, at least, he knew where it was. Among a hundred sections, a hundred thousand file banks, dozens of vista rooms with their three-dimensional maps of all corners of the known cosmos, among museum halls with their displays of artifacts of great, strange, dead, new, dangerous, utterly mysterious cultures of the past and present, there was a course-coin for Revelo—a little button of a thing which a man could hide in his hand, and which bore the skills to pilot him to the Proscribed planet, and through which, like light through a pinhole, all his being must now pass, to fan out on the other side and place him in a picture of wealth beyond imagining. He glanced at the girl walking so confidently beside him and knew again that whatever she was worth, she wasn't important enough to turn him aside, precious enough to spare if she got in his way. And this made him inexpressibly sad.

He saw the banks of course-coin dispensers, where any planet's coin could be acquired by anyone . . . well, almost any planet by almost anyone. Spell out the name of the planet on a keyboard, and in seconds the coin would drop into a glass chamber below the board. Inspect it through the glass, and if it bore the right name, press your thumb into a depression at the right (your thumb would identify you for billing later) and the chamber opened. Or if you'd miscued it and saw the wrong coin, or changed your mind, hit the reject button and the coin would be returned to the bank.

So he punched out K-E-T-H, and a blank disk dropped into the chamber. *Proscribed*, a lighted sign under the chamber announced.

"Oh, my goodness, you don't want that one!" cried the girl.

"No," said Deeming truthfully—of all planets in the universe, Keth was the most unspeakable. "I just wanted to see what happened if you punched for it."

"You draw a blank," said the girl, touching the reject button and clearing the chamber. "Proscribed coins aren't even in this area. They're kept separately in a guarded file room. Do you want to see it? Angel Abdasel is the guard; he's so nice."

Deeming's heart leaped. "Yes, I'd like that. But . . . don't make me talk to an Angel. They make me feel . . . you're not going to like this . . ."

"Tell me."

"They make me feel small."

"I'm not angry at that!" She laughed. "They make me feel small too! Well, come on."

They took a gray tube and floated to the upper level of the low building, then walked through a labyrinth of corridors and through a door marked STAFF ONLY, which the girl opened for him, waving him through with mock gestures of pride and privilege. At the end of this corridor was a stairway leading down; Deeming could see the corner of an outer exit down there, and floodlit shrubbery. Near the top of the stairs was an open doorway; through it Deeming got a glimpse of gold. There was an Angel in there. Deeming stepped close to the wall, out of the Angel's line of sight. "Is this the place?"

"Yes," she said. "Come on—don't be shy; Abdasel's ever so nice." She tapped at the doorpost. "Abdasel . . ."

The resonant voice in the room was warm and welcoming. "Tandy! Come in, child."

So her name's Tandy, thought Deeming dully.

She said, "I've brought a friend. Could we . . .?"

"Any friend of——"

Deeming had Rockhard's specially designed needler out before he moved to the doorway. He rested it against the doorframe and put his head forward only far enough to sight it with one eye. He fired, and the needle disappeared silently into the broad golden chest. There had been no warning for the Angel, and no time. He bent his head in amazement as if to look at his chest while a hand rose to touch it. The hand simply stopped. The whole Angel stopped.

"Abdasel . . .?" whispered the girl, puzzled. She stepped into the room. "Angel Ab——" She must then have sensed something new in her companion's tense posture. She turned to him and eyed the needler in his hand, and the frozen Angel. "Did . . . did you——?"

"Too bad, Tandy," he rasped. "Too damn bad." He was breathing hard and his eyes burned. He dashed tears away from them with his free hand furiously.

"You hurt him," she said dazedly.

"He never felt a thing. He'll get over it. You know I have to kill you?" he blurted in sudden agony.

She didn't scream, or faint, or even look horrified. She simply said, "Do you?" in open puzzlement.

He got her out of the way then, not daring to wait a second more for fear he might debate the matter. He closed his mind down to a single icy purpose and lived solely with it while he pawed over the Angel's desk for an index. He found it—a complete list of Proscribed planets. He recognized the small keyboard beside the computer for what it was, a junior version of the dispensers downstairs, lacking the thumb plate which identified the purchaser.

He took the Angel's hand. The long arm was heavy, stiff, and noticeably cold—not surprising considering the amount of heat-absorbing *athermine* particles which the needle was even yet feeding into his blood stream. It was enough to freeze an ordinary human solid in minutes, but he had Rockhard's assurance that it would not kill an Angel. Not that he cared, or Rockhard either. For his purposes, the special needle was just as good either way.

He lifted the heavy hand and used one of its fingers to punch out the names of eight Proscribed planets, among them, of course, Revelo. He scooped them out of the receiving chute and dropped them in his pocket. Then he went to the door and stood holding his breath and listening intently. No sign of anyone in the corridor.

He whipped off his jacket and reversed it, slipped the inserts in his heels, removed the mustache and contact lenses, and stepped out into the corridor. He did not look back (because all he could see whether he looked or not was what lay crumpled on the floor smiling. *Smiling,* through some accident of spasm . . . a cruel accident which would mark his inner eye, his inner self, forever).

He went downstairs and out into the night, not hurrying.

He walked toward the park, numb inside except for that old, cold unhappiness which always signalized his successes. He remembered thinking that this was only because the take was so small. Well, he needed to think of a better one than that now.

His sky pressed down on his skull and nape. He watched each step he took and knew which step to take next.

It was very dark.

He found the road and then the milepost by the bridge. The people he had passed paid him no attention. When he was quite sure he was unobserved he slipped into the underbrush and through it to the meadow. He found the sloping ridge at the lip of the gully and moved along it, seeing mostly with his leg muscles and his semicircular canals. He drew his needler because it was better to have it and not need it than to need it and not have it; he moved silently because there was such a thing as a statistical improbability, and when he reached the point over the hiding place of his boat, he got down on his stomach and lay still, listening.

He heard only the gurgle of the water.

He got out his pencil torch, and held it in the same hand as the needler, clamping them tightly together and parallel, so that anywhere the light beam struck could be the exact target for a needle. Then walking his elbows, worming his abdomen, he crept to the edge and looked down.

Pitch black. Nothing.

He aimed the needler and torch as close as he could to where the ship ought to be, put his thumb ready on the stud, and with his other hand found the light switch and clicked it on.

The narrow beam shot downward. He was well oriented. The circle of white picked out the boat and the ground around it, and the figure of the Angel who sat in a patient posture on top of the boat.

The Angel looked up and smiled. "Hello, friend."

"Hello," said Deeming, and shot him. The Angel sat where he was, smiling up into the light, his eyes puckered from the glare. For a long moment nothing happened, and then, with head still up, and still smiling, the Angel toppled rigidly off the lifeboat and pitched backward into the rocky stream bed.

Deeming turned out the light and clambered slowly down into the dark. He fumbled his way to the boat, unlocked the canopy with the pre-set palm pattern, and climbed in. Then he cursed and climbed out again and found the water's edge and fumbled along it until his hands found the soft, strong folds of the golden cloak. He blinked his light once, briefly, and studied the scene as it faded from his retinas. The Angel lay on his back, turned from the hips so that his legs still held the sitting position he had been in when shot. His head was still back, but Deeming had not seen the head; it was under water.

He heaved the big body, lifted it, shifted it until he was sure it was placed the way he wanted it. A man as big as this Angel would have been a sizable load to move around; the Angel was a third again as heavy as that. (What *are* they, anyway?)

Then he got back into the boat and buttoned it up. He took his stolen course-coins and racked them neatly with the ones the ship already had. And for a while he sat and thought.

Hello, friend.

Her name was Tandy.

(Old eyes, pleading.)

"There's a lot of money in Yinyang weed."

He shifted in annoyance and pressed his thumbs to his eyes until he saw sparks. These weren't the thoughts he was after.

He ran his hand over the coin rack and slipped his fingers behind it to touch the new flicker-frequency coil which he had plugged in back there. In these tiny objects he had a potential possessed probably by no human being since time began. He had free and secret access to eight Proscribed planets, on some of which there was certainly material that someone, somewhere, would pay for exorbitantly—completely aside from yinyang weed. He could assume that he could not be traced from Ybo . . . no—no he couldn't. Say rather that as far as he knew he couldn't be traced; as far as he knew he had not been observed. The stories that were told about the Angels, how they could read minds, even newly dead minds . . . and then, for all their strength and confidence, for all their public stature, did they really feel that one Angel guarding the Proscribed coins would by his sole presence be sufficient to protect such potential devastation as those little disks represented? If he, Deeming, were setting up that office, Angels or no Angels, he'd put in cameras and alarms and various interlocks, like a particular rhythm pattern for keying the wanted disks which no outsider could know about.

The more he pursued this line of thought, the less confidence he had that his trail was cold. The more he thought of this, the more sure he became that even if they could not follow immediately, they would have nets spread in more places than even his growing fear could conjure up.

What would he do if he were an Angel and wanted to catch the likes of Deeming?

First of all, he'd cordon off the Proscribed planets (assuming that the keyboard had made a record of what coins were taken; and it was unthinkable that it had not).

Then he'd put a watch on every place known to have

been a haunt of the criminal—on the growing assumption that they could very soon find out who he was.

If they found out who he was, then special watches would be put on Rockhard, because the deal with Rockhard would certainly be discovered; it was too complex and involved too many people to be hidden for long, once the Angels had any lead at all.

Which meant that Earth was out, the Proscribed planets were out, Ybo and Bluebutter and anywhere else he'd ever been were out. He had to go to a new place, somewhere he had never been, where no one would know him, where there were lots of people to disappear among. Somehow, some way, he could think his way through to Don Rockhard and some, anyway, of the riches the old man had promised him.

He sighed and pawed through the coins on the rack until he came to the one marked Iolanthe. A big planet, a little hard on the muscles for comfort, but well crowded and totally new to him.

He dropped it into the slot and coined out of there.

Iolanthe was really up to the minute. He came out of flicker with about a mile of altitude and took a quick look around before he flicked to the nightside. With a design as unique as the ship's, he wouldn't want to leave it where it would cause comment. So he hung in the sky and fanned through the communications the planet had to offer.

They were plenty. There was a fine relief map of the planet on perpetual manation in conjunction with the space beacon, and a wonderful radio grid, so it was easy to place himself. There was an entertainment band and best of all, a news band—a broad one, set up in video frames, each with its audio loop of comment. He could tune in any page of the entire sequence. It was indexed and extremely well edited to cover both current news and background, local and intercultural events.

He started with the most recent bulletins and worked backward. There was nothing, and nothing, and nothing that might apply to him, not even a date line from anywhere he'd been. Until suddenly he found himself gaping into the face of Richard E. Rockhard.

He turned up the audio.

". . . indicted yesterday by C Jury of Earth High Court," said the announcer suavely, "on one hundred and eleven counts of restraint of trade, illegal interlocked directorates, price pegging, monopoly, market manipulation . . ." on and on and on. Apparently the old pirate had blown his balloon too big. ". . . estimated value of Mr. Rockhard's estate and holdings has been estimated in excess of two and three quarter billions, but in the face of these charges it is evident that the satisfaction of invoices outstanding, accounts receivable, taxes, and penalties will in all likelihood total to a far higher figure than the assets. These assets are, of course, in government hands pending a detailed accounting."

Slowly, his hand shaking, Deeming reached for the control and turned the communicator off. He watched, fascinated, as the ruddy, cold-eyed face of the old man faded away under his hand, distorted suddenly, and was gone. A trick of his mind, or of the fading electrons, shattered the picture as it was extinguished, and for the tiniest fraction of a second it assumed the wordless pleading which had moved him so deeply before.

"Stupid, clumsy old swine," he growled, too shocked to think of anything really foul to say.

No money. There wasn't anything except what the government held. He could see himself going to the government with a claim like his.

He pawed through the money the old man had given him for incidentals. He had used none of it so far, but it no longer looked like a lot. He crammed it back into his pocket and then shook himself hard.

I got to do something. I got to get down there and disappear.

He cut in the penetroscope and switched it to the video. The instrument resolved night views considerably better than it did images through beryl steel. He aimed it downward and got a good sharp focus on the ground and began hunting out a place to hide his boat. He would want hilly or rocky ground, a lot of vegetative cover, access to road or river, and perhaps——

Something golden flashed across the screen.

Deeming grunted and slapped at a control. The camera angle widened and the picture details shrank as the viewpoint gained altitude. He caught them, lost them, caught and hung on to them—three Angels, flying in V formation close to the ground, with their backpack geo-gravs. They were swiftly covering the ground in a most efficient area-search looking for—well, something concealed down there, small enough to justify that close scrutiny, sitting mum enough to justify a visual hunt. Something, say, about the size of his boat.

On impulse he cut in the ship detectors. The picture reeled and steadied and reeled again as the detectors scanned and selected, and then gave him a quick rundown of everything it had found, in order of closest estimated arrival time at a collision point with him.

To the north and northeast, two small golden ships converging.

To the east, another, and directly above it, another, apparently maneuvering to fly cover on its partner.

To the south, a large—no, that was nothing, just a freighter minding its own business. But no—it was launching boats. He zoomed the video on them. Fighter boats streaking toward him.

To the southeast—— The hell with the southeast! He pawed the Revelo coin out of the rack and banged it down on the slot of the coin box. It bounced out of his fingers and fell to the deck. He pounced on it and scrabbled it wildly into his hand.

A luminescent pink cloud bloomed suddenly to his right, another just behind him. Its significance: stand by for questioning, or else.

His hull began to hum, and, impressed on this vibration as a signal on a carrier; his whole craft spoke hoarsely to him: "Halt in the name of Angels. Stand by for tow beam."

"Yeah, sure," said Deeming, and this time got the coin to the slot. He banged the button and the scene through ports and video alike disappeared.

He switched off everything he didn't need and lay back, sweating.

He wouldn't even glance at the remote, wanly hopeful possibility that they had mistaken him for someone else. They knew who he was, all right. And how long had it taken them to draw a bead on him on a planet to which they could not possibly have known he was going? Thirty minutes?

He found himself staring out of the port, and became shockingly aware that he was still in hyperspace. He had never been in the gray so long before; where in time was this Revelo place anyway?

He began to sweat again. Was something wrong with the field generator? According to the telltales on the control panel, no; it seemed all right.

Still the queasy, deeply frightening gray. He blanked out the ports and shivered in his seat, hugging himself.

What had made him pick Revelo anyhow?

Only an unconfirmed guess that one man had managed to stay alive there. The other Proscribed planets were death for humans in one form or another; he had no idea which. Revelo probably was too, for that matter, but Don Rockhard would hardly have chanced it if it was certain death.

And then maybe—just barely maybe—the new flicker coil really would work so well in the Revelo death-field that he could slip through without detection. Maybe, for a while, for a very little while, he could be in a sheltered place where he could think.

There was a shrill rushing sound from the hull. He stared at the ports but could see nothing. He switched on the detector and then remembered the port blanks. He opened them and let the light of Revelo flood in.

He had never seen a sky like this. Masses of color, blue, blue-green, pink, drifted above him. The dim zenith was alive with shooting sparks. A great soft purple flame reached from the eastern horizon and wavered to invisibility almost directly overhead. It pulsed hypnotically.

Deeming shuddered. He set the detector to the task of finding Don Rockhard's boat and let it cruise. He started the exterior air analyzer and sat back to wait.

Since the missing boat was so small and the planet so large, he had to set his detector's discriminator very wide and its sensitivity high. And it found all sorts of things for him—great shining lumps of metallic copper and molybdenum jutting from the ragged hills, a long wavering row of circular pools of molten lead, and even the Angel's warning beacon and death-field generator. It was obviously untended, and understandably so; it was self-powered, foolproof, and set in a case that a hydrogen explosion wouldn't nick.

He had to sleep after a while, so he set the buzzer to its loudest and lay back to sleep. It seemed that each time he slept he dreamed and each time he dreamed, no matter how it began, it always ended with his coming face to face with a smiling Angel, unarmed, pleasant, just sitting waiting for him. Each time the buzzer sounded, he leaped frantically to see what it was reporting. The need to spend a moment with someone else beside himself, someone else's ideas besides his turgid miasmas of flight and dead smiles and kind relentless Angels became urgent, hysterical, frantic. Each time the buzzer sounded it was rich ore or a strange electrical fog between two iron crags, or nothing at all, and, at last, Donald Rockhard's lifeboat.

By the time he found it he was in a numb and miserable state, the retreat which lives on the other side of hysteria. He was riding a habit pattern of sleep and dream, wake and stare; hear the buzzer, lurch at the screen, get the disappointment, slap the reject button, and go on. He actually rejected the other lifeboat twice before he realized it, but his craft began to circle it and the strong fix made it impossible for the buzzer to be silent. He switched it off at last and hovered, staring dully at the tiny bronze ball below, and pulling himself back to reality.

He landed. The craziest thing of all about this crazy place was that the atmosphere at ground level was Earth normal, though a bit warm for real comfort. He unbuttoned the canopy and climbed stiffly out.

There was no sign of Donald Rockhard.

He walked over to the other boat and stooped to look in. The canopy was closed but not locked. He opened it and leaned inside. There were only three course-coins in the rack, Earth and Bootes II and Cabrini in Beta Centauri. He fumbled behind the rack and his fingers found a flat packet. He opened it.

It contained a fortune—a real fortune in large notes. And a card. And a course-coin.

The card was of indestructible hellenite, and bore the famous symbol of the surgeons of Grebd, and in hand script, by some means penetrating all the way through the impenetrable plastic, like ink through a paper towel, the legend: *Class A. Paid in full. Accept bearer without interrogation.* It was signed by an authoritative squiggle and overstamped with the well-known pattern of the Grebdan Surgical Society.

The coin was, of course, to Grebd.

Deeming clutched the treasure into his lap and bent over it, hugging it, and then laughed until he cried—which he did almost immediately.

The Grebd, for a new face, a new mind if he wanted it—a tail, wings, who cares? The sky's the limit.

(The sky—your sky—has always been the limit.)

And then, new face and all, with that packet of loot, to any place in the cosmos that I think is good enough for me.

"Hey! Who are you? What do you think you're doing? Get out of my boat! And drop those things!"

Deeming did not turn. He put up his hands and stopped his ears like a little child in the birdhouse at the zoo.

"Out, I said!"

Deeming lifted the treasure in shaking hands, rumpling and spilling it. "Out!" barked the voice, and out he came, not attempting to pick anything up. He turned tiredly with his hands raised somewhat less than shoulder height, as if they were much, much too heavy for him.

He faced a hollow-cheeked, weather-beaten young man with the wide-set frosty eyes of Richard Rockhard. At his feet a cloth sack lay where he had dropped it on seeing someone in his boat. In his hand, steady as an I-beam, rested a sonic disrupter aimed at Deeming's midsection.

Deeming said, "Donald Rockhard."

Rockhard said, "So?"

Deeming put down his hands, and croaked, "I've come to paint your belly blue."

Rockhard was absolutely motionless for a long moment, and then as if they were operated from the same string, his gun arm slowly lowered while slowly his smile spread. "Well, damn me up and back!" he said. "Father sent you!"

"Man," said Deeming exhaustedly, "I'm sure glad you ask questions first and shoot later."

"Oh, I wouldn't've shot you, whoever you were. I'm so glad to see another face that I—— Who are you, anyway?"

Deeming told him his name. "Your father found out that when a boat like yours busts through the Angel's death-field, it turns it inside out. Or some such. Anyway, if you'd coined out of here you never would have come down anywhere."

Donald Rockhard looked up into the mad sky, paling. "You don't say." He wet his lips and laughed nervously. It was not a funny sound. "And now that you've come to tell me, how do you get out?"

"Don't look at me like no hero," said Deeming with the shade of a grin. "It's only a matter of plugging in a new freak coil. 'That's what I was doing when I bumped into all that cabbage. I know I had no business looking it over, but then how often do you bump into four million in negotiable good cash money?"

"Can't blame you, at that," Rockhard admitted. "I suppose you saw what else was in there."

"I saw it."

"The theory is that if you plan to go to Grebd, no living soul should know about it."

Deeming glanced at the disrupter hanging from the young man's hand. The hand was slack, but then, he hadn't pulled the weapon anyway either. He said, "That's up to you. Your father trusted me with the information, though; you ought to know that."

"Well, all right," said Rockhard. He put the gun away. "How is he?"

"Your father? Not so good. I'd say he needs you about now."

"Needs me? Why, if I showed up in the same solar system and the Angels found out, it'd cost him."

"No, it wouldn't," said Deeming. He told them what had happened to the old man's towering structure of businesses. "Not that a lousy four million'd do much good."

Rockhard bit his lip. "What do you think I could get for the card?"

Deeming closed his eyes. "That might help," he nodded.

"I've got to get out of here," said young Rockhard. "You finished with that coil?"

"Just got the old one out."

"Finish it up, will you? I'll just sort out one or two of these." He dumped the contents of his sack on the ground and hunkered down over them.

"That what you're looking for?" asked Deeming, going to his own boat for the coil.

The other snorted. "Who knows? They might be potsherds and then again they might be fossilized mud puddles. I'll just take the best of 'em for analysis. You think archaeologists are crazy, Deeming?"

"Sure," said Deeming from the other boat. "But then, I also think everybody's crazy." He lay belly down on the seat of Rockhard's boat and began picking up money. He got it all and the card and stacked them neatly and slipped them into their packet. Rockhard glanced in at him.

"You taking some of that for yourself?"

Deeming shook his head. He put the packet on its shelf behind the coin rack. "I've been taken care of." He got out of the boat.

Rockhard got in, and looked up over his shoulder at him. "You better take some. A lot."

"I won't be needing it," said Deeming tiredly.

"You're a funny guy, Deeming."

"Yuk, yuk."

"Will I see you again?"

"No."

When Rockhard had no answer to that flat syllable Deeming said, "I'll swing your canopy." Under cover of reaching for the canopy, he got out his needler and concealed it in his sleeve, with the snout just protruding between the fingers of his closed fist. His little finger rested comfortably on the stud. He leaned on the fist, resting on the cowling right back of Rockhard's ear.

He said, "Good-by, Rockhard."

Rockhard didn't say anything.

Deeming stood for a long time looking down at the needler in a kind of dull astonishment. *Why didn't I shoot?* Then, when Rockhard's ship had flickered and gone, he let his shoulders hang and he slogged through the hot sand to his boat.

God he was tired.

"Why didn't you shoot?"

Deeming stopped where he was, not even finishing a stride; one foot forward, the other back. Slowly he raised his head and faced the golden giant who leaned casually, smiling, against his boat.

Deeming took a deep breath and held it and let it out painfully. Then in a harsh flat voice he said, "By God, I can't even say I'm surprised."

"Take it easy," said the Angel. "You're going to be all right now."

"Oh sure," said Deeming bitterly. They'd scrape out his brains and fill his head with cool delicious yogurt, and he'd spend the rest of his placid life mopping out the Angel's H.Q., wherever that might be. "Here," he said, "I guess you won this fair and square," and he tossed his needler to the Angel, who waved a negligent hand. The weapon ceased to exist in mid-air halfway between them. Deeming said, "You have a whole *bag* of tricks."

"Sure," said the Angel agreeably. "Why didn't you shoot young Rockhard?"

"You know," said Deeming, "I've been wondering about that myself. I meant to. I was sure I meant to." He raised hollow, bewildered eyes to the Angel. "What's the matter with me? I had it made, and I threw it away."

"Tell me some more things," said the Angel. "When you shot that Angel on Ybo and he fell with his head underwater, why did you take the trouble to drag him out and stretch him on the bank?"

"I didn't."

"I saw you. I was right there watching you."

"The hell you were," said Deeming, looked at the Angel's eyes, and knew that the Angel meant what he said. "Well, I—I don't know. I just did it, that's all."

"Now tell me why you knocked out that girl with your fist instead of killing her and covering your tracks."

"Her name was Tandy," said Deeming reflectively. "That's all I remember about it."

"Let's go way back," said the Angel easily. "When you left old Rockhard's place for an evening to clean up your affairs, you put a watch in a package and put it in the mail. Who'd you send it to?"

"Can't recall."

"I can. You mailed it back to the woman you stole it from. Why, Deeming?"

"Why, why, why! I always did that, that's why!"

"Not always. Only when it was a watch which was all the woman had left of her dead husband, or when it was something of equal value. You know what you are, Deeming? You're a softy."

"You're having yourself a time."

"I'm sorry," said the giant gently. "Deeming, I didn't win, as you just put it. *You've* won."

"Look," said Deeming, "you've caught up with me and I'll get mine. Let's let it go at that and skip the preaching, all right? Right. Let's go. I'm tired."

The Angel put out both hands, fingers slightly spread. Deeming tingled. He distinctly heard two sharp cracks as his spine stretched and reseated itself. He looked up sharply.

"Tired now?" smiled the Angel.

Deeming touched his own forearms, his eyelids. "No," he breathed. "By God, no, I'm not." He cocked his head and said reluctantly, "That's the first one of your tricks I've liked, shorty." He looked again at the jovial golden man. "Just what *are* you guys, anyway? Oh, all right," he said immediately, "I know, I know. That's the question you never answer. Skip it."

"*You* can ask it." Disregarding Deeming's slack-jawed astonishment at that, the Angel said, "Once we were a strong-arm squad. Sort of a small private army, if you can understand that. All through history there've been mercenaries. Once there was a thing called the Pinkerton man. You wouldn't know about that—it was before your time. Our outfit was operated originally by a man called Angell—with two Ls, and we were called Angell's, with a 'postrophe S. So the name really came before the fancy clothes and the Sunday-school kind of activity we go in for now.

"And as time went on we recruited more carefully and improved our rank and file more, and in the meantime our management became less and less, until finally we didn't have a management. Just us, and an idea that we could stop a lot of trouble if we could make people be kind to one another."

"You've sometimes got an offbeat way of being kind!"

"People used to shoot a horse with a broken leg. It was kind," said the Angel.

"So why do you tell me all this?"

"I'm recruiting."

"*What?*"

"Recruiting," the Angel said clearly. "Mustering new men. Making new Angels. Like you, if you want to."

"Aw, now wait a mucking minute here," said Deeming. "You're not going to stand there and tell me you can turn me into an Angel! Not me, you're not."

"Why not?"

"Not me," said Deeming doggedly. "I'm not the Angel type."

"You're not? What type is a man so big he can't live one life at a time but has to play the inverted *and* upside-down Robin Hood for the people? Were you aware that you never stole from anyone who did not, in the long run, benefit by it, learn something from it, and, if he'd lost something of real importance, he always got it back?"

"Is that really so?"

"I can show you a case history of every single one of them."

"You've been onto me for that long?"

"Since you were in third grade."

"Cut it out," said Deeming. "You'd have to be invisible."

The Angel disappeared. Blinking, Deeming walked slowly over to the hull and ran his hand over it.

"Not that that's so marvelous, once you know how it's done. Do you know any reason why a flicker-field shouldn't be refined down to something the size of your fist?" demanded the Angel's voice from mid-air. Deeming whirled and saw nothing. He backed against the boat, wide-eyed. "Over here," said the Angel cheerfully, and reappeared to the right. He drew back his cloak and turned down his waistband. Deeming briefly glimpsed a small, curved, flat plastic pack of some kind.

"You've got to understand," said the Angel, "that human beings, by and large, are by nature both superstitious and reverent. If you substitute science for their theology, they'll just get reverent about their science. All we do is give them what they want anyway. We never pretend to be anything special, but neither do we deny anything they think about us. If they think we're power-hungry slave traders, we prove they're wrong. If they think we're demigods or something, we don't say anything at all.

"It works out. There hasn't been a war in so long that half the population couldn't define the word. And we came along when we were needed most, believe me. When man was expanding against and through extra-terrestrial cultures. The word had to be spread, or damn well else."

"Just exactly what is the word? What are you really after?"

"I've already told you, but it sounds so confounded simple that nobody will believe it until they see it in action, and then they find something else to describe it. I'll try you again," said the Angel, chuckling. "The word is, *be kind to each other*. It opened the sky."

"I have to think about that," said Deeming, overwhelmed. He shook it off. "Later, I'll think about it. . . . I hear things about you people. I hear you don't eat."

"That's so."

"Or sleep."

"True. We don't breed either; we haven't been able to get our treatment to take on women, though we'll make it someday. We're not a species or a race, or supermen, or anything like that. We're descendants, out of sadism by technology, of the yinyang weed."

"Yinyang!"

"Our dark and deadly secret," said the Angel, laughing. "You know what the stuff does to people who take it uncontrolled. In the right hands, it's no more addictive than any other medicine. And you see, Deeming, you don't, you just *don't* increase intelligence by a factor of five and fail to see that people must be kind to one another. So the word, as I've called it, isn't a doctrine as such, or a philosophy, but simply a logical dictate. By the way, if you decide against joining us, don't go clacking in public about Yinyang, or you'll get yourself clobbered out of thin air."

"What did you say? What?" shouted Deeming. "If I decide against ... Have I a choice?"

"Can you honestly conceive of our forcing you to get people to be kind to each other?" asked the Angel soberly.

Deeming walked away and walked back again, eyes closed, pounding a fist into his other hand. "Well, you don't force me; fine. But I still have no choice. I'll take your word for it—though it'll be months before it really sinks in—that you boys are off my back. But I can't go back to that mess on Earth, with all old Rockhard's affairs churning around and the government poking into all his associations, and——"

"What mess did you say?" asked the Angel, and laughed. "Deeming, there isn't any mess."

"But Rockhard——"

"There isn't any Rockhard. Did you ever hear of any Rockhard before that fat boy called on you that night?"

"Well, no, but that doesn't mean—— Oh, by golly, it *does* mean ... yeah, but what about the big smashup, all Rockhard's affairs; it was in all the newscasts, it said right there——"

"In how many newscasts?"

"When I was on Iolanthe! I saw it myself when—oh. Oh. A private showing."

"You were in no position to be suspicious," the Angel excused him kindly.

"I'll say I wasn't. Your flyboys were about to knock me out of the sky. I could've been killed."

"Right."

"Matter of fact, suppose I'd kept my mouth shut when I was welded up in the landing foot of that ship? I might be there yet!"

"Correct."

"And if I'd bobbled that job on Ybo I could have caught a disrupter beam."

"Just get used to it and you won't be so indignant. Certainly you were in danger. Everything was set up so that you had right and wrong choices to make, and a great deal of freedom in between. You made the right choices and you're here. We can use you. We couldn't use a man who might jump the wrong way in an emergency."

"They say you're immortal," said Deeming abruptly.

"Nonsense!" said the Angel. "That's just a rumor, probably based on the fact that none of us has died yet. I don't doubt that we will."

"Oh," said Deeming, and started to think of something else. Then the full impact of what he had just heard reached him. He whispered, "But there have been gold-cloaked Angels around for two thousand years!"

"Twenty-three hundred," said the Angel.

"For that you stop breeding," said Deeming, and added rudely, "tell me, Gramps, is it worth it?"

"In all kindness," beamed the Angel, "I do believe you should have three or your teeth knocked down your throat, to guard you against making such remarks in the presence of someone who might take it less kindly than I do."

"I withdraw the remark," said Deeming, bowing low; and when he straightened up his face was puckered up like that of a child wanting to cry but hanging on tight. "I have to make gags about it, sir. Can't you see that? Or I—I——"

"All right, boy. Don't let it worry you . . . it's a big thing to meet without warning. D'ye think I've forgotten that?"

They stood for a while in companionable silence. Then, "How long do I have to make up my mind?"

"As much time as it takes. You've qualified, you understand that? Your invitation is permanent. You can only lose it by breaking faith with me."

"I can't see myself starting a movement to persuade people to hate each other. Not after this. And I'm not likely to talk. Who'd listen?"

"An Angel," said the golden one softly, "no matter whom you were talking to. Now—what do you want to do?"

"I want to go back to Earth."

The Angel waved at the boat. "Help yourself."

Deeming looked at him and bit his lip. "Don't you want to know why?"

The Angel silently smiled.

"It's just that I have to," blurted Deeming protestingly. "I mean, all my damn miserable years I've been afraid to live more than half a life at a time. Even when I created a new one, for kicks, I shut off the original while it was going on. I want to go back the way I am, and learn how to be as big as I am." He leaned forward and tapped the Angel's broad chest. "That—is—pretty damn big. If I let you make me into what you are, I'd go back larger than life size. I want to be life size for a time. I think that's what I mean. You don't have to be an Angel to be big. You don't have to be any more than a man to live by the word, for that matter." He fell silent.

"How do you know what it's like to be what you call 'life size'?"

"I did it for about three minutes, standing on the steps of the Astro Central on Ybo. I was talking to——"

"You could go back by way of Ybo."

"She wouldn't look my way, except to have me arrested," said Deeming. "She saw me shoot an Angel."

"Then we'll have that same Angel arrest you, and restore her faith in us."

Deeming never reached Earth. He was arrested on Ybo and the arresting Angel draped him over a thick forearm and displayed him to the girl Tandy. She watched him stride off with his prisoner and ran after them.

"What are you going to do with him?"

"What would you do?"

They looked at each other for a time, until the Angel said to Deeming, "Can you tell me honestly that you have something to learn from this girl, and that you're willing to learn it?"

"Oh yes," said Deeming.

"Teach him what?" cried the girl, in a panic. "Teach him how?"

"By being yourself," Deeming said, and when he said that the Angel let go of him.

"Come see me," the Angel said to Deeming, "three days after this is over."

It was over when she died and after they had lived together on Ybo for seventy-four years, and in three days he was able to sit among his great-grandchildren and decide what to do next.

A Touch of Strange

He left his clothes in the car and slipped down to the beach.

Moonrise, she'd said.

He glanced at the eastern horizon and was informed of nothing. It was a night to drink the very airglow, and the stars lay lightless like scattered talc on the background.

"Moonrise," he muttered.

Easy enough for her. Moonrise was something, in her cosmos, that one simply knew about. He'd had to look it up. You don't realize—certainly *she'd* never realize—how hard it is, when you don't know anything about it, to find out exactly what time moonrise is supposed to be, at the dark of the moon. He still wasn't positive, so he'd come early, and would wait.

He shuffled down to the whispering water, finding it with ears and toes. "Woo." Catch m' death, he thought. But it never occurred to him to keep *her* waiting. It wasn't in her to understand human frailties.

He glanced once again at the sky, then waded in and gave himself to the sea. It was chilly, but by the time he had taken ten of the fine strong strokes which had first attracted her, he felt wonderful. He thought, oh well, by the time I've learned to breathe under water, it should be no trick at all to find moonrise without an almanac.

He struck out silently for the blackened and broken teeth of rock they call Harpy's Jaw, with their gums of foam and the floss of tide-risen weed bitten up and hung for the birds to pick. It was oily calm everywhere but by the Jaw, which mumbled and munched on every wave and spit the pieces into the air. He was therefore very close before he heard the singing. What with the surf and his concentration on flanking the Jaw without cracking a kneecap the way he had that first time, he was in deep water on the seaward side before he noticed the new quality in the singing. Delighted, he trod water and listened to be sure; and sure enough, he was right.

It sounded terrible.

"Get your flukes out of your mouth," he bellowed joyfully, "you baggy old guano-guzzler."

"You don't sound so hot yourself, chum," came the shrill falsetto answer, "and you know what type fish-gut *chum* I mean."

He swam closer. Oh, this was fine. It wasn't easy to find a for-real something like this to clobber her with. Mostly, she was so darn perfect, he had to make it up whole, like the time he told her her eyes weren't the same color. Imagine, he thought, *they* get head-colds too! And then he thought, well, why not? "You mind your big bony bottom-feeding mouth," he called cheerfully, "or I'll curry your tail with a scaling-tool." He could barely make her out, sprawled on the narrow seaward ledge—something piebald dark in the darkness. "Was that really you singin' or are you sitting on a blowfish?"

"You creak no better'n a straight-gut skua gull in a sewer sump," she cried raucously. "Whyn'cha swallow that seaslug or spit it out, one?"

"Ah, go soak your head in a paddlewheel," he laughed. He got a hand on the ledge and heaved himself out of the water. Instantly that was a high-pitched squeak and a clumsy splash, and she was gone. The particolored mass of shadow-in-shade had passed him in mid-air too swiftly for him to determine just what it was, but he knew with a shocked certainty what it was not.

He wriggled a bare (*i.e.*, mere) buttock-clutch on the short narrow shelf of rock and leaned over as far as he could to peer into the night-stained sea. In a moment there was a feeble commotion and then a bleached oval so faint that he must avert his eyes two points to looward like a sailor seeing a far light, to make it out at all. Again, seeing virtually nothing, he could be sure of the things it was not. That close cap of darkness, night or no night, was not the web of floating gold for which he had once bought a Florentine comb. Those two dim blotches were not the luminous, over-long, wide-spaced (almost side-set) green eyes which, laughing, devoured his sleep. Those hints of shoulders were not broad and fair, but slender. That salt-spasmed weak sobbing cough was unlike any sound he had heard on these rocks before; and the (by this time) unnecessary final proof was the narrow hand he reached for and grasped. It was delicate, not splayed; it was unwebbed; its smoothness was that of the plum and not the articulated magic of a fine wrought golden watchband. It was, in short, human, and for a long devastated moment their hands clung together while their minds, in panic, prepared to do battle with the truth.

At last they said in unison, "But you're not—"

And let a wave pass, and chorused, "I didn't know there was anybod—"

And opened and closed their mouths, and said together, "Y'see, I was waiting for—" "Look!" he said abruptly, because he had found something he could say that she couldn't at the moment. "Get a good grip, I'll pull you out. Ready? One, two—"

"No!" she said, outraged, and pulled back abruptly. He lost her hand, and down she went in mid-gasp, and up she came strangling. He reached down to help, and missed, though he brushed her arm. "Don't touch me!" she cried, and doggy-paddled frantically to the rock on which he sat, and got a hand on it. She hung there coughing until he stirred, whereupon: "Don't touch me!" she cried again.

"Well all right," he said in an injured tone.

She said, aloud but obviously to herself, "Oh, *dear* . . ."

Somehow this made him want to explain himself. "I only thought you should come out, coughing like that, I mean it's silly you should be bobbing around in the water and I'm sitting up here on the—" He started a sentence about he was only trying to be—, and another about he was *not* trying to be—, and was unable to finish either. They stared at one another, two panting sightless blots on a spume-slick rock.

"The way I was talking before, you've got to understand—"

They stopped as soon as they realized they were in chorus again. In a sudden surge of understanding he laughed—it was like relief—and said, "You mean that you're not the kind of girl who talks the way you were talking just before I got here. I believe you. ... And I'm not the kind of guy who does it either. I thought you were a—thought you were someone else, that's all. Come on out. I won't touch you."

"Well..."

"I'm still waiting for the—for my friend. That's all."

"Well..."

A wave came and she took sudden advantage of it and surged upward, falling across the ledge on her stomach. "I'll manage, I'll manage," she said rapidly, and did. He stayed where he was. They stayed where they were in the hollow of the rock, out of the wind, four feet apart, in darkness so absolute that the red of tight-closed eyes was a lightening.

She said, "Uh ..." and then sat silently masticating something she wanted to say, and swallowing versions of it. At last: "I'm not trying to be nosy."

"I didn't think you ... Nosy? You haven't asked me anything."

"I mean staying here," she said primly. "I'm not just trying to be in the way, I mean. I mean, I'm waiting for someone too."

"Make yourself at home," he said expansively, and then felt like a fool. He was sure he had sounded cynical, sarcastic, and unbelieving. Her protracted silence made it worse. It became unbearable. There was only one thing he could think of to say, but he found himself unaccountably reluctant to bring out into the open the only possible explanation for her presence here. His mouth asked (as it were) while he wasn't watching it, inanely, "Is your uh friend coming out in uh a boat?"

"Is yours?" she asked shyly; and suddenly they were laughing together like a brace of loons. It was one of those crazy sessions people will at times find themselves conducting, laughing explosively, achingly, without a specific punchline over which to hang the fabric of the situation. When it had spent itself, they sat quietly. They had not moved nor exchanged anything, and yet they now sat together, and not merely side by side. The understood attachment to someone —something—else had paradoxically dissolved a barrier between them.

It was she who took the plunge, exposed the Word, the code attachment by which they might grasp and handle their preoccupation. She said, dreamily, "I never saw a mermaid."

And he responded, quite as dreamily but instantly too:

"Beautiful." And that was question and answer. And when he said, "I never saw a—" she said immediately, "Beautiful." And that was reciprocity. They looked at each other again in the dark and laughed, quietly this time.

After a friendly silence, she asked, "What's her name?"

He snorted in self-surprise. "Why, I don't know. I really don't. When I'm away from her I think of her as *she,* and when I'm with her she's just . . . *you.* Not you," he added with a childish giggle.

She gave him back the giggle and then sobered reflectively. "Now that's the strangest thing. I don't know *his name* either. I don't even know if they have names."

"Maybe they don't need them. She—uh—they're sort of different, if you know what I mean. I mean, they know things we don't know, sort of . . . feel them. Like if people are coming to the beach, long before they're in sight. And what the weather will be like, and where to sit behind a rock on the bottom of the sea so a fish swims right into their hands."

"And what time's moonrise."

"Yes," he said, thinking, you suppose they know each other? you think they're out there in the dark watching? you suppose *he'll* come first, and what will he say to me? Or what if *she* comes first?

"I don't think they need names," the girl was saying. "They know one person from another, or just who they're talking about, by the feel of it. What's your name?"

"John Smith," he said. "Honest to God."

She was silent, and then suddenly giggled.

He made a questioning sound.

"I bet you say 'Honest to God' like that every single time you tell anyone your name. I bet you've said it thousands and thousand of times," she said.

"Well, yes. Nobody ever noticed it before, though."

"I would. My name is Jane Dow. Dee owe doubleyou, not Doe."

"Jane Dow. Oh! and you have to spell it out like that every single time?"

"Honest to God," she said, and they laughed.

He said, "John Smith, Jane Dow. Golly. Pretty ordinary people."

"Ordinary. You and your mermaid."

He wished he could see her face. He wondered if the mer-people were as great a pressure on her as they were on him. He had never told a soul about it—who'd listen?

Who'd believe? Or, listening, believing, who would not interfere? Such a wonder . . . and had she told all her girl-friends and boyfriends and the boss and what-not? He doubted it. He could not have said why, but he doubted it.

"Ordinary," he said assertively, "yes." And he began to talk, really talk about it because he had not, because he had to. "That has a whole lot to do with it. Well, it has everything to do with it. Look, nothing ever happened in my whole entire life. Know what I mean? I mean, nothing. I never skipped a grade in school and I never got left back. I never won a prize. I never broke a bone. I was never rich and never hungry. I got a job and kept it and I won't ever go very high in the company and I won't ever get canned. You know what I mean?"

"Oh, yes."

"So then," he said exultantly, "along comes this mermaid. I mean, to *me* comes a mermaid. Not just a glimpse, no maybe I did and maybe I didn't see a mermaid: this is a real live mermaid who wants me back again, time and again, and makes dates and keeps 'em too, for all she's all the time late."

"So is *he*," she said in intense agreement.

"What I call it," he said, leaning an inch closer and lowering his voice confidentially, "is a touch of strange. A touch of strange. I mean, that's what I call it to myself, you see? I mean, a person is a person all his life, he's good to his mother, he never gets arrested, if he drinks too much he doesn't get in trouble he just gets, excuse the expression, sick to his stomach. He does a day's good work for a day's pay and nobody hates him or, for that matter, nobody likes him either. Now a man like that has no *life;* what I mean, he isn't *real*. But just take an ordinary guy-by-the-millions like that, and add a touch of strange, you see? Some little something he does, or has, or that happens to him, even once. Then for all the rest of his life he's *real*. Golly. I talk too much."

"No you don't. I think that's real nice, Mr. Smith. A touch of strange. A touch . . . you know, you just told the story of my life. Yes you did. I was born and brought up and went to school and got a job all right there in Springfield, and—"

"*Spring*field? You mean Springfield Massa*chu*setts? That's my town!" he blurted excitedly, and fell off the ledge into the sea. He came up instantly and sprang up beside her, blowing like a manatee.

"Well no," she said gently. "It was Springfield, Illinois."

"Oh," he said, deflated.

She went on, "I wasn't ever a pretty girl, what you'd call, you know, pretty. I wasn't repulsive either, I don't mean that. Well, when they had the school dances in the gymnasium, and they told all the boys to go one by one and choose a partner, I never got to be the first one. I was never the last one left either, but sometimes I was *afraid* I'd be. I got a job the day after I graduated from high school. Not a good one, but not bad, and I still work there. I like some people more than other people, but not very much, you know? . . . A touch of strange. I always knew there was a name for the thing I never had, and you gave it a good one. Thank you, Mr. Smith."

"Oh that's all right," he said shyly. "And anyway, you have it now . . . how was it you happened to meet your . . . him, I mean?"

"Oh, I was scared to *death*, I really was. It was the company picnic, and I was swimming, and I—well, to tell you the actual truth, if you'll forgive me, Mr. Smith, I had a strap on my bathing suit that was, well, slippy. Please, I don't mean too *bad*, you know, or I wouldn't ever have worn it. But I was uncomfortable about it, and I just slipped around the rocks here to fix it and . . . there he was."

"In the daytime?"

"With the sun on him. It was like . . . like . . . There's nothing it was like. He was just lying here on this very rock, out of the water. Like he was waiting for me. He didn't try to get away or look surprised or anything, just lay there smiling. Waiting. He has a beautiful soft big voice and the longest green eyes, and long golden hair."

"Yes, yes. *She* has, too."

"He was so beautiful. And then all the rest, well, I don't have to tell *you*. Shiny silver scales and the big curvy flippers."

"Oh," said John Smith.

"I was scared, oh yes. But not *afraid*. He didn't try to

come near me and I sort of knew he couldn't ever hurt me . . . and then he spoke to me, and I promised to come back again, and I did, a lot, and that's the story." She touched his shoulder gently and embarrassedly snatched her hand away. "I never told anyone before. Not a single living soul," she whispered. "I'm so glad to be able to talk about it."

"Yeah." He felt insanely pleased. "Yeah."

"How did you . . ."

He laughed. "Well, I have to sort of tell something on myself. This swimming, it's the only thing I was ever any good at, only I never found out until I was grown. I mean, we had no swimming pools and all that when I went to school. So I never show off about it or anything, I just swim when there's nobody around much. And I came here one day, it was in the evening in summer when most everyone had gone home to dinner, and I swam past the reef line, way out away from the Jaw, here. And there's a place there where it's only a couple of feet deep and I hit my knee."

Jane Dow inhaled with a sharp sympathetic hiss.

Smith chuckled. "Now I'm not one for bad language. I mean I never feel right about using it. But you hear it all the time, and I guess it sticks without you knowing it. So sometimes when I'm by myself and bump my head or whatnot I hear this rough talk, you know, and I suddenly realize it's me doing it. And that's what happened this day, when I hurt my knee. I mean, I really hurt it. So I sort of scrounched down holding on to my knee and I like to boil up the water for a yard around with what I said. I didn't know anyone was around or I'd never.

"And all of a sudden there she was, laughing at me. She came porpoising up out of deep water to seaward of the reef and jumped up into that sunlight, the sun was low then, and red; and she fell flat on her back loud as your tooth breaking on a cherry-pip. When she hit, the water rose up all around her, and for that one second she lay in it like something in a jewel box, you know, pink satin all around and her deep in it.

"I was that hurt and confused and startled I couldn't believe what I saw, and I remember thinking this was some la—I mean, woman, girl like you hear about, living the life and bathing in the altogether. And I turned my back on her to show her what I thought of that kind of goings-on, but looking over my shoulder to see if she got the message, and I thought then I'd made it all up, because there was nothing there but her suds where she splashed, and they disappeared before I really saw them.

"About then my knee gave another twinge and I looked down and saw it wasn't just bumped, it was cut too and bleeding all down my leg, and only when I heard her laughing louder than I was cussing did I realize what I was saying. She swam round and round me, laughing, but you know? there's a way of laughing *at* and a way of laughing *with*, and there was no bad feeling in what she was doing.

"So I forgot my knee altogether and began to swim, and I think she liked that; she stopped laughing and began to sing, and it was . . ." Smith was quiet for a time, and Jane Dow had nothing to say. It was as if she were listening for that singing, or to it.

"She can sing with anything that moves, if it's alive, or even if it isn't alive, if it's big enough, like a storm wind or neaptide rollers. The way she sang, it was to my arms stroking the water and my hands cutting it, and me in it, and being scared and wondering, the way I was . . . and the water on me, and the blood from my knee, it was all what she was singing, and before I knew it it was all the other way round, and I was swimming to what she sang. I think I never swam in my life the way I did then, and may never again, I don't know; because there's a way of moving where every twitch and wiggle is exactly right, and does twice what it could do before; there isn't a thing in you fighting anything else of yours. . . ." His voice trailed off.

Jane Dow sighed.

He said, "She went for the rocks like a torpedo and just where she had to bash her brains out, she churned up a fountain of white-water and shot out of the top of it and up on the rocks—right where she wanted to be and not breathing hard at all. She reached her hand into a crack without stretching and took out a big old comb and began running it through her hair, still humming that music and smiling at me like—well, just the way you said *he* did, waiting, not ready to run. I swam to the rocks and climbed up and sat down near her, the way she wanted."

Jane Dow spoke after a time, shyly, but quite obviously from a conviction that in his silence Smith had spent quite enough time on these remembered rocks. "What . . . did she want, Mr. Smith?"

Smith laughed.

"Oh," she said. "I do beg your pardon. I shouldn't have asked."

"Oh please," he said quickly, "it's all right. What I was laughing about was that she should pick on me—me of all people in the world—" He stopped again, and shook his head invisibly. No, I'm not going to tell her about that, he decided. Whatever she thinks about me is bad enough. Sitting on a rock half the night with a mermaid, teaching her to cuss . . . He said, "They have a way of getting you to do what they want."

It is possible, Smith found, even while surf whispers virtually underfoot, to detect the cessation of someone's breathing; to be curious, wondering, alarmed, then relieved as it begins again, all without hearing it or seeing anything. *What'd I say?* he thought, perplexed; but he could not recall exactly, except to be sure he had begun to describe the scene with the mermaid on the rocks, and had then decided against it and said something or other else instead. Oh. Pleasing the mermaid. "When you come right down to it," he said, "they're not hard to please. Once you understand what they want."

"Oh yes," she said in a controlled tone. "I found that out."

"You did?"

Enough silence for a nod from her.

He wondered what pleased a merman. He knew nothing about them—nothing. His mermaid liked to sing and to be listened to, to be watched, to comb her hair, and to be cussed at. "And whatever it is, it's worth doing," he added, "because when they're happy, they're happy up to the sky."

"Whatever it is," she said, disagreeably agreeing.

A strange corrosive thought drifted against his consciousness. He batted it away before he could identify it. It was strange, and corrosive, because of his knowledge of and feeling for, his mermaid. There is a popular conception of what joy with a mermaid might be, and he had shared it— if he had thought of mermaids at all—with the populace . . . up until the day he met one. You listen to mermaids, watch them, give them little presents, cuss at them, and perhaps learn certain dexterities unknown, or forgotten, to most of us, like breathing under water—or, to be more accurate, storing more oxygen than you thought you could, and finding still more (however little) extractable from small amounts of water admitted to your lungs and vaporized by practiced contractions of the diaphragm, whereby some of the dissolved oxygen could be coaxed out of the vapor. Or so Smith had theorized after practicing certain of the mermaid's ritual exercises. And then there was fishing to be eating, and fishing to be fishing, and hypnotizing eels, and other innocent pleasures.

But innocent.

For your mermaid is as oviparous as a carp, though rather more mammalian than an echidna. Her eggs are tiny, by honored mammalian precedent, and in their season are placed in their glittering clusters (for each egg looks like a tiny pearl imbedded in a miniature moonstone) in secret, guarded grottos, and cared for with much ritual. One of the rituals takes place after the eggs are well rafted and have plated themselves to the inner lip of their hidden nest; and this is the finding and courting of a merman to come and, in the only way he can, father the eggs.

This embryological sequence, unusual though it may be, is hardly unique in complexity in a world which contains such marvels as the pelagic phalange of the cephalopods and the simultaneity of disparate appetites exhibited by certain arachnids. Suffice it to say, regarding mermaids, that the legendary monosyllable of greeting used by the ribald Indian is answered herewith; and since design follows function in such matters, one has a guide to one's conduct with the lovely creatures, and they, brother, with you, and with you, sister.

"So gentle," Jane Dow was saying, "but then, so rough."

"Oh?" said Smith. The corrosive thought nudged at him. He flung it somewhere else, and it nudged him there, too. ... It was at one time the custom in the Old South to quiet babies by smearing their hands liberally with molasses and giving them a chicken feather. Smith's corrosive thought behaved like such a feather, and pass it about as he would he could not put it down.

The mer*man* now, he thought wildly ... "I suppose," said Jane Dow, "I really am in no position to criticize."

Smith was too busy with his figurative feather to answer.

"The way I talked to you when I thought you were ... when you came out here. Why, I never in my life—"

"That's all right. You heard *me,* didn't you?" Oh, he thought, suddenly disgusted with himself, it's the same way with her and her friend as it is with me and mine. Smith, you have an evil mind. This is a nice girl, this Jane Dow.

It never occurred to him to wonder what was going through her mind. Not for a moment did he imagine that she might have less information on mermaids than he had, even while he yearned for more information on mermen.

"They *make* you do it," she said. "You just have to. I admit it; I lie awake nights thinking up new nasty names to call him. It makes him so happy. And he loves to do it too. The . . . things he says. He calls me 'alligator bait.' He says I'm his squashy little bucket of roe. Isn't that awful? He says I'm a milt-and-water type. What's milt, Mr. Smith?"

"I can't say," hoarsely said Smith, who couldn't, making a silent resolution not to look it up. He found himself getting very upset. She seemed like such a nice girl. . . . He found himself getting angry. She unquestionably *had* been a nice girl.

Monster, he thought redly. "I wonder if it's moonrise yet."

Surprisingly she said, "Oh dear. Moonrise."

Smith did not know why, but for the first time since he had come to the rock, he felt cold. He looked unhappily seaward. A ragged, wistful, handled phrase blew by his consciousness: *save her from herself.* It made him feel unaccountably noble.

She said faintly, "Are you . . . have you . . . I mean, if you don't mind my asking, you don't have to tell me . . ."

"What is it?" he asked gently, moving close to her. She was huddled unhappily on the edge of the shelf. She didn't turn to him, but she didn't move away.

"Married, or anything?" she whispered.

"Oh gosh no. Never. I suppose I had hopes once or twice, but no, oh gosh no."

"Why not?"

"I never met a . . . well, they all . . . You remember what I said about a touch of strange?"

"Yes, yes . . ."

"Nobody had it. . . . Then I got it, and . . . put it this way, I never met a girl I could tell about the mermaid."

The remark stretched itself and lay down comfortably across their laps, warm and increasingly audible, while they sat and regarded it. When he was used to it, he bent his head and turned his face toward where he imagined hers must be, hoping for some glint of expression. He found his lips resting on hers. Not pressing, not cowering. He was still, at first from astonishment, and then in bliss. She sat up straight with her arms braced behind her and her eyes wide until his mouth slid away from hers. It was a very gentle thing.

Mermaids love to kiss. They think it excruciatingly funny. So Smith knew what it was like to kiss one. He was thinking about that while his lips lay still and sweetly on those of Jane Dow. He was thinking that the mermaid's lips were not only cold, but dry and not completely flexible, like the carapace of the soft-shell crab. The mermaid's tongue, suited to the eviction of whelk and the scything of kelp, could draw blood. (It never had, but it could.) And her breath smelt of fish.

He said, when he could, "What were you thinking?"

She answered, but he could not hear her.

"What?"

She murmured into his shoulder, "His teeth all point inwards."

Aha, he thought.

"John," she said suddenly, desperately, "there's one thing you must know now and forever more. I know just how things were between you and *her*, but what you have to understand is that it wasn't the same with me. I want you to know the truth right from the very beginning, and now we don't need to wonder about it or talk about it ever again."

"Oh you're fine," John Smith choked. "So fine. . . . Let's go. Let's get out of here before—before moonrise."

Strange how she fell into the wrong and would never know it (for they never discussed it again), and forgave him and drew from that a mightiness; for had she not defeated the most lawless, the loveliest of rivals?

Strange how he fell into the wrong and forgave her, and drew from his forgiveness a lasting pride and a deep certainty of her eternal gratitude.

Strange how the moon had risen long before they left, yet the mermaid and the merman never came at all, feeling things as they strangely do.

And John swam in the dark sea slowly, solicitous, and Jane swam, and they separated on the dark beach and dressed, and met again at John's car, and went to the lights where they saw each other at last; and when it was time, they fell well and truly in love, and surely that is the strangest touch of all.

The Other Celia

If you live in a cheap enough rooming house and the doors are made of cheap enough pine, and the locks are old-fashioned single-action jobs and the hinges are loose, and if you have a hundred and ninety lean pounds to operate with, you can grasp the knob, press the door sidewise against its hinges, and slip the latch. Further, you can lock the door the same way when you come out.

Slim Walsh lived in, and was, and had, and did these things partly because he was bored. The company doctors had laid him up—not off, up—for three weeks (after his helper had hit him just over the temple with a fourteen-inch crescent wrench) pending some more X-rays. If he was going to get just sick-leave pay, he wanted to make it stretch. If he was going to get a big fat settlement—all to the good; what he saved by living in this firetrap would make the money look even better. Meanwhile, he felt fine and had nothing to do all day.

"Slim isn't dishonest," his mother used to tell Children's Court some years back. "He's just curious."

She was perfectly right.

Slim was constitutionally incapable of borrowing your bathroom without looking into your medicine chest. Send him into your kitchen for a saucer and when he came out a minute later, he'd have inventoried your refrigerator, your vegetable bin, and (since he was six feet three inches tall) he would know about a moldering jar of maraschino cherries in the back of the top shelf that you'd forgotten about.

Perhaps Slim, who was not impressed by his impressive size and build, felt that a knowledge that you secretly use hair-restorer, or are one of those strange people who keeps a little mound of unmated socks in your second drawer, gave him a kind of superiority. Or maybe security is a better word. Or maybe it was an odd compensation for one of the most advanced cases of gawking, gasping shyness ever recorded.

Whatever it was, Slim liked you better if, while talking to you, he knew how many jackets hung in your closet, how old that unpaid phone bill was, and just where you'd hidden those photographs. On the other hand, Slim didn't insist on knowing bad or even embarrassing things about you. He just wanted to know things about you, period.

His current situation was therefore a near-paradise. Flimsy doors stood in rows, barely sustaining vacuum on aching vacuum of knowledge; and one by one they imploded at the nudge of his curiosity. He touched nothing (or if he did, he replaced it carefully) and removed nothing, and within a week he knew Mrs. Koyper's roomers far better than she could, or cared to. Each secret visit to the rooms gave him a starting point; subsequent ones taught him more. He knew not only what these people had, but what they did, where, how much, *for* how much, and how often. In almost every case, he knew why as well.

Almost every case. Celia Sarton came.

Now, at various times, in various places, Slim had found strange things in other people's rooms. There was an old lady in one shabby place who had an electric train under her bed; used it, too. There was an old spinster in this very building who collected bottles, large and small, of any value or capacity, providing they were round and squat and with long necks. A man on the second floor secretly guarded his desirables with the unloaded .25 automatic in his top bureau drawer, for which he had a half-box of .38 cartridges.

There was a (to be chivalrous) girl in one of the rooms who kept fresh cut flowers before a photograph on her nighttable—or, rather, before a frame in which were stacked eight photographs, one of which held the stage each day. Seven days, eight photographs: Slim admired the system. A new love every day and, predictably, a different love on successive Wednesdays. And all of them movie stars.

Dozens of rooms, dozens of imprints, marks, impressions,

overlays, atmospheres of people. And they needn't be odd ones. A woman moves into a room, however standardized; the instant she puts down her dusting powder on top of the flush tank, the room is *hers*. Something stuck in the ill-fitting frame of a mirror, something draped over the long-dead gas jet, and the samest of rooms begins to shrink toward its occupant as if it wished, one day, to be a close-knit, form-fitting, individual integument as intimate as a skin.

But not Celia Sarton's room.

Slim Walsh got a glimpse of her as she followed Mrs. Koyper up the stairs to the third floor. Mrs. Koyper, who hobbled, slowed any follower sufficiently to afford the most disinterested witness a good look, and Slim was anything but disinterested. Yet for days he could not recall her clearly. It was as if Celia Sarton had been—not invisible, for that would have been memorable in itself—but translucent or, chameleonlike, drably re-radiating the drab wall color, carpet color, woodwork color.

She was—how old? Old enough to pay taxes. How tall? Tall enough. Dressed in . . . whatever women cover themselves with in their statistical thousands. Shoes, hose, skirt, jacket, hat.

She carried a bag. When you go to the baggage window at a big terminal, you notice a suitcase here, a steamer-trunk there; and all around, high up, far back, there are rows and ranks and racks of luggage not individually noticed but just *there*. This bag, Celia Sarton's bag, was one of them.

And to Mrs. Koyper, she said—she said— She said whatever is necessary when one takes a cheap room; and to find her voice, divide the sound of a crowd by the number of people in it.

So anonymous, so unnoticeable was she that, aside from being aware that she left in the morning and returned in the evening, Slim let two days go by before he entered her room; he simply could not remind himself about her. And when he did, and had inspected it to his satisfaction, he had his hand on the knob, about to leave, before he recalled that the room was, after all, occupied. Until that second, he had thought he was giving one of the vacancies the once-over. (He did this regularly; it gave him a reference-point.)

He grunted and turned back, flicking his gaze over the

room. First he had to assure himself that he was in the right room, which, for a man of his instinctive orientations, was extraordinary. Then he had to spend a moment of disbelief in his own eyes, which was all but unthinkable. When that passed, he stood in astonishment, staring at the refutation of everything his—hobby—had taught him about people and the places they live in.

The bureau drawers were empty. The ashtray was clean. No toothbrush, toothpaste, soap. In the closet, two wire hangers and one wooden one covered with dirty quilted silk, and nothing else. Under the grime-gray dresser scarf, nothing. In the shower stall, the medicine chest, nothing and nothing again, except what Mrs. Koyper had grudgingly installed.

Slim went to the bed and carefully turned back the faded coverlet. Maybe she had slept in it, but very possibly not; Mrs. Koyper specialized in unironed sheets of such a ground-in gray that it wasn't easy to tell. Frowning, Slim put up the coverlet again and smoothed it.

Suddenly he struck his forehead, which yielded him a flash of pain from his injury. He ignored it. "The bag!"

It was under the bed, shoved there, not hidden there. He looked at it without touching it for a moment, so that it could be returned exactly. Then he hauled it out.

It was a black gladstone, neither new nor expensive, of that nondescript rusty color acquired by untended leatherette. It had a worn zipper closure and was not locked. Slim opened it. It contained a cardboard box, crisp and new, for a thousand virgin sheets of cheap white typewriter paper surrounded by a glossy bright blue band bearing a white diamond with the legend: *Nonpareil the writers friend 15% cotton fiber trade mark registered.*

Slim lifted the paper out of the box, looked under it, riffled a thumbful of the sheets at the top and the same from the bottom, shook his head, replaced the paper, closed the box, put it back into the bag and restored everything precisely as he had found it. He paused again in the middle of the room, turning slowly once, but there was simply nothing else to look at. He let himself out, locked the door, and went silently back to his room.

He sat down on the edge of his bed and at last protested, "Nobody *lives* like that!"

His room was on the fourth and topmost floor of the old house. Anyone else would have called it the worst room in the place. It was small, dark, shabby and remote and it suited him beautifully.

Its door had a transom, the glass of which had many times been painted over. By standing on the foot of his bed, Slim could apply one eye to the peephole he had scratched in the paint and look straight down the stairs to the third-floor landing. On this landing, hanging to the stub of one of the ancient gas jets, was a cloudy mirror surmounted by a dust-mantled gilt eagle and surrounded by a great many rococo carved flowers. By careful propping with folded cigarette wrappers, innumerable tests and a great deal of silent mileage up and down the stairs, Slim had arranged the exact tilt necessary in the mirror so that it covered the second floor landing as well. And just as a radar operator learns to translate glowing pips and masses into aircraft and weather, so Slim became expert at the interpretation of the fogged and distant image it afforded him. Thus he had the comings and goings of half the tenants under surveillance without having to leave his room.

It was in this mirror, at twelve minutes past six, that he saw Celia Sarton next, and as he watched her climb the stairs, his eyes glowed.

The anonymity was gone. She came up the stairs two at a time, with a gait like bounding. She reached the landing and whirled into her corridor and was gone, and while a part of Slim's mind listened for the way she opened the door (hurriedly, rattling the key against the lock-plate, banging the door open, slamming it shut), another part studied a mental photograph of her face.

What raised its veil of the statistical ordinary was its set purpose. Here were eyes only superficially interested in cars, curbs, stairs, doors. It was as if she had projected every important part of herself into that empty room of hers and waited there impatiently for her body to catch up. There was something in the room, or something she had to do there, which she could not, would not, wait for. One goes this way to a beloved after a long parting, or to a deathbed in the last, precipitous moments. This was not the arrival of one who wants, but of one who needs.

Slim buttoned his shirt, eased his door open and sidled through it. He poised a moment on his landing like a great moose sensing the air before descending to a waterhole, and then moved downstairs.

Celia Sarton's only neighbor in the north corridor—the spinster with the bottles—was settled for the evening; she was of very regular habits and Slim knew them well.

Completely confident that he would not be seen, he drifted to the girl's door and paused.

She was there, all right. He could see the light around the edge of the ill-fitting door, could sense that difference between an occupied room and an empty one, which exists however silent the occupant might be. And this one *was* silent. Whatever it was that had driven her into the room with such headlong urgency, whatever it was she was doing (*had* to do) was being done with no sound or motion that he could detect.

For a long time—six minutes, seven—Slim hung there, open-throated to conceal the sound of his breath. At last, shaking his head, he withdrew, climbed the stairs, let himself into his own room and lay down on the bed, frowning.

He could only wait. Yet he *could* wait. No one does any single thing for very long. Especially a thing not involving movement. In an hour, in two—

It was five. At half-past eleven, some faint sound from the floor below brought Slim, half-dozing, twisting up from the bed and to his high peephole in the transom. He saw the Sarton girl come out of the corridor slowly, and stop, and look around at nothing in particular, like someone confined too long in a ship's cabin who has emerged on deck, not so much for the lungs' sake, but for the eyes'. And when she went down the stairs, it was easily and without hurry, as if (again) the important part of her was in the room. But the something was finished with for now and what was ahead of her wasn't important and could wait.

Standing with his hand on his own doorknob, Slim decided that he, too, could wait. The temptation to go straight to her room was, of course, large, but caution also loomed. What he had tentatively established as her habit patterns did not include midnight exits. He could not know when she might come back and it would be foolish indeed to jeopardize his hobby—not only where it included her, but all of it—by being caught. He sighed, mixing resignation with anticipatory pleasure, and went to bed.

Less than fifteen minutes later, he congratulated himself

with a sleepy smile as he heard her slow footsteps mount the stairs below. He slept.

There was nothing in the closet, there was nothing in the ashtray, there was nothing in the medicine chest nor under the dresser scarf. The bed was made, the dresser drawers were empty, and under the bed was the cheap gladstone. In it was a box containing a thousand sheets of typing paper surrounded by a glossy blue band. Without disturbing this, Slim riffled the sheets, once at the top, once at the bottom. He grunted, shook his head and then proceeded, automatically but meticulously, to put everything back as he had found it.

"Whatever it is this girl does at night," he said glumly, "it leaves tracks like it makes noise."

He left.

The rest of the day was unusually busy for Slim. In the morning he had a doctor's appointment, and in the afternoon he spent hours with a company lawyer who seemed determined to (a) deny the existence of any head injury and (b) prove to Slim and the world that the injury must have occurred years ago. He got absolutely nowhere. If Slim had another characteristic as consuming and compulsive as his curiosity, it was his shyness; these two could stand on one another's shoulders, though, and still look upward at Slim's stubbornness. It served its purpose. It took hours, however, and it was after seven when he got home.

He paused at the third-floor landing and glanced down the corridor. Celia Sarton's room was occupied and silent. If she emerged around midnight, exhausted and relieved, then he would know she had again raced up the stairs to her urgent, motionless task, whatever it was . . . and here he checked himself. He had long ago learned the uselessness of cluttering up his busy head with conjectures. A thousand things might happen; in each case, only one would. He would wait, then, and could.

And again, some hours later, he saw her come out of her corridor. She looked about, but he knew she saw very little; her face was withdrawn and her eyes wide and unguarded. Then, instead of going out, she went back into her room.

He slipped downstairs half an hour later and listened at her door, and smiled. She was washing her lingerie at the handbasin. It was a small thing to learn, but he felt he was making progress. It did not explain why she lived as she did, but indicated how she could manage without so much as a spare handkerchief.

Oh, well, maybe in the morning.

In the morning, there was no maybe. He found it, he found it, though he could not know what it was he'd found. He laughed at first, not in triumph but wryly, calling himself a clown. Then he squatted on his heels in the middle of the floor (he would not sit on the bed, for fear of leaving wrinkles of his own on those Mrs. Koyper supplied) and carefully lifted the box of paper out of the suitcase and put it on the floor in front of him.

Up to now, he had contented himself with a quick riffle of the blank paper, a little at the top, a little at the bottom. He had done just this again, without removing the box from the suitcase, but only taking the top off and tilting up the banded ream of *Nonpareil-the-writers-friend*. And almost in spite of itself, his quick eye had caught the briefest flash of pale blue.

Gently, he removed the band, sliding it off the pack of paper, being careful not to slit the glossy finish. Now he could freely riffle the pages, and when he did, he discovered that all of them except a hundred or so, top and bottom, had the same rectangular cut-out, leaving only a narrow margin all the way around. In the hollow space thus formed, something was packed.

He could not tell what the something was, except that it was pale tan, with a tinge of pink, and felt like smooth untextured leather. There was a lot of it, neatly folded so that it exactly fitted the hole in the ream of paper.

He puzzled over it for some minutes without touching it again, and then, scrubbing his fingertips against his shirt until he felt that they were quite free of moisture and grease, he gently worked loose the top corner of the substance and unfolded a layer. All he found was more of the same.

He folded it down flat again to be sure he could, and then brought more of it out. He soon realized that the material was of an irregular shape and almost certainly of one piece, so that folding it into a tight rectangle required care and great skill. Therefore he proceeded very slowly, stopping every now and then to fold it up again, and it took him more than an hour to get enough of it out so that he could identify it.

Identify? It was completely unlike anything he had ever seen before.

It was a human skin, done in some substance very like the real thing. The first fold, the one which had been revealed at first, was an area of the back, which was why it showed no features. One might liken it to a balloon, except that a deflated balloon is smaller in every dimension than an inflated one. As far as Slim could judge, this was life-sized—a little over five feet long and proportioned accordingly. The hair was peculiar, looking exactly like the real thing until flexed, and then revealing itself to be one piece.

It had Celia Sarton's face.

Slim closed his eyes and opened them, and found that it was still true. He held his breath and put forth a careful, steady forefinger and gently pressed the left eyelid upward. There was an eye under it, all right, light blue and seemingly moist, but flat.

Slim released the breath, closed the eye and sat back on his heels. His feet were beginning to tingle from his having knelt on the floor for so long.

He looked all around the room once, to clear his head of strangeness, and then began to fold the thing up again. It took a while, but when he was finished, he knew he had it right. He replaced the typewriter paper in the box and the box in the bag, put the bag away and at last stood in the middle of the room in the suspension which overcame him when he was deep in thought.

After a moment of this, he began to inspect the ceiling. It was made of stamped tin, like those of many old-fashioned houses. It was grimy and flaked and stained; here and there, rust showed through, and in one or two places, edges of the tin sheets had sagged. Slim nodded to himself in profound satisfaction, listened for a while at the door, let himself out, locked it and went upstairs.

He stood in his own corridor for a minute, checking the position of doors, the hall window, and his accurate orientation of the same things on the floor below. Then he went into his own room.

His room, though smaller than most, was one of the

few in the house which was blessed with a real closet instead of a rickety off-the-floor wardrobe. He went into it and knelt, and grunted in satisfaction when he found how loose the ancient, unpainted floorboards were. By removing the side baseboard, he found it possible to get to the air-space between the fourth floor and the third-floor ceiling.

He took out boards until he had an opening perhaps fourteen inches wide, and then, working in almost total silence, he began cleaning away dirt and old plaster. He did this meticulously, because when he finally pierced the tin sheeting, he wanted not one grain of dirt to fall into the room below. He took his time and it was late in the afternoon when he was satisfied with his preparations and began, with his knife, on the tin.

It was thinner and softer than he had dared to hope; he almost overcut on the first try. Carefully he squeezed the sharp steel into the little slot he had cut, lengthening it. When it was somewhat less than an inch long, he withdrew all but the point of the knife and twisted it slightly, moved it a sixteenth of an inch and twisted again, repeating this all down the cut until he had widened it enough for his purposes.

He checked the time, then returned to Celia Sarton's room for just long enough to check the appearance of his work from that side. He was very pleased with it. The little cut had come through a foot away from the wall over the bed and was a mere pencil line lost in the baroque design with which the tin was stamped and the dirt and rust that marred it. He returned to his room and sat down to wait.

He heard the old house coming to its evening surge of life, a voice here, a door there, footsteps on the stairs. He ignored them all as he sat on the edge of his bed, hands folded between his knees, eyes half closed, immobile like a machine fueled, oiled, tuned and ready, lacking only the right touch on the right control. And like that touch, the faint sound of Celia Sarton's footsteps moved him.

To use his new peephole, he had to lie on the floor half in and half out of the closet, with his head in the hole, actually below floor level. With this, he was perfectly content, any amount of discomfort being well worth his trouble—an attitude he shared with many another ardent hobbyist, mountain-climber or speleologist, duck-hunter or bird-watcher.

When she turned on the light, he could see her splendidly, as well as most of the floor, the lower third of the door and part of the washbasin in the bathroom.

She had come in hurriedly, with that same agonized haste he had observed before. At the same second she turned on the light, she had apparently flung her handbag toward the bed; it was in mid-air as the light appeared. She did not even glance its way, but hastily fumbled the old gladstone from under the bed, opened it, removed the box, opened it, took out the paper, slipped off the blue band and removed the blank sheets of paper which covered the hollowed-out ream.

She scooped out the thing hidden there, shaking it once like a grocery clerk with a folded paper sack, so that the long limp thing straightened itself out. She arranged it carefully on the worn linoleum of the floor, arms down at the side, legs slightly apart, face up, neck straight. Then she lay down on the floor, too, head-to-head with the deflated thing. She reached up over her head, took hold of the collapsed image of herself about the region of the ears, and for a moment did some sort of manipulation of it against the top of her own head.

Slim heard faintly a sharp, chitinous click, like the sound one makes by snapping the edge of a thumbnail against the edge of a fingernail.

Her hands slipped to the cheeks of the figure and she pulled at the empty head as if testing a connection. The head seemed now to have adhered to hers.

Then she assumed the same pose she had arranged for this other, letting her hands fall wearily to her sides on the floor, closing her eyes.

For a long while, nothing seemed to be happening, except for the odd way she was breathing, very deeply but very slowly, like the slow-motion picture of someone panting, gasping for breath after a long hard run. After perhaps ten minutes of this, the breathing became shallower and even slower, until, at the end of a half hour, he could detect none at all.

Slim lay there immobile for more than an hour, until his body shrieked protest and his head ached from eyestrain. He hated to move, but move he must. Silently he backed out of the closet, stood up and stretched. It was a great luxury and he deeply enjoyed it. He felt moved to think over what he had just seen, but clearly and consciously decided not to—not yet, anyway.

When he was unkinked, again, he crept back into the closet, put his head in the hole and his eye to the slot.

Nothing had changed. She still lay quiet, utterly relaxed, so much so that her hands had turned palm upward.

Slim watched and he watched. Just as he was about to conclude that this was the way the girl spent her entire nights and that there would be nothing more to see, he saw a slight and sudden contraction about the region of her solar plexus, and then another. For a time, there was nothing more, and then the empty thing attached to the top of her head began to fill.

And Celia Sarton began to empty.

Slim stopped breathing until it hurt and watched in total astonishment.

Once it had started, the process progressed swiftly. It was as if something passed from the clothed body of the girl to this naked empty thing. The something, whatever it might be, had to be fluid, for nothing but a fluid would fill a flexible container in just this way, or make a flexible container slowly and evenly flatten out like this. Slim could see the fingers, which had been folded flat against the palms, inflate and move until they took on the normal relaxed curl of a normal hand. The elbows shifted a little to lie more normally against the body. And yes, it was a body now.

The other one was not a body any more. It lay foolishly limp in its garments, its sleeping face slightly distorted by its flattening. The fingers fell against the palms by their own limp weight. The shoes thumped quietly on their sides, heels together, toes pointing in opposite directions.

The exchange was done in less than ten minutes and then the new filled body moved.

It flexed its hands tentatively, drew up it knees and stretched its legs out again, arched its back against the floor. Its eyes flickered open. It put up its arms and made some deft manipulation at the top of its head. Slim heard another version of the soft hard click and the now-empty head fell flat to the floor.

The new Celia Sarton sat up and sighed and rubbed her hands lightly over her body, as if restoring circulation and sensation to a chilled skin. She stretched as comfortably and luxuriously as Slim had a few minutes earlier. She looked rested and refreshed.

At the top of her head, Slim caught a glimpse of a slit through which a wet whiteness showed, but it seemed to be closing. In a brief time, nothing showed there but a small valley in the hair, like a normal parting.

She sighed again and got up. She took the clothed thing on the floor by the neck, raised it and shook it twice to make the clothes fall away. She tossed it to the bed and carefully picked up the clothes and deployed them about the room, the undergarments in the washbasin, the dress and slip on a hanger in the wardrobe.

Moving leisurely but with purpose, she went into the bathroom and, except from her shins down, out of Slim's range of vision. There he heard the same faint domestic sounds he had once detected outside the door, as she washed her underclothes. She emerged in due course, went to the wardrobe for some wire hangers and took them into the bathroom. Back she came with the underwear folded on the hangers, which she hooked to the top of the open wardrobe door. Then she took the deflated integument which lay crumpled on the bed, shook it again, rolled it up into a ball and took it into the bathroom.

Slim heard more water-running and sudsing noises, and, by ear, followed the operation through a soaping and two rinses. Then she came out again, shaking out the object, which had apparently just been wrung, pulled it through a wooden clothes-hanger, arranged it creaselessly depending from the crossbar of the hanger with the bar about at its waistline, and hung it with the others on the wardrobe door.

Then she lay down on the bed, not to sleep or to read or even to rest—she seemed very rested—but merely to wait until it was time to do something else.

By now, Slim's bones were complaining again, so he wormed noiselessly backward out of his lookout point, got into his shoes and a jacket, and went out to get something to eat. When he came home an hour later and looked, her light was out and he could see nothing. He spread his overcoat carefully over the hole in the closet so no stray light from his room would appear in the little slot in the ceiling, closed the door, read a comic book for a while, and went to bed.

The next day, he followed her. What strange occupation she might have, what weird vampiric duties she might disclose, he did not speculate on. He was doggedly determined to gather information first and think later.

What he found out about her daytime activities was, if anything, more surprising than any wild surmise. She was a clerk in a small five-and-ten on the East Side. She ate in the store's lunch bar at lunchtime—a green salad and a surprising amount of milk—and in the evening she stopped at a hot-dog stand and drank a small container of milk, though she ate nothing.

Her steps were slowed by then and she moved wearily, speeding up only when she was close to the rooming house, and then apparently all but overcome with eagerness to get home and . . . into something more comfortable. She was watched in this process, and Slim, had he disbelieved his own eyes the first time, must believe them now.

So it went for a week, three days of which Slim spent in shadowing her, every evening in watching her make her strange toilet. Every twenty-four hours, she changed bodies, carefully washing, drying, folding and putting away the one she was not using.

Twice during the week, she went out for what was apparently a constitutional and nothing more—a half-hour around midnight, when she would stand on the walk in front of the rooming house, or wander around the block.

At work, she was silent but not unnaturally so; she spoke, when spoken to, in a small, unmusical voice. She seemed to have no friends; she maintained her aloofness by being uninteresting and by seeking no one out and by needing no one. She evinced no outside interests, never going to the movies or to the park. She had no dates, not even with girls. Slim thought she did not sleep, but lay quietly in the dark waiting for it to be time to get up and go to work.

And when he came to think about it, as ultimately he did, it occurred to Slim that within the anthill in which we all live and have our being, enough privacy can be exacted to allow for all sorts of strangeness in the members of society, providing the strangeness is not permitted to show. If it is a man's pleasure to sleep upsidedown like a bat, and if he so arranges his life that no one ever sees him sleeping, or his sleeping-place, why, batlike he may sleep all the days of his life.

One need not, by these rules, even *be* a human being. Not if the mimicry is good enough. It is a measure of Slim's odd personality to report that Celia Sarton's ways did not frighten him. He was, if anything, less disturbed by her now than he'd been before he had begun to spy on her. He knew what she did in her room and how she lived. Before, he had not known. Now he did. This made him much happier.

He was, however, still curious.

His curiosity would never drive him to do what another man might—to speak to her on the stairs or on the street, get to know her and more about her. He was too shy for that. Nor was he moved to report to anyone the odd practice he watched each evening. It wasn't his business to report. She was doing no harm as far as he could see. In his cosmos, everybody had a right to live and make a buck if they could.

Yet his curiosity, its immediacy taken care of, did undergo a change. It was not in him to wonder what sort of being this was and whether its ancestors had grown up among human beings, living with them in caves and in tents, developing and evolving along with *homo sap* until it could assume the uniform of the smallest and most invisible of wageworkers. He would never reach the conclusion that in the fight for survival, a species might discover that a most excellent characteristic for survival among human beings might be not to fight them but to join them.

No, Slim's curiosity was far simpler, more basic and less informed than any of these conjectures. He simply changed the field of his wonderment from *what* to *what if?*

So it was that on the eighth day of his survey, a Tuesday, he went again to her room, got the bag, opened it, removed the box, opened it, removed the ream of paper, slid the blue band off, removed the covering sheets, took out the second Celia Sarton, put her on the bed and then replaced paper, blue band, box-cover, box, and bag just as he had found them. He put the folded thing under his shirt and went out, carefully locking the door behind him in his special way, and went upstairs to his room. He put his prize under the four clean shirts in his bottom drawer and sat down to await Celia Sarton's homecoming.

She was a little late that night—twenty minutes, perhaps. The delay seemed to have increased both her fatigue and her eagerness; she burst in feverishly, moved with the rapidity of near-panic. She looked drawn and pale and her hands shook. She fumbled the bag from under the bed, snatched out the box and opened it, contrary to her usual measured movements, by inverting it over the bed and dumping out its contents.

When she saw nothing there but sheets of paper, some with a wide rectangle cut from them and some without, she froze. She crouched over that bed without moving for an interminable two minutes. Then she straightened up slowly and glanced about the room. Once she fumbled through the paper, but resignedly, without hope. She made one sound, a high, sad whimper, and, from that moment on, was silent.

She went to the window slowly, her feet dragging, her shoulders slumped. For a long time, she stood looking out at the city, its growing darkness, its growing colonies of lights, each a symbol of life and life's usages. Then she drew down the blind and went back to the bed.

She stacked the papers there with loose uncaring fingers and put the heap of them on the dresser. She took off her shoes and placed them neatly side by side on the floor by the bed. She lay down in the same utterly relaxed pose she affected when she made her change, hands down and open, legs a little apart.

Her face looked like a death-mask, its tissues sunken and sagging. It was flushed and sick-looking. There was a little of the deep regular breathing, but only a little. There was a bit of the fluttering contractions at the midriff, but only a bit. Then—nothing.

Slim backed away from the peephole and sat up. He felt very bad about this. He had been only curious; he hadn't wanted her to get sick, to die. For he was sure she had died. How could he know what sort of sleep-surrogate an organism like this might require, or what might be the results of a delay in changing? What could he know of the chemistry of such a being? He had thought vaguely of slipping down the next day while she was out and returning her property. Just to see. Just to know *what if*. Just out of curiosity.

Should he call a doctor?

She hadn't. She hadn't even tried, though she must have known much better than he did how serious her predicament was. (Yet if a species depended for its existence on secrecy, it would be species-survival to let an individual die undetected.) Well, maybe not calling a doctor meant that she'd be all right, after all. Doctors would have a lot of silly questions to ask. She might even tell the doctor about her other skin, and if Slim was the one who had fetched the doctor, Slim might be questioned about that.

Slim didn't want to get involved with anything. He just wanted to know things.

He thought, "I'll take another look."

He crawled back into the closet and put his head in the hole. Celia Sarton, he knew instantly, would not survive this. Her face was swollen, her eyes protruded, and her purpled tongue lolled far—too far—from the corner of her mouth. Even as he watched, her face darkened still more and the skin of it crinkled until it looked like carbon paper which has been balled up tight and then smoothed out.

The very beginnings of an impulse to snatch the thing she needed out of his shirt drawer and rush it down to her died within him, for he saw a wisp of smoke emerge from her nostrils and then—

Slim cried out, snatched his head from the hole, bumping it cruelly, and clapped his hands over his eyes. Put the biggest size flash-bulb an inch from your nose, and fire it, and you might get a flare approaching the one he got through his little slot in the tin ceiling.

He sat grunting in pain and watching, on the insides of his eyelids, migrations of flaming worms. At last they faded and he tentatively opened his eyes. They hurt and the after-image of the slot hung before him, but at least he could see.

Feet pounded on the stairs. He smelled smoke and a burned, oily unpleasant something which he could not identify. Someone shouted. Someone hammered on a door. Then someone screamed and screamed.

It was in the papers next day. Mysterious, the story said. Charles Fort, in *Lo!*, had reported many such cases and there had been others since—people burned to a crisp by a fierce heat which had nevertheless not destroyed clothes or bedding, while leaving nothing for autopsy. This was, said the paper, either an unknown kind of heat or heat of such intensity and such brevity that it would do such a thing. No known relatives, it said. Police mystified—no clues or suspects.

Slim didn't say anything to anybody. He wasn't curious about the matter any more. He closed up the hole in the closet that same night, and next day, after he read the story, he used the newspaper to wrap up the thing in his shirt drawer. It smelled pretty bad and, even that early, was too far gone to be unfolded. He dropped it into a garbage can on the way to the lawyer's office on Wednesday.

They settled his lawsuit that afternoon and he moved.

The Pod
in the Barrier

A lousy mission. Of course, it was a volunteer (i.e., suicide) mission, and for that you take what comes. They may wine you and dine you and honor you and your tribe for three generations coming and going, in the days before you start. But once you're on your way, you can't expect it to be a pleasure. Everything about suicide is death, not just the final part.

Potter pinched his nostrils and didn't know he was doing it, even while he was looking you straight in the eye, talking to you at the time. Try shipping out with that. That's what bothered me the most, anyway.

Most of the others seemed to be bugged by Donato. He had a psychosomatic cough that passed all the preflight medics for the simple reason that he had never had such a thing before, probably because he had never gone out to die before. Me, I guess I have soaked up enough of that "profound compassion" of the Luanae to defend me against that kind of annoyance. But Potter the Pincher now—that got to me, I admit it.

Little Donato was always trying to please. Some people are annoying because once in a while they just don't go out of their way to make things a little happier for anyone else. Donato hit the other extreme, always making way, never disagreeing, forever finding some way to help or get a cushion or move back or bring or say or not-say whatever anyone else might want, until you wanted to scuttle the ship just so it would take him with the lot of you.

The main trouble was, he was so helpful he never gave you anything to complain about. Time after time, I would see one or the other of the crew suddenly wheel on him out of a dead silence and roar at him to get the hell out.

"Why, sure, friend," Donato would always say, and smile, and get the hell out, leaving whoever it was beating himself on the temples.

Potter was a specialist in field mechanics and Donato was a top ballistics man. England was an ugly man with big ears and wet eyes who kept to himself pretty much, only he ate loud. He was an expert in missile control. And I'm Palmer; I heard there was a man in Alpha Sigma IV once who knew more about trans-spatial stress than I do, but I don't believe it.

The four of us had four different ideas for breaking the Luanae Barrier and that's what we were on our way to do. All four ideas were pretty far-fetched and the odds were much in favor of the Barrier's getting us, but it had to be done. After everything reasonable has been tried on something that must be done but can't be done, you have to start calling in the crackpots. I had to bring along my perfectly valid theories with the three crackpots because it was the only way they would ever get tried.

And that was the expedition personnel. The other were just operations. A skipper, Capt. Steev, strictly ferryboat, who knew everything he had to know about running the ship and getting her there, and didn't know, didn't care, wouldn't talk about anything else. Some of the others griped about the kind of skipper we had, but not me. He had to be expendable and he was. He had to know his job and he did. So?

The utility monkey was funny for about half an hour of anybody's time, and forever after that just unpleasant to have around. He was sort of misshapen, with a head much too big for his body and a left leg with too much bounce in it. It's been so many hundreds of years, I guess, since anyone had anything drastic wrong physically that nobody can get used to it any more. You know how to be polite about it when you do encounter it, and back home you know how to forget you saw it pretty thoroughly, but on a spacecan you never get the chance.

Personally, I think we should have shipped without a utility man. I don't know if I feel so strongly about it that I'd have done the dirty work on the ship myself, but maybe one of the others would. I don't care how much humanity progresses, there is always a little room somewhere for the unskilled hand, lifting and mopping and cleaning out the sewer lines when something gets stuck. This monkey we had went by the name of Nils Blum, and nobody paid much attention to him.

And then we had the unemployed CG. Did you ever hear of an unemployed crew's girl—on a ship? I don't mean kicking around the spaceports waiting to ship out, unemployed that way. I mean right there aboard, she had nothing to do.

CGs as a whole are a dowdy bunch. There's no point in putting cute clothes, cute tricks and heady perfume aboard a spacecan. You don't need to stimulate anything; that takes care of itself as time goes by. They keep themselves clean and wait around till they're needed. They're a thick-skinned, slow-witted lot because there's no sense in sensitivity in their line. It just makes trouble.

This Virginia we shipped, she came from the bottom of the underside of the sump. She was everything that distinguishes a CG from a real Earthside female woman. She had a wide face that was closed and bland as a bank-vault door on the Sabbath, and a build that was neither this nor that but sort of statistically there. With a normal personality, or none at all, she might have had a job to do, and would have done it. But with the personality she had . . .

Well, at first you just didn't like her, and after a while you couldn't abide her, and finally you got the feeling about her that she was a lower animal, that you couldn't stand what the others might think of you if you went near her. There was a lot of difference of opinion aboard on a lot of subjects, but not on that one.

So that's what we had, believe it or not, an unemployed CG.

I read someplace about an Arctic explorer back in the days where the poles of Old Earth were covered with ice. He used to bring along the ugliest woman he could find to cook. Her other function was to inform him when he'd been away from civilization too long, which she did by beginning to look good to him. Well, maybe, given time enough, we'd have found something for this Virginia to do. But given that much time, we'd all be dead.

Oh, she was a great help aboard, Virginia was.

That personality. I thought a lot about that personality of hers, just because on a long haul you have time to think a lot about everything . . . I knew a kid in school who had a face so insulting, so all-fired arrogant when it was relaxed that the teachers used to throw him out of the class just for sitting there. At least until they learned it was only physical and had him remodeled. Well, maybe Virginia's personality was something like that. Maybe she couldn't help it.

She had a way of carrying a cloud of what Potter once called "retroactive doubt." When she was anywhere near you, you breathed it. You'd say something and she would repeat it, and by the way she did it—I can't describe it at all, but I'm telling you the truth—by the way she did it, she made whatever you'd said into a falsehood. Sometimes it suddenly sounded like a lie and sometimes like a mistake and sometimes like something you could be expected to believe because you were ignorant. I mean just repeating your own words.

You'd say, "Back home, I've got a silver-headed walking stick," and she'd say, "Yeah, you've got a silver-headed walking stick," in that dull flat drone of hers, and, by damn, you'd find yourself arguing with her that you *did* have one. I mean fighting, defending yourself, the way you only can when you doubt something yourself. Then she'd go away and you'd sit and stew about the walking stick, wondering where it was you last saw it, wondering if you actually did have it any more, if the head of it was real silver.

It didn't have to be something that was important at all; she could make you feel that way. When it *was* important . . . shipmate, better not mention it around her. I think you could tell her your name and she'd make you doubt it.

As a matter of fact, now I think of it, she did just that to me, the day I first saw her (which is traditionally the day after upship). I walked up to her in the messhall and said, "My name's Palmer," and she looked at me without blinking and said flatly, "Your name's Palmer," and made me say, before I could stop myself, "No—really it is," and then skulk off feeling damn strange.

We'd taken off with a null-grav tug and slipped into second-order matrix within six hours—all very fast and painless, thanks to the Luanae. Both devices were theirs, and so was the ship's power plant, and so was the sub-etheric communication we could get loud and clear for almost four full days after upship. Do you know how far that would be in miles? Here, figure it out—four days is enough to take you halfway to Sirius, and that's a powerful long reach for a communicator phasing out of normal space and finding your receiver.

I recall especially that fourth day's bulletins, because we all gathered around to soak them up and chew them thoroughly. We knew that we'd hear nothing else from Earth Worlds from there on for the six ship-weeks it took us to get out to the Luanae Barrier, way out on the other side of the Coalsack.

We cheered the whiffleball scores and the chess results and laughed too loud at the human-interest bit about the kid who brought the Nova Mars stinkdog into school; and then there was the last real news we heard, that Chicago had been frozen from Northern Ontario Parish clear south to the Joplin city limits, back on Old Earth.

Everybody tsk-tsked.

"Well," said Potter, looking at his finger, "I guess there's no other way."

"But people always get killed in a freeze," said big-eared England.

"More people get killed in a riot," I remember saying.

About then, the signal faded, very abruptly, as it does when you get out of range in sub-space, and we all sat around worrying a bit.

It was funny, that news of all news being the last we heard. It was like a nudge, a send-off. A reminder.

Old Earth wasn't the only place where there were riots, not by a sight. Of eighteen planets in the two so-called Earth Galaxies, only Ragnarok and Luna-Luna were not bulging at the seams, and they'd be as bad as the others in a generation. By and large, people behaved themselves . . . but there were so *many* of them! The law of averages dictated that, in that number, there had to be so many trouble makers, there were bound to be so many riots—and there had to be more trouble-makers and riots all the time.

Unless we broke the Luanae Barrier.

We owe the Luanae a lot. As I said before, a good deal of our most advanced technology is built on transmissions from the Luanae. A very old people, ancient before old Sol the First was a sun. Wise and compassionate. That was the real cliché: the compassionate Luanae. True enough, though.

No one had ever seen them, of course—the Barrier took care of that. No one understood the exact method of their

A TOUCH OF STRANGE

transmissions, though they tried their best to explain. You'd get in range and then there it was, they were talking to you, inside your head. What they said was true—that you could bank on, swear by, hang your hat or your life on.

Some things have to be proved. But not anything the Luanae said. You might not believe it if you heard about something they said, from me, say. But go hear it from them —you'll *know* it's so. Never in the three hundred years of contact had anything they said turned out to be anything but exactly—really exactly—so.

They say that at first humanity took it with a dose of salts —we are a suspicious species. But although the Luanae couldn't give us the specs of a machine like theirs—they insisted that their thought transmitter was only a machine —they were able to describe an odd little recorder that would play back and "sound" like the original. When a few million of those had been made and distributed, there wasn't any suspicion any more. It just blew away.

But population-pressure rioting isn't as easy to dispose of as inbred suspicion. Put enough people in a limited area and you'll have trouble. Put too much in the same area and —look out. Now we had sixteen worlds with too much humanity, and two more with almost enough to start trouble. And all we could do was watch and feel, and freeze whole sections when the thing boiled over.

After each freeze, the United Planet men would spread through the countryside, picking up the mangled corpses from ground-cars and aircraft which had smashed up when everyone blacked out, and making the millions of others comfortable where they lay. They'd wake up in due course, with no sense of time passed, but the dead would have been long buried and the trouble-makers located and treated, and the immediate causes of the riot, whatever they might be (it didn't take much) adjudicated and put right.

It was generally suspected that the UP boys declared riot and froze sections on somewhat less excuse than they really needed, but most people didn't object. At least it kept a few million people, each time, from breeding any more for six to eight months. But nobody denied that this was pure stopgap.

As to halting reproduction altogether for a while, the suggestion came up monotonously in the Council sessions and was as monotonously knocked down. Enforced sterility is counter to the most basic civil rights, and the Earth Worlds would die before they would relinquish any basic right.

They were dying, too.

And there, hanging just out of reach, were the Luanae Earths—eight fine Earth-type planets circling three suns in Galaxy Three. Eight beautiful worlds, ready and waiting; we wanted them and the Luanae wanted us to have them. And all we could do was watch them swing by and feel wistful, because of the Barrier.

The Luanae are not terrestrial. As far as can be understood, they have a boron metabolism and compete in no way with us hydrocarbon types. They need nothing from us and wouldn't take it if they did need it.

When they say they have those worlds to give us, when they say the worlds are suitable, and they say for sure that those are the only planets left in this entire quadrant of the Universe—why, you can bet on it. (They're the ones who found Luna-Luna and Ragnarok for us, when the Earth Worlds had despaired of ever finding another terrestrial planet.) We also have their assurance that in the other quadrants are literally thousands of terrestrial planets; but we will need a totally new technology to reach them, and that will take us maybe four centuries to acquire, even with their help.

Well, the Earth World wouldn't last four centuries without the Luanae planets. With them, though—with them, it might be done. All we had to do was reach them. All we had to do was penetrate the Barrier.

The Barrier was a sphere in space—not a thing, exactly, just a place which could be represented on a cosmimap as a sphere. It was a fair-sized sphere; it englobed a third of the Luanae Galaxy, including, of course, the three little Luanae home-planets and the eight lovely, unreachable Luanae Earths.

All it did, that Barrier, was to draw a line. Anything outside of it was left strictly alone. Anything penetrating it was instantly tracked, hunted and smashed by Luanae missiles. And anything that got cute enough to duck inside and out again was destroyed by the Barrier itself, which had the simple ability of reversing the terrene-sign of a random third of the atoms in any matter it touched.

You can imagine what happened to anything from a micrometeorite to a sun that got exposed to it. Shot through and through with contra-terrene matter. Disappeared in a single ferocious flash.

The Luanae Galaxy was discovered three hundred years ago by a creaky old Earth survey ship powered by Teller-formula atomics and a primitive subspace drive which barely quadrupled effective light-velocity.

The first thing the ship—it was called the *Luanae*, after its skipper's wife and daughter, both of whom were named Luana—the first thing they saw was the Luanae Galaxy, a long narrow elliptical one with a dark band, the perfect arc of a circle, a third of the way down the long axis. It looked artificial, so they hobbled over there to investigate.

It was artificial, all right. It was the Barrier, or, rather, the segment of space through which the Barrier had removed all impinging matter. And when they got within a dozen light-years of it, they were in range of the beings who came to be known by the same name as the ship and the galaxy—the Luanae.

They said *Stop*.

They said it simultaneously inside the heads of everyone aboard. They said it with that encasement of utter truth and total believability. They said it (they told us later) with an automatic machine set up eons ago, to warn away any intelligent life from their Barrier. But when the ship *Luanae* responded (by stopping), it wasn't any machine that spoke next. The strange creatures set up such a welcome, such a warm, admiring, congratulatory flood of thought that they say all hands looked at each other in amazement and started to weep.

And along with the welcome—a warning. *Don't come any closer*.

They threw a few million cubic meters of rubble up from the inside of the Barrier and let the astonished crew watch the near margins of the invisible Barrier light up with a hellish three-hour show of destruction. They urged experiment, suggesting that the survey ship throw something at the Barrier.

The ship did. Whatever matter penetrated was overtaken and destroyed by what appeared to be tiny hunting missiles. Whatever matter was angled through the Barrier's skin, so that it would cut a chord and emerge again, splashed into flame as it left. The men on the ship knew, down to the marrow, that they were welcome—thirstily, ardently welcome.

And they knew that they were warned.

The ship hung outside the Barrier for over a year, setting down what turned out to be the greatest treasure ever brought home by a vessel since time began. Knowledge—the knowledge that put cold-fusion power plants on all the Earth planets, in all the factories. New designs. New principles of mathematics and spatial mechanics. New methods, new ideas, much of it material Earth possibly might have discovered for itself in a thousand years, most of it material we never could have found unaided.

And every bit of it was valid. Every bit of it held out the promise of more, once we had assimilated this incredible cargo.

When the survey ship Luanae reached the Earth Worlds, they say that the suspicion was thicker than anyone alive today could readily understand. They say they were going to court-martial the skipper for wasting all that time out there making up stories. And they say there was a powerful movement to suppress everything they brought back, out of fear that the new technology might in some way be a Trojan horse.

But sheer cussed human curiosity got the better of all that and, though they started slowly, it wasn't too long before the Luanae devices and principles proved themselves out—spectacularly.

And in a few years, humanity was back again. In force. The main idea was to breach the Barrier—peaceably if possible, but breach it. Most of the ships, most of the men, did not make the attempt, so great was the impact of the Luanae truth and fellow feeling.

Some did try, though, ramming, bombing, bringing up hypermagnetic generator ships to try warping the intangible structure of the Barrier. All failed; those who touched it died. Whenever that happened, there was a great soundless cry of mourning from the Luanae, but the Barrier remained.

When the survey ship discovered them, the Luanae had explained simply and clearly why the Barrier was there and why it stayed. It seemed too simple a story, and buried as it was in such a mass of other data, it was overlooked or disbelieved. Mind you, that was before the Luanae had been recorded, before the human millions could "hear" for themselves what a transmission from them was really like. Probably the Luanae realized this; at any rate, the story of the

Barrier was the first Luanae recording to be widely distributed and its impact was huge.

Such a simple story . . . a people in some ways like humanity, perhaps a little swifter technologically, perhaps in some ways less demanding . . . well, they lived a good deal longer, took a good deal less from the land to keep themselves alive.

They had some things to be proud of—an art that can only be imagined outside the Barrier, and music of a kind. They did "send" some of their literature, as you know . . . ah.

Then they had a number of things to be ashamed of. Some wars, big ones. Three times they all but destroyed themselves, and climbed back up again. Then there was a long flowering, which seemed like something good, something fine. They developed a compassion, a philosophy of respect for the living and harmony with the laws of the Universe— more than a religion, more than simply a way of life and thought. Through it, a good many things became unnecessary to them and they forgot they had hands . . .

When they were attacked from space (this happened countless thousands of years ago), they could not defend themselves at all. They had forgotten the largest part of their fabulous technology; their machines were corroded, their skills had died, and worst of all, they had forgotten how to organize, how to be many men under one man's hand—for the duration.

So they were enslaved.

They broke their chains at length—at some thirty thousand years' length. When they had driven out the invader, and followed him and destroyed him and all his worlds, they were a frightened and sobered people. Their taste of quiet, of personal and individual fulfillment, was a touch of paradise to them and they deeply resented its loss.

Their return to material power was (in their minds), a descent and a degradation. Yet they had learned a lesson and learned it well. They made up their minds to defend themselves in such a way that never again—positively, absolutely and forever—never again would they be attacked, no matter how long it might be, no matter how deep and distantly they buried their souls in their nameless, nebulous delights.

So, after due consideration, they decided on the Barrier. They threw their total productivity—enormous, after their last war—and all their ingenuity into a defense to end all defenses. They marked out a segment of the surrounding space, purposely enclosing ten times the volume which their computers specified as the most that they could conceivably ever need for themselves.

They built a planetoid and stabilized it in an orbit around a dead sun not far from their cultural hub. This control planetoid, in ways as yet too advanced for humanity to grasp, generated and maintained the Barrier itself. In addition, it gathered up cosmic debris and sucked it in and, with its mammoth automatic machinery, transmuted and smelted and cast and machined flight after flight of missiles—large and small. These were racked and stored by the hundreds of thousands, stationed throughout the Barrier-protected space in a myriad of automatically computed orbits.

And so it was that anything which penetrated the Barrier, from any quarter, was instantly hunted down and killed.

There was some alarm at first over the fact that the Barrier, by its nature, must destroy anything leaving, as the missiles destroyed everything entering. But there seemed no valid answer to the question "Why not?" The Luanae weren't going anywhere. They had space enough, and ten times space enough, for any roaming they chose to do. And they chose to do very little, for their orientation was back toward those golden years of introspection, of contemplative, inward self-realization, and their hunger for it was very great.

And so they locked the Universe out and themselves in—
And threw away the key.

The control planetoid was a machine—automatic, self-repairing, powered by cold fusion of two isotopes of hydrogen, and it could always get hydrogen. It made missiles and used them. When it used them, it gathered up the dust that was left and salvaged it and made more. When any outbound matter was destroyed by the inner surface of the Barrier, it gathered up the radiant energy of the pyre, and the ashes, and brought them in and used them. It was impregnable, inexhaustible, tireless and immortal. It brought safety; it brought peace.

It brought death to a nomad people, so vastly superior in intellect and in what has been translated from the Luanae "sendings" as "size-of-soul" that the Luanae, by that time steeped again in their unthinkable metaphysics, awoke to watch them approach, awe-struck, alive and aware of them. What they were can never now be known. Even the Luanae do not know. They say only that their thirty thousand years of slavery to the creatures who invaded them was but a scratch, a toe-stub, compared to the wound they suffered in the realization that they caused the destruction of these nameless nomads.

The creatures swept down on the Barrier, unable to detect something unique in the Universe, unwarned and unprepared, and were swallowed up by it.

It is impossible to describe the impact of this event on the Luanae. Already deeply involved in their ancient philosophy, in tune with the Universe and respecting all natural things—compassionate, life-reverent, humble and kind—they watched the destruction of their infinite superiors with an infinite horror. They realized then the extent of their folly, their crime in the creation of the Barrier.

Already far gone again away from their technological peak, they again restored it. They surpassed it. They mobilized to pull down what they had put up, driven by guilt and horror at the thing they had done. It was the crucifixion of crucifixions, the murder of murders with the Messiah of Messiahs their irreplaceable victim.

And they failed. They had built too well. The planetoid destroyed everything that approached it. It was surrounded by miniature versions of the great Barrier, some turned inside out so that the disintegrating surface was encountered first. It picked apart, in a microsecond, everything they threw at it, ate it, digested it, and was nourished.

The Luanae then undertook a frightening sacrifice, an appalling expense. In an effort to overload the planetoid's defenses, they flung up thousands of missiles, ships, lumps of rock and debris, hurling it every which way between their stars and planets. Implacably the planetoid located the intrusive matter, compared it with its matrix of stored information on allowable bodies and their permitted circlings, and sought out and destroyed the offending ones, quite uncaring that many of them, tragically many, were manned ...

And, in time, the Luanae discovered that the planetoid was producing missiles and energy past its original capacity, consuming more than it had originally been designed to handle, computing more things more quickly. At that, they ceased to attack it, realizing belatedly that they had forced it to enlarge and strengthen itself—the only course open to a self-repairing machine stressed beyond its original endurance.

They fell back then on the only thing left for them to do, as creatures of efficient conscience. They sent out warnings.

They devised transmissions which covered the entire spectra of intelligence, transcending language, surpassing even symbolism. They set up automatic beacons to radiate the warning in all directions, each beam overlapping the next. Bitterly, they organized a trade of monitors to watch over the automatic machines, which they never again would trust. The monitors were ritualized like a priesthood, drilled like slave-legions, marinated in the impulses of duty.

Once that was done and tested past any conceivable fault or failure, they settled to a new level of life, neither blindly mechanical, like that which had produced the planetoid, nor vegetative and contemplative, like that which had left them open to slavery, but a middle ground, based on the ancient convictions of respect for life and its ways in the rigid and marvelous frame of the Universe; and implemented it by an unrusting technology.

So it was that the Luanae were at last in a position to make their greatest and most mature discovery—a thing known to each of them as individuals, but until now unrealized in terms of lifegroups:

A man cannot exist alone. He must be a member of something, a piece, an integer of some larger whole. Men plus men make cities, which band together to form states, then countries, then worlds, and never can a sole unit exist alone and unsupplied. Communication and intercourse are necessary and vital; without them, the lone unit is a brief accident unnoticed by the Universe and forever forgotten.

So, behind their gigantic ghastly barricade, the Luanae at last acknowledged membership in a grouping greater than species, and declared themselves belonging to Life and dedicated to the survival of its total membership.

This, then, was the self-imprisoned people discovered by an Earth scout ship, in the business of locating terrestrial planets for humanity. The Luanae rose with a shout at the sight of them. This was Life—life to aid and life to share. For until Earth came to them, they saw themselves dying like a surrounded city, like a lone traveler, like an amputated limb, like any other life separated from its sustaining body.

Earth brought life to the Luanae, and the Luanae enlisted themselves in Earth's search for life.

A lousy trip. A suicide trip, with a skipper and utility monkey horse-blindered by their duties, three crackpots and an unemployed and unusable CG. And me, Palmer, with what could be the answer.

I had faith in my solution; I liked its math. I had little or no hope that it would be tried—really tried full-scale, and done right. People don't know enough. They don't think really straight. They turn the wrong valves and push the wrong buttons. Palmer should have a thousand hands and the ability to be simultaneously in a thousand places. Then this business of being the wasp-waist in the history of Life and the Lives of the two cultures—this would make more sense.

I shall be bungled out of history, I told myself as we ground along in the nothingness of subspace—the Luanae subspace, given us by Luanae cold-fusion generators. I'm coming, I'm coming, I told the Luanae silently, but I bring the enemy; I bring bungling; and, my marvels, you'll succumb to stupidity as will I, for it's the last and strongest enemy of them all, against which you and I might not prevail.

I watched Potter pinching away at his nose tip, and I silently bore Donato's cough, and I gave my approval to big-eared England because he had so little to say to anybody; I tried to remember what exactly it was that made Nils Blum, the utility monkey, funny to me when I saw him first; I hoped to recapture it and laugh again, but I never made it. I swore sometimes at Donato's eternal helpfulness and I ignored the skipper, because who wants to talk all the screaming time about ship's business and the business of ships gone by?

. . . I said nothing where the CG could hear me, and tightened up in painful empathy when I saw one or another of the ship's company floundering and defending and doubting when she repeated his words.

I did nothing about any of these annoyances, except maybe the time I suggested to the skipper that he feed the CG at times other than our mess, so I wouldn't have to witness her purposeless wreckage of even the little things men believe in. He bought that, and it had a double advantage. We not only were spared the sight of her at meals, but she took to spending her time aft in the "monkey's cage" among the mops and drums of cleaning aerosol and sewerline scrapers. If Nils Blum objected, then, monkeylike, he could pass it off by scratching and chewing a straw.

. . . I came through there once and saw them sitting across from each other at Blum's little table, elbows almost touching, not speaking and not looking at each other. And, by the Lord, she was crying, and I must say it did me good. I had a mind to go ask the monkey how he managed it, but I don't involve myself with the unskilled.

We got where we were going and snapped out of the nothing into the something. We took a bearing on the Luanae Galaxy and it was quite a sight, a long irregular sausage of an island galaxy, with its unmistakable signpost, the long regular black swatch of the Barrier's edge where it impinged on, and shut out, the rest of the bodies in the formation. We ducked under again for half an hour and came up again too close to see the swatch, but close enough at last to get the Luanae greeting.

That I can't tell you about.

Captain Steev piped us all into the messhall in mid-morning, which would have annoyed me if I could think of anything I'd rather be doing—but there just wasn't anything to do, or to want to do, instead. So I shuffled in with the rest of them—Potter, England, Donato. Blum and the CG were back with the mops, I imagine. The captain let us all be seated and stood at the end of the table and knocked on a coffee mug self-consciously.

He said, "We have arrived at our site of operations. We have, among the four of you, four different specialists with, as I understand it, four attacks on the problem of penetrating the Luanae Barrier. I need not," he says, and then went right on as if he needed to anyway, "need not tell you of the vital importance of this task. The entire history of humanity might—not might, *does*—depend on it. If you, or men like you, fail to solve this problem soon, we can expect our entire civilization to explode, like a dying sun, through the internal pressures of its own contracting mass."

He coughed to cover up the floridity of his phrasing, and little Donato happily joined in. I saw one of England's wide flat hands move on the table, to cover the other and hold it down.

"Now, then," said the captain. He bent from the waist and removed his hand from his side pocket. In it was a sleek little remote mike. "This is for the record, gentlemen. You first, Mr. Palmer?"

"Me first what?" I wanted to know.

"Your plan, sir. Your approach, attack, whatever it pleases you to call it. Your projected method of cracking the Barrier."

I looked around at what passed for an audience, coughing, picking, glowering wetly.

I said, "In the first place, my plan has been fully detailed and filed with the proper authorities—men who are in a position to understand my specialty. I believe that copies of these papers are on file with you. I suggest that you look at them and save us both the trouble."

"I'm afraid you don't understand," said the captain, looking flustered. He gestured at the mike. "This is for the record. I've got to have the oral rundown. It's—it's—well, for the record."

"Then I say to the recording, for the record," I barked, right into the mike, "that I am not accustomed to being asked to make speeches before a lay audience, which cannot be expected to understand one word in ten of what I have to say. And I refer the recording and its auditors, whoever they may be, to the files in which my detailed report is presented, for proof not only of my project but of the fact that these assembled, and no doubt those listening to this record, would in all likelihood not know what I was talking about. Not at all."

I glared up at the skipper. "Does that satisfy the record, Lieutenant?"

"Captain," corrected the captain mildly. "Really."

"A mistake," I allowed. "I never make mistakes accidentally, you understand." I waved at the mike. "Let's let the record stand with that, do you mind?"

"Mr. Potter," said the captain, and I leaned back, pleased with myself.

Potter removed and immediately replaced his perennial pinch. "Well I don't bind tellig you bine," he said adenoidally. "I'm in field bechanics, as you dough. I have bade certain calculations which indicate that the stresses present in the barrier skin are subject to bobentary distortion under the stress of sball area, high intenstidty focused bagnetic fields of about one hudred billion gauss per square centimeter at focus. That's *billion*," he amended, "dot *billion*."

I wondered how the record would make out the difference.

"Very good, Mr. Potter," said the captain. "Unless I am mistaken, you propose to breach the Barrier momentarily with a high-intensity focused magnetic field. Is that correct?

Potter nodded, a gesture which carried through his right wrist.

"Very well," said the captain.

I blew disgustedly through my nostrils, looking at Potter. His business was as disgusting as his hobby of picking at his cuticles. If I knew as little about my specialty as he did about his, I'd never get trapped into talking about it.

"Mr. Donato?"

"Yes, Captain Steev, yes, sir!" Donato cried, all blushes and eagerness. "Well, sir, I'm in ballistics. What I propose is a two-part missile aimed to graze the Barrier in such a way that, at the moment of contact, it separates, one segment glancing back outside, the other entering and proceeding inward. This is on the theory that, although the control planetoid reacts instantaneously, its sensors report only one event at one locality at a given moment. I feel I have a fifty-fifty chance, then, of slipping one part through while the other part is being reported grazed and gone. I think a minimum of one hundred thirty shots, fired in four groups and at four slightly different approach angles, would establish whether or not the theory is tenable."

"Tenable?" I gasped. "Why, you—nincompoop!" That's the first time in my entire life I ever called anyone that, but as I looked at him, blushing and grinning and wanting to do right, there just wasn't another applicable term. "What makes you think—"

"Mr. England?" said the skipper, much louder than I have ever heard him speak before.

I confess I was startled. Before I could quite recover myself, England answered.

"In the area of mis," he said in a whispery voice which at that point failed him. He swallowed with all his might and then made a weak, flickery smile. "In the field of missiles, my chief concern is, first, a series of tests to determine the exact nature of the internal control pulses in the hunting missiles, the frequency and wave-height of the command pulses in the guided missiles, with a view to jamming or redirecting them. Second, I plan to lob some solids through the Barrier at low velocities in order to study the metallurgical content of the missiles, with a view to the design of sensing-dodging equipment, and possibily some type of repulsion field, designed to force the missiles into a near miss."

"Very succinct," said the captain, and I wondered how he knew what was succinct or not about a specialty. "Now that we've got the swing of this little discussion, perhaps, Mr. Palmer, you would like to reconsider and join it."

"Perhaps I would at that," I said, stopping to think it over.

After all, a little sense ought to be added to this exhibition of maundering incompetence, if only for balance.

"Then if you must know," I said, "the only tenable method of approaching the problem lies in the area of explosive stress. No one but myself seems to have noticed the almost perfectly spherical shape of the Barrier. A sphere in any flexing material is a certain indication of some dynamic tension, a container and the contained in equilibrium, with the analog of some fluid differential like the air inside and outside an inflated balloon. You don't follow me."

"Go on," said the captain, holding his head as if he was listening.

"Why, all it will take is a toroidal mass equipped with a subspace generator and an alternator. If this is placed upon the Barrier margin and caused to vibrate into and out of the subspace state, there will be a portion of the Barrier—that which is surrounded by the toroid—which will be included in the vibration. The effect then is in causing a circular section of the Barrier to be in nonexistence for part of the time. It is my conclusion that this small breach will cause the Barrier to collapse like that toy balloon I mentioned. Q.E.D. Lieutenant." I leaned back.

"Captain," said the captain tiredly. Then he looked me in the eye and said, "I regret to inform you, Mr. Palmer, that you are completely wrong. Blum!" he bellowed suddenly. "Coffee out here!"

"Hah!" came the monkey's voice. It was as near as he ever let himself get to aye-aye, sir.

He must have had the tray ready before the skipper called, because he came out with it loaded and steaming. He set it down in the middle of the table and retired to a corner. At the side of my eye, I saw the CG sidle out of the "cage" and go to stand silently beside him.

But I wasn't in a mood for anything but this preposterous allegation from the captain. I got to my feet so I could look down at him.

"Did I understand you to say," I ground out, cold as Neptune, "that in *your* opinion *I* am wrong?"

"Quite wrong. The Barrier is a position, an infinite locus, not a material substance, and is therefore not subject to the laws and treatments of matter per se."

I have been known to splutter when I am angry, unless I try not to. I found myself trying very hard not to.

"I have reduced every observation on that surface known to Man," I informed him, "to mathematical symbology, and from it have written a consecutive sequence of occasions which proves beyond doubt that the surface is as I say and will act as I say. You seem to forget that this is on the record, Admiral, and this may mean you are making a permanent rather than a temporary fool of yourself."

I sat down, feeling better.

"Captain," said the captain wearily.

He turned and took a paper from the stack of folders which I noticed for the first time lay there. He flashed it; at first glance, it looked like a page of figures over which a child superimposed a crude and scratchy picture of a Christmas tree in red.

He said, "Equation number 132, four pi sigma over theta plus the square root of four pi sigma quantity squared." I could not help noticing that, as he reeled it off, he was waving the paper, not reading from it.

I said, "I recognize the equation. Well?"

"Well nothing," snapped the captain. "Unwell, I'd call it. Heh." He slid the sheet over to me. "If you will observe, to be consistent with the preceding series, the integer sigma is not whole but factorial, in view of which an increasing error is introduced wherein—but see for yourself."

I looked. What resembled a crude picture of a Christmas tree was the correction, in red, of the symbol he had mentioned, and the scrawled figures of three corrected factors in the next equation and seven in the third following, until the red marks became a whole line.

I said, "Might I ask who has had the effrontery to scribble all over these calculations?"

"Oh, I did," said the captain. "I thought it might be a good idea to rework the whole series, just in case, and I'm glad I did. You ought to be, too."

I looked again at the sheet and swallowed sand. A man has to major for a considerable time in some highly creative math to be able to do what had been done here. A thing or two came to my lips, but I would not say them, because they were for my figures and against his, yet it could not be denied that his were right.

To save something out of this, I growled at him, "I think, sir, you owe me an explanation as to why you have chosen publicly to humiliate me."

"I didn't humiliate you. Those figures humiliated you, and they're your figures," he said, and shrugged.

I glanced at Potter and England. They were grinning broadly. I looked up suddenly and caught the CG's flat gray stare.

"They're your figures," she murmured, and anyone hearing her would swear she knew for certain that I had copied them from somebody else's work. There was such a flame of insistence burning up in me that they were *so* my figures that I could barely contain it. But contain it I did; they were not figures I was anxious to claim at the moment.

I was very confused. I slumped down in my chair.

"You're next, Mr. Potter. I'm sorry to have to inform you that although, in theory, the Barrier does yield under the stress of a magnetic field such as you describe, it would take a generator somewhat larger than this ship to supply it; the affected area would be just about what you said—a square centimeter; and, finally, it wouldn't be a hole in the Barrier, but what you might call a replacement patch. In other words, the affected area will, when surrounded by the so-called Barrier skin, act precisely like part of that skin in all respects."

Potter put his hobby finger out for inspection and was so distressed he forgot to look at it. "Are . . . are you sure?"

"That's what happened the last seven times it was tried."

Potter made a wordless sound, a sort of moan, or sigh. I did not feel like grinning at him as he had at me. England did not grin, either, because I think he realized what was coming. He just sat there wondering how it would come.

It came at Donato first. "Mr. Donato—"

"Yes, *sir*, Cap'n."

"You propose a two-piece missile. You seem to forget, as many another has before you, that the Barrier offers no resistance to penetration and therefore needs no complicated hanky-panky to get something inside. In addition, it's unimportant whether or not an object is sensed by the skin and reported to control, or whether it's picked up a minute or hour later by one of the hunting missiles. You've attacked the whole problem with a view to getting something inside, which isn't a problem, and overlooked what to do inside, which is."

"Oh, Cap'n, I'm sorry," said Donato, stricken. He burst into a sharp series of barking coughs. There were tears in his eyes. "Oh, I'm sorry. I'm sorry."

"Nothing to be sorry about," the captain said. "Got it yet, Mr. England?"

"Whuh? Oh," said the missile expert. "I guess I was off base about the jamming. Suddenly it seems to me that's so obvious, it must have been tried and it doesn't work."

"Right, it doesn't. That's because the frequency and amplitude of the control pulses make like purest noise—they're genuinely random. So trying to jam them is like trying to jam FM with an AM signal. You hit it so seldom, you might as well not try."

"What do you mean, random? You can't control anything with random noise."

The captain thumbed over his shoulder at the Luanae Galaxy. "They can. There's a synchronous generator in the missiles that reproduces the *same random noise,* peak by pulse. Once you do that, modulation's no problem. I don't know *how* they do it. They just do. The Luanae can't explain it; the planetoid developed it."

England put his head down almost to the table. "The same random," he whispered from the very edge of sanity.

As if anxious to push him the rest of the way, the captain said cheerfully, "Good thinking on that proposal to study the metal content of the missiles. Only there isn't any. They're a hundred per cent dielectric synthetics—God knows exactly what. The planetoid can transmute, you know. What little circuitry the missiles have is laid out in fluid-filled pipes, capillary coils, things like that. There seems to be some sort of instantaneous transition from solid to liquid and back. The liquid conductors are solid dielectrics again just as soon as they have passed whatever current they're supposed to pass, and that's done in microseconds."

"Radar-transparent," concluded England dolefully.

"For all practical purposes," agreed the captain. "Well, that seems to be that, gentlemen."

"Just you tell me one thing," I said before I could stop myself. "Precisely what in hell are we doing here at all?"

"Precisely what you came to do." The captain picked up his folders. "Blum, I sense that these four gentlemen might be happier without an audience, even us."

"Come on, Virginia."

The captain started out forward and the monkey and the CG headed aft. We all sat where we were.

After a time, England said, "Why didn't he tell me he knew so much about missiles?"

"Did you ask him?" snapped Potter.

That was the question and answer I had been humbly formulating, too. I said, "What did he mean, we are here to do what we came to do?"

"Maybe he wants us to get oriented, is all," said Donato sheepishly. "Get off theory, you know. Like field work."

"If he thinks he's jolting my inspiration, he's crazy," gloomed England. He wiped his wet eyes with the backs of his hands, leaving them still wet. "The jolt, I got all right. The inspiration, I can't find."

"He should have told us before, right at the start. Maybe by now we'd have a whole new set of figures." Donato caught my sharp look and immediately said, "Theories, I mean, friend. I didn't mean to say figures."

Somehow that didn't help.

"Get out of here, Donato," I said.

"Sure, friend, sure," he said and got out like always, smiling. He went into his room and closed the door. We could hear him coughing.

"Like a box you have in your room ten years," Potter was muttering adenoidally, "it all of a sudden goes boing and there's a jumpid-jack." I was going to ask him what he was talking about and then realized he was talking about the captain. I saw his point. Why *hadn't* he called this meeting weeks ago?

"He must like things to look futile," I said. "I'm going back to bed."

"Be, too," said Potter.

I got up. Potter and England stayed where they were. They were going to talk about me.

I just didn't care.

I dreamed I was walking in a meadow, smelling the sweet fresh odor of snowdrops, when all of a sudden they grew taller and taller, or I grew smaller and smaller, and I saw that instead of stems, the snowdrops were growing on a sequence of equations. I began to read them off, but they got all twisted and jumbled and started to grab at my feet. I fell and grunted and caught hard at the edges of the bunk and was totally awake.

I turned over and looked at the overhead. I felt clear-headed but lethargic. I thought I could still smell the snowdrops.

Then I noticed the whine. It was far away, but persistent. The lights looked funny. They seemed to be flickering slightly, but when you looked straight at them, they were steady. I didn't like it. It made me feel dizzy.

I got up and went out into the corridor. Nobody was around. Then a timid voice said behind me, "Virginia in there?"

I jumped and turned. It was the monkey, cringing against the bulkhead.

"You think I'm *that* bad off?" I answered him in disgust, but as I turned away, he leaned forward and peered into my room anyway.

I went into the messhall and knocked on the decanter and, when it steamed, poured coffee. Somewhere in the background, I heard a wistful murmur, and then Potter's shocked voice: "In *here?* Monkey, didn't they tell you? I like *girls.*" In a moment, he came shuffling in and headed for the coffee. "What time is it, Palmer?"

I shrugged. I looked at the clock, but it didn't seem to make any sense to me.

"God," said Potter, and sniffed noisily. "I feel all . . . disconnected. I got a buzzing in my ears. My eyes—it's sort of flickery."

I looked at him curiously, wondering what it must be like to be a man who so readily relates everything around him to himself. "That isn't your flicker. It's ours. Same with the buzz, though I'd call it a sort of whine."

He looked very relieved. "You hear it, too. What happens here, anyway?"

A TOUCH OF STRANGE

I drank some coffee and looked at the clock again. "What's the matter with that clock?" I demanded.

Potter craned to look at it. "Can't be. Can't be."

Donato came in, his face scrubbed and shining. "Morning, Palmer. Potter. Well, I wondered which one of us would fall first, and I guess I know now, and who'd a' thunk it." He nodded aft and began coughing.

We looked. The monkey was stepping off one foot and onto the other in front of England's door.

"You ought to mind your own business, Don."

"Oh, sure," said Donato agreeably. "Guess you're right at that."

Just then, England flung his door open, saw Nils Blum crouching there, and recoiled with an odd high squeak.

Immediately he growled, in his deepest bass, "Don't hang around me, monk," and pushed past the utility man without a backward glance.

We watched, looking past him as he approached. Blum ducked his head inside England's door, withdrew it, took a step toward us and stopped, his jaw working silently, his big wrinkled head held a little askew.

"But hungry, I'm hungry," England said. "Whatever time is it?"

"Clock's busted." Potter suddenly laughed. We all looked at him. "Well," he said, pointing at England, "it's not him, either."

"You were just saying to Don, he ought to mind his own business," I snapped. I wonder, I thought to myself, if he knows I cut at him because he twiddles his nose?

"What business? What goes?" England demanded.

"By holy creepin' Kramden," said Donato to himself. He looked aft at the miserable figure there and forward at the closed door to the wardroom and control. "What do you know."

"He is a very surprising man," I said.

"Who? Who? The skipper? What's he done now?" England insisted.

"Virginia seems to be missing," said Donato.

Hearing her name, Blum ran three steps toward us and then stopped in the messhall door, looking timidly at our faces, one by one.

"Well," said England, "rank has its privileges."

Potter blew sharply through his nostrils, expressing a

great deal and disposing of the matter. He glanced at the clock. "What'd you say is wrong with it?"

"Nothing's wrong with it."

We turned abruptly and faced the captain. There was an oddness about him, a set to his jaw, a certain hard something in his eye that hadn't been there at all before. Or maybe it had, there at the table this morning. (Was that this morning? What the clock said just made no sense at all.) I looked at the captain and past him, through his open door, through the wardroom with his neat bunk at the side, on forward to the control console and observation blister.

There wasn't anybody up there.

From the other doorway, the utility monkey whispered, "Sir . . . ?"

"Something the matter with the lights, Captain," Donato said.

"It's all right," said the captain shortly. He went to the messhall peeper and switched it on. He dialed for starboard view and stepped back.

We crowded around it. Everything looked about the same out there, the wide vein of jewels straggling across the sky, then the unrelieved black.

"Show you something," said the captain. He moved the controls and the view zoomed in toward the stars. At close to peak magnification, he switched to the fine tuning and got the cross-hairs where he wanted them. "Know what that is?"

It was a ball, shiny, golden. It was impossible to say how big. Then I heard England gasp.

"I've seen that before. Pictures. That's the Barrier Control—the planetoid!"

"So close?" I asked.

"Just because the Barrier is a sphere," said the captain, "everyone assumes the control has to be in the center. Well, it isn't. It's right here at the edge, and heaven help anything that goes in there in a rush, trying to converge on the center!"

"Sir . . ." came the whisper.

"Now look," said the captain, winding the zoom handle again. The view backed away from the golden sphere until it was almost lost. Suddenly the screen filled with a flat-topped, streamlined—

"A pod, a ship's pod!" said England.

The captain stepped back a pace and watched the pod

with glowing eyes. His hands were pressed tight together and some great suppressed excitement yearned in him to burst free. We looked from him to the peeper.

Under his breath, the captain said, "Git'm! Go git'm!"

"Sir . . ."

"Shut up, monk."

"That pod's inside the Barrier!" somebody said. Me, I think. "Look! Look there!"

It was like a segment of ivory knitting needle. It was turning slowly end over end. It approached the pod slowly, high, passed close by and drifted out of the picture.

"A missile, a big one."

"My God, what's happened?" gasped Donato.

"The Barrier's down," said the captain, as if he couldn't hold the words inside any longer. "It's down, you see? It's gone and the missiles are all dead."

"Sir, oh, Cap'n . . . I can't find Virginia. Where's Virginia, Cap'n?"

"You're looking at her, Blum. You're looking right at her," said the captain, his eyes fixed on the screen.

Something hit us, scattered us. For a moment, the messhall was a swirl of grunts and outraged yells, and then the utility monkey had tumbled us aside and was standing in front of the peeper, one hand on each side frame. He seemed a half a head taller, all at once, and his one hairy arm, where it passed close by me, had cords on it I hadn't known about before; his head was a lion's head.

Suddenly he barked, "What'd you do? What'd you do?" He was talking to the captain, who kept looking over Blum's shoulder at the picture and was laughing softly. Then the monkey whirled from the screen, turning as if to turn was to tear something, and he faced the captain and said again, "What'd you do? What'd you do with Virginia?"

The captain stopped laughing altogether and was a captain duty-talking to a utility monkey. "I gave her her orders and I put her in that pod and sent her on her way. Any objections, mister?"

Blum's eyes began to protrude—honestly, you could see them press outward. His mouth opened slowly, slowly, and a dribble suddenly scored the corner of the mouth and down the side of the chin; the hands came up, clawed, half-grasping. The nostrils trembled, trembled . . . and then he screamed, so loud, so close to us, it was like a big dazzling light flashing to blind us.

We reared back from that scream, pawing at it.

Next thing was Blum, crouched over and peering ahead as he ran, trying to go somewhere, not knowing how. He ran crazily to the airlock hatch and hit it with his fists, and turned with his back to it and screamed again. "You send me, you hear? You send me with Virginia, you hear me, Cap'n?"

Donato strolled over toward him and, smiling, said the stupidest thing I ever heard squirted into a violent silence: "Aw, come on, monkey, let's all be chums."

Blum screamed again and Donato didn't wait to get turned around. He ran straight backward until he hit me, and I caught him and held him up so he didn't fall.

"Captain, sir," Donato said, squinching his head around as he dangled from my hands, "he won't mind me at all, Captain."

"Get to your quarters, Blum," said the captain from way back in his throat.

"You bring her back or you send me out with her, one," slavered Blum. "You hear me?"

"Get—to—your—quarters."

Blum put up his claws. He began walking toward the captain, chewing on his own mouth parts, and his eyes were crazy. The captain bent a little low and put his arms out a little from his sides, and moved very slowly toward Blum. We all got back out of the way.

Blum said, "Now! You hear me?" very softly, and leaped.

The captain stepped aside and hit him. I thought it was on the head, but England told me later it was on the side of the neck, toward the back. The monkey was in midair when the captain hit him, and he went right down on the deck on his face, and he didn't put out his hands to stop himself, and he didn't move.

We all looked at him and then at each other.

"Take him to his quarters," said the captain.

His voice startled me because it wasn't where I thought it was, standing by the sprawled-out monkey. He was already across the room staring into the peeper. For him, the thing was finished; probably his heart wasn't quick any more. He was back with his work, his job. The rest of us had poundings in the sides of our necks and we didn't know what to do.

"Go on, go on. Get him out of here. You, Palmer. You're the biggest."

I was going to splutter, but I held on tight to it and didn't. I said, "See here, I don't have to—"

From back in his throat, like before, the captain spoke to me. It was a different thing, being the one he spoke to like that and not watching somebody else get it.

He said, "*You* see here—you do have to. Whatever I say, you have to, not only you, Palmer, but all four of you clowns. The party's over and the work's done, and from now on out, you mind me and think first of what I want. At all times. Is that clear, mister?"

I said, loud, "Well, I—" and the skipper ripped his eyes away from the screen, almost like Blum, tearing something, and looked at me. So I picked up the monkey's shoulders and dragged him back to his cabin.

It was just like ours, only he didn't have quite so much stuff lying around, or anyway what there was was in square stacks.

I tumbled him into the bunk and closed the door, because that was the only clear place to lean back against, and I leaned on it and tried to get my breath back.

The monkey started to make a scratchy sound in the rear of his throat. I looked down at him. His head was twisted to one side. It was jammed against the pillow. His eyes were open.

"Cut that out, monk." He went right on doing it. "That noise, cut it out, hear me? I said, you hear me, mister?"

That "mister" didn't sound a bit like the skipper's. I was embarrassed.

The monkey's eyes stayed open and I realized he wasn't blinking them; he wasn't seeing out of them. I couldn't stand that breathing noise, so finally I straightened out his head and put the pillow under it. He stopped the noise right away. He closed his eyes.

I still couldn't get my breath. He had blood on his face; maybe that was it.

He didn't open his eyes, but he began to talk, very fast, very soft. It was like being too far away from someone to understand what was being said, and then it was like coming closer . . .

". . . all she had to do was let herself and she couldn't do it, she couldn't just stop fighting and believe. It was like she'd die if she believed anything. She wanted to. More than anything she wanted to. But it was like someone told her, if you believe in anything, you'll die."

He opened his eyes suddenly and saw me and closed them again.

"Palmer. You Palmer you, you saw it your own self, the time she cried. All that time, all those weeks, those gray eyes still and hiding whatever it was she had inside her, and me begging her and begging: 'Virginia, oh, Virginia, I don't care what you think of me. I wouldn't want you to love me, Virginia. But only believe me; you can so be loved, you're worth loving, I love you. I do, Virginia; just you believe that once, because it's true, and after that you'll be able to believe other things . . . little ones at first; I'll help you with them, and always tell you the truth.'

"I said, 'Don't love me, Virginia, or think about it at all. I wouldn't know what to do with it if you gave me anything like that.' I said, 'Just trust me is all I want, so you can ask me what's the truth and I'll tell you. But believe I love you; I'm not much, Virginia, so I guess that's not too much to start on. Believe I love you, Virginia, will you just do that?' And she . . ."

He lay with his eyes open for a long time and I thought he was unconscious again, but then he blinked his eyes and went on.

". . . she cried, all at once, all over, and she said, 'Monkey, monkey, you're tearing me up, can't you see? I want to believe you. I want to believe you more than anything in the world. But I can't, I don't know how, I'm not supposed to, I'm not allowed.' That's what she said. And she cried again and said, 'But I want to believe you, monkey. You just don't know how much I want to believe that. Only . . . nothing is what it looks like, nothing is what it's supposed to be, no one really wants what they say they want. I can't believe them and I can't believe you.'

"She said, 'Suppose I believed you and then the day came when things were all straight and true, and they let you see everything; and suppose I found out then that everything you said wasn't so; found out maybe there was no you at all, monkey . . . what about that? I couldn't stand that. I don't dare believe you, because I want to. If I don't believe anything about anything or anyone, then if things get all true, I can start there and be all right without losing anything.' And she cried some more and then you, Palmer, you came in, and in a second she was back inside her flat gray eyes. So she didn't believe me and that's why."

I couldn't get my breath. Blum couldn't get his breath. I leaned on the door and he lay on the bed and we panted.

"There was a difference," he whispered, chasing some thought he was having. "She had a way of making you doubt anything you said. I told her my mother could cook. She said, 'Your mother could cook' in that flat way, and you know, I had to think and wonder if my mother really could. That's what I mean. But I said to her, 'Virginia, you know, I love you,' and she said, 'You love me' in that same way, like who ever heard of such a thing?

"But what I'm trying to say, that didn't touch me, when she did that when I said I love you. I looked into how I felt and I felt the same no matter what she said. So about that, there was a difference. That's how it was all right to say, 'Believe me, believe me about that.' I knew that things could change. I knew that almost anything I told her could be wrong, some way. But not that. She could trust me with that. And she wanted to. At least I got that."

I leaned against the door, feeling embarrassed, and then I could turn it to anger.

I said, "You're stupid, monkey, you know? You're crew, she's CG. She couldn't stop you. Why didn't you just go right ahead? That's what she's aboard for."

But that didn't make him angry. He looked up at the ceiling and said quietly, "Yeah, she said that, too. She said, 'You don't know what you want, monkey,' she said. She said, 'This is what you want. So go ahead, only stop talking about it.' I said no. I said there could be a time—I hadn't thought about it yet; I wanted something else first—I wanted her to believe me. She said I was crazy and to keep away from her then, but after, you saw it, Palmer. After, she said she wanted to believe me, more than anything."

He was quiet at last, breathing easily, thinking about something to smile at. I spoke to him, but he didn't answer. He was asleep, I guess. I opened the door quietly and closed it on him and went back to the messhall.

They were all there by the peeper, watching.

I said, "He's asleep now, but there's going to be particular hell to pay when he wakes up and really understands she isn't here."

The skipper looked away from the screen at me and then back again. He wouldn't spit on the messhall deck, but he might as well, the way his face looked. He couldn't worry about that monkey.

I asked Potter, "What goes?"

Potter said, "Whether to get mad or glad, I don't know. You specialist, Palmer—you're a clown. And England. Donato. Me, too. Virginia, she was the specialist all along. She was the one this whole thing is for. How much farther?" he called out.

"A few meters," said Donato, absorbed.

I looked at the peeper. The ship's pod, that long false underbelly we'd hauled all the way from the Earth Worlds, it was drifting in close to that golden ball. That ball, I could see now, it was big as a supership if you could roll a supership into a ball. It was big as some moons. There were pale sticks drifting all over, dozens of them.

"Dead missiles, you see?" said Potter, watching the screen. "All dead. Every single cold-fusion power plant and explosive in a thousand kilometers is dead. Maybe more. Ours, too."

"Ours?"

"That hum, that flicker. We're not tapping a cold-fusion plant now, Palmer. We're taking off a steam turbine, water superheated by a parabolic mirror from that sun yonder."

"Steam turbine take us home?"

"Stupid!"

Donato chimed in. It was weird. Everybody talking whispery, as if loud noises would spoil something in the peeper. Nobody looked at anybody to talk, just kept watching the peeper, some of them moving the mouth all to one side to talk to one, to the other side to talk to someone else.

Donato said, "Little turbine wouldn't move this can half a length."

"It's all right," England said. "What she's doing, she's going in there to leech on to that planetoid. First there's a catalyst that will crumble a pit in the armor, because a bomb'll hardly scratch it. Then, when the skin's thin enough, she's got a bomb there. It goes off and no more Barrier."

"He said the Barrier's gone."

"Sure. She damped it. She's holding it dead. If she let go,

bango, back comes the Barrier and all those missiles come to life."

"What's this damped, holding it dead, letting go—what is all this?" I was getting impatient.

The skipper saw fit to say something. "We call it the D-field because—" he was quiet a long time—"because that way it sounds like something we know about, can know about."

He flicked a quick glance at all of us, as if somebody was going to laugh. Nobody was going to laugh.

"What it is," said the skipper, hating to say it, "it's doubt. A field of doubt. I mean—well, doubt, that's all."

Nobody said anything. Doubt, all right. But doubt has a way of getting invisible after a captain makes all those loud captain noises like he did.

I imagine he knew that. None of it was our business, not any more, but he didn't want to be doubted, not even by us specialists—us clowns.

He said, "What we did, we found Virginia trying to commit suicide. She had this doubt thing on her back, naturally. She didn't want to go on, because she had nothing she could believe in. Or just plain believe. Well, we took her and gave her some treatments . . . I'm a skipper, I don't know the details . . . Anyway, she came out of it with what she had when she went in, but more so. Much more. You all felt it— don't tell me you didn't. She could make a man doubt his own name."

I said, "Yeah . . ." only realizing when I heard it that I'd said it aloud.

Captain Steev watched the screen for a while and said under his breath, "That's right . . . atta girl . . ." and then to us, "It was a tricky problem. Given that a concentrated disbelief in things could have an effect like this—just for the sake of argument—if you want someone to stop a big power plant from a great distance with this faculty, how do you transport that someone in a ship powered with the same type of plant?"

"If it was a machine now," said England, "I'd say assemble it only when you wanted to use it."

"That's the way they did with the first fission bombs," said Donato knowledgeably. "They didn't put it together until it was due to blow. They blew it *by* putting it together. But doing that with a person, now . . ."

"You have the idea. You can't disbelieve in anything until you know what it is, or at least what people think it is. I can't believe or disbelieve that *pyoop* is the word for godmother in High Martian. I just don't know. Well, Virginia didn't know one way or another about a cold-fusion plant, thought I swear ours gasped a time or two on the way out. She has a large amount of control over it."

England said with sudden impatience, "Excuse me, Captain, but the only reason I can stand here talking about this is I see it working."

"Let me tell you, then. The cold-fusion plant is a Luanae idea. It's real simple-minded. Anybody can understand it once it's explained to them. Everything was set up when we came out here, including you four. The crackpot experts who knew more than people who've been in this all their lives. But as far as she was concerned, you were experts right up to the time I set you up and knocked you down—factorial sigma and the square-centimeter magnetic field, hah!

"She doubted you were experts when she first saw you, just because she doubted everything. When she saw what I did to you, she felt she was right to doubt. She reached a . . . sort of peak of disbelief. My God, didn't you feel it? . . . Look there, she's leeched down. Now the catalyst will be working on the armor. It won't be long now."

"I still don't see how just plain disbelief can shut down power plants," I argued.

"Not power plants. Just cold-fusion plants. Well, let me tell you and you'll understand. I put a shot of sleep-gas in your ventilators and got you all out of the way. Then—"

"Snowdrops," I said, remembering.

"Then I put her in the pod and told her to ride it, that's all. Except I . . . armed her . . . like you arm a bomb, you see? I told her what a cold-fusion plant is. She didn't care one way or the other, mind, but she listened while I explained it to her, all the parts. Then I gave her a paper and told her this is exactly what happens. I told her to read it as soon as the red light on the panel went on, which would be when she was clear of the ship."

"Read what?" somebody asked, after it got too quiet.

It was a long wait, watching that pod leeched to the planetoid and nothing happening but white sticks drifting, rocks, bits of stuff the planetoid had pulled in and hadn't been able to eat . . .

"Read what?" the captain finally repeated. "The cold-fusion formula, that's all. Written out in words of one cylinder. When Hydrogen One and Hydrogen Two are in the presence of mu mesons, they fuse into Helium Three with an energy yield in electron volts of 5.4 times ten to the fifth power. That's what was on the paper. She knew, piece by each, what the parts were—what mu mesons and Helium Three are and what is meant by that many electron volts. She had all that buried deep in her before we left the Earth Worlds. She'd had no occasion to put them together, that's all.

"And here I come saying (on paper), 'This gadget does exactly such and such.' Well, she just out and out doesn't believe it. That would make no never mind to a turbine or a power drill, but when you get into subatomic particles, clouds of them, involved in a catalysis—untouched in the long run, but I imagine pretty edgy . . . and you slam them with this thing, whatever it is she has . . ."

Suddenly impatient, he rapped, "Who am I trying to convince? It works, you see?"

I said, "Get off my foot, monk," and went on watching the screen. I don't think anyone else noticed the utility man. I hardly did myself.

"Hey," Donato said suddenly, "our generators are out, right? How do we get out of here?"

"When the bomb blows—no more D-field. Simple."

England barked, just as suddenly, "And what about all those missiles with the damper gone? They shoot off in every—"

"Dry up, clown," said the skipper. "And keep your panic to yourself. Every one of those missiles is triggered from one place and one place only—that planetoid. How do you think they were kept inside the Barrier and off the Luanae Earths all this time? Who cares if they get their power and explosives again? There'll be nobody in the driver's seat any more. Now shut up. It ought to blow pretty quick."

"Blow how? If it's right in the middle of the—uh—damping field—"

"I said shut up! That isn't a cold-fusion bomb. It's a hairy old thermonuclear that doesn't give a damn what anybody believes."

"What *is* it? What's going to *happen? What's* out there? *Where*—"

"Go on back to bed, monk," I said out of the side of my mouth, watching the screen. I meant it to sound kind—he'd had a bad time—but it didn't come out kind. I guess I'll never get used to talking to them.

It let go.

Oh, my God.

Captain Steev was wrong. There was triggering, somewhere, in some part of that split-second of hell. Because all the missiles went, too. They didn't fly; they didn't hunt. The warheads went.

It took a long time for our eyes to come back. The peeper screen was gone for good.

The turbine moaned down and down the scale and stopped. The lights stopped that annoying side-of-the-eye flicker.

"We got to go out and get Virginia," was the first complete sentence anyone said.

Somebody laughed. Not a funny laugh.

England's voice was harsh. "Don't be stupider'n you have to be, monkey. Don't you see we're back on our cold-fusion plant?"

"That makes no difference to him," I told England. "He wasn't around when the skipper explained."

"Who wasn't around?" barked the captain. "Damn it, Blum, nobody told you to leave your quarters. You're confined, you understand that? You, Palmer, can't I trust you to—"

"Wait!" The scream was almost more than a man could take. It was almost like that flare of light.

The monkey stood there in the middle of the messhall, going mad again. "Wait, wait, *wait!* I got to know. You all know. I don't. What *happened?*"

"Come on, Blum," I said quickly. I was afraid of him, but I think I was more afraid of the captain. He had a look on his face I never want to see any more.

He brought the face close to Blum and said, "You want to know, well, okay, and I don't see why I should waste time or pity on a goddam monkey. That bomb knocked off the planetoid and the Barrier, which is what we came here for, and it knocked off your Virginia because that's what she was sent out for. Okay?"

"What you want to kill her for?" Blum whispered.

"You wouldn't happen to know any other way to bring

back our power plant, now would you?" snarled the captain.

I tried to explain to the utility monkey. "She didn't believe the plant could work, Blum. So it couldn't work."

"I could make her believe. I could. I could."

We looked at him, the big tilted head, the trembling nostrils. He wasn't going to get crazy mad, after all. He was going into something else. It scared me more than his going crazy mad would.

He said, "It was you, wasn't it, fixed it so she wouldn't believe anything?"

"She had a head start," said the skipper, and turned his back. "Come on, Potter. Donato. You're crew now, like it or not. Let's get this can the hell home. We got news for the people."

"I never thought human beings could be like that," Blum said very quietly. "I never believed they could."

"Get to bed, monk," I said. And before I could stop myself, I begged him. "Please. Please, Blum—get out of his way."

He looked up into my face for a long time. Suddenly he said, "All right, Palmer." Then he just left.

I felt a lot better. Does you good to know you can handle people.

"Bunk in, men. We jump in five minutes." The captain went forward to check his controls.

"Well, don't stand there!" I barked at them. "Bunk in, men!"

"You know what, Palmer, you're a jerk," Donato told me. Then we all bunked down.

Four minutes went by. Five. I heard the whir of machinery.

The lights went out. The whir was a moan, then a whine. The light came on dim, then bright, and flickering at the edges of the eyes.

I didn't figure it was any of my business, so I just lay there and waited. Pretty soon the captain came back. He leaned against my cabin door and looked at me.

"Something the matter?" I wanted to know, trying to sound intelligent.

"Power plant's out, is all."

"Oh," I said. "Uh—what's wrong with it?"

He heaved a slow sigh. "Nothing. Only it doesn't work."

"I guess I better get up," I said.

"Why?" he asked me, and went away.

I got up anyway and went and told Donato and Potter and England. They stayed where they were. They didn't like this quiet skipper with the quiet voice and no arguments.

"You know, if he can't fix it, we don't go anywhere. The Luanae have no ships and we can't reach any of their planets," England told me. I'd as soon he hadn't.

I went to see Blum, for something to do.

He had his eyes open without seeing anything and he was mumbling to himself. I tried to hear.

". . . a little kid, they say you have the same chance as everybody else, you believe them. 'I'll hold your bag,' they say, 'while you get the tickets. Don't worry, I'll be here when you get back,' and you believe them . . . 'Got a great job for you, son. Light work, big tips—' "

"Monkey," I said.

He looked up at me. "You know what, Palmer? She said if you don't believe anything at all, you lose nothing when it all comes straight at last. It's all come straight for me now, Virginia. I can be safe now, Virginia, not believing. They can't take anything away from you that way. You're so right."

He went on talking like that for a long time. I left and walked forward and found the captain. He was in the control room jiggling a handle back and forth and not looking at it.

I said, "Captain, that D-field the girl had—now could a person fall into that by himself—I mean without those Earth Worlds doctors and all?"

"You sure you have to come bother me about it?" he asked in a whisper, not looking at me.

I backed way off and said, "I think I do. I think the monkey's got a case of the same."

"Now that's crazy! He'd have to have a real shock to get into a state like that. The monkey's okay. Beat it."

"He's mumbling how he doesn't believe in anything."

So the captain went aft with me. He watched the utility monkey for a time and then said, "Well, we'll fix it so he doesn't believe one way or another," and hit the man in the bed on the jaw so he slid up and banged his head on the inboard bulkhead.

I could hear the monkey breathing and I could hear the steam turbine, on and on.

I said, "I guess being unconscious doesn't make any difference to what you believe."

"You should know," said the captain. "All right, Palmer, pick him up and bring him along."

"Where?"

"Shut up."

He walked out. I guessed I'd better go along with him. I heaved and grunted the monkey up over my shoulder. I almost fell down with him. The captain was waiting in the corridor. He started to walk when I came out, so I followed him. We went down to pod level and forward to the airlock. Captain Steev began to undog the inner lock.

"What you going to do?" I asked him.

"Shut up," said the captain.

"You fixing to kill this monkey?"

"You want to get home?"

"I don't know," I said, and thought about it.

The captain flung back the inner door and stood up. He said, "What's your trouble, Palmer?"

I said, "I don't think I'm going to let you do this, Captain. There's some other way. You don't have to kill a little utility man."

"Put him in, Palmer."

I stood there with the limp monkey on my shoulder and glared at the captain while he glared back. I don't know how that might have ended—I do, only I'm ashamed to say it— but there was a noise and a voice, and somebody stood up out of the lock.

"Well, it's about time," Virginia complained. "You had the inner lock dogged and I've been lying in there for an hour. I guess I went to sleep. Who's that? What's the matter with Nils?"

The captain looked like a man with a cup of flour in the face. *"Who told you to leave the pod?"*

"The Luanae," she said calmly. "Inside my head, like. It was funny. Told me how to get into the flight-suit and how to get the gas bottles and strap them all together and use them to jet clear of the pod and that big gold thing. I got a long way away and then they told me to get back of a big piece of rock floating there. There was a lot of light. They told me when to go again, after the pieces stopped flying by.

It was easier then. There's a jet unit built right into the suit, did you know that? The Luanae told me how I was supposed to use it."

I got my jaw working and said, "What made you think you could make it go?"

"Well, it's the same kind of unit that brought us here, isn't it? You can't help believing your own eyes."

At last the captain moved. Before he could say a word, I slung the monkey down to the deck and pushed him. I bet the captain has been hit in his life, and maybe kicked, but I don't believe anyone just up and pushed him in the chest. He sat right down like a child with his legs spraddled out, looking up at me.

"Now you just stay there and shut up yourself," I told him. "You're always doing everything with these people the wrong way."

Virginia was kneeling beside the monkey. "What is it? What happened to him?"

I said, "He got a bump, that's all. Listen, if you don't mind me asking, do you believe he loves you?"

"Oh, yes!" she said immediately.

"Then I tell you what. You stay right here with him and rock him back and forth a little till his eyes open, hear? Then tell him that—tell him you believe him. That's all."

The captain scrambled to his feet and opened his mouth to bellow. I bellowed first. I don't know where it came from, but I believed I could do it, and it was a time to believe things.

"You! You get up forward and check your controls. This can's going to take off like a scalded eel if you've left the controls open, and I don't want these folks shaken up. Go on, quick! You're the only one here who knows how to do that. I'm the only one who knows how to do this other. Right? Right!" I said and pushed him.

He growled at me, but he went right up the ladder.

I hunkered down beside those two people and looked them over. I felt fine, very fine.

I said, "Virginia, you know what this is? This is the day everything all comes out straight. Right? Right."

"You're a funny sort of man, Mr. Palmer."

"A clown, ma'am."

I made a face at her and went up the ladder. About the

time I reached the top, the ship began to move. I fell right back down again, but they don't think it was funny. They didn't even seem to see me.

I climbed back up quietly and went back to my cabin.

The Girl Had Guts

The cabby wouldn't take the fare ("Me take a nickel from Captain Gargan? Not in this life!") and the doorman welcomed me so warmly I almost forgave Sue for moving into a place that had a doorman. And then the elevator and then Sue. You have to be away a long time, a long way, to miss someone like that, and me, I'd been farther away than anyone ought to be for too long plus six weeks. I kissed her and squeezed her until she yelled for mercy, and when I got to where I realized she was yelling we were clear back to the terrace, the whole length of the apartment away from the door. I guess I was sort of enthusiastic, but as I said . . . oh, who can say a thing like that and make any sense? I was glad to see my wife, and that was it.

She finally got me quieted down and my uniform jacket and shoes off and a dish of ale in my fist, and there I lay in the relaxer looking at her just the way I used to when I could come home from the base every night, just the way I'd dreamed every off-duty minute since we blasted off all those months ago. Special message to anyone who's never been off Earth: Look around you. Take a good *long* look around. You're in the best place there is. A fine place.

I said as much to Sue, and she laughed and said, "Even the last six weeks?" and I said, "I don't want to insult you, baby, but yes: even those six weeks in lousy quarantine at the lousy base hospital were good, compared to being anyplace else. But it was the longest six weeks I ever spent; I'll give you that." I pulled her down on top of me and kissed her again. "It was longer than twice the rest of the trip."

She struggled loose and patted me on the head the way I don't like. "Was it so bad really?"

"It was bad. It was lonesome and dangerous and—and disgusting, I guess is the best word for it."

"You mean the plague."

I snorted. "It wasn't a plague."

"Well, I wouldn't know," she said. "Just rumors. That thing of you recalling the crew after twelve hours of liberty, for six weeks of quarantine . . ."

"Yeah, I guess that would start rumors." I closed my eyes and laughed grimly. "Let 'em rumor. No one could dream up anything uglier than the truth. Give me another bucket of suds."

She did, and I kissed her hand as she passed it over. She took the hand right away and I laughed at her. "Scared of me or something?"

"Oh Lord no. Just . . . wanting to catch up. So much you've done, millions of miles, months and months . . . and all I know is you're back, and nothing else."

"I brought the Demon Lover back safe and sound," I kidded.

She colored up. "Don't talk like that." The Demon Lover was my Second, name of Purcell. Purcell was one of those guys who just has to go around making like a bull moose in fly-time, bellowing at the moon and banging his antlers against the rocks. He'd been to the house a couple or three times and said things about Sue that were so appreciative that I had to tell him to knock it off or he'd collect a punch in the mouth. Sue had liked him, though; well, Sue was always that way, always going a bit out of her way to get upwind of an animal like that. And I guess I'm one of 'em myself; anyway, it was me she married. I said, "I'm afraid ol' Purcell's either a blow-hard or he was just out of character when we rounded up the crew and brought 'em all back. We found 'em in honky-tonks and strip joints; we found 'em in the buzzoms of their families behaving like normal family men do after a long trip; but Purcell, we found him at the King George Hotel—" I emphasized with a forefinger— "alone by himself and fast asleep, where he tells us he went as soon as he got earthside. Said he wanted a soak in a hot tub and 24 hours sleep in a real 1-G bed with sheets. How's that for a sailor ashore on his first leave?"

She'd gotten up to get me more ale. "I haven't finished this one yet!" I said.

She said oh and sat down again. "You were going to tell me about the trip."

"I was? Oh, all right, I was. But listen carefully, because this is one trip I'm going to forget as fast as I can, and I'm not going to do it again, even in my head."

I don't have to tell you about blastoff—that it's more like drift-off these days, since all long hops start from Outer Orbit satellites, out past the Moon—or about the flicker-field by which we hop faster than light, get dizzier than a five-year-old on a drug store stool, and develop more morning-sickness than Mom. That I've told you before.

So I'll start with planetfall on Mullygantz II, Terra's best bet to date for a colonial planet, five-nines Earth Normal (that is, .99999) and just about as handsome a rock as ever circled a sun. We hung the blister in stable orbit and Purcell and I dropped down in a superscout with supplies and equipment for the ecological survey station. We expected to find things humming there, five busy people and a sheaf of completed reports, and we hoped we'd be the ones to take back the news that the next ship would be the colony ship. We found three dead and two sick, and knew right away that the news we'd be taking back was going to stop the colonists in their tracks.

Clement was the only one I'd known personally. Head of the station, physicist and ecologist both, and tops both ways, and he was one of the dead. Joe and Katherine Flent were dead. Amy Segal, the recorder—one of the best in Pioneer Service—was sick in a way I'll go into a minute, and Glenda Spooner, the plant biologist, was—well, call it withdrawn. Retreated. Something had scared her so badly that she could only sit with her arms folded and her legs crossed and her eyes wide open, rocking and watching.

Anyone gets to striking hero medals ought to make a platter-sized one for Amy Segal. Like I said, she was sick. Her body temperature was wildly erratic, going from 102 all the way down to 96 and back up again. She was just this side of breakdown and must have been like that for weeks, slipping across the line for minutes at a time, hauling herself back for a moment or two, then sliding across again. But she knew Glenda was helpless, though physically in perfect shape, and she knew that even automatic machinery has to be watched. She not only dragged herself around keeping ink in the recording pens and new charts when the seismo's and hygro's and airsonde recorders needed them, but she kept Glenda fed; more than that, she fed herself.

She fed herself *close to fifteen thousand calories a day*. And she was forty pounds underweight. She was the weirdest sight you ever saw, her face full like a fat person's but her abdomen, from the lower ribs to the pubes, collapsed almost against her spine. You'd never have believed an organism could require so much food—not, that is, until you saw her eat. She'd rigged up a chopper out of the lab equipment because she actually couldn't wait to chew her food. She just dumped everything and anything edible into that gadget and propped her chin on the edge of the table by the outlet, and packed that garbage into her open mouth with both hands. If she could have slept it would have been easier but hunger would wake her after twenty minutes or so and back she'd go, chop and cram, guzzle and swill. If Glenda had been able to help—but there she was, she did it all herself, and when we got the whole story straight we found she'd been at it for nearly three weeks. In another three weeks they'd have been close to the end of their stores, enough for five people for anyway another couple of months.

We had a portable hypno in the first-aid kit on the scout, and we slapped it to Glenda Spooner with a reassurance tape and a normal sleep command, and just put her to bed with it. We bedded Amy down too, though she got a bit hysterical until we could make her understand through that fog of delirium that one of us would stand by every minute with premasticated rations. Once she understood that she slept like a corpse, but such a corpse you never want to see, lying there eating.

It was a lot of work all at once, and when we had it done Purcell wiped his face and said, "Five-nines Earth Normal, hah. No malignant virus or bacterium. No toxic plants or fungi. Come to Mullygantz II, land of happiness and health."

"Nobody's used that big fat *no*," I reminded him. "The reports only say there's nothing bad here that we know about or can test for. My God, the best brains in the world used to kill AB patients by transfusing type O blood. Heaven help us the day we think we know everything that goes on in the universe."

We didn't get the whole story then; rather, it was all there but not in a comprehensible order. The key to it all was Amy Segal's personal log, which she called a "diary," and kept in hentracks called shorthands, which took three historians and a philologist a week to decode after we returned to Earth. It was the diary that fleshed the thing out for us, told us about these people and their guts and how they exploded all over each other. So I'll tell it, not the way we got it, but the way it happened.

To begin with it was a good team. Clement was a good head, one of those relaxed guys who always listens to other people talking. He could get a fantastic amount of work out of a team and out of himself too, and it never showed. His kind of drive is sort of a secret weapon.

Glenda Spooner and Amy Segal were wild about him in a warm respectful way that never interfered with the work. I'd guess that Glenda was more worshipful about it, or at least, with her it showed more. Amy was the little mouse with the big eyes that gets happier and stays just as quiet when her grand passion walks into the room, except maybe she works a little harder so he'll be pleased. Clement was bed-friends with both of them, which is the way things usually arrange themselves when there's an odd number of singles on a team. It's expected of them, and the wise exec keeps it going that way and plays no favorites, at least till the job's done.

The Flents, Katherine and Joe, were married, and had been for quite a while before they went Outside. His specialty was geology and mineralogy and she was a chemist, and just as their sciences supplemented each other so did their egos. One of Amy's early "diary" entries says they knew each other so well they were one step away from telepathy; they'd work side by side for hours swapping information with grunts and eyebrows.

Just what kicked over all this stability it's hard to say. It wasn't a fine balance; you'd think from the look of things that the arrangement could stand a lot of bumps and friction. Probably it was an unlucky combination of small things all harmless in themselves, but having a critical-mass characteristic that nobody knew about. Maybe it was Clement's sick spell that triggered it; maybe the Flents suddenly went into one of those oh-God-what-did-I-ever-see-in-you phases that come over married people who are never separated; maybe it was Amy's sudden crazy yen for Joe Flent and her confusion over it. Probably the worst thing of all was that Joe Flent might have sensed how she felt and caught fire too. I don't know. I guess, like I said, that they all happened at once.

Clement getting sick like that. He was out after bio specimens and spotted a primate. They're fairly rare on Mullygantz II, big ugly devils maybe five feet tall but so fat they outweigh a man two to one. They're mottled pink and gray, and hairless, and they have a face that looks like an angry gorilla when it's relaxed, and a ridiculous row of little pointed teeth instead of fangs. They get around pretty good in the trees but they're easy to outrun on the ground, because they never learned to use their arms and knuckles like the great apes, but waddle over the ground with their arms held up in the air to get them out of the way. It fools you. They look so damn silly that you forget they might be dangerous.

So anyway, Clement surprised one on the ground and had it headed for the open fields before it knew what was happening. He ran it to a standstill, just by getting between it and the trees and then approaching it. The primate did all the running; Clement just maneuvered it until it was totally pooped and squatted down to wait its doom. Actually all the doom it would have gotten from Clement was to get stunned, hypoed, examined and turned loose, but of course it had no way of knowing that. It just sat there in the grass looking stupid and ludicrous and harmless in an ugly sort of way, and when Clement put out his hand it didn't move, and when he patted it on the neck it just trembled. He was slowly withdrawing his hand to get his stun-gun out when he said something or laughed—anyway, made a sound, and the thing bit him.

Those little bitty teeth weren't what they seemed. The gums are retractile and the teeth are really not teeth at all but serrated bone with all those little needles slanting inward like a shark's. The jaw muscles are pretty flabby, fortunately, or he'd have lost an elbow, but all the same, it was a bad bite. Clement couldn't get loose, and he couldn't reach around himself to get to the stun-gun, so he drew his flame pistol, thumbed it around to "low," and scorched the primate's throat with it. That was Clement, never wanting to do any more damage than he had to. The primate opened its mouth to protect its throat and Clement got free. He jumped back and twisted his foot and fell, and something burned him on the side of the face like a lick of hellfire. He scrambled back out of the way and got to his feet. The primate was galloping for the woods on its stumpy little legs with its long arms up over its head—even then Clement thought it was funny. Then something else went for him in the long grass and he took a big leap out of its way.

He later wrote very careful notes on this thing. It was wet and it was nasty and it stunk beyond words. He said you could search your memory long afterwards and locate separate smells in that overall stench the way you can with the instruments of an orchestra. There was butyl mercaptan and rotten celery, excrement, formic acid, decayed meat and that certain smell which is like the taste of some brasses. The burn on his cheek smelt like hydrochloric acid at work on a hydrocarbon; just what it was.

The thing was irregularly spherical or ovoid, but soft and squashy. Fluids of various kinds oozed from it here and there—colorless and watery, clotted yellow like soft-boiled eggs, and blood. It bled more than anything ought to that needs blood; it bled in gouts from openings at random, and it bled cutaneously, droplets forming on its surface like the sweat on a glass of icewater. Cutaneously, did I say? That's not what Clement reported. It looked skinless—flayed was the word he used. Much of its surface was striated muscle fibre, apparently unprotected. In two places that he could see was naked brown tissue like liver, drooling and dripping excretions of its own.

And this thing, roughly a foot and a half by two feet and weighing maybe thirty pounds, was flopping and hopping in a spastic fashion, not caring which side was up (if it had an up) but always moving toward him.

Clement blew sharply out of his nostrils and stepped back and to one side—a good long step, with the agony of his scalded cheek to remind him that wherever the thing had come from, it was high up, and he didn't want it taking off like that again.

And when he turned like that, so did the thing, leaving behind it a trail of slime and blood in the beaten grass, a curved filthy spoor to show him it knew him and wanted him.

He confesses he does not remember dialing up the flame pistol, or the first squeeze of the release. He does remember circling the thing and pouring fire on it while it squirmed and squirted, and while he yelled sounds that were not words, until he and his weapon were spent and there was nothing where the thing had been but a charred wetness adding the smell of burned fat to all the others. He says in his unsparing report that he tramped around and around the thing, stamping out the grass-fire he had started, and shaking with revulsion, and that he squatted weakly in the grass weeping from reaction, and that only then did he think of his wounds. He broke out his pioneer's spectral salve and smeared it liberally on burns and bite both. He hunkered there until the analgesic took the pain away and he felt confident that the wide array of spansuled antibiotics was at work, and then he roused himself and slogged back to the base.

And to that sickness. It lasted only eight days or so, and wasn't the kind of sickness that ought to follow such an experience. His arm and his face healed well and quickly, his appetite was very good but not excessive, and his mind seemed clear enough. But during that time, as he put it in the careful notes he taped on the voicewriter, he felt things he had never felt before and could hardly describe. They were all things he had heard about or read about, foreign to him personally. There were faint shooting pains in his abdomen and back, a sense of pulse where no pulse should be—like that in a knitting bone, but beating in his soft tissues. None of it was beyond bearing. He had a constant black diarrhoea, but like the pains it never passed the nuisance stage. One vague thing he said about four times: that when he woke up in the morning he felt that he was in some way different from what he had been the night before, and he couldn't say how. Just . . . different.

And in time it faded away and he felt normal again. That was the whole damned thing about what had happened—he was a very resourceful guy, Clement was, and if he'd been gigged just a little more by this he'd have laid his ears back and worked until he *knew* what the trouble was. But he wasn't pushed into it that way, and it didn't keep him from doing his usual man-and-a-half's hard work each day. To the others he was unusually quiet, but if they noticed it at all it wasn't enough to remark about. They were all working hard too, don't forget. Clement slept alone these eight or nine days, and this wasn't remarkable either, only a little unusual, and not worth comment to either Glenda or Amy, who were satisfied, secure, and fully occupied women.

But then, here again was that rotten timing, small things on small things. This had to be the time of poor Amy Segal's trouble. It started over nothing at all, in the chem lab where she was doing the hurry-up-and-wait routine of a lengthy titration. Joe Flent came in to see how it was going, passed the time of day, did a little something here, something there with the equipment. He had to move along the bench just where Amy was standing, and, absorbed in what he was doing, he put out his hand to gesture her back, and went on with what he was doing. But—

She wrote it in her diary, in longhand, a big scrawl of it in the middle of those neat little glyphs of hers: "He *touched* me." All underlined and everything. All right, it was a nothing: I said that. It was an accident. But the accident had jarred her and she was made of fulminate of mercury all of a sudden. She stood where she was and let him press close to her, going on with his work, and she almost fainted. What makes these things happen . . . ? Never mind; the thing happened. She looked at him as if she had never seen him before, the light on his hair, the shape of his ears and his jaw, the—well, all like that. Maybe she made a sound and maybe Joe Flent just sensed it, but he turned around and there they were, staring at each other in some sort of mutual hypnosis with God knows what flowing back and forth between them. Then Joe gave a funny little surprised grunt and did not walk, he ran out of there.

That doesn't sound like anything at all, does it? Whatever it was, though, it was enough to throw little Amy Segal into a flat spin of the second order, and pop her gimbal bearings. I've read that there used to be a lot of stress and strain between people about this business of sex. Well, we've pretty well cleared that up, in the way we humans generally clear things up, by being extreme about it. If you're single you're absolutely free. If you're married you're absolutely bound. If you're married and you get an external itch, you have your free choice—you stay married and don't scratch it, or you scuttle the marriage and you do scratch it. If you're single you respect the marriage bond just like anyone else; you don't, but I mean you *don't* go holing somebody else's hull.

All of which hardly needs saying, especially not to Amy Segal. But like a lot of fine fools before her, she was all mixed up with what she felt and what she thought she should feel. Maybe she's a throwback to the primitive, when everybody's concave was fair game to anyone else's convex. Whatever it was about her, it took the form of making her hate herself. She was walking around among those other people thinking, I'm no good, Joe's married and look at me, I guess I don't *care* he's married. What's the matter with me, how could I feel this way about Joe, I must be a monster, I don't deserve to be here among decent people. And so on. And no one to tell it to. Maybe if Clement hadn't been sick, or maybe if she'd had it in her to confide in one of the other women, or maybe—well, hell with maybe's. She was half-blind with misery.

Reading the diary transcript later I wished I could put time back and space too and tap her on the shoulder and say come along, little girl, and then put her in a corner and say listen, knothead, get untied, will you? You got a yen, never mind, it'll pass. But as long as it lasts don't be ashamed of it. Damn it, that's all she needed, just a word like that. . . .

Then Clement was well again and one night gave her the sign, and she jumped at it, and that was the most miserable thing of all, because after it was over she burst into tears and told him it was the last time, never again. He must've been no end startled. He missed the ferry there. He could've got the whole story if he'd tried, but he didn't. Maybe . . . maybe he was a little changed from what happened to him, after all. Anyway, poor Amy hit the bottom of the tank about then. She scribbled yards about it in her book. She'd just found out she responded to Clement just like always, and that proved to her that she couldn't love Joe after all, therefore her love wasn't real, therefore she wasn't worth loving, therefore Joe would never love her. Little bubblehead! and the only way out she could see was to force herself to be faithful to somebody, so she was going to "purify her feelings"—that's what she wrote—by being faithful to Joe, hence no more Clement and of course no Joe. And with that decision she put her ductless glands in a grand alliance with her insanity. Would you believe that anyone in this day and age could have such a pot boiling inside a fuzzy skull?

From that moment on Amy Segal was under forced draft. Apparently no one said anything about it, but you just don't build up incandescence in small dark places without somebody noticing. Katherine Flent must have tumbled early, as women do, and probably said nothing about it, as some women sometimes don't. Ultimately Joe Flent saw it, and what he went through nobody will ever know. I know he saw it, and felt it, because of what happened. Oh my God, what happened!

It must have been about now that Amy got the same strange almost-sickness Clement had gone through. Vague throbbings and shiftings in the abdomen, and the drizzles, and again that weird thing, about feeling different in the morning and not knowing why. And when she was about halfway through the eight-day siege, damn if Glenda Spooner doesn't seem to come down with it. Clement did the reporting on this; he was seeing a lot more of Glenda these days and could watch it. He noticed the similarity with his own illness all right, though it wasn't as noticeable, and called all hands for a report. Amy, possibly Glenda, and Clement had it and passed it; the Flents never showed the signs. Clement decided finally that it was just one of those things that people get and no one knows why, like the common cold before Billipp discovered it was an allergy to a gluten fraction. And the fact that Glenda Spooner had had such a slight attack opened the possibility that one or both Flents had had it and never known it—and that's something else we'll never know for sure.

Well, one fine day Clement headed out to quarter the shale hills to the north, looking for petroleum if he could find it and anything else if he couldn't. Clement was a fine observer. Trouble with Clement, he was an ecologist, which is mostly a biologist, and biologists are crazy.

The fine day, about three hours after he left, sprung a leak, and the bottom dropped out of the sky—which didn't worry anyone because everyone knew it wouldn't worry Clement.

Only he didn't come back.

That was a long night at the base. Twice searchers started out but they turned back in the first two hundred yards. Rain can come down like that if it wants to, but it shouldn't keep it up for so long. Morning didn't stop it, but as soon as it was dark grey outside instead of total black, the Flents and the two girls dropped everything and headed for the hills. Amy and Glenda went to the west and separated and searched the ridge until mid-afternoon, so it was all over by the time they got back. The Flents took the north and east, and it was Joe who found Clement.

That crazy Clement, he'd seen a bird's nest. He saw it because it was raining and because the fish-head stork always roosts in the rain; if it didn't its goofy glued-together nest would come unstuck. It's a big bird, larger than a terran stork, snow-white, wide-winged and easy to see, especially against the black shale bluff. Clement wanted a good look at how it sheltered its nest, which looks like half a pinecone as big as half a barrel—you'd think too big for the bird to keep dry. So up he went—and discovered that the fish-head stork's thick floppy neck conceals three, maybe four S-curves underneath all that loose skin. He was all of nine feet away from the nest, clinging to the crumbly rock wall, when he discovered it, the hard way. The stork's head shot out like a battering ram and caught him right on the breastbone, and down he went, and I guess that waterlogged shale was waiting for just this, because he started a really good rock-slide. He broke his leg and was buried up to the shoulder blades. He was facing up the cliff, with the rain beating down on him almost enough to tear his eyelids. He had nothing to look at except the underside of the nest, which his rock-slide had exposed, and I imagine he looked at it until he understood, much against his will, that the nest was all that was holding up more loosened rock above it; and he put in the night that way, waiting for seepage to loosen the gunk that stuck the nest up there and sent those tons of rock smack in his face. The leg was pretty bad and he probably passed out two or three times, but never long enough to suit him . . . *damn* it! I got a list this long of people who ought to have things like that happen to them. So it has to happen to Clement.

It was still raining in the morning when Joe Flent found him. Joe let out a roar to the westward where his wife was combing the rocks, but didn't wait to see if she'd heard. If she didn't, maybe there was a sort of telepathy between them like Amy said in her diary. Anyway, she arrived just in time to see it happen, but not in time to do anything about it.

She saw Joe bending over Clement's head and shoulders where they stuck out of the rock pile, and then she heard a short, sharp shout. It must have been Clement who shouted; he was facing uphill and could see it coming, nest and all. Katherine screamed and ran toward them, and then the new slide reached the bottom, and that was that for Clement.

But not for Joe. Something else got Joe.

It seemed to explode out of the rocks a split second before the slide hit. It took Joe Flent in the chest so hard it lifted him right off his feet and flung him down and away from the slide. Katherine screamed again as she ran, because the thing that had knocked Joe down was bouncing up and down in a crazy irregular hop, each one taking it closer to Joe as he lay on his back half stunned, and she recognized it for the thing that had attacked Clement the day the primate bit him.

She logged this report on the voicewriter and I heard the tape, and I wish they'd transcribe it and then destroy it. Nobody should hear a duty-bound horror-struck soul like that tell such a story. Read it, okay. But that torn-up monotone, oh God. She was having nine agonies at once, what with her hands all gone and what happened to Joe out there, and what he'd said . . . arrgh! I can't tell it without hearing it in my head.

Well. That stinking horror hopped up on Joe and he half sat up and it hopped again and landed right over his face and slumped there quivering, bleeding and streaming rain and acid. Joe flipped so hard his feet went straight up in the air and he seemed to hang there, standing on the back of his head and his shoulder-blades with his arms and legs doing a crazy jumping-jack flailing. Then he fell again with the monstrosity snugger that ever over his face and neck and head, and he squirmed once and then lay still, and that was when Katherine got to him.

Katherine went at that thing with her bare hands. One-half second contact, even in all that rain, was enough to pucker and shrivel her skin, and it must have felt like plunging her hands into smoking deep-fat. She didn't say what it felt like. She only said that when she grabbed at the thing to tear it away from Joe's face, it came apart in small slippery handfuls. She kicked at it and her foot went in and through it and it spilled ropy guts and gouted blood. She tore into it again, clawing and batting it away, and that was probably when she did the most damage to her hands. Then she had an idea from somewhere in that nightmare, fell back and took Joe's feet and dragged him twenty feet away—don't ask me how—and turned him over on his face so the last of that mess dropped off him. She skinned out of her shirt and knelt down and rolled him over and sat him up. She tried to wipe his face with the shirt but found she couldn't hold it, so she scooped her ruined hand under it and brought it up and mopped, but what she mopped at wasn't a face any more. On the tape she said, in that flat shredded voice, "I didn't realize that for a while."

She put her arms around Joe and rocked him and said, "Joey, it's Katherine, it's all right, honey. Katherine's here." He sighed once, a long, shuddering sigh and straightened his back, and a hole bigger than a mouth opened up in the front of his head. He said, "Amy? Amy?" and suddenly fought Katherine blindly. She lost her balance and her arm fell away from his back, and he went down. He made one great cry that raised echoes all up and down the ridge: "A . . . meeeee . . ." and in a minute or two he was dead.

Katherine sat there until she was ready to go, and covered his face with the shirt. She looked once at the thing that had killed him. It was dead, scattered in slimy bits all over the edge of the rock-fall. She went back to the base. She didn't remember the trip. She must have been soaked and chilled to the bone-marrow. She apparently went straight to the voicewriter and reported in and then just sat there, three, four hours until the others got back.

Now if only somebody had been there to . . . I don't know. Maybe she couldn't have listened, after all that. Who knows what went on in her head while she sat there letting her blood run out of her hands on to the floor? I'd guess it was that last cry of Joe's, because of what happened when Glenda and Amy came in. It might have been so loud in her head that nobody else's voice could get in. But I still wish somebody had been there, somebody who knows about the things people say when they die. Sometimes they're already dead when they say those things; they don't mean anything. I saw an engineer get it when a generator threw a segment. He just said, "Three-eighths . . . three-eighths . . ."

What I'm trying to say, it didn't have to mean anything . . . Well, what's the difference now?

They came in dripping and tired, calling out. Katherine Flent didn't answer. They came into the recording shack, Amy first. Amy was half across the floor before she saw Katherine. Glenda was still in the doorway. Amy screamed, and I guess anyone would, seeing Katherine with her hair plastered around her face the way it had dried, and blood all over her clothes and the floor, and no shirt. She fixed her crazy eyes on Amy and got up slowly. Amy called her name twice but Katherine kept on moving, slow, steady, evenly. Between the heels of her ruined hands she held a skinning knife. She probably couldn't have held it tightly enough to do any damage, but I guess that didn't occur to Amy.

Amy stepped back toward the door and with one long step Katherine headed her off and herded her toward the other corner, where there was no way out. Amy glanced behind her, saw the trap, covered her face with her hands, stepped back and dropped her hands. "Katherine!" she screamed. "What is it? What is it? Did you find Clement? Quick!" she rapped at Glenda, who stood frozen in the doorway. "Get Joe."

At the sound of Joe's name Katherine moaned softly and leaped. She was met in mid-air by the same kind of thing that had killed her husband.

The soft horror caught Katherine off the floor in mid-leap and hurled her backward. Her head hit the corner of a steel relay-rack . . .

The stench in the small room was quite beyond description, beyond bearing. Amy staggered to the door, pushing an unresisting Glenda ahead of her. . . .

And there they were as we found them, Purcell and me: one fevered freak that could out-eat six men, and one catatonic.

I sent Purcell out to the shale hill to see if there was enough left of Clement and Joe Flent for an examination. There wasn't. Animals had scattered Joe's remains pretty thoroughly, and Purcell couldn't find Clement at all, though he moved rocks till his hands bled. There had probably been more slides after that rain. Somehow, in those weeks when she maintained the basic instrumentation single-handed, Amy

Segal had managed to drag Katherine out and bury her, and clean up the recording room, though nothing but burning would ever get all that smell out of it.

We left everything but the tapes and records. The scout was built for two men and cargo, and getting her off the ground with four wasn't easy. I was mighty glad to get back on the bridge of the flicker-ship and away from that five-nines hell. We stashed the two girls in a cabin next to the sick bay and quarantined them, just in case, and I went to work on the records, getting the story in about the order I've given it here.

And once I had it, there wasn't a thing I could do with it. Amy was at all times delirious, or asleep or eating; you could get very little from her, and even then you couldn't trust what you got. From Glenda you got nothing. She just lay still with that pleasant half-smile on her face and let the universe proceed without her. On a ship like ours we are the medical division, the skipper and the officers, and we could do nothing for these two but keep them fed and comfortable; otherwise, we mostly forgot they were aboard. Which was an error.

Status quo, then, far as I knew, from the time we left the planet until we made earthfall, the crew going about its business, the two girls in quarantine with Purcell filling the hopper with food for the one and spoon-feeding the other, and me locked up with the records, piecing and guessing and trying to make sense out of a limbless, eyeless monstrosity which apparently could appear from nowhere in mid-air, even indoors (like the one that killed Katherine Flent); which looked as if it could not live, but which still would attack and could kill. I got no place. I mulled over more theories than I'll go into, some of 'em pretty far-fetched, like a fourth-dimensional thing that . . . well, on the other hand, Nature can be pretty far-fetched too, as anyone who has seen the rear end of a mandrill will attest.

What do you know about sea-cucumbers, as another nauseating example?

We popped out of the flicker-field in due time, and Luna was good to see. We transferred to a rocket-ferry at Outer Orbit and dropped in smoothly, and came into the base here in quarantine procedure, impounding ferry and all. The girls were at last put into competent hands, and the crew were given the usual screening. Usual or not, it's about as thorough as a physical examination can get, and after they'd all been cleared, and slept six hours, and gone through it again and been cleared again, I gave them 72-hour passes, renewable, and turned 'em loose.

I was more than anxious to go along too, but by that time I was up to the eyeballs in specialists and theorists, and in some specialties and theories that began to get too fascinating for even a home-hungry hound like me to ignore. That was when I called you and said how tied up I was and swore I'd be out of there in another day. You were nice about that. Of course, I had no idea it wouldn't be just one more day, but another six weeks.

Right after the crew was turned loose they called me out of the semantics section, where we were collating all notes and records, into the psych division.

They had one of the . . . the things there.

I have to hand it to those guys. I guess they were just as tempted as Clement was when he first saw one, to burn it into nothing as fast as it could be burned. I saw it, and that was my first impulse. God. No amount of clinical reporting like Clement's could give you the remotest idea of just how disgusting one of those things is.

They'd been working over Glenda Spooner. Catatonics are hard to do anything with, but they used some high-potency narcosyntheses and some field inductions, and did a regression. They found out just what sort of a catatonic she was. Some, you probably know, retreat like that as a result of some profound shock—after they have been shocked. It's an escape. But some go into that seize-up in the split second *before* the shock. Then it isn't an escape, it's a defense. And that was our girl Glenda.

They regressed her until they had her located out in the field, searching for Clement. Then they brought her forward again, so that in her mind she was contacting Amy, slogging through the rain back to the base. They got to where Amy entered the recording shack and screamed, seeing Katherine Flent looking that way. There they located the exact split second of trauma, the moment when something happened which was so terrible that Glenda had not let herself see it.

More dope, more application of the fields through the helmet they had her strapped into. They regressed her a few minutes and had her approach that moment again. They tried it again, and some more, making slight adjustments each time, knowing that sooner or later they would have the exact subtle nudge that would push her through her self-induced barrier, make her at last experience the thing she was so afraid to acknowledge.

And they did it, and when they did it, the soft gutty *thing* appeared, slamming into a technician fifteen feet away, hitting him so hard it knocked him flat and slid him spinning into the far wall. He was a young fellow named Petri and it killed him. Like Katherine Flent, he died probably before he felt the acid burns. He went right into the transformer housing and died in a net of sparks.

And as I said, these boys had their wits about them. Sure, someone went to help Petri (though not in time) and someone else went after a flame pistol. He wasn't in time either; because when he got back with it, Shellabarger and Li Kyu had the glass bell off a vacuum rig and had corralled the filthy thing with it. They slid a resilient mat under it and slapped a coupling on top and jetted the jar full of liquid argon.

This time there was no charred mass, no kicked-apart, rain-soaked scatter of parts to deal with. Here was a perfect specimen, if you can call such a thing perfect, frozen solid while it was still alive and trying to hop up and down and find someone to bubble its dirty acids on. They had it to keep, to slice up with a microtome, even to revive, if anyone had the strong guts.

Glenda proved clearly that with her particular psychic makeup, she had chosen the right defense. When she saw the thing, she died of fright. It was that, just that, that she had tried to avoid with catatonia. The psycho boys breached it, and found out just how right she had been. But at least she didn't die uselessly, like Flent and Clement and poor Katherine. Because it was her autopsy that cleared things up.

One thing they found was pretty subtle. It was a nuclear pattern in the cells of the connective tissue quite unlike any of them had seen before. They checked Amy Segal for it and found the same thing. They checked me for it and didn't. That was when I sent out the recall order for the whole crew. I didn't think any of them would have it, but we had to be sure. If that got loose on Earth . . .

All but one of the crew had a clean bill when given the

new test, and there wasn't otherwise anything wrong with that one.

The other thing Glenda's autopsy revealed was anything but subtle.

Her abdomen was empty.

Her liver, kidneys, almost all of the upper and all of the lower intestine were missing, along with the spleen, the bladder, and assorted tripe of that nature. Remaining were the uterus, with the Fallopian tubes newly convoluted and the ovaries tacked right to the uterus itself; the stomach; a single loop of what had once been upper intestine, attached in a dozen places to various spots on the wall of the peritoneum. It emptied directly into a rectal segment, without any distinctive urinary system, much like the primitive equipment of a bird.

Everything that was missing, they found under the bell jar.

Now we knew what had hit Katherine Flent, and why Amy was empty and starved when we found her. Joe Flent had been killed by . . . one of the . . . well, by something that erupted at him as he bent over the trapped Clement. Clement himself had been struck on the side of the face by such a thing—and whose was that?

Why, that primate's. The primate he walked into submission, and touched, and frightened.

It bit him in panic terror. Joe Flent was killed in a moment of panic terror too—not this, but Clement's, who saw the rock-slide coming. Katherine Flent died in a moment of terror—not hers, but Amy's, as Amy crouched cornered in the shack and watched Katherine coming with a knife. And the one which had appeared on earth, in the psych lab, why, that needed the same thing to be born in—when the boys forced Glenda Spooner across a mental barrier she could not cross and live.

We had everything now but the mechanics of the thing, and that we got from Amy, the bravest woman yet. By the time we were through with her, every man in the place admired her g—uh, dammit not that. Admired her fortitude. She was probed and goaded and prodded and checked, and finally went through a whole series of advanced exploratories. By the time the exploratories began, about six weeks had gone by, that is, six weeks from Katherine Flent's death, and Amy was almost back to normal; she'd tapered off on the calories, her abdomen had filled out to almost normal, her temperature had steadied and by and large she was okay. What I'm trying to put over is that she had some intestines for us to investigate—*she'd grown a new set.*

That's right. She'd thrown her old ones at Katherine Flent. There wasn't anything wrong with the new ones, either. At the time of her first examination everything was operating but the kidneys; their function was being handled by a very simple, very efficient sort of filter attached to the ventral wall of the peritoneum. We found a similar organ in autopsying poor Glenda Spooner. Next to it were the adrenals, apparently transferred there from their place astride the original kidneys. And sure enough, we found Amy's adrenals placed that way, and not on the new kidneys. In a fascinating three-day sequence we saw those new kidneys completed and begin to operate, while the surrogate organ which had been doing their work atrophied and went quiet. It stayed there, though, ready.

The climax of the examination came when we induced panic terror in her, with a vivid abreaction of the events in the recording shack the day Katherine died. Bless that Amy, when we suggested it she grinned and said, "Sure!"

But this time it was done under laboratory conditions, with a high-speed camera to watch the proceedings. Oh God, did they proceed!

The film showed Amy's plain pleasant sleeping face with its stainless halo of psych-field hood, which was hauling her subjective self back to that awful moment in the records shack. You could tell the moment she arrived there by the anxiety, the tension, the surprise and shock that showed on her face. "Glenda!" she screamed, "Get Joe!"—and then . . .

It looked at first as if she was making a face, sticking out her tongue. She was making a face all right, the mask of purest, terminal fear, but that wasn't a tongue. It came out and out, unbelievably fast even on the slow-motion frames on the high-speed camera. At its greatest, the diameter was no more than two inches, the length . . . about eight feet. It arrowed out of her mouth, and even in mid-air it contracted into the roughly spherical shape we had seen before. It stuck the net which the doctors had spread for it and dropped into a plastic container, where it hopped and hopped, sweated, drooled, bled and died. They tried to keep it alive but it wasn't meant to live more than a few minutes.

On dissection they found it contained all Amy's new equipment, in sorry shape. All abdominal organs can be compressed to less than two inches in diameter, but not if they're expected to work again. These weren't.

The thing was covered with a layer of muscle tissue, and dotted with two kinds of ganglia, one sensory and one motor. It would keep hopping as long as there was enough of it left to hop, which was what the motor system did. It was geotropic, and it would alter its muscular spasms to move it toward anything around it that lived and had warm blood, and that's what the primitive sensory system was for.

And at last we could discard the fifty or sixty theories that had been formed and decide on one: That the primates of Mullygantz II had the ability, like a terran sea-cucumber, of ejecting their internal organs when frightened, and of growing a new set; that in a primitive creature this was a survival characteristic, and the more elaborate the ejected matter the better the chances of the animal's survival. Probably starting with something as simple as a lizard's discarding a tail-segment which just lies there and squirms to distract a pursuer, this one had evolved from 'distract' to 'attract' and finally to 'attack.' True, it took a fantastic amount of forage for the animal to supply itself with a new set of innards, but for vegetarian primates on fertile Mullygantz II, this was no problem.

The only problem that remained was to find out exactly how terrans had become infected, and the records cleared that up. Clement got it from a primate's bite. Amy and Glenda got it from Clement. The Flents may well never have had it. Did that mean that Clement had bitten those girls? Amy said no, and experiments proved that the activating factor passed readily from any mucous tissue to any other. A bite would do it, but so would a kiss. Which didn't explain our one crew-member who "contracted" the condition. Nor did it explain what kind of a survival characteristic it is that can get transmitted around like a virus infection, even between species.

Within that same six weeks of quarantine, we even got an answer to that. By a stretch of the imagination, you might call the thing a virus. At least, it was a filterable organism which, like the tobacco mosaic or the slime mold, had an organizing factor. You might call it a life form, or a com-

plex biochemical action, basically un-alive. You could call
it symbiote. Symbiotes often go out of their way to see to
it that the hosts survive.

After entering a body, these creatures multiplied until
they could organize, and then went to work on the host.
Connective tissue and muscle fiber was where they did most
of their work. They separated muscle fibers all over the
peritoneal walls and diaphragm, giving a layer to the entrails and the rest to the exterior. They duplicated organic
functions with their efficient, primitive little surrogate organs and glands. They hooked the ilium to the stomach
wall and to the rectum, and in a dozen places to their new
organic structures. Then they apparently stood by.

When an emergency came every muscle in the abdomen
and throat cooperated in a single, synchronized spasm, and
the entrails, sheathed in muscle fiber and dotted with nerve
ganglia, compressed into a long tube and was forced out
like a bullet. Instantly the revised and edited abdomen got
to work, perforating the new stomach outlet, sealing the old,
and starting the complex of simple surrogate to work. And
as long as enough new building material was received fast
enough, an enormously accelerated rebuilding job started,
blue-printed God knows how from God knows what kind of
a cellular memory, until in less than two months the original
abdominal contents, plus revision, were duplicated, and all
was ready for the next emergency.

Then we found that in spite of its incredible and complex
hold on its own life and those of its hosts, it had no defense
at all against one of humanity's oldest therapeutic tools,
the RF fever cabinet. A high frequency induced fever of
108 sustained for seven minutes killed it off as if it had
never existed, and we found that the "revised" gut was in
every way as good as the original, if not better (because
damaged organs were replaced with healthy ones if there was
enough of them left to show original structure)—and that
by keeping a culture of the Mullygantz 'virus' we had the
ultimate, drastic treatment for forty-odd types of abdominal cancer—including two types for which we'd had no
answer at all!

So it was we lost the planet, and gained it back with a
bonus. We could cause this thing and cure it and diagnose
it and use it, and the new world was open again. And that
part of the story, as you probably know, came out all over

the newsfax and 'casters, which is why I'm getting a big hello from taxi drivers and doormen. . . .

"But the 'fax said you wouldn't be leaving the base until tomorrow noon!" Sue said after I had spouted all this to her and at long last got it all off my chest in one great big piece.

"Sure. They got that straight from me. I heard rumors of a parade and speeches and God knows what else, and I wanted to get home to my walkin' talkin' wettin' doll that blows bubbles."

"You're silly."

"C'mere."

The doorbell hummed.

"I'll get it," I said, "and throw 'em out. It's probably a reporter."

But Sue was already on her feet. "Let me, let me. You just stay there and finish your drink." And before I could stop her she flung into the house and up the long corridor to the foyer.

I chuckled, drank my ale and got up to see who was horning in. I had my shoes off so I guess I was pretty quiet. Though I didn't need to be. Purcell was roaring away in his best old salt fashion, "Let's have us another quickie, Susie, before the Space Scout gets through with his red carpet treatment tomorrow—miss me, honey?" . . . while Sue was imploringly trying to cover his mouth with her hands.

Maybe I ran; I don't know. Anyway, I was there, right behind her. I didn't say anything. Purcell looked at me and went white. "Skipper . . ."

And in the hall mirror behind Purcell, my wife met my eyes. What she saw in my face I cannot say, but in hers I saw panic terror.

In the small space between Purcell and Sue, something appeared. It knocked Purcell into the mirror, and he slid down in a welter of blood and stinks and broken glass. The recoil slammed Sue into my arms. I put her by so I could watch the tattered, bleeding thing on the floor hop and hop until it settled down on the nearest warm living thing it could sense, which was Purcell's face.

I let Sue watch it and crossed to the phone and called the commandant. "Gargan," I said, watching. "Listen, Joe. I found out that Purcell lied about where he went in that first liberty. Also why he lied." For a few seconds I couldn't seem to get my breath. "Send the meat wagon and an ambulance, and tell Harry to get ready for another hollowbelly. . . . Yes, I said, one dead. . . . Purcell, dammit. Do I have to draw you a cartoon?" I roared, and hung up.

I said to Sue, who was holding on to her flat midriff, "That Purcell, I guess it did him good to get away with things under my nose. First that helpless catatonic Glenda on the way home, then you. I hope you had a real good time, honey."

It smelled bad in there so I left. I left and walked all the way back to the Base. It took about ten hours. When I got there I went to the Medical wing for my own fever-box-cure and to do some thinking about girls with guts, one way or another. And I began to wait. They'd be opening up Mullygantz II again, and I thought I might look for a girl who'd have the . . . fortitude to go back with me. A girl like Amy.

Or maybe Amy.

- [ ] **THE 1978 ANNUAL WORLD'S BEST SF.** An all-star selection including Haldeman, Ellison, Bishop, Varley, etc.
(#UJ1376—$1.95)

- [ ] **THE 1977 ANNUAL WORLD'S BEST SF.** Featuring Asimov, Tiptree, Aldiss, Coney, and a galaxy of great ones. An SFBC Selection. (#UE1297—$1.75)

- [ ] **THE 1976 ANNUAL WORLD'S BEST SF.** A winner with Fritz Leiber, Brunner, Cowper, Vinge, and more. An SFBC Selection. (#UW1232—$1.50)

- [ ] **THE DAW SCIENCE FICTION READER.** The unique anthology with a full novel by Andre Norton and tales by Akers, Dickson, Bradley, Stableford, and Tanith Lee.
(#UW1242—$1.50)

- [ ] **THE BEST FROM THE REST OF THE WORLD.** Great stories by the master of sf writers of Western Europe.
(#UE1343—$1.75)

- [ ] **THE YEAR'S BEST FANTASY STORIES: 3.** Edited by Lin Carter, the 1977 volume includes C. J. Cherryh, Karl Edward Wagner, G.R.R. Martin, etc. (#UW1338—$1.50)

DAW BOOKS are represented by the publishers of Signet and Mentor Books, THE NEW AMERICAN LIBRARY, INC.

THE NEW AMERICAN LIBRARY, INC.,
P.O. Box 999, Bergenfield, New Jersey 07621

Please send me the DAW BOOKS I have checked above. I am enclosing
$_____(check or money order—no currency or C.O.D.'s).
Please include the list price plus 35¢ per copy to cover mailing costs.

Name_____

Address_____

City_____State_____Zip Code_____

Please allow at least 4 weeks for delivery